Also by Vaughn Heppner

Fenris series:
Alien Honor
Alien Shores

Doom Star series:
Star Soldier
Bio-Weapon
Battle Pod
Cyborg Assault
Planet Wrecker
Star Fortress
Planetary Assault (with
  BV Larson and David VanDyke)

Invasion America series:
Invasion: Alaska
Invasion: California
Invasion: Colorado
Invasion: New York

Ark Chronicles:
People of the Ark
People of the Flood
People of Babel
People of the Tower

Extinction Wars series:
Assault Troopers
Planet Strike

Lost Civilizations series:
Giants
Leviathan
Tree of Life
Gog
Behemoth
Lod the Warrior
Lod the Galley Slave

Other novels:
Accelerated
I, Weapon
Strontium-90
Death Knight
Assassin of the Damned
The Dragon Horn
Elves and Dragons
The Assassin of Carthage
The Great Pagan Army
The Sword of Carthage
The Rogue Knight

ALIEN SHORES

ALIEN SHORES

A FENRIS NOVEL

VAUGHN HEPPNER

Text copyright © 2014 Vaughn Heppner

Published by 47North, Seattle

www.apub.com

Amazon, the Amazon logo, and 47North are trademarks of Amazon.com, Inc., or its affiliates.

ISBN-13: 9781477823842
ISBN-10: 1477823840

Illustrated by Maciej Rebisz

Library of Congress Control Number: 2014930970

Printed in the United States of America

To my beautiful wife, Cyndi Heppner

1

Like a flea on a warrior's leg, Klane scaled down a vast cliff face as he descended into the Valley of the Demons.

Klane panted as the air burned his lungs. His side ached, his hands were sore, and the big toe on his right foot had begun to bleed. Swallowing in a dry throat, he made the mistake of glancing down to see how far he had to go to the next ledge. His stomach tightened, and vertigo threatened. The next shelf was over three hundred feet below. Beyond it to the bottom, he could see wispy clouds drifting as a gat soared through thermals.

He closed his eyes and his fingers gripped harder against the rough granite. Maybe he shouldn't have taken this route. Maybe he should have gone the long way to the Mountain that was a Machine. Even here, as the wind whistled past him, he could hear the thunderous churning of the demon-made mountain.

Opening his eyes, Klane gazed across the chasm to the other side. The great boxlike mountain stood there with vast funnels spewing white vapors into the air. Gigantic hoses attached to the mountain reached to the icebergs beside it. Rockets from space had brought the ice to the fantastic Machine Mountain, what the seeker had once called a terraforming convertor.

Klane swallowed again and looked up at the banded moon filling much of the sky. The seeker had told him before that he had come from there, from space. The seeker had informed him of the terrible reason why he was not like the others of Clan Tash-Toi.

The others in his clan were big and strong and possessed large lungs and tough skin not easily scratched or penetrated. Even after his long quest across the plains, Klane remained a pasty white color and became winded far too easily.

He was unlike them in other ways, too: he often brooded, and spent too much time alone, and he was curious about everything. As they neared adulthood, the other young men had refused to wrestle with the weakling or include him in the hunts. Besides, he practiced magic, using the power of his junction-stone and the wisdom of the seeker.

Don't dwell on that now. Climb down to the ledge. Concentrate on the task at hand.

A bleak grimace twisted his features. He wore leather garments like a warrior and a pack on his back. In the pack rested his water bottle. He desperately wanted a drink, but not so badly that he would try to shrug off the pack and get the flask. He needed to reach the ledge first. Then he could slake his parched throat.

As the Mountain that was a Machine churned, as the wind whistled and his hands threatened to cramp, Klane continued the descent.

His precious junction-stone was also in the pack, wrapped in a gat oil–soaked rag. With the stone, he had slain demons. Doing so had been the greatest event of his life.

They had slid through the air in their sky vehicle, the demons with their vile jaws. The knife at his belt had been fashioned from the torn metal of the sky vehicle. The metal had powerful mojo and it gave him courage.

Desiring vengeance for the slain demons, other monsters had come. They had come to take away the demonslayer, arriving in more sky vehicles. The seeker, his great friend, had raced out to them, using magic to attack. The demons had captured the seeker in a net, lifting him into the belly of one of the cars, no doubt to conduct hideous tortures on his flesh in their dread valley.

Klane could not abide the thought. For fear of further demon attacks, the clan had relocated into the Jumbles, there to hide from new depredations. Klane could have remained with them as the clan seeker. Instead, he had told the hetman that he would go to the Valley of the Demons to rescue his friend. It seemed an impossible goal.

Who was he to think that he could perform such a bold and mighty feat?

I am the demonslayer.

As he clung to the cliff face, Klane concentrated on the thought, using it to supply him with resolve. *A demonslayer ignores pain. He ignores tiredness. He continues on the death path . . .*

Klane paused. He was on the death path. Yes, he should have recognized that from the beginning. He was heading into the lair of the terrible enemy. He would wreak vengeance on them. Likely, he would fail in freeing the seeker, but he would make the streets of the demon abode run red with blood.

He knew they had red blood because he had seen their twisted, torn bodies in the wreckage of the sky vehicle that he had brought down through his power.

The grimace on his face turned into a fierce grin. It gave his aching hands strength, and it eased the burning in his throat. Sweat slicked his body, and that made the climb many times more dangerous.

I am on the death path. I am the demonslayer.

He did not lose track of time or effort. Each second hurt. Each moment felt as if it could be his last. In places, the cliff face had jutting rocks that pushed against his chest as he tried to negotiate it. He panted, and his fingers become slippery. The grin faded and weariness threatened to dull his senses into fatal miscalculation.

At last, the final particles of strength fled his body. He panted against the rock face, and it was all he could to do to hang onto his position. With agonizing slowness, he twisted his head and looked down. Tufts of skeleton grass grew on the ledge fifty feet below. If he could reach the grand oasis, he would be able to lie down and sleep. Oh, that would be glorious indeed.

Lines deepened on his forehead. How could he reach the ledge? His biceps quivered with exhaustion. If he attempted to scale down, he would lose his grip and fall. He would likely strike the ledge hard enough to bounce off it to his death, or he might break a bone. Yet he couldn't rest here. As he clung to the rock, he could feel the remaining strength drain out of his flesh.

With the weakness came a dulling of his mind and a lessening of his willpower. This was too much for the pale-skinned lad. The others had been right to exclude him from their wrestling matches and from the hunts. He was pitifully weak. Any Tash-Toi youth could have scaled this cliff . . .

No. You're wrong. They would not have been mad enough to attempt such a thing. I'm descending into the Valley of the Demons. I am a fool.

Klane resolved in that second to end the game as a fool then. If he had the junction-stone in hand, he would have attempted a Levitating Spell. He did not hold the stone, but he would attempt to summon its magic and perform this final feat.

He took a last breath, and in that second, he realized how desperately he wanted to live. He loved life. He had to avenge his friend—the only friend he'd ever had, and his father figure.

"Let's get this over with," he said aloud.

Klane didn't have an audience, but he decided to attempt the foolish feat with determination. He released his grip and slid his left foot from the precarious ledge, causing bits of gravel to fall. He concentrated as well as an exhausted fool could hope to do.

I am a feather. I will float to the ledge. I will levitate.

He dropped like a rock, fast. He cried out in dismay, and he scratched for a hold, tearing out a fingernail and cutting his hands. It

4

slowed his descent minimally. He had the presence of mind to look down, saw the ledge rush up, and readied himself.

He hit with sickening force. His legs crumpled under him, but he managed to absorb some of his velocity. Still, he toppled, hit his left shoulder, and began to roll, to bounce toward the edge and over it.

"No!" he howled, and he rotated his body. Instead of flipping off the ledge, he landed on his back, one shoulder blade on the stony outcropping and the other hanging over empty space. He froze, and he felt himself balanced on a knife-edge of existence. With a muscular contortion, he heaved himself toward the cliff face. It was barely enough, but it proved successful. Both shoulder blades rested on hard rock.

Klane lay there, sobbing with relief and utter exhaustion. The shock of the fall robbed him of any other feelings.

I'm alive. I'm alive. I can't believe I'm alive.

He didn't do anything but rest and breathe. Finally, he felt throbbing pain in his fingers and hands. He tried to lift his arms, but that proved too difficult.

His muscles quivered and finally, exhaustion drove him to sleep. He awoke to dusk and cold and found himself shivering.

The stars had begun appearing in the heavens, and for once the moon did not stare down at him. The world felt empty without sight of the moon.

He forgot about it as he continued shivering: he was freezing. Slowly, with tight muscles complaining painfully, he sat up and eased toward the cliff. As he slid on his backside, he worked his shoulders, but realized it would be impossible for him to remove his pack now. He drew the demon-metal knife and cut one of the straps. The pack swung free and he let the other strap slide down his arm. Soon he leaned against the rock face and sat there panting.

Uncorking the flask, he sipped water. He wanted to gulp it all in a flash, but he restrained himself, sipped again, and corked it. It felt as if his body absorbed the liquid. He would need much more than that before he reached the bottom.

In fact, as he shivered in the gloom, he realized that he would never be able to scale all the way down into the valley. It was simply too far. He had hoped to come across a ledge or path that would let him walk the rest of the way. Now, he wasn't so sanguine concerning his chances.

You can't rely on luck. You must think. You must scheme. You are the demonslayer.

He added the last thought to bolster his morale. What a stupid way to die: stuck on a ledge with dwindling strength.

While eating dried jerky, he decided that if he was going to die, he might as well feel satisfied one last time. He took out his flask and drained it. Ah, now that felt good.

He grew sleepy, but shivered himself to greater alertness.

If you fall asleep now, you'll likely freeze to death. It will only get colder as true night comes. You have to do something soon if you're going to do anything at all.

Yet what could he do?

Drowsiness threatened again. He had eaten and drunk enough that his body wanted to shut down and repair itself. He was young. Give him a day and he would start again.

I don't have a day. I have to do something tonight. No, make that right now. Whatever I'm going to do, it has to be now.

Easing onto his stomach, he crawled to the edge. He poked his head over and scanned as far as he could. Would it be possible, now that he could clutch the junction-stone, to levitate all the way to the bottom?

Klane didn't think so. The spell was not meant for such a use. That would almost be flying. Levitation was for soft landings. So where did that leave him?

Sliding back to the cliff, Klane rummaged in his pack. He untied the knots around his gat oil–soaked rag. Unfolding the cloth, he dumped the smooth junction-stone into his palm. He had oiled it for countless hours in the seeker's tent. He had spent many days filling it with his power and polishing it until it glowed with a sheen.

As he sat there, Klane recalled the first time he'd known real power. It had been near here; in fact, on the other side of the chasm. The seeker had taken him to a cave system. There had been metal tubes with strange etchings on them. He had listened to the singing gods, and they had filled him with magical potency. That day, he had cast a Teleport Spell. It had—

Klane sat up and his eyes widened. *That* was his way to life. He must teleport again.

He laughed bleakly. There was a problem. He didn't know how to teleport. He had listened to the singing gods and they had filled him with the vital force. The seeker had tricked him that day into attempting the teleportation.

The singing gods are near. They lie under the terraforming convertor, under the Mountain that was a Machine. All I must do is travel with my mind to the cave. I must listen to them again.

With the inspiration came a surge of hope. He might survive his foolish decision to scale down to the Valley of the Demons. He might gain a second chance.

With trembling fingers, he clutched the junction-stone, wincing as it pressed against a raw blister. He breathed in and out. Composing himself, he searched with his magical power. Nothing happened, so he almost opened his eyes and gave up.

Try this until you die, because unless you succeed, you are dead.

He had slain demons by destroying the mechanisms in their sky vehicles. He had reached out with his mind. Now he must reach out again. Then, immediate peril had made him desperate. He—

It happened then as he sat on the ledge. His mind roved outward. Like a soaring gat, it flew to the other side of the chasm. It reached the Mountain that was a Machine. Part of him wanted to go inside. He had always wanted to see what occurred within. He resisted the temptation to check. He had more important business this pregnant night. Instead, his thoughts descended the real mountain. He sought for landmarks, things he had seen the last time he'd been here with the seeker.

Ah. He spied a boulder formation, hurried there, and found a faint trail. With his mind, he sought . . . there! He spied a greater darkness. It was the entrance to the cave. He raced there in his thoughts, and a feeling of danger threatened his concentration.

High up on the other side of the chasm, on the ledge, Klane gripped his junction-stone with fierce strength. It made the muscles on his forearms leap up like cables.

His thoughts hovered before the cave entrance. The danger caused fear to quicken his heartbeat. He plunged in because he had no other choice. In the darkness he retraced the old route with accuracy. Soon his consciousness hovered before giant pipes embedded on the top and bottom into rock. Strange symbols were etched into the metal.

Klane didn't need to think about reaching out to the singing gods. His consciousness plunged into what seemed like cold water. He heard odd sounds, almost like voices, and he bobbed along like a cork in a raging mountain torrent.

An instinctive part of him realized that he could die here. He needed to act.

Power—I need power and more power.

Something heard, or his mind flipped onto the right channel or stream. Power filled him. It felt as if some other being shoved a funnel into his mouth and poured liquid into him. His belly swelled, and if the process would have continued long enough, it might have caused him to burst.

Klane felt as if he shook his head, and he gasped, spewing some of the liquid.

I want to stand by the etchings. I want to be near the singing gods.

His mind twisted. The power of the singing gods motivated an unused portion of his thoughts. He didn't see how, but his mind or his magic warped reality.

A loud ripping sounded. Klane vanished from the ledge on the other side of the chasm. With a roar of displaced air, Klane appeared before the strange pipes deep in the caves under the mountain. Blood gushed from his nostrils, flowing onto his lips. He coughed, and he spat blood as something tore inside him.

With a groan Klane toppled onto his side. He lay there, gasping and bleeding. His brain throbbed and he twitched. Agony exploded in his stomach.

The singing gods were angry with him. He felt them coming. He—

Klane surged to his feet. In the pitch-blackness of the caves, he blundered away from the metal pipes. He crashed against stone, against boulders. He kept trying to flee as he tried to dampen the threatening panic. Slamming full against a wall, he hit his bloody nose. With a groan, he crouched, holding his nose, enduring the pain until it subsided.

The singing gods were searching for him. He could hear them in his mind.

Klane crawled on his hands and knees. He fled from them, and in time the mental sound of their approach faded. He had escaped them for the moment.

At that point, Klane reached the end of his endurance. Flopping onto his stomach, he closed his eyes. He ached and hurt all over. He had pushed himself further than he would have ever believed possible. Now he needed to rest. Curling into a fetal ball, with the junction-stone still clenched in his hand, Klane fell into a deep slumber. The singing gods were hunting him, and they might find him fast asleep. Maybe he should set up protective magic . . .

He tried to come back to awareness, but failed as he continued sleeping as one dead.

2

There was nothing fair in the Fenris System, nothing easy and nothing nice.

Cyrus Gant hated everything about Fenris, but that didn't mean he was going to quit. He was from Level 40 Milan, a former Latin King, and an artist with the vibrio-knife. He also happened to be a Special, and Earth's only hope of receiving the dreadful news of these freakish aliens.

He was in a needle-ship and now gave the scanner the finger. An Attack Talon braked hard, spewing a long exhaust tail. From the angle of its approach, the Kresh military vessel must have originated from High Station 3. That gave it a high probability that the Attack Talon hunted them.

Cyrus glanced at Skar 192, their needle-ship's pilot. Skar was a gene-warped soldier for the Kresh, or he had been until he'd secretly joined the Resisters. The soldier was short, broad-shouldered, with dangling arms like an ape, and had incredible vitality and strength. For the past three weeks the two of them had shared the tiny vessel, journeying through the void of lonely space.

Over the years, Resisters on High Station 3 had secretly constructed the needle-ship out of stealth material for such a time as this. The spacecraft had a toilet and a narrow main chamber. It flew via magnetic propulsion, making it incredibly slow, useful only for traveling in a planet's outer gravity well.

"Do they see us?" Cyrus asked.

"I am unsure," Skar said in his clipped manner.

Cyrus loathed the tight ball that was his gut. He had helped bring Teleship *Discovery* across two hundred and thirty light years from Earth's solar system. Humanity had found how to use discontinuity windows, or DW, man-made rips in space joining two distant points. A DW joined two points up to 8.3 light years apart. Usually it was less. Still, a Teleship jumped the distance in a moment. The process needed advanced AI systems and Specials: psionic individuals with telepathic, telekinetic, and other mental abilities. As of last count, Sol had a little fewer than one hundred and fifty such individuals, out of billions.

Until now, the Fenris System aliens, the Kresh, had lacked Teleships and discontinuity window tech. It had become more than likely they could reverse engineer Earth's captured Teleship. With their vast number of psi-masters, the Kresh could and likely would launch a large scale attack on Sol. Earth had one hundredth the number of psionics as the aliens. This disparity would put humanity at a grave disadvantage if it came to an interstellar war. An alien surprise attack might be devastating.

"This is terrible," Cyrus said.

"The Attack Talon does complicate our situation," Skar agreed.

Cyrus squinted at the scanner. He was a lean young man with muscles like strings of steel. As Specials went, his abilities were minor. He had learned a mind-null trick three weeks ago while escaping from High Station 3, one that let him hide from psi-able searchers. The null might come in handy today, provided the Kresh didn't just laser them out of existence.

Do they see us? Are they hunting for our ship?

After weeks of inaction, of studying the memory crystal and doing a thousand isometric exercises to keep in shape, Cyrus wasn't ready to enter combat again.

Their needle-ship crawled toward Jassac. The moon was a reddish ball, looking much like Mars, only bigger. Jassac was a satellite of

Pulsar, a Jupiter-like gas giant. High Station 3 also orbited Pulsar, but over several million kilometers away. The station was a Kresh habitat, a vast, cylindrical installation. The rest of *Discovery*'s crew and colonists were still prisoners there, those who had survived the battle against other Attack Talons when the Teleship had first arrived in the system.

Cyrus had few illusions about freeing his friends from the Kresh. If he could, he would, certainly. At the moment, he doubted he would survive the next few hours. If he did survive, he had a completely different goal in mind.

Cyrus snorted with disbelief. His goal was insane, really, far-fetched and surreal. An earlier human colonizing ship had arrived at Fenris approximately one hundred and fifty years ago, having departed Earth about four hundred years ago. As far as Cyrus knew, Earth had no record of the journey. Those ancient mariners had crossed the many light years using Bussard ramjet technology. The Kresh had captured the ship and scooped out every female ovary for the eggs, starting the gruesome practice of gene warping and breeding humans to suit various alien needs.

Gene warping was primarily used to create the Vomags, soldiers like Skar, or the genetically altered Bo Taw like the Reacher, who had given Cyrus the "keys" to this needle-ship. Millions of soldiers like Skar fought on the second and third planets of the Fenris System. Those two were Earth-like planets. The soldiers went into the tunnels of the Chirr, intelligent insects at war with the Kresh. The Bo Taw were psi-masters, tall, arrogant humanoids with psionic abilities who had been conditioned to love the Kresh. A few psi-masters had secretly resisted the aliens. A few of those had been clairvoyants, having pre-cognitive visions or dreams. A key vision was that of someone called the Anointed One. That hero was supposed to free humanity from the Kresh.

To Cyrus it all seemed like holo-vid dramas come to life. Maybe the idea was inborn to the human spirit. Cyrus hoped the vision was true. Otherwise, humanity was screwed and the universe really was a dark, dark place.

A beep sounded from Skar's panel, and a red light began to wink. With a deadpan stare, Skar glanced up at Cyrus. "Doesn't that indicate enemy radar lock-on?" Cyrus asked.

"Yes, it—" Those were Skar's last words. His eyes glazed over and he became abnormally rigid.

"Psi-masters," Cyrus hissed. A second later he felt an oily sensation. It came from a gene-warped Kresh tool reaching across space using mental power. The humanoid slave did the aliens' bidding.

Cyrus concentrated his thoughts, and he strove for a tranquil feeling. He had practiced this "going null" many times during the three-week journey. He had been certain he knew how to achieve the state he needed. Now he wasn't sure. It was possible he'd been fooling himself. That was an easy thing to do for a Special. Solipsism was an occupational hazard for his kind.

"Breathe," he whispered.

Cyrus's eyelids fluttered. He breathed in and out, and he relaxed his shoulders. The oily sensation increased and seemed to press down against his skull as if it were in a vise. The psi-master almost had achieved firm contact with him. Cyrus might be able to shield himself from the enemy in the regular psi manner, at least stopping the Bo Taw from taking control of him, but the attacker would know that an Earth Special was here on this ship. In other words, the Kresh would have found him. He needed to use the null.

You're a block of ice. You're like glass.

The oily sensation reached toward his mind like a drill, and Cyrus wanted to spit. Then the feeling was gone. Just like that, snap of the fingers. He'd done it. He had gone null and disappeared from the other's mental sight.

Cyrus kept himself from gloating in any manner. He had to keep up the effect and remain hidden.

You are ice. You are glass. You reflect like a polished surface.

Skar woodenly moved his neck as if he were a puppet. He brought his head about toward Cyrus.

He's going to look at me. Right! The psi-master is going to use Skar's eyes to see if anyone else is in here. This psi-master must have gone against other nulls before.

There came a moment's indecision. Cyrus wasn't sure how to play this. Deciding, he grabbed Skar's nearest forearm. The flesh was like iron. He clutched his friend's limb and mentally wrapped the null around the soldier.

Skar blinked, unfroze from psionic control, and looked up at Cyrus.

"Psi-master," Cyrus whispered. "He's from the Attack Talon."

"They know it's us?"

"I guess so," Cyrus said.

Skar contemplated for all of three seconds. On the fourth, his fingers blurred across the panel.

"Strap in," Skar said.

Cyrus dropped onto the seat beside Skar's piloting chair. He buckled in, listening to the clicks, and fended off another mind search.

I know how to do this. I'm a null. How about that?

The magnetic propulsion came online, pushing the craft. Cyrus's head snapped back, and he almost lost hold of the null. The little needle-ship leapt toward Jassac. The maneuver ruined their last several days of slow but steady deceleration.

"What's the plan?" Cyrus asked.

"We must reach the planet before they reach us."

"Moon," Cyrus said. "It's a moon."

"Yes," Skar said. "We must reach the moon and land. That is the first priority."

In the clairvoyant dreamworld of the Resisters—the rebellious humanoid slaves of the Kresh—a fantasy had emerged, perhaps a prophecy: the Anointed One would save them. How he would do this, no one had any idea.

First, however, someone had to find the Anointed One. That person was the Tracker. The Reacher on High Station 3—the chief Resister there—had informed him a little over three weeks ago that Cyrus himself was the Tracker. It was Cyrus's duty, his prophetic purpose, to find the man who would destroy the Kresh.

The Anointed One had a name: Klane. He was believed to be a Stone Age primitive—a test-subject human for the Kresh—living free in the barren highlands of Jassac. Apparently, the aliens wanted to see how untainted people reacted to certain stimuli, so they had created a game preserve on one of the planetoids they were busy terraforming.

The whole thing was confusing, totally strange to Cyrus. Even after three weeks, it was difficult to wrap his mind around the entire idea of this star system with its competing alien races and gene-warped humans.

"Can you shear off their radar lock?" Skar asked.

"Are you serious? You mean with my psi-ability?"

With a stubby finger, Skar indicated the blinking red light showing the radar fix.

"Are they in range to fire at us?" Cyrus asked.

"We have inferior tech," Skar said.

Cyrus rubbed his forehead. While in their power several weeks ago, an alien machine had force-fed him their language. The process had killed others of *Discovery*'s crew, but Cyrus had survived. So, he could understand Skar's words. Unfortunately, he didn't always comprehend the idioms . . . like now, for instance.

"What do you mean, we have inferior tech?" Cyrus asked.

"My indicators aren't precise," Skar said. "I'm uncertain concerning their present distance and velocity."

"You don't know if they're in range to hit us with their lasers?"

"Correct," Skar said.

"Give me your best guess then."

Skar manipulated the panel, and he spoke slowly. "They appear to be out of laser range."

"That's good."

"Agreed," said Skar. He bent over the scanner, intently studying it.

"Is there a problem?" Cyrus asked.

Skar gestured at the scanner.

Cyrus squinted at it. Okay. That didn't look good. A dot detached from the braking Attack Talon. The dot moved quite a bit faster than the Kresh military vessel.

"Is it a missile?" Cyrus asked.

"I give that a high probability," Skar said.

"Is it a proximity missile or a nuclear-pumped X-ray type?"

"I cannot tell."

Cyrus watched the monitoring device. The Attack Talon was teardrop shaped and at the edge of the scanner's range. The needle-ship was hardly bigger than the dot and almost touched the huge mass of Jassac.

"How much time until we reach the moon?" Cyrus asked.

Skar tapped the controls, reading alien symbols. "We should reach the atmosphere in another two hours."

"How about if we don't bother braking first?" Cyrus asked.

Skar's head twitched. "I have computed for a meteoric landing."

"Uh . . ." Cyrus had to decipher mentally for the idiom again. "Oh, okay, you mean we're going to slash into the atmosphere as we descend at high speed?"

"That is a possibility," Skar said.

"What is? Why don't you make sense for once?"

"One possibility is that we will slash into the atmosphere like a meteor," Skar said. "The other is that we will skip like a stone off water and head back out into space."

This isn't good at all. Cyrus scratched his left cheek. The situation had turned ugly fast. Maybe Skar was right with his decision. It was time to gamble with their lives because capture likely ended everything.

In other words, it would be better to burn up in the atmosphere than to let the Kresh grab them. The aliens had things like agonizers and mind extractors.

Cyrus suppressed a shudder and squinted at the dot on the scanner, at the missile already gaining on the needle-ship. "I'd have figured they would want to capture us. The way they're doing it now—"

The comm unit squawked, signaling a caller. Were psi-masters somehow reading his thoughts?

Skar's left index finger hovered over a receive switch on the screen. "What should I do?" he asked.

Cyrus had been through this before on Teleship *Discovery*. The aliens had hailed them, and when the captain had opened channels, he had made it a thousand times easier for the enemy psi-masters to mind attack *Discovery*'s crew. Somehow, the comm signals helped the telepaths. The psi-masters liked to freeze people, as they had just done to Skar a moment ago, or put them to sleep. What should he do? What was the best decision?

Cyrus hated indecision. It was death during a knife fight. He knew how to play it then with the flash of vibrating steel. Now . . . if he answered, it might amplify another psi-assault. If he ignored them, the missile would keep gaining on the ship.

"What should I do?" Skar asked.

"Can you answer without putting them on the screen?"

"Of course," Skar said.

Cyrus bit his lower lip. Capture was the worst scenario. Dying came in as a bad second. If he died, Earth would never learn about the Kresh. Earth had to learn or . . . what? If the Kresh got the jump on the solar system, that might mean the end of free humanity.

"Let's roll the dice," Cyrus said.

Skar gave him a look of incomprehension.

"It's not so fun when the shoe is on the other foot, is it?" Cyrus asked.

"I do not understand you," Skar said. "What should I do concerning the comm hail?"

"Answer it," Cyrus said. "Let's see what they want."

Skar tapped "Receive," but the comm unit simply hissed with noise. The soldier hunched over the panel, adjusting the controls.

Cyrus tried to relax. He had to keep rolling his shoulders as he waited for another psi-attack. The null was a superb tactic, especially for someone of his limited abilities. If he'd been Venice or Jasper—

The hissing quit and a man's voice came online. "You must immediately cease acceleration and await a boarding party."

Skar stiffened.

How did they get to him so fast? I didn't even feel the psi-attack this time. What happened?

"You have launched a missile at our vessel," Skar said, hotly. "That is an aggressive enemy action. Detonate the missile and give us a reason why we should comply with your demand."

Oh. Skar isn't being controlled, he's just angry.

"You fool," the man said. "I belong to Attack Talon *Valiant*, the personal vessel of Chengal Ras the 109th. You are his property and engaged in unlawful space travel. That is against the Protocols of Ten Fourteen."

"Who are you?" Skar said.

"That is immaterial," the man said. "Will you comply with the lawful order or must you force the Revered One's Talon?"

"Let me ingest your words," Skar said. His hand hovered over the cutoff switch.

Cyrus had been waiting for something psionic to happen. When it did, it almost caught him by surprise. Instead of a second's advance warning, an avalanche of thought hit like tons of mental boulders. It was loud to his mind, disorienting and confusing. The null began to slip away from him.

Skar went rigid. Then his head whipped around and his eyes bulged outward.

"*You,*" Skar said, in a higher-pitched voice than normal. The features of his bullet-shaped head seemed to melt and distort. Then his lips drew back, revealing his teeth. He attempted to lunge upward and attack Cyrus, but the buckles and straps of his piloting chair restrained him.

As enemy mind bolts flashed and crashed around Cyrus, seeking to latch onto him, his thoughts ran riot.

They never did it like this before. Is this a new type of mind assault? Are they using the A team now? How do I get out of this? How—turn off the comm unit, you idiot.

Skar, or the psi-master controlling him, hissed with frustration and tried to lurch the Vomag up again. The soldier's strong hands flailed at the buckles, attempting to rip and tear them apart. But not even he was that strong. Still, the savagery of it daunted Cyrus.

It took an effort of will, but Cyrus reached for the cutoff switch.

"No!" Skar shouted. He grabbed Cyrus's wrist. "Chengal Ras wishes to examine you."

Cyrus leaned his weight for the switch, shoving his arm toward it. Skar gripped cruelly, and the wrist bones ground together. At the same time the mind bolts flashed harder, attempting to hit the hidden null through luck.

They can't see me, but are attacking in my vicinity. If they ever get a lock on my mind . . .

One of the buckles clicked free and a strap fell away. Cyrus realized Skar, or the psi-master controlling his friend, had finally realized what to do.

"We'll surrender," Cyrus said, in a rush. "Do you hear me? I want to know your terms."

"No terms," Skar said. Yet he eased up on the pressure, no longer grinding Cyrus's wrist bones.

Taking the opening, as small as it was, Cyrus shot an elbow against Skar's stony face. The eyes flashed with rage. Sometimes, when one had powerful control of another, the Special or psi-master felt unexpected pain.

The soldier shoved Cyrus away from him. Cyrus crashed against the panel. The small of his back exploded with agony. He grunted, and then swiveled eel-like and slapped the switch, cutting communications with *Valiant*.

It wasn't over, though. The enemy had established the link. As Skar unlatched the last buckle, stood, and brought his other hand into play, Cyrus took a gamble. He broadened his null again, thereby weakening it. He might become barely visible to the enemy, showing them an outline of his mind. He heard enemy thoughts in his head, indistinct noises. For a second, he could see the chief psi-master in the alien Attack Talon. He was a human with an elongated head. A sliver *baan* encircled the cranium and was pressed against amplifier discs. Cyrus almost caught the psi-master's name.

Disappear, he told himself. *Go null—*

Skar's hands latched onto his throat. The soldier choked him, the ironlike fingers digging into flesh.

Despite that, Cyrus held onto the null. As a thumb dug deep, the whispering minds in his head snapped off. The mental images vanished and the pressure against his throat immediately quit.

"Cyrus, I—"

The Special from Milan opened his eyes. Skar slumped into the pilot's chair. The soldier turned away and wouldn't look at Cyrus.

Massaging his raw throat, coughing, Cyrus eased off the panel and sat down. That had been too close. What had he been thinking? It never paid to talk to the bastards. They always tried tricks. They had no sense of honor.

His gaze wandered to the scanner. The incoming missile kept accelerating even as the Attack Talon decelerated. *Valiant* had a greater velocity than their needle-ship, even with them accelerating. How long would it be before their vessel was in laser range of the enemy?

"It must be a nuclear-pumped missile that will fire X-rays," Cyrus said.

Skar still said nothing. It appeared he brooded.

"Don't worry about it," Cyrus said. "You didn't have a choice. They controlled your mind."

Skar's head snapped up and his mouth twisted with distaste as if he had sucked on a lemon. "Don't you understand? I despise my weakness. I acted contrary to my will. They controlled a Vomag soldier. I am a liability to you, to the cause."

"No you're not."

"I almost killed you."

"How does your face feel where I hit it?"

There was a red mark on the left side of the nose.

"You used a clever trick," Skar muttered. "I congratulate you."

"Look, I can teach you how to defend against mind control."

"I do not possess such abilities," Skar said.

"Right, you're not a Special, you're a . . ." Cyrus almost said "Normal." But Skar wasn't really normal. In a fight between them, Skar would win unless Cyrus could do something tricky. Maybe Argon could win a fight against Skar, but no regular human had a chance.

Argon had been the chief monitor aboard *Discovery*. The man had the blood of the Highborn in him. Cyrus hoped Argon was still alive. Out of all the Normals he'd known, Argon had the best mind shield.

"There's a way to shield against mind control and reading," Cyrus said. "Thinking about mathematical formulas, going over them again and again in your thoughts, is one of the best ways."

"That would shield me against them?" Skar asked, sounding dubious.

"Not completely," Cyrus admitted. "The math formulas make it harder. It's like static or the hissing just now. The mind controller would have to work harder to pierce your running computations. Sometimes repeating an endless litany in your thoughts helps, too. If you're really stubborn, that also helps."

"He dominated me so easily," Skar said.

"They hit us with something new, something more powerful than before. Personally, I think Chengal Ras brought along his best psi-master." Cyrus nodded. "They must want me—want the two of us—really badly, more than I realized."

The comm signal beeped again.

"No way," Cyrus said. "They can't believe we're that stupid."

"We are cattle to the Kresh," Skar said, glumly.

"Yeah," Cyrus said. "Tell me about it."

Their words dwindled, and they kept watching the scanner. Soon, the comm signal stopped. The missile didn't, though—it kept coming for them.

This is depressing, watching death accelerate for us.

Cyrus got up, went to the head, came out, and sat down at his station. A *baan* was there, a metal-colored band. It sat next to what looked like amplifying discs, but was really a reader. Two long prongs curved up out of it with discs at the end for him to press the *baan* against once it encircled his forehead. He'd been doing just that for the past three weeks. He had one memory crystal. The Reacher had given it to him on High Station 3. The crystal held information about the Anointed One, about Klane as a baby when first inserted into Clan Tash-Toi.

Big, muscular, reddish-skinned humans inhabited the stony highlands of Jassac. They were the Tash-Toi, and they lived like primitives, with clubs, spears, and a ruling hetman. The crystal had shown Cyrus the seeker, a shamanistic individual with obvious mind powers. Cyrus had reviewed the crystal repeatedly, studying in depth everything it had shown him. Unfortunately, the crystal hadn't given him many clues. How was he supposed to track down this Klane on a moon the size of Earth? Clearly, the psi-masters aboard *Valiant* would be hunting him, provided Cyrus and Skar even made it down onto the planetoid.

How old was Klane now, anyway? How old was the crystal? How had the Reacher gotten hold of the information?

Cyrus shrugged. He didn't know the answers. Maybe the Reacher had gotten the information through a clairvoyant. Anyway, except for Klane's age, the questions hardly mattered at this point.

"Any change in status?" Cyrus asked.

"No," Skar said, who had maintained his post.

"Should we get ready?"

"What do you suggest we do?" Skar asked.

Cyrus sighed, got up, and approached their sole window. Jassac filled the view. High clouds drifted over the red moon's surface. The place boasted fantastic mountain ranges and valleys like knife slashes.

"I'm surprised the Kresh on Jassac don't just fire missiles or ground-based lasers at us," Cyrus said.

"Perhaps Chengal Ras has not yet contacted them about us."

"I find that hard to believe," Cyrus said.

"Why is that?" Skar asked.

"It should be obvious why."

Skar shook his head.

Maybe the soldier had a point. The Kresh were unfathomable. Well, they were aliens and didn't appear or act like humans. An individual Kresh stood about nine feet tall and looked like an intelligent raptor wearing leather straps and metallic streamers. The aliens lacked psionic abilities, but apparently were intensely logical. They hungered for facts, and they had something called the *Codex of All Knowledge*.

Cyrus wasn't sure what that was supposed to be. Maybe the codex was a running encyclopedia or a vast computer program. The Kresh fiercely competed for rank. Despite their warm-blooded dinosaur bodies, they were hyperindividualists. The top one hundred Kresh ran the star system. Unimaginatively, the Kresh called that group "the Hundred." It seemed they ranked each other exactly. Thus, when the

VAUGHN HEPPNER

humanoid earlier referred to Chengal Ras the 109th, that meant the
Kresh was the 109th highest ranked among his species.

Cyrus wasn't sure, and Skar hadn't been able to enlighten him much
on the subject, but it seemed as if each Kresh had his or her precise area
of authority or responsibility. The Reacher had told him a few things
about the aliens. Each Kresh seemed to act like an independent king or
lord. Therefore, it was just conceivable that Chengal Ras hadn't yet
informed the Jassac-bound aliens about the runaway needle-ship.

"How much time do we have until impact?" Cyrus asked.

"A little over an hour until we reach the upper atmosphere," Skar
said.

"Are we going to try to land our vessel?"

"Not at these speeds," Skar said.

"Do we parachute out then while we're screaming down?"

"Negative," Skar said.

The soldier, like the other gene-warped humans Cyrus had met
so far, seemed to be devoid of humor.

"We have one antigravity sled," Skar said. "The needle-ship builders
did not incorporate normal antigrav plates onto our vessel." The soldier
shrugged. "I do not know why, perhaps to conserve weight or because
they lacked the hardware. Luckily, the Reacher or one of his people put
an antigrav sled into storage, and therefore we have some hope."

"I haven't seen any storage chamber aboard our ship," Cyrus said.

"Naturally," Skar said. "It is outside the vessel."

"So . . ."

"We will need to don vacc-suits, go outside, and climb onto the sled."

"And it can float us down to the planet?"

"In theory it should," Skar said.

"What could go wrong?"

"The sled is a one-person device, and there are two of us." Skar
looked away. He stood, and he nodded crisply. "I will, of course,
remain on the vessel as you—"

24

"No you won't," Cyrus said.

Skar turned in obvious surprise. "I am a danger to you. The enemy has locked onto my mind patterns—"

"Forget it, Skar. I'm not wandering the Jassac wastelands alone. You're coming with me."

"The sled—"

"We're going to make it work," Cyrus said.

"The danger—"

"You're my bodyguard, soldier. Are you attempting to shirk your duty?"

A sour look crossed Skar's features.

"I didn't think so," Cyrus said. "Now, I don't want to hear any more about it. You have to pilot us down to the surface. That's your task. Mine will be keeping the psi-masters off of us as we do it."

"If we reach Jassac in time," Skar said.

"Let's get ready," Cyrus said. "That will be better than sitting here watching the scanner."

"Agreed," said Skar.

Cyrus headed back to his station to pack what he'd need, or had room to take. They had to stay alive, and then they had to find the Anointed One.

Was Klane still alive? How old is he, anyway? And where in the heck is he on this barren wasteland of a planetoid?

3

The hour passed quickly as Cyrus and Skar watched the missile on the scanner.

Each wore a silvery vacc-suit, with a bubble helmet attached to the back of the neckband. Under the suits, each had a survival pack and weapons.

"If it's an X-ray missile, it is now in range," Skar said.

Jassac filled the window, and the mountains on the moon showed themselves as high, daunting, and widespread on the surface.

How am I supposed to find the Anointed One? Cyrus wondered. *Do we just bump into each other or what?*

The comm unit light blinked on and off again. It hadn't been doing that for some time. The aliens were hailing them one more time.

"Are you ready?" Skar asked.

"Yeah, sure," Cyrus said.

Each sat in his respective chair. After strapping in, Cyrus fixed his eyes on the scanner. He expected to see the missile detonate a nuclear warhead. Rods at the tip of the missile would channel the X-rays as a beam before the nuclear explosion obliterated the aiming devices.

Before that happened, Skar tapped the panel. Side jets maneuvered the needle-ship, rotating them. The planetoid moved, or at least it seemed as if it did to Cyrus. Soon, stars appeared in profusion, and still the needle-ship rotated. Jassac disappeared, and then colorfully banded Pulsar filled the window. The ship's single exhaust port now aimed at Jassac.

"I'm giving it full thrust," Skar said, as he tapped the panel.

The magnetic propulsion came online, slowing their velocity. Cyrus felt himself pressed against his seat, and it felt as if an anvil shoved against his lungs. Breathing became a chore. This was the strongest thrust of the journey, much greater than he would have thought possible.

"I'm burning out our propulsion," Skar said in a strained voice. "The engine will not last long."

"It doesn't have to," Cyrus gasped. He kept his eyes glued on the scanner, on the missile.

"This could work," Skar said.

Cyrus didn't want to bet on it. In the next few minutes, the Kresh missile would probably end all their dreams, and his life. He wished now that Earth's Psi Force had never hunted for him. They should have left him in Level 40 Milan. He'd been moving up in rank in the Latin Kings. He'd become a gunman, a gang enforcer. It had been a hard life, a brutal one, even.

Would I have survived the Red Blades? Likely, the answer would have been no. Several enemy gang members had trapped him the day Jasper and the cops had saved his sorry butt. Maybe joining Psi Force hadn't been the problem. Why had Jasper told him all those things? Why had he picked Spartacus as a hero? Did wearing a slave collar, the lock on his mind, really matter so much? If he—

The heck with this. How does bitching and moaning help anything?

"It's been a fun ride," Cyrus wheezed. "I'm glad I knew you, Skar."

The soldier was too busy adjusting the controls to answer.

"Too bad—" Cyrus said. He saw it then. Sight of the red line stole his words. The missile did not explode. Rather, it continued on its course just as before. Instead, a laser beam struck from *Valiant* and burned against the needle-ship.

Metal melted, making a churning, grumbling sound inside the chamber. Cyrus turned and shoved upward so he could peer over his headrest. A meter-wide area glowed red-hot to the side of the ship. It took a second for Cyrus to understand what he witnessed.

"Laser breach!" he shouted.

At the same instant, the laser penetrated the skin and beamed through the ship, hitting the other side. Metal melted, drops falling like rain, making a silvery puddle on the deck plates. In a microsecond, the laser burned through, making a second hole.

Several things happened at once. A gale-force sound whipped through the compartment as air shoved through the two holes and into the vacuum of space. Violent decompression followed. The beam also knocked out the magnetic propulsion. The g-forces stopped and they no longer shoved Cyrus against his padded chair.

"Put on your helmet!" Cyrus shouted.

In the violent wind, he reached up and slammed the bubble helmet into place, twisting it, attaching the locks. He pressed his air tank valve and heard the whoosh of air in his helmet. He looked over, and saw Skar doing the same thing. Then Cyrus's gaze shifted back to the scanner. It continued to show *Valiant* lasering them—the red line.

Is the missile a trick then? That doesn't make sense. No. The missile is a threat. Chengal Ras wants to capture us—capture me.

Cyrus nodded to himself. The Kresh meant to cripple the needle-ship so Chengal Ras could grab them. That was the only thing that made sense. Maybe if they reached the planetoid's surface, Skar and he would be out of Chengal Ras's authority. Some other alien might have jurisdiction on Jassac.

We have to use that crack between areas of authority to make like mice and slip out of sight.

Cyrus turned on the short-range suit emitter, linking the two of them for communication.

"We have to get out of here," Cyrus said.

"We have too much velocity," Skar said over the helmet's comm.

"There's nothing we can do now but try our best."

Skar unlatched himself. "Yes. I agree."

The laser no longer slashed through their vessel. *Valiant* had fired the one burst, disabling them. Now the alien waited.

The comm light blinked for their attention.

As the needle-ship raced down toward Jassac, Cyrus unbuckled, climbed his seat, and jumped after Skar. The soldier sailed smoothly through the chamber. Cyrus did likewise. He had trained in zero G maneuvers, practicing at times with *Discovery*'s space marines.

Anchoring himself with a magnetized palm, Skar opened the hatch. No air escaped because all of it had already fled into space through the twin laser holes.

"Turn on your boots," Skar said.

Cyrus bent down and tapped the magnetic boot controls. He felt the soles vibrate to a new setting.

"Follow me and watch your step," Skar said. "If you float free, there will be nothing I can do to help you."

"I got it," Cyrus said.

"What?"

"I understand."

The soldier nodded. Then he walked onto the metallic skin of the needle-ship.

Cyrus followed him onto the outer hull, planting his feet on the stealth surface. The sight daunted him. There was banded Pulsar on one side and vast red Jassac on the other. It was crazy beautiful. Everywhere else, the stars blazed in diamond splendor.

"Do you think *Valiant*'s crew can see us?" Cyrus asked.

"No," Skar said. "We climbed out the side hidden from them."

Once more, Cyrus was impressed by a soldier's tactical sense. "What side is the outer chamber on?" he asked.

"We have been granted a boon," Skar said. "It is on the hidden side."

"We won't be hidden once we drift off the needle-ship."

"We must hope atmospheric disturbance will aid us then," Skar said.

"Do we even have a chance, at the velocity we're traveling?"

"We breathe," Skar said. "Therefore, we have a chance.

"More soldier philosophy, eh?"

"I do not understand you," Skar said.

"Never mind. Let's do it," Cyrus said.

"That is sound advice."

The two men clanked along the needle-ship's hull. As they did, *Valiant* fired again, more steadily this time. The laser moved upward like a saw, and in moments it had sheared the ship into two halves. The laser didn't stop even then, but it began slicing their half in two.

"Run!" Skar said. He pumped his legs, dashing along the remaining side of the dying needle-ship.

Cyrus did likewise, and for a moment, both boots left the skin of the half ship. He might have floated away, but the suit's designer must have foreseen such an incident. The magnetic attraction of his boots increased enough to pull him down. He clanged into place with both boots. Yet it happened so quickly that he still tried to run. He wrenched his muscles by the exertion, and he toppled so his torso bent toward the ship.

Skar ran ahead of him.

You'd better think fast, Cyrus, or you're staying here forever.

Despite the throbbing of his joints, he reached and dialed down the magnetic strength of his boots. He also tapped in an override code, making sure his boots wouldn't do that again.

As Skar worked the hatch lock, the laser continued to slice and dice the sections of needle-ship. Cyrus ran along the hull. He reached Skar just as the other pulled out a pole and a standing pad big enough for one man. The pad was deep. It was the antigrav plate and likely had enough battery juice to help a man land. There were two of them, though, and hardly enough room for each to put a foot on.

"Are you ready?" Skar asked.

Cyrus twisted around and looked at Jassac below them. This was higher than a crazy space-jump stunt. This was the two of them in orbital space, going down much too fast—

"Let's do it before we chicken out," Cyrus said.

"Settle yourself onto the pad," Skar said.

Cyrus had a premonition, and he grabbed Skar's left arm. "Swear me a soldier oath you're not staying behind. Swear you'll join me on this."

"There is no time," Skar said.

"Swear it."

"You are the Tracker. Your life is more important—"

"Swear it," Cyrus said, "or I'm staying here with you."

"That is illogical."

"Yeah," Cyrus said.

In the light of Jassac, Skar studied him. Finally, the soldier said, "I swear."

Cyrus climbed onto the antigrav sled. Skar grabbed the pole with both hands, and he ran along the hull. He shoved the antigrav sled and Cyrus, building up velocity. Finally, he reached the end of the hull.

Cyrus grew tense. Would Skar keep his oath?

Yes! The soldier leaped, hung onto the pole, and climbed up beside Cyrus. The two of them each had a foot on the pad and clung to the pole. There was a control panel, a very small one, at the top.

They drifted away from the slowly spreading wreckage of the needle-ship.

Cyrus's jaw opened then. He visualized *Valiant*'s relative position in space. He realized that Skar had shoved them into the best spot possible, using the debris to hide them from the Attack Talon's scanners. That wouldn't last long, but it helped them just a fraction.

"You're a tactical genius, my friend," Cyrus said.

"I am a soldier."

"I guess that's saying the same thing, huh?"

Skar looked up at the wreckage. "They have stopped firing."

They drifted down toward Jassac. The needle-ship, in its component pieces, drifted after them.

"Do you have any preferences where we should land?" Skar asked.

Cyrus had studied the memory crystal for hours, for days, really. It had shown Clan Tash-Toi and Klane as a baby. It had also shown the surrounding territory. He thought about everything he'd cataloged: the soil, the height of the clan members, their stone weapons, and the complexity of their headgear.

He remembered a few of the things the Reacher had said: The aliens had terraformed the moon. Pulsar as a planet was quite far from the system's sun. That meant the planetoid was much colder than Earth would be. The deep valleys would be the most hospitable places so far, with the thickest atmosphere and the warmest weather. The little he'd seen of the Kresh led him to believe they would like warmer climes versus colder.

The real question was: Where would Klane be? And how could they find him?

I need a hunch, Cyrus realized. *I'm the Tracker, right? Doesn't it make sense I'm supposed to have some . . . ability to find this Klane?*

Cyrus thought about Klane as a baby. He had been white-skinned versus the reddish hue of Clan Tash-Toi. Klane had shown psi-abilities even then, pulling a blanket onto him to cover his nakedness.

Squeezing his eyes shut, knowing he was a weak telepath, Cyrus reached with his mind: *Klane.*

At that point, Cyrus felt minds searching for him. Several of the searchers called his name. He directed his thoughts toward them— then, with sickening speed, he drew back and practiced the null.

The enemy minds shot telepathic bolts toward him.

"What's wrong?" Skar asked. "You look worried."

Cyrus couldn't afford to answer. He concentrated on the null. He included Skar in it, and he made himself glass, a smooth surface. He had accidently shown himself to Chengal Ras's psi-masters. What an idiot.

"Look," Skar whispered.

Something in the soldier's voice caused Cyrus to open his eyes. A laser speared past them and toward the planet.

I caused that. Chengal Ras knows we're still alive.

"It is time," Skar said.

"Time to do what?" Cyrus asked.

"Hang onto the pole and do not let go," Skar said. "Do not lose your footing, either."

"Do you think we can do this?"

"I do," the soldier said.

Cyrus wrapped his arms around the pole, pressing his chest against it. This was madness. *I can't mind call Klane. I have to use logic to find him. What makes the most sense?*

He had no idea. He didn't know how reaching Klane would make one iota of difference. Besides, if the Resisters had clairvoyants, couldn't the psi-masters have some as well?

"Drop us near a valley," Cyrus said.

"In a valley?" Skar asked.

"No! The Kresh must live in the valleys. That's my guess, anyway. We don't want to land on top of them, but beside them."

Stone-faced, Skar adjusted the controls.

Cyrus had no idea if he'd guessed right or wrong. If he was hoping for intuition, he had none. If he had special skills to help him find Klane, he didn't know what they were.

"Ten seconds until we begin," Skar said.

"Will using the sled's power make us visible to those on *Valiant*?"

"The possibility exists," Skar said. The seconds lengthened until the soldier said, "Three, two, one, zero." He tapped the controls, and the wild ride down to the surface began.

4

Chengal Ras the 109th watched the large screen in Attack Talon *Valiant*. He had a three-Kresh crew in the control chamber with him. Outlying modules held a host of human techs and psi-able personnel, and a squad of Vomags for special purposes.

He was several inches taller than nine Earth feet, and rested his raptor-like bulk against an upright station. It was a Kresh acceleration couch. A dry, musky odor pervaded the chamber. Like the others here, Chengal Ras was huge but graceful, poised on two large legs, each ending with curved talons. He wore metallic streamers from his waist and neck, and wore smaller streamers around his two arms. The arms ended in smaller talons like large fingers, three of them. Chengal Ras wore a belt around his dinosaur-like waist. From it dangled various weapons and control devices.

"There is an urgent call for you, Excellency," one of the crew said.

"Put her on the main screen," Chengal Ras said.

The wreckage of the needle-ship disappeared. In its place appeared the image of Zama Dee the 73rd, a philosopher king—one of the Hundred. She was in charge of the moon of Jassac. She was large, with an old core burn across her snout, a whitish color that did not look good against her yellow and black hide.

"The Creator has granted you a safe voyage?" Zama Dee asked.

"I bless His kindness, yes," Chengal Ras said.

"You are wise."

"You are radiant."

Zama Dee clicked the talons of her right arm, indicating the ritual greeting at end. Behind her, an unclassified human carried a package, stepping into and out of visual. "My observers inform me you have fired a class-three laser at a survival boat entering Jassac orbit."

"It is so," Chengal Ras said.

"I would like an explanation for this aggressive behavior."

"Of course," Chengal Ras said. "I was about to inform you." He did not glance at his crew. They were vetted, but he hadn't taken any of them into his confidence. "I have conducted an emergency seek-and-destroy mission. I postulated an escapee from High Station 3, giving the stealth-craft several days' lead time. My crew acted flawlessly, finding and destroying the small vessel. I am in the process now of awarding codex points." He added the last for his crew's benefit, letting them realize that he would award the points for their silence as to the true nature of the chase.

"I see," Zama Dee said. "On the face of it, I find it odd that a near Hundred such as you would engage in such a routine endeavor. Perhaps you are collecting data for a new treatise?"

"I am in the process of collating ideas for a new paper, yes, but not concerning security work. I have found it practical to engage in routine endeavors as a reminder, a memory aid to myself."

"I do not follow your reasoning."

"I am not in the Hundred," Chengal Ras said.

"No," Zama Dee said. "I do not accept humility from you. Your zeal for . . . ah, *knowledge*, shall we say, is well known."

Chengal Ras grew wary. He could not believe that Zama Dee would so openly sneer at him. Yes, he strove to enter the Hundred. He did not mask that. His zeal, as she said, caused many to scorn him and belittle his efforts. He did that for a reason. Their scorn kept them from examining his actions too closely. Since he couldn't keep his zeal hidden—most would reason—he could not keep anything hidden. They were wrong. How wrong he would show them soon enough, if the Creator kept out of his way.

"Your stealth-craft came near my authorized ice-hauler corridor," Zama Dee was saying. "It could have caused an incident."

"I thank the Creator it did not," Chengal Ras said.

Zama Dee closed her mouth and eyed him critically. "Return to High Station 3, or wherever it is that you practice your syllogisms. We do serious work on Jassac for the furtherance of the Race. I do not approve of unsolicited laser fire here."

"I have overstepped myself—"

"Desist! I do not have time to listen to . . . to your excuses."

Chengal Ras bristled. Would she openly mock him before his crew? This was unseemly, a challenge to his authority, to his status.

"I must return to my laboratory. Thus, I am leaving," she said.

"May radiance shine on you," Chengal Ras managed to say.

A moment later the connection ended, and the large screen retuned to showing the wreckage of the needle-ship.

Not for the first time, Chengal Ras made a mental note of one of the Hundred who would taste his wrath in the days of his elevation. He would remind Zama Dee of her mockery as he dismembered her limbs and removed her organs. He would ask her to mock him then.

"The two High Station 3 cattle are free-falling toward Jassac, Excellency," Dez Rek said. She was the Attack Talon's pilot and ranked 828,002nd.

Chengal Ras made no reply. He could see that for himself quite well.

"Should I contact Jassac Central?" Dez Rek asked.

Chengal Ras knew a moment of igniting rage as the tip of his tail twitched. Could the pilot have actually formulated those words? She had just heard his conversation with Zama Dee. Yes, the pilot was ranked high enough that he would expect her to be more intelligent.

She must have realized he had diverted from full disclosure of the truth for a critical reason.

Yet now she suggested he tell Jassac Central, which meant tell Zama Dee, about the two prized cattle? Either the pilot tested him—a bad idea for one in her position—or she played a deeper game. He must tease out her reasoning and act accordingly.

"Your suggestion is premature," Chengal Ras told her.

"The cattle have entered the Jassac atmosphere," Dez Rek said. "The Concordat Treatise of Fifty-Two Sigma declares we are honorbound to inform the governing authority of such an event. Our window for subterfuge has legally ended."

Chengal Ras turned away from the screen, the better to regard *Valiant*'s pilot. He had not anticipated Dez Rek's attempt to climb rank this soon in her apprenticeship. She tried to push him, tried to force her will against his. He had already openly hinted of bribing them with codex points to remain silent. Logically, since there were three of them, it could only be a small number of points for each. Now it appeared she attempted a greater gain. Granted, it seemed like an opportune moment for her to inflict the concordat on him. She must surmise his desire to keep this secret for as long as he could. Yet might she have a stealth contract with Zama Dee?

He should have studied her profile in greater depth.

"Excellency," she said, showing her lack of remorse, "I should note for the record that the two strays have engaged the antigravity sled. I compute a 63 percent chance of success on their part. Jassac Central would wish to know about High Station 3 strays on their game preserve."

The other two Kresh in the chamber kept silent. By their stances, Chengal Ras knew they listened keenly to the exchange. There was a reason he hadn't taken any of them into his confidence yet. Oh, yes, there was a most logical and precise reason why he flew alone among the Kresh.

He had attained the dizzying rank of 109th far in advance of others his age. He had climbed with quickness, trampling any who stood in his way. It was true he had a sharply logical mind even for a Kresh. His papers and treatises were legendary among the younger set. And his stubbornness of purpose—it was greater than all but the highest ten.

Even with all that in his favor, he had climbed higher and faster than a Kresh like him should have been able to achieve.

The explanation was simple. He had been born on the outer asteroids to the Seven Sisters, and therefore been a declared rogue. During his formative years, the Hundred had also declared the Seven as outcast, hunting and slaughtering them one by one. Due to his age, Chengal Ras had been spared after his capture, and they had given him a second-class education in the 2020 Gymnasium, a place of decidedly inferior quality.

Seething at the indignity of the constant slights and the setbacks of his life, he had sworn a secret oath. He would climb and beat the best of them. Three years later, Chengal Ras had discovered a shortcut to rank. With logical and unerring precision, he had taken it.

In a word—two words—he cheated.

He obeyed the honor codes and customs of the Kresh *most* of the time. He departed the codes and customs at strategic moments of pregnant opportunity. This possibly was such a time. Now a climber in his personal retinue chose to reveal herself. It was too soon. She should have waited for maximum gain and to protect her life. Now he would have to make a deal with her or he would have to take a drastic step.

The odds for advancement here were astronomical. In fact, he believed this the opportunity of a lifetime. Once one reached the final thousand, higher rank became most difficult to achieve. Reaching 109th was a fantastic feat. To get even one rank higher would be many times harder than what he had achieved so far.

Therefore, he would give Dez Rek one chance to reform. He didn't believe there was anything he could say to change her opinion. He would have to let her own mind do the arguing for her.

Thus he waited, watching the two cattle attempt a landing at high velocity and with a single antigravity sled to aid them. Under normal circumstances, he would not give them high odds. These two, however, were different. Dez Rek must have considered that while computing their odds. They were unique specimens. The one actually came from out-system, much, much farther than the outer asteroids. Cattle inquisitors had discovered the name of the humanoid's home system: Sol, two hundred and thirty light years distant. These cattle were different from the machine-oriented humanoids that had attacked Fenris several years ago.

Yes, these two had escaped out of High Station 3. It had been cleverly done, with aid from the vermin, the Humanity Ultimates in the slums.

"Excellency," Dez Rek said, "time is critical."

Chengal Ras gazed at her. She would persist. She was a climber, indeed. He had gauged her wrongly. That was unusual. He had a gift for reading Kresh and for reading cattle, too. Apparently, she did not understand that she could go farther riding his tail to greatness. She was an egotist. He knew the signs well, because he was a full-blown egotist himself. Under normal circumstances, the Hundred would have long ago ordered his destruction. He had hidden his gross egotism through what the highest considered buffoonery.

The Race could not long survive many category-one egotists in their midst. Chengal Ras had destroyed several category-two egotists in his time. One such was still in his employ, although not on *Valiant*. That was too bad.

"I do not wish to appear insistent," Dez Rek said. "But time is limited, and these two are level-three hazards. They could possibly implement the Grand Rebellion as written by the Second."

If the pilot tried to dazzle him with her knowledge, she failed dismally. Chengal Ras had not only read about the Grand Rebellion, he had added an addendum to it that had won him critical acclaim. In fact, it had propelled him from 110th to 109th. It was likely Dez Rek was aware of the addendum. A climber usually knew her selected target. Therefore, what was she hinting at?

"You are rational and rigorous," Chengal Ras said. "I would reward you for your insight."

The other two Kresh turned away from their stations to glance at him in surprise.

"The ribbons I'm wearing are too paltry to show my proper appreciation," Chengal Ras said, indicating those on his body. "I would bring you a red."

A red indicated many codex points. An accumulation of codex points was how one gained rank. He could only give her points out of his own vault. Therefore, Kresh only paid out points in a miserly manner.

"I . . . do not comprehend," Dez Rek said.

He knew she did not because he had just acted out of character. He was counting on a climber's greed to blind her long enough for him to act decisively. "It will take two minutes."

"I will contact Jassac Central in your absence," the pilot said.

"No. You will patch me through only while in my presence. One, I would have them record the codex points as I award them, as that is the proper ceremony. Two, it is my responsibility to tell Jassac Central of the danger."

"This is true—" Dez Rek stopped abruptly. She had almost insulted him.

"Two minutes," Chengal Ras said.

"Of course, Excellency," Dez Rek said. "I await your commands."

Chengal Ras stalked toward the hatch, with his talons scraping against the deck plates. He kept from glancing at the others. They might recognize his unease if they saw his eyes. This was a new step for him on his road to the Hundred. He knew that once he reached the exalted state, that he would attempt to gain entrance into the Ten. Still, to do what he planned . . . it was difficult for him. It would set him on the hard path to the top. Yet he must take it, for he refused to be denied preeminence. He would win, and he would do it at all costs.

This was a prime warship. The personnel were his best. He would miss them, including the crack soldiers, the Vomag cattle, and his best Bo Taw.

He should have taken a different Attack Talon.

Chengal Ras hardened his resolve as he entered a lift. He rode it down to a seldom-used corridor, strode to his special single-ship, and climbed into it. The hatch clanged shut behind him. Seconds went by, and sudden acceleration pressed him against the upright couch as the single-ship launched out of the Attack Talon and into space. He waited.

"Excellency," Dez Rek said over a comm unit. "I have you on my scanner. You have left *Valiant*. May I ask why?"

"The answer should be obvious," he said. He pressed a switch, and he waited a few moments longer.

"Excellency, I can only conclude—"

Dez Rek never had a chance to finish her thought. Attack Talon *Valiant*'s nuclear-powered engine detonated. Everyone aboard the ship died in the blast, including the three Kresh in the control chamber.

Chengal Ras exhaled sharply, riding ahead of the spreading radioactive zone. He had done it, and it felt evil to him. He shuddered and wished there could have been another way. Dez Rek had badly miscalculated and forced him to this. He sighed, and he pressed a beacon, summoning aid from Jassac Central.

Now he would hunt the two cattle on his own. He could not let them get away. It would be harder with the 73rd watching him, but he would outwit any who thought to thwart his rise to power.

He had made his own study of the Grand Rebellion. The addendum he'd written had propelled him from 110th to 109th. Yet he had left out the most important finds. These he used for himself, as well as the underground network of Resisters. Oh yes, he planned to use them in the furtherance of his goal of attaining the Hundred and then the Ten. If he could, he would even reach for First. Chengal Ras, First of the Kresh.

To gain such an exalted rank would take great cunning and heightened cheating. It might even take a massive disruption of the Fenris System. Possibly, it could weaken the Kresh hold on the Chirr planets.

Chengal Ras was willing to gamble because he would do anything to rise. His will for power was absolute. He was the egotist of egotists, self above all.

His leathery lips slid upward, revealing his gleaming teeth. He was Chengal Ras, and he would use these Humanity Ultimates to remake the rankings into something more to his liking.

5

Cyrus Gant expected death at any moment. The atmosphere might help them a little, yet he doubted it was thick enough to distort a military laser.

They rode the antigravity sled, the small vehicle shaking wildly as if trying to loosen his grip around the pole. Then the bottom of his foot became hot, concentrating on the ball of his left sole.

"Do you feel that heat?" he asked.

"Yes," Skar said.

Apparently, the soldier didn't have any more time to speak. His gloved fingers kept playing over the controls. Cyrus didn't know what Skar did exactly, but it had kept them alive so far.

It might have been beautiful, the fast descent toward the surface, but he kept wondering if he was about to die. Towering, stony peaks stood beside vast, slashing valleys like those on Mars or the Grand Canyon on Earth.

Lights glowed in some of the valleys. That seemed to indicate high technology. The upper plains looked bleak, a red desert of windswept stone, sand, and dirt. Seeing that the system's sun was so far away, he wondered what kept the planet warm enough for people to survive here.

The heat coming through the sole of his boot became too much. He switched feet, and he nearly lost his grip on the pole while making the exchange.

"Let me explain the sled's workings," Skar said.

"Why? You're doing fine."

"I must leave you, my friend. The sled—"

"If you step off this thing, I'm stepping off it, too," Cyrus said.

"That does not make sense," Skar said. "You must warn your home system of the Kresh. I wish to aid you in that."

"Are you tired of living?"

"No. That is not—"

"I didn't think you soldiers believed in suicide."

"Why do you attempt to belittle my sacrifice?" Skar asked.

"Work the sled," Cyrus said. "Ask me philosophical questions once we're down."

The antigravity sled shook even worse than before. The heat under Cyrus's foot became unbearable. He switched feet again. Skar adjusted the controls. Whatever he did made it worse. Smoke began billowing out of the antigrav plate. The machine lurched, and lurched again, taking them down faster.

"It cannot handle two of us, not at this velocity," Skar said.

"Burn it out. Make the bastard work for its death."

Skar stared at him through his bubble helmet. At last, the soldier shrugged. He adjusted the controls, and Cyrus nearly shouted at the heat burning through his sole.

The smoke intensified, and the next lurch almost threw him off. Then, moment by moment, the smoke went from black to gray to whitish, and then it became a trickle. The heat dissipated, and a grin spread across the soldier's face.

"I'm eating up battery power," Skar explained. "We may not have enough juice to land."

Cyrus watched the mountains, and then concentrated on one range in particular, the one closest to them. A huge zigzagging crack showed the valley beside it.

"I can steer for a time," Skar said. "Do you have any suggestions?"

What made the most sense? Then Cyrus had it. "Yeah," he said. "If you see any primitives—humans—land near them."

"You wish to land near a clan on the uplands?" asked Skar.

"Exactly," Cyrus said.

"I can see nothing from this height."

"I realize that. So steer for the plains."

For the next few minutes, they floated down toward the surface. The sled lurched again, and a high-pitched whine began. It told Cyrus they were farther down then he realized, deep in the atmosphere. Clearly, the sled didn't have long to live.

The mountain range, seemingly underneath them, shifted to the left. The same thing happened with the deep valley.

"How far away from the mountains do you wish to be?" Skar asked.

"Two days' march, I guess," Cyrus said.

The antigravity sled began swaying back and forth like a swing. The trickle of smoke increased, and it became black-colored again. If the sled gave out, they were dead. It was as simple as that.

"Too bad we couldn't have landed the needle-ship," Cyrus said.

"We live," the soldier said.

Something about that, or the way Skar said it, struck him as funny. Cyrus threw back his head and laughed. Yeah, he lived all right. Despite everything, this was just plain cool. He rode an antigravity sled down from space. If he couldn't enjoy this, then what could he enjoy? The aliens had shot their ship to pieces and he was still alive. Screw them, anyway.

"Are you well?" Skar asked.

Cyrus looked down at the nearing red plains. He spied a field of boulders and then tall, spindly grass. "I'm great!" he shouted. "We're going to make it, my friend. We escaped from High Station 3 and we reached the damn planetoid. I don't know about you, but I think that's fantastic."

"The odds were against us, certainly," Skar said.

"We're going to win," Cyrus said, as fierce resolve beat in his chest. "We're going to warn Earth. I don't know how, but I know I'm not quitting, ever. If we can jump off orbital wreckage and land here on the surface—"

The antigravity sled gave the worst lurch yet, and it dropped.

"What just happened?" Cyrus shouted.

"You cursed us," Skar said. "You celebrated before the victory had been achieved. That always brings bad luck."

Cyrus watched the ground rush up. At the same time, Skar's hands blurred across the controls. The antigrav plate shuddered, shuddered again, and the thing billowed smoke. Yet it floated again.

"All we need is another minute," Cyrus said.

Skar must have worked a miracle. The ground floated up toward them. Then, through the smoke, Cyrus noticed movement in the distance.

"Hey!" he shouted. "What do you see over there?" He dared to point.

Skar twisted around. "Natives," he said. "I count five primitives with spears. They're racing here."

Neither man had time for speech after that. The antigravity sled plummeted the last one hundred feet toward the rock-hard surface below.

Cyrus knew they were traveling too fast. Fifty feet, forty, thirty, twenty—

"Jump!" Skar roared.

The soldier sprang off the sled. Cyrus followed a second later. Relieved of their combined weight, the antigravity sled slewed to the right, and it moved more slowly. Cyrus fell. His stomach tightened and he tried to ready himself. The jump had thrown him off, though. He struck with his side, bounced up, and hit again. He groaned in agony, twisting on the ground. What had he broken? His entire side felt as if it were on fire. He tried to breathe, but his lungs locked. He groaned again, twisted again. Then Cyrus Gant blacked out from the pain.

||||||||||

Cyrus's eyes fluttered as an odd, dusty odor permeated his nostrils. His entire left side throbbed and felt numb at the same time. Breathing was a chore.

"Can you hear me?"

Cyrus wondered who spoke to him. He was disoriented, dizzy, and—oh. He was in an alien star system. He had landed on an Earth-sized moon. The air was cold, crisp in his lungs, and it tasted different from anything he'd known. He was on a foreign moon in a different star system. He might be the first human to have reached another world like Earth.

Well, no, that didn't make sense. The first colonizing ship from the solar system would have held the first people to do that.

His eyes finally came into focus, and he saw Skar staring down at him. The soldier had shed his vacc-suit and he wore his brown uniform with red shoulder taps. Skar had a thicker chest than anyone Cyrus had known. In reality, the soldier didn't really have a neck. With his helmet and alert eyes, Skar seemed like an alien, especially with those gorilla-like arms. He had a sidearm and a short-handled axe dangling from his belt. Cyrus recalled the first time he'd seen Vomags, inside the belly of a Kresh military vessel. He was glad the soldier was on his side.

"Can you understand me?" Skar asked.

"Yeah," Cyrus whispered. He noticed Skar had twisted off the bubble helmet—he could breathe the planetary air. So, Cyrus took off his own helmet, figuring the air was good.

"The natives approach," Skar said. "You must get up."

"I don't know if I can."

"Are any bones broken?"

"Maybe. I hurt like hell. Does that count?"

"No," Skar said. "Broken bones—"

"I'm joking. How about helping me out of this suit?"

Skar reached down and pulled. Cyrus yelled and flinched from the contact. The soldier frowned. "I will try again, more slowly this time."

"Yeah," Cyrus wheezed.

Bit by bit, Skar, with Cyrus's help, removed the vacc-suit. There wasn't any blood, nor did any bones stick out of his flesh. That was good, right?

Cyrus wore a sidearm and had a High Station 3 knife. It wasn't a vibrio-knife from Earth, but it had good balance, at least.

The big test came a moment later. With Skar's help, Cyrus climbed to his feet. Standing made his left side throb even more, and his neck had stiffened into near immobility, but at least he could balance on his own two feet.

"Spit," Skar said.

Cyrus wondered what for, but he did it.

Skar examined the spittle on the red ground. "I don't think you have internal bleeding," the soldier said.

"That's something."

"What are your plans for the natives?" Skar asked.

"Let me sit down," Cyrus said. Without moving his head or neck, he managed to sit on the ground. He leaned on his right side and sipped from the canteen Skar handed him. After capping it, he moved his eyes and looked up at the wispy clouds. He could hardly believe they had come down from outer space to land on dirt. He would have laughed, but that would have pained his left side too much.

"How come you're not hurt?" Cyrus asked.

"I have space dropped before," Skar said. "It was part of my training."

"I bet you landed on your feet like a cat."

"What is a cat?" Skar asked.

"How far away are the natives?" Cyrus asked, ignoring the soldier's question.

Skar shaded his eyes from the rising sun. "I can see their dust."

Cyrus managed to twist around. Yeah, he could see dust, too. In a little while he saw the outlines of men. Yeah, they were headed this way.

"How did you see they had spears earlier?" Cyrus asked.

"My helmet had a HUD. It shorted out, unfortunately."

"We get all the luck, don't we?"

"We live," Skar said.

The crash had welded Cyrus's neck muscles into place. There was no way he would try to nod in agreement. That didn't matter now, anyway. He had to think. Cyrus closed his eyes and opened them thirty seconds later. "The way I see it, we have one clue. We know the Anointed One's name. I'm hoping Klane is older than a baby. The Reacher never told me how old he's supposed to be now. I guess there are many things the Reacher never explained. But if Klane is the hero of this holo-vid drama, the big savior of the human race, he must have done a few things already to show his greatness."

"What kind of things?" Skar asked.

"Good question. I have no idea. I'm just speculating."

"I see," Skar said.

"Unfortunately, that's all we have. That's our clue: the name Klane. I'll ask them if they've heard about him. If they have, I'll ask how we can get ahold of him. If they haven't . . . we're crap out of luck."

"We wait for them, then?" Skar asked.

"What's troubling you?"

Skar glanced in the natives' direction. "We are strangers. How do the Tash-Toi or other clan members treat strangers on Jassac?"

"You think they'll attack us?"

"There are five of them and two of us."

Cyrus thought about that. "One of my teachers once told me that intercity gangs act like primitives. I happen to know a little bit about gangs. Yeah, maybe this is their territory and they're coming to chase us off. But I'm not too worried. We have guns. We ought to be able to make them listen to us."

Skar folded his arms, watching the dust, no doubt watching the outlines grow. "We will not need guns to deal with them."

Gingerly reaching up, Cyrus attempted to massage his neck, particularly a hard knot the size of his eye. When he touched the bruised flesh, he winced, dropping his arm. He thought about lying down, but wondered if he'd be able to get up again anytime soon. He might stiffen into a log. That would be bad, especially if any Kresh came to inspect the wreckage.

"We can't stay here," Cyrus said, indicating the antigravity sled in the distance. "In fact, we'd better leave before the Kresh show up."

"Can you walk?" Skar asked.

"I don't have a choice, not if I want to remain free. Let's go."

"Do we head toward them or away?" Skar asked.

You'd better think really hard here. This isn't a game. This is life or death for you and for your friends in High Station 3. It could even be life or death for the solar system. He knew what he should do, but just how hardened a survivor was he? He knew about making the tough choices. He'd been doing it all his life in Level 40 Milan. The schooling he'd received in Crete had given him a veneer of civilization, nothing more. At all costs, he had to remain free of the aliens.

"We need native clothing," Cyrus said.

Skar gave him a level stare.

"The Kresh came after us from High Station 3," Cyrus said. "I don't know what that means exactly, but it shows they're taking us seriously. You and I stick out like sore thumbs out here. We have to blend in better if we're going to hide from the Kresh."

"I doubt the natives will give us their clothing."

"Yeah, I know," Cyrus said. He'd been an enforcer for the Latin Kings. He'd used a gun before, and knives, and he'd made penniless people hurt for failing to make the vig, the interest on loan-sharked credits. "Let's get this over with," he said.

He got up and they started walking. It made his left side throb, and he soon found himself panting, with sweat staining his clothes. Despite his injury, he didn't believe he was that out of shape. Then it came to him.

"This place must have a thin atmosphere," Cyrus wheezed.

Skar glanced at him. The soldier seemed the same as ever, a block of hardened muscle who could endure anything.

For a moment, Cyrus hated the shorter man. *You'd better be glad for what you have and exploit it to the max.* With that resolved, he concentrated on the landscape and the approaching natives.

The mountains towered to the left. A field of ten-foot spindly grasses waved far to his right. The approaching warriors kicked up dust, having come from a vast open expanse. They ran in a line, thickly muscled men standing taller than either Skar or him. Their reddish-brown skin looked tough, like cracked leather. They had dark eyes, slashes for mouths, and hooked noses. Each warrior wore leather garments and complex conical helmets of fur and bits of bone and black rock. Uniformly clad, each clan member carried a leather shield, what looked like a stone-shod spear, and a heavy flint dagger strapped against his chest.

Wait a minute. The last one looked different. Instead of a man, she was a woman. And instead of blocky muscles, she was lithe, with long legs, and she wore a knit cap. She also happened to be well endowed, a regular barbarian princess.

The others seemed similar to what he'd viewed in the reader these past three weeks. Were they Tash-Toi, or were they from another tribe? How likely was it he had landed in the right spot?

"Do they speak our language?" Skar asked.

"We're going to find out soon enough," Cyrus said.

The lead warrior halted, pointing his spear at them. The other warriors and the woman, the barbarian princess, halted beside the first man. Each native glared with open defiance, possibly hatred. They were roughly a hundred yards away.

"What do you want in our land, demons?" the first warrior, the largest of the group, shouted. He had a booming voice. "Be gone from us. Return to your valley of evil."

"They speak our language," Skar said.

Cyrus found it difficult to raise his left arm, but he managed to cup his hands around his mouth. "We're not demons," he shouted. "We're men just like you."

The biggest warrior glanced at his fellows. Warily, he approached closer. After he had taken five steps, the others reluctantly followed. The leader halted fifty yards away.

"You have the guise of men," the leader shouted. "But we saw you float down from the sky. Only demons possess such magic."

"You're wrong," Cyrus shouted. "We're men and we floated down from space. Surely, your legends tell of a time when people flew in the void."

The big warrior stubbornly shook his head. "You cannot deceive us, demons. We are the Berserkers, the fiercest warriors on the plains. Other clans run from us and hide. We do not accept your deception. Go! I, Stone Fist, demand it."

"Have you heard of Klane?" Cyrus shouted.

"Is that the name of your chief demon?" Stone Fist shouted. "Do you attempt to conjure a spell with his name? Know, demon, that I am unimpressed and do not fear your paltry spells. Your sky vehicle crashed. You are weak and therefore easy prey."

"We're not demons," Cyrus said. "Can't you accept the evidence of your own eyes?"

"He mocks you," the woman shouted.

Stone Fist raised his spear. "I give you your last warning, demon-spawn. Run from us while you can."

Skar unclipped his gun and handed it to Cyrus. Then the soldier drew his small-handled axe and strode toward Stone Fist.

"What deception is this?" Stone Fist shouted. "You dare to challenge the Berserkers on their own land?"

"I am a man," Skar said. "And I will defeat you in fair combat. Then you will see we are men like you."

Several of the warriors backed away, and they looked uneasy. One of them spoke quietly to Stone Fist.

"Stay here," Cyrus called to Skar. "It's better to talk this out."

The soldier shook his head and continued stalking toward the primitives.

Stone Fist bellowed and shook his spear. Then he beckoned his fellow warriors. With a roar, the Berserkers charged Skar. They towered over the shorter soldier; their shoulders were broader and their muscles seemed denser. Cyrus didn't see how Skar had a chance.

Skar didn't back off, though. Instead, he broke into a sprint, charging them.

Cyrus took in the situation. On one side was a Kresh-trained soldier with his axe, with gene-warped strength and speed. Despite that, he'd seen Argon toss soldiers like boys. The Berserkers looked powerful, and each side had equivalent weapons. Was Skar five times better than the primitives? Cyrus didn't want to bet on it, and he needed the soldier.

Cyrus's chest tightened. He didn't want to do this. But the needs of Earth, of humanity, demanded he take action. Lifting the soldier's gun, gripping it with both hands, Cyrus fired. He'd expected it to act like the other heat guns he'd seen before on High Station 3. Instead, Skar's pistol held exploding pellets. The first shot went wide, and blew a puff of dirt near the primitives. Two of the Berserkers noticed, and they looked surprised. It didn't slow them down any, though, and that's what counted.

Cyrus adjusted and fired again. This time, the leader's chest exploded, and the force knocked the Berserker to the ground. Without waiting, Cyrus retargeted. He caused the next native's head to explode with gory results.

That did it. The last three skidded to a halt. Cyrus shot again, killing the third native, blowing him onto the dirt. The last two Berserkers pivoted and sprinted like mad to get away, although they held onto their weapons.

Cyrus hesitated. He knew he should kill. They would tell their clan what had happened. Later, other clan members might hunt them, using their primitively honed skills. He'd have to kill a woman in cold blood, though. The hesitation lasted long enough that the last two sprinted out of easy range. Cyrus wasn't sure he could hit them even if he did fire, and he didn't want to waste precious ammo.

Lowering the gun, Cyrus moved in his uneasy gait to a watching Skar. The soldier finally slid the axe into its belt holder.

"I could have defeated them," Skar said, stonily.

"Defeat all five?" Cyrus asked.

"I am trained. They are primitives."

"Underestimating your foe is a bad idea."

"Given your action," Skar said, "you should have killed the last two."

"Yeah, I suppose." Cyrus handed the soldier the gun. He felt soiled, and he wished he hadn't murdered them. Just gunning them down—

"We've got to ditch our clothes," Cyrus said. "We'll wear their leathers so we can blend in."

"Neither of us have their reddish skin," Skar said. "I am clearly a Vomag, and you look exactly like what you are, an out-system human. We will fool no one."

"We wouldn't fool a Vomag, perhaps," Cyrus said. "But we might fool a Kresh."

"That is even less likely," Skar said.

"Do you have a better idea?"

"No."

"I didn't think so. Now let's hurry. I want to get out of here, and I don't want to keep looking at their corpses. I feel bad enough as it is."

Skar gave him a blank look before heading to the corpses.

A second later, Cyrus followed. He was stuck in an alien star system. He had to do what he had to do. That didn't mean he had to like it. No, murder was never easy. Now they had to get far away before the Kresh showed up.

6

Chengal Ras brooded as his single-ship orbited Jassac. He was having second thoughts concerning his precipitous action. Perhaps he should have taken Dez Rek into his confidence and slain her later at a more opportune moment. He could have saved *Valiant* and the prime cattle specimens. Now they were gone.

Yet revealing secrets to Dez Rek would have been a gamble, perhaps a bad odds hazard. He would have needed to trust her, and she had been a climber *and* an egotist. She might have attempted to leverage more out of him. It's what he would have done under similar circumstances. In fact, he had done exactly that several years ago.

His screen blipped. He tapped it, and Zama Dee regarded him.

Chengal Ras knew even greater unease. He reminded himself that she was 73rd for a reason. Some might believe her more logical and more clever than he. Her rank supported such a thesis, naturally. But he rejected the hypothesis out of hand. He was Chengal Ras. He was a prodigy, one hidden from the Hundred and from the Ten. Even from this inferior position today, he would play the game with utmost skill and outmaneuver the arrogant interloper.

"I have just been informed of a tragic accident," Zama Dee said. "Your Attack Talon unexpectedly exploded."

He heard her gloating tone. She thought him a buffoon to have lost his vessel. Should he play that role and use that angle to trick her?

"Just before the end," he said, "I detected sabotage."

She stiffened. "I hope that is not an accusation directed toward me."

"I would not be so rash as to accuse you," he said.

"That implies you mean not to openly accuse me," Zama Dee said. "Thus, you secretly accuse me in your heart, or at least suspect I or one of my confederates had something to do with your ship and crew's destruction."

"I am at your mercy, clearly. I have—"

"Chengal Ras," she said. "We will settle this issue here and now. Do you accuse me or my confederates of sabotage?"

"I have no evidence to base such a claim," he said.

"Am I to believe that you intuit such a thing?"

"No, of course not," he said.

"Will you sign an affidavit to that effect?" she asked.

"Is that your price for allowing me to land?"

"Do not be absurd," she said. "You have every legal right to land and request transfer to another locale."

"I have already placed a summons to High Station 3. A second Attack Talon will leave the station in several hours and rendezvous with me here."

"Do you wish—" Zama Dee glanced to her left as someone spoke in a low voice. The whitish core burn on her snout deepened in color. She regarded him again. "Survivors escaped your High Station 3 prey-craft. My observers have reason to believe your cattle have landed on the surface."

"I find that interesting," Chengal Ras said.

"I am sending an investigation team at once. I demand purity in my tests, and your cattle represent a possible contamination of my Jassac game preserves, infecting my primitives with new ideas. Possibly, you inserted your cattle here to warp my findings. Is that your hidden game?"

"I am not so foolish," Chengal Ras said. He was impressed, however, with the depth of her paranoia. Yes, she had made it to 73rd for a reason. He would adjust his actions accordingly.

"It appears your cattle have landed among the primitives in the Factor Three Reserve," she said. "Because you claim they arrived by accident, are there any unusual attributes concerning these two that I or my wardens should be aware of?"

Chengal Ras hesitated. There were several unusual attributes to those two. Of that, there was no doubt. They had escaped High Station 3 and successfully reached Jassac. At all costs, he must acquire them and extract everything each of them knew. Would Zama Dee claim the Sol native if her wardens captured him? Yes, unquestionably she would. He might possibly bring the case before the Hundred, but they usually decided legal cases in favor of one of their own. Even if he won legally, it might be months or even years before Zama Dee returned the Sol native to him.

Logically then, it would not pay to tell her the truth. What were the odds of her investigation team capturing them? The odds would be high, indeed. Yet those two were unique. Well, the one creature was different from the regular run of cattle. The other, if his facts were correct, was a Vomag.

"Your hesitation does not reflect well on you," Zama Dee said.

"I find that an odd comment. It is, in fact, slanderous in nature."

"You tread on dangerous ground, 109th."

He switched tack because he realized she was right, and she had a deep pool of paranoia. He respected that. "I hesitate because I am attempting to remember their classification."

"Your memory is legendary. Therefore, your hesitation implies duplicity."

"I assure you it is otherwise," he said. "The sabotage, the loss of *Valiant*—"

"The incident has upset your mental facilities?" Zama Dee asked. "Is that your claim?"

"I received an injury during the blast," Chengal Ras said.

"You appear well."

"Thank you," he said.

"That is not—oh, never mind. Continue your explanation," she said.

Good, good, she had returned to believing him a buffoon. His smoke screen had worked, at least to a degree. "To answer your query, one of the cattle is a soldier—"

"A Vomag?" Zama Dee asked.

"Precisely."

"And the second?"

"A high-grade pilot of human norm appearance," he said.

"What species?"

"Ungraded, as I've implied," he said.

"What made it such a good pilot?"

"That is precisely what I am endeavoring to discover."

"Chengal Ras, I must now inform you that I perceive deception. I have taken the liberty of monitoring certain of your bodily functions. I mean your breathing rate, the twitch of your eyeballs, and the nearly imperceptible changing hue of your facial hide."

"I protest this invasion of privacy," he said. She had lulled him. He would remember that. Had she become his enemy? How could he destroy her?

"I note your protest, and have logged it now." On screen, she tapped a panel before her. "However, I am the authority on Jassac. I find the sudden destruction of your Attack Talon to be highly suspicious. The bodily indicators show me you are not without—"

"Zama Dee the 73rd," he said, formally.

Her manner changed and she stood taller, taking a more imperious stance.

Chengal Ras thought at a furious pace. He had been reckless with his statements. Now she doubted him, and she used science to pierce his lies. He would remember her reliance upon machinery. Now he

59

must summon the power of his supreme egotism. Several years ago, he had tested a theory on his humans and had discovered a most interesting truth. The best liars believed their own lies. It gave them the semblance of telling the truth.

I believe. I have already started the paper. How dare she attempt to thwart powerful research.

"I must confess," he said. "Before the Creator, I will acknowledge my secret treatise. The unclassified specimen has shown me something interesting."

"I'm listening," Zama Dee said.

"Must you strip my data from me?" he asked. "It is a codex point—"

"Listen to me well, Chengal Ras," she said. "I have grown weary of your continued intent to sow confusion. You practice subterfuge at a dubious moment, to wit: directly after the destruction of prized property. It makes me wonder if you caused the destruction."

"This is outrageous," he said.

"For a normal Kresh, yes, I agree. But let me boldly state the obvious. You are the offspring of the Seven Sisters. They were notorious for having non-Kresh attributes. I'm afraid that I detect such anomalies in you."

If he could, Chengal Ras would have killed the 73rd right then. For these insults, he yearned to see her blood gush from her hide.

No, no, maintain decorum. She is recording me. She is analyzing my reactions. I am at a disadvantage in several categories. I must use my superior intellect to full effect or face a possible loss of rank.

"It would appear that you are susceptible to heightened emotions," Zama Dee said. "My indicators show you are angry."

"I have a tainted family line," Chengal Ras said, as smoothly as he could. "It plagues me no matter how hard I try to expunge it from my chromosomes."

"Interesting," Zama Dee said. "Is this a play for sympathy?"

"No. It is simply a bald statement of fact."

"Hmm, the indictors show you are bringing your emotions under control."

"I note you feel free to imply insults," he said. "Does this not indicate an emotive state upon you?"

"I grow weary of this exchange," she said. "I believe I have the evidence I need—"

"My treatise is simple," Chengal Ras said. "I believe human norms have advantages in certain situations, at least over the modified species."

"That is a dubious hypothesis," she said. "Our genetic-molders have improved upon the humanoids, giving us better soldiers, psionic-capable inquisitors, and—"

"In precise environments, the selected humanoid has greater utility," Chengal Ras said. "In a Chirr tunnel, for instance, one would use a soldier. But I am testing a different theory. Given changing environments, which humanoid has the highest survival value? I have begun to suspect the unmodified norms have a greater chance to succeed at a multiplicity of tasks than the gene-warped specimens."

"What does any of this have to do . . . ?"

"By your pause I see your intellect has already made the leap," Chengal Ras said. "I have included one soldier in the prey-craft and one unmodified norm. I had wished to continue testing the two of them."

"You expect me to believe this is why you practiced deceit here and now with me?"

This is the moment to lie to the best of my ability. I believe what I am about to say as the Creator's own truth.

"It is a simple treatise," Chengal Ras said, "but I believe it will have a revolutionary impact on our breeding programs. In truth, I see it elevating me two or maybe even three new levels."

"You attempt to reach 106th in a grand leap?"

"More than that," he said.

Zama Dee glanced at something unseen, likely the indictors of his eye rate and breathing. "Hmm, I see."

"As I have bared my secrets to you, I now formally request a landing permit and the results of your investigation team."

"Granted," she said.

"I would also like my property returned to me so I may continue further studies," he said.

Zama Dee stood motionless. At last, she said, "I grant that, too, on a provisional basis. First, my investigation team must apprehend your cattle."

"That should prove simplicity itself."

"Let me ask you, Chengal Ras. Would you care to wager any codex points on which humanoid my team captures first?"

"How many codex points?" he asked.

Zama Dee revealed her glistening teeth. The inner ones looked polished. "Let us make it one hundred points. I believe the team will capture the unmodified human first."

He blanched inwardly at the amount, and he seethed in secret at her. She could afford such a princely sum. For him—

"Yes, of course," he said. "One hundred codex points is acceptable. Your team will capture the soldier first."

"Interesting," she said, "very interesting." She tapped her panel. "I have recorded the wager. And you have made me more than attentive to those two cattle. I will be monitoring the situation closely."

Chengal Ras felt sick inside. He may have overplayed what little hand he had. Well, he must forge ahead and be ready to extract every benefit he could from the coming troubles. He had already destroyed one of his own Attack Talons. He would have no hesitation destroying more property in the furtherance of his quest.

7

Cyrus and Skar barely made it into the tall, spindly grass that towered above them as a Kresh sky vehicle slid through the air.

They both wore Berserker clan garments, including the tall, conical hats. Unfortunately, Cyrus had discovered that Jassac was too chilly to wear only the leather straps, buckles, and medallions. He still wore his regular shirt and pants, and wore the clan accoutrements over them.

"It will fool no one," Skar had informed him earlier.

The soldier wore the primitive outfit and carried his old garments in a carryall he swung at his side.

"Down," Cyrus hissed.

Despite his stiff neck, he'd looked back by turning his entire torso. He saw a dark object sliding low through the sky, coming from the direction of the nearest valley.

In silence, the two of them watched the sky vehicle.

"We should return to the edge of the grass in order to get a better understanding of the situation," Skar said.

Cyrus wanted to keep wading through the sea of grass, but he realized that Skar was right. They needed information.

Skar led the way. He moved like a jungle cat, never breaking stiff stalks or crushing the grass at the base. After his passing, the grass looked as it had before his coming.

Cyrus, on the other hand, blundered about. Except for the two years at the institute at Crete, he had lived either underground in Milan or aboard the corridors of a Teleship. This was alien, indeed, living rough in the wilds. He'd never had any experience at it. Thus, he broke stalks and crushed bases. By watching the soldier, he was starting to get the hang of it. Would it be soon enough, though?

"Be careful," Skar called out from ahead. "We're almost at the edge of the field."

Seconds later, Cyrus crouched down beside the soldier. The two of them peered through a last screen of stalks. They saw the crashed antigravity sled a little over a kilometer away. They'd also left the three corpses where they'd fallen. Skar had suggested they slash and hack the bodies to make it look as if the primitives had died through native weaponry. Cyrus hadn't believed it would fool anyone, nor had he wanted to cut up the dead.

"It's small," Cyrus said, pointing at the Kresh sky vehicle.

It had a thin, boxy shape, although somewhat curved at the front. On the top middle was a bubble canopy with a single Kresh operator underneath. The craft was half the size of the main chamber aboard the destroyed needle-ship.

"It's a capture-craft," Skar said. "I have seen them before."

"Capture . . . how?" Cyrus asked.

"Notice the front mount."

Cyrus squinted. He might have detected a hump on the front hood. It was hard to tell at this distance.

"I suspect it throws a net or fires a paralysis ray," Skar said.

The sky vehicle approached the antigravity sled and soon hovered over it by one hundred meters. After half a minute, the sky vehicle turned in a complete circle, began turning again, and slid toward the corpses. The vehicle descended to a man's height, stayed there for a minute, and finally came to a rest on the surface, sending up a puff of dust. The Kresh had parked near the three corpses.

The bubble canopy slid open and a Kresh climbed out of the car. Its resemblance to a raptor seemed uncanny to Cyrus. The alien opened a trunk in back and extracted poles. In its raptor-stalking manner, the alien approached the corpses. It appeared as if the alien recorded something with a handheld device.

"I wish we had binoculars," Cyrus said.

Skar grunted agreement.

After it had finished recording, the Kresh used the poles, neatly shoving something under one of the corpses. Effortlessly, the alien lifted the first dead primitive and carried it to the back trunk, sliding the body inside. The alien soon deposited all three corpses into the sky vehicle. The Kresh thoroughly examined the area. Afterward, the dinosaur-like creature put on a helmet and reexamined the ground.

"Is that an infrared-vision helmet?" Cyrus whispered.

"Be careful you make no sudden motions," Skar whispered. "It is always easier to spy movement than immobility."

"Do you think it can see us?"

"One must always assume the helmet has zoom capability."

The Kresh stalked back to where Cyrus imagined he'd been standing while firing Skar's gun. He had combed the area before leaving. Skar had, too. They had tried to take everything technological with them. They hadn't been able to take the antigravity sled.

The Kresh froze for thirty seconds. Perhaps the alien was speaking into a recorder or to someone back at its base. Then, the creature climbed back into the sky vehicle and flew to the antigravity sled. The vehicle landed in another puff of dust. The Kresh climbed out and seemed to test the sled, poking it with a pole. Eventually, the alien carried the sled to the car and put it in the trunk.

"What's next?" Cyrus asked.

"Patience will likely reward us with an answer," Skar said.

The sky vehicle lifted and hovered over the site. Finally, the Kresh raced away in the direction of the plain. Cyrus found it ominous that the sky vehicle took off in the exact direction the two surviving primitives had taken.

"Do you think it's tracking them?" Cyrus asked.

"I do."

"That means the alien can track us."

"At least to here," Skar said. They both stood. "You must move more carefully through the grass," the soldier said.

"Let's get started," Cyrus said.

They did. Time passed; Cyrus's left leg became tired, and he started to limp. How in the world could he find Klane, anyway? This was going to be impossible. Well, surviving a free fall onto a planet should have been impossible, but the two of them had done it. Why couldn't they find Klane, too?

Walking became monotonous. Nothing changed. The grass hissed against their garments, and every once in a while a blade caught on their clothes.

"I imagine you could make good rope out of this stuff," Cyrus said, as he shoved a long blade out of his way.

Skar said nothing. The soldier marched as if he were late for a battle. It was a relentless step.

"Do you hear that?" Cyrus asked.

Skar stopped, and he raised his head. Then he turned fast, and motioned Cyrus to duck. With his legs, the soldier lowered himself like a submariner bringing the periscope down.

Instead of listening to Skar's advice, Cyrus looked up over his shoulder. The sky vehicle slid into view. Profanity exploded out of his mouth and he hit the ground. The stalks around him shook, and his neck burned red-hot with agony at the sudden motion.

Like a crab, Skar scuttled away from Cyrus as his garments whispered against grass.

The sky vehicle slid closer, and Cyrus could hear its mechanisms. Panic threatened as fear thudded through him, along with a flood of shame for blundering like a fool just now. Was this how he was going to save Earth from the aliens? The flying machine came even closer, and Cyrus scrambled to his feet.

His left side and his neck throbbed, but panic washed adrenaline into his system. He stood and saw the reptilian Kresh inside the bubble canopy. The creature was huge like all the others of its kind. Yet there was something lesser about this one. It was hard to pinpoint the difference, but Cyrus certainly felt it.

Without any visible emotions, the Kresh manipulated its controls. A gun popped out of the front hump of the sky vehicle. The weapon swiveled around to point at Cyrus. Time seemed to slow down for him even as Cyrus reacted as fast as he could. He used his mind powers and attempted to short something within the sky vehicle.

Instead of causing the sky vehicle to crash, the bubble canopy slid open. The Kresh looked up in surprise. A second later, the alien concentered on its task of shooting the human.

Cyrus tried to focus his thoughts for another stab of telekinetic power. He lacked time for the opportunity. The orifice of the gun on the front mount lit up. A microsecond later, Cyrus froze, and then he toppled. He couldn't make his mouth move in order to shout or to make his vocal cords vibrate enough to mutter his rage. Like a falling log, he crushed stalks and slammed against the ground. His nerve endings silently screamed their complaint at the pain. He wanted to rave and roar. Instead, he lay on his back, unable to move, but watching the sky vehicle.

He heard Skar's gun then, the *phutt* sounds it made. One pellet exploded harmlessly against the half-open canopy. Then blood sprayed and bone chips blew into the air. The angle was bad, but the topmost part of the Kresh's head disappeared as blood spurted upward.

The Kresh slumped forward. Cyrus dearly wanted to squirm out of the way or even open his eyes wider in wonder. The sky vehicle slid toward him. Then it passed overhead like Death's shadow, and several seconds later he heard it plow into the ground. Things crumpled and shattered, and a burnt electrical smell billowed into existence.

From his location on the ground, Cyrus heard sizzling, zapping sounds. They intensified until the crackle of grass fire drowned them out.

How long would the paralysis hold? Cyrus was defenseless. What if Skar couldn't find him in the vast maze of grass?

He heard the soldier running, with stalks cracking in half.

Skar, Skar, I'm over here. Panic threatened again. What would it feel like, burning to death while he couldn't move?

The intense crackling sounds of fire grew louder, and out of the corner of his eyes, Cyrus saw leaping flames. Would the entire sea of grass become a wild fire?

There was shouting, banging, and more shouting. What was going on?

I don't want to die like this. I can't believe it. After crossing two hundred and thirty light years, I'm going to roast to death on the first alien world I reach.

Cyrus strove to move. He strained, but nothing worked. After that, as the flames leaped higher, he struggled to maintain his calm. Maybe he could use his psionics to break the paralysis. For the next few minutes, he did what he could. Unfortunately, his mind felt sluggish. Did the paralysis ray affect it in some way?

"Cyrus!" Skar shouted. "Cyrus, where are you?"

Here, here, I'm over here. Don't leave me, Skar. Search for me.

"He could be dead," a woman said.

"He's not dead," Skar said, harshly. "The Kresh hit him with a paralysis ray."

"What is that?" the woman asked.

"The demon cast a spell over him, freezing his muscles," Skar said.

"The demons are evil," the woman said in an agreeing tone.

That must be the barbarian princess speaking. Yes, of course. The

Kresh must have tracked down the last two Berserkers and captured them. Skar had no doubt freed them from captivity.

"You are a demonslayer," the woman said in admiration.

"Help me find my friend," Skar said.

Cyrus could hear them beating the grasses, shouting his name. All the while the fire grew. He could feel the heat against his face.

"Here! I've found your friend."

Cyrus saw the woman bend over him. She looked young, even though she had sunburnt skin. She had brown eyes and a raw gash over the bridge of her nose. Despite that, she was beautiful, with a full figure and long brown hair. She wore fur garments and had smooth limbs like a triathlete.

Cyrus wondered if she would take the opportunity to kill him silently.

Her eyes showed curiosity, interest perhaps. She opened her mouth, and he wondered what she meant to ask.

Skar appeared then, limping into view. "Cyrus," he shouted. "Can you hear me?"

Cyrus could only stare.

"He is under a terrible spell," the woman said. She glanced toward the flames. "Do you want me to put him out of his misery?"

"No!" Skar said.

"The fire grows," the woman said, as if making an argument.

Skar snarled, and he pointed a finger at her. "We're carrying him out of here."

"Impossible," she said. "The fire grows and will become wild in minutes. We will be lucky to save ourselves."

"You'll carry him," Skar said in an ugly voice. "My left leg feels as if it's burning. I saved you from the belly of the demons. Now you owe me your life."

The woman stared at the shorter soldier. Cyrus wondered what went on inside her head.

"Yes," she said. "You speak the truth. We will take turns carrying him. I will do so first because I am unhurt."

She turned her back on Cyrus and bent down. Skar grabbed Cyrus under the armpits and hauled him onto the woman. She adjusted for his weight. She was stronger than she looked, and grabbed his dangling arms. She was lithe and beautiful, and he felt the strength in her.

Now, for the first time, Cyrus saw the fire in full bloom. Orange flames leapt into the air. The flames jumped and crackled, heading in the direction of the wind. The three of them would have to flee toward the antigravity sled's landing zone, heading into the wind.

The woman shoved up. Cyrus could feel her strain. Then the soldier and the primitive began to run through the grass, carrying Cyrus away from danger.

They were in the race of their lives.

||||||||||

The paralysis wore off by degrees. Cyrus felt tingling in his fingers and toes first as the flames' heat scorched his back. His clothes smoldered, and it felt as if the skin there melted.

"Turn around," he said through half-frozen lips.

The woman shouted, and she dropped Cyrus, letting him tumble from her back and smack onto the ground. With a bound, she was several feet away, with a stone-bladed knife in her hand. She stood trembling.

"What are you doing?" Skar shouted.

"He spoke to me," she said.

"Help me," Cyrus said. The fall hurt, but he was terrified of the approaching fire. He could feel the heat on his face and saw flames leaping and crackling skyward.

Skar scrambled to him, dragging Cyrus from the fire. "Put him on my back," the soldier said. "Now we're going to move."

Sullenly, the woman sheathed her knife and helped deposit Cyrus onto the soldier's back. Skar ran like a machine, his short legs moving like pistons. The tall, individual stalks blurred as Cyrus passed them. Before long, the woman panted, with sweat glistening on her face.

"You are more powerful than you look," she said.

"Save your breath for running," Skar told her.

Eventually, Cyrus made it easier for Skar by holding on instead of Skar hanging onto his dangling arms. Finally, the soldier and the woman burst out of the spindly grass and onto the plains. The roaring flames crackled behind them. They staggered for another hundred meters. Then Skar slid Cyrus off his back. The soldier stretched out, closed his eyes, and promptly fell asleep.

The woman fell onto her hands and knees, gasping for air. Drops of sweat dripped onto the ground.

Cyrus slowly moved his arms and legs. He felt numb in places, but he was beginning to feel normal again.

"We can't stop here," he said.

The woman lifted her head, staring at him. With her tousled hair, she was achingly beautiful.

Struggling to a sitting position, Cyrus asked, "Do you have a name?"

"Are you a demon-spawn?" she asked in a raw voice.

"No. I'm human just like you."

"Then why are you so pale and thin?"

"Different skin color is all."

She shook her head. "Your pale skin shows your weakness, your strangeness."

"Do you think he's weak?" Cyrus asked, pointing at Skar.

"He's a demonslayer. He is a prodigy among men."

"And I'm his friend. My name is Cyrus Gant."

"You are two-named," she said in awe. "I did not realize. No wonder he wished to save you."

Her simplicity surprised Cyrus. "You have only one name, I take it."

"Of course," she said, as she brushed back hair with her fingertips. It was artfully done. Cyrus found it alluring.

"What do you want me to call you?" he asked.

She switched to a sitting position. Gathering her long hair, she tied it into a ponytail. She regarded him closely as anger showed in her intense brown eyes. Her mouth turned downward. "You slew my companions with your spell wand. I should slay you now in vengeance while I have the chance."

Cyrus didn't doubt her, and he wondered if he could draw his gun in time. He would be slow and she correspondingly fast. He needed to talk his way out of this. "Don't you remember that you five attacked us? We did not attack you?"

"I remember, but it changes nothing."

How could he maneuver his right hand closer to his gun without her noticing? He needed a diversion. All he had were his words. "Why did you attack us before?" he asked.

"You were there. Stone Fist believed you were demons. You had floated down from the sky. Only demons can do that."

Cyrus didn't like the way her nostrils flared. He wasn't sure he wanted to debate with her primitive logic. "Whatever else you can say, Skar saved you from the demon's sky vehicle."

She appeared to think about that, and nodded an affirmative.

"The demons are called Kresh, by the way," Cyrus said.

"Kresh demons," she said, as if tasting the word. She regarded him anew, and there was something different in her eyes. "You know strange things, interesting lore. Where did you learn such wisdom?"

"I came from a far place," he said, "a place where there are no Kresh."

Her eyes widened. "No Kresh?"

"Men and women live free on their own."

"We live free, but the demons—the Kresh—hunt us for their vile games."

"You still haven't answered my question, by the way. What do you want me to call you?"

She nodded slowly, as if coming to a decision. Her eyes shone as she said, "I am Jana. No one can twirl a sling better than me or track a beast with greater ease."

"Thanks for your help, Jana. I appreciate it."

"It is strange," Jana said. "I owe him my life. Otherwise, I would have killed you while you were under the demon spell. I do not trust someone so pale. Now that I hear your lore and know that you are two-named . . ."

Was she coming on to him? He wouldn't mind that. *You have to keep focused, man. Quit staring at her and start thinking.* He cleared his throat. "What happened to your friend in the demon vehicle?"

Jana looked away, finally saying, "He died during the crash. He broke his neck."

He shouldn't have asked that. It was only a short connection to the other dead friends, the ones he'd shot. "It seems that you truly hate the demons."

Jana glared at him. "The Kresh demons, you said."

"Actually, I said just 'Kresh.' You call them demons. They've been molesting your clan for some time, is that right?"

"For all time," Jana said. "They have always attacked our clan."

"That's what I thought—we thought. We're here to destroy them."

Jana peered at him, and she cocked her head. "The demonslayer has great courage. I saw him attack us: one man against five. Not even Stone Fist would have done such a thing. The slayer must have skills to challenge the demons. You used magic to kill three of us. Yet now your magic has proven less than demon spells. The Kresh demon froze you. You did not freeze him. Is it possible for you to defeat even one demon?"

"I didn't mean just me or even the two of us," Cyrus said. "We have powerful friends. Some of them live in space."

Jana frowned.

"Up there in the stars," Cyrus said.

"I know where space is. But you said you are humans, not demons. Only demons live in space."

"Have you ever been into space?" Cyrus asked.

"I belong to Berserker Clan. I live here." Jana touched her hair, and her eyes widened. "Is your question an insult?"

"No," Cyrus said. "I just wondered how you knew everyone in space was a demon if you haven't actually been there."

Jana thought about that. "I spoke common knowledge."

"It is wrong knowledge," Cyrus said. "Only those who have been to a place can tell you who is there."

Jana shook her head almost as if surprised. "Your words *seem* wrong, yet there is wisdom in what you say."

"Not everyone living up there is a demon. I'm from there. He's from there. You saw us coming down from space, so you know my words are true."

Jana glanced at Skar before scratching her head and looking at Cyrus. "Your words are strange, but they have the ring of truth. Why did you ask us about Klane before?"

"Have you heard of Klane?" Cyrus asked, trying to keep the excitement out of his voice.

"No."

"He is pale-skinned like me," Cyrus said.

"He, too, is from space?"

"Klane has lived among the Tash-Toi—"

Jana sprang to her feet, and she drew her stone blade. "We have fought the Tash-Toi. They are a strong clan, but not stronger than the Berserkers."

Hope flared in Cyrus's breast. He needed a break like this. "Do you know where the Tash-Toi live?"

"I know their range," Jana said. "It is far on the other side of the mountains. It is many, many sleeps from here."

That didn't sound good. "How large is a clan range?"

Jana shrugged. "It changes with the seasons and with the years. We fought the Tash-Toi long ago. No one has forgotten it, though. We await the chance to challenge them again."

"How many sleeps would you estimate they are from here?" Cyrus asked.

Jana shrugged. "It could be ten sleeps. It could be twenty. After such a long time, it could be a hundred."

"Do you follow migrating herd animals then?" Cyrus asked.

"Sometimes we follow the bosk," Jana said. "All the clans follow the bosk at some time or another."

Cyrus didn't want to hear that the Tash-Toi could be one hundred sleeps away. In the memory crystal on the needle-ship, the seeker had obviously been a Special, a psionic. Could one seeker speak to another?

"Does your tribe . . . your clan, have a seeker?" Cyrus asked.

Jana sheathed the blade, bent down, and picked up several pebbles, shaking them in her fist. She stared at the ground as she said, "No. The Tash-Toi have the seeker. They are an arrogant people due to that. They believe themselves better than the Berserkers."

Cyrus frowned. Was she lying? Why would she lie about something like that? He didn't know enough about the clans. "Well," he said, "is it possible you could help us find Clan Tash-Toi?"

"Never!" Jana said, dropping the pebbles and standing. She redrew the knife and pointed it at Cyrus. "I should kill you for suggesting that I'm a traitor to my people." She took a step toward Cyrus.

Cyrus didn't hesitate. He dragged out his gun, drawing as quickly as he could. Unlike Skar's heavier pistol, Cyrus had a flattish heat gun.

Jana shouted in alarm as she kicked sand and gravel at Cyrus.

Particles stung his eyes. He envisioned her lunging at him. She was beautiful, but he'd rather live. Cyrus lifted the heat gun and fired where he'd last seen her. The weapon made a sizzling sound. He expected to hear the thud of Jana's falling body striking the ground. He didn't hear that, however. Cyrus rubbed his eyes and dared fire again in a different location. He tensed, expecting a knife to plunge into him.

"Cyrus!" Skar shouted.

Cyrus finally managed to clear his eyes. The primitive raced away, kicking up dust with each step.

"What happened?" Skar asked. "Why did you fire your gun?"

Cyrus told the soldier what had happened.

Jana kept running, although she halted after a kilometer. She lifted an arm, and she made a strange undulating cry directed at them.

"You should have killed her," Skar said. "I think she's telling us this isn't over."

"I didn't want to shoot her. I was just trying to keep her from killing me."

"We've made an enemy," Skar said. "By what you just told me, she has learned our goals." The soldier clutched his axe. "If she didn't have such a long head start, I'd chase her down and finish it."

"Let her go," Cyrus said.

The soldier eyed him.

"The Tash-Toi live somewhere on the other side of the mountain range," Cyrus said. "They could be ten sleeps away or one hundred. It isn't much, but at least we have a direction. We have to get out of here before more Kresh show up."

Jana gave another cry. Then she turned and began jogging away.

"And we have to reach the other side of the mountains before Jana brings the rest of the Berserkers against us," Cyrus said.

"You are right," Skar said. "We must leave."

As the grass fire continued to rage behind them, Cyrus climbed to his feet. The two of them set off for the mountains and the valley that divided the present plains from the next.

8

Klane groaned in the darkness. He felt sick and ached all over. He lay on cold stone, and he held something in his right hand. With an effort of will he forced his frozen fingers to move. With his left hand he felt around his palm and discovered pieces of junction-stone.

The stone broke? I couldn't have crushed it with my flesh. The power pouring through it must have shattered the stone.

He'd never heard of such a thing happening before. It must have had something to do with the singing gods.

Anguish washed over him so Klane wanted to weep. He'd lost his precious junction-stone. Yes, he'd managed to get off the cliff ledge, but now he was lost in the darkness of a strange cave system. Perhaps as bad, something had torn inside him and—

He felt his forehead. It radiated with heat. He had a fever, too. He needed water. His throat was parched. He must have been unconscious for longer than he realized.

I must escape from these caverns. I must find water.

Klane began to crawl through the darkness, sliding his aching body across the stone floor. As he crawled, he sensed the singing gods as a distant stream. They were like an icy river gurgling over stones and boulders. He knew that in reality whatever gurgled did so through the metal pipes.

What or who exactly were the singing gods? What were the pipes? Klane didn't think the Kresh had installed them deep under the Mountain that was a Machine. No. Klane had sensed terrible age among the singing gods, old, old, old beyond his understanding. Did they live as he did, or were they ancient memories, spirits of a long-dead race?

Klane coughed, and he felt wetness on his tongue. He tasted the wetness, a coppery sensation.

That's my blood. I'm coughing up blood. Maybe I'm dying.

He paused in his crawl and rested his forehead against stone. Somehow, he had torn his body while teleporting across the chasm and deep into these caves.

He could never do that again. He managed a wry chuckle. He didn't think he would do anything ever again. His life force ebbed away.

If I die, will my spirit go into the pipes? Will I join the singing gods in death?

Something about that terrified him. He didn't want to spend death in the darkness of the mountain. To remain with the alien singing gods—

No. If I die, let me die cleanly under the sun.

He raised himself up onto his elbows and spat blood. He wasn't dead yet. His friend, the seeker, had sacrificed himself to the demons. If Klane was going to die, he would die killing more demons and setting the seeker free. Clan Tash-Toi needed the seeker. He couldn't let the old man down and he couldn't let his clan down. The eternal war of man against demon had sucked him into the abyss of the singing gods. Now he had to escape this place.

Klane wasn't sure the spirits in the pipes were good. Maybe these were the singing demons. Maybe the seeker had been wrong about this place. It was evil and dark, hidden from the light of the sun.

I will live. I will prevail.

Klane thrust his elbows forward, crawling through the darkness. Time became one monotonous agony of burning limbs and coughing and spitting up blood. Memories returned of his childhood: the endless mockery from older, stronger boys. With the memories of the abuse, his stubbornness grew. He would prevail. He would not die as a weakling in the caves.

In the darkness, with the throb of stubbornness, his thoughts began to magnify. With his power he reached outward, upward and saw the Machine that was a Mountain. He could go inside it with his mind and finally see the inner workings.

"No," he whispered, down in the darkness of the caves. "I must use my strength wisely." Who knew how long this would last?

He turned his powers inward and he plunged his consciousness into his body. He used his mind to heal ruptured parts of flesh. He listened to the blood swish through him and to his heart beating like a drum. He repaired himself, using magic without a junction-stone. He had never known this was possible.

At last, weariness stole upon him. He ignored it and mended interior flesh, knitting it together one particle at a time.

Without warning, ahead of him, rocks tumbled against each other.

Klane's eyes snapped open. He found himself on his hands and knees. A cold draft blew over him. He squinted, because light nearly blinded him. He endured, and he realized that he was still in the cave. Craning his neck, he peered upward at the spark of light. It didn't seem so great now. His eyes were adjusting to it instead of the bitter darkness.

What had happened to cause this? He didn't understand.

As he knelt there, he began to reel off his memories, playing them back. His ears had heard something earlier, while his hands had felt . . . yes, yes, the singing gods had just tried to kill him. They had started a rockslide, tumbling the heavy boulders at him. He had reflexively shielded himself, using his powers, a Telekinetic Spell, to create a shield. Quite far away from him, the boulders had slid aside. Through the palms of his hands, he had felt them striking the floor. This was amazing.

Now, because of the rockslide, he viewed a distant opening up there.

He laughed until he felt something new. The singing gods raged at him, and they considered striking directly this time.

I must leave this place at once, but I don't dare practice a Teleport Spell. That would kill me.

Wearily, Klane climbed to his feet. He concentrated on tasting the inside of his mouth. No more blood came up. He had healed the rupture inside him. His mind no longer felt hazy, either. He was thirsty and very hungry, but he was whole again.

He realized something else: his mind had become like a junction-stone.

In that moment, understanding filled him. The junction-stone had always been a crutch. In the teleportation, he presumed that the singing gods had done something to his mind. Now he was different, more powerful, and could think more clearly or quickly.

I have thrown away childish things. Now I am a man.

He sensed the singing gods. They gathered strength and they gathered resolve. He must flee or they would surely overpower him and bury him here with them.

Klane licked his lips. He was weak, but he must attempt this or lose his life. The seeker would also lose, and in some fashion that Klane didn't understand, humanity would lose forever.

"Now," Klane whispered.

With his eyes open, as he stared at the distant opening, Klane willed himself upward. Very slowly, his feet levitated off the floor. Realization of his rise caused him to sway. He swung his arms, and his torso went back and forth, but he managed to keep his balance. He concentrated and levitated higher, faster. Then he rose swiftly, and felt godlike. He also sensed the strain to his mind and his power. If he did this too long, he would rupture something inside himself again. He might have a fatal heart attack this time.

Concentrate, Klane, he told himself.

He did, and he flew higher yet. The young man of Clan Tash-Toi levitated until the opening bathed his body in light and sun-warmed heat. That felt good. He glanced at his hands, at his bloody clothes. Then he stared upward at the opening, and he levitated through it and onto a ledge on the mountainside.

He deposited himself on rock and let his mind rest. His shoulders slumped and he crumpled to his knees. Sweat dotted his forehead, and he shivered uncontrollably.

Despite the sun's heat, the wind made it cold up here, and he still felt feverish. Even so, Klane's lips parted and he grinned wolfishly. He had escaped the mountain ledge on the other side of the chasm. He had also escaped the darkness of the caves, and he had escaped from the singing gods.

He frowned for a moment, for he heard laughter in his mind. It seemed to come from the singing gods.

Ignore their laughter, he told himself. *The gods—maybe new kinds of demons—are angry. They attempt to shatter your newfound confidence through mockery, but I refuse to let them sway me.*

Klane exhaled the air in his lungs. He needed water and he needed food. Then he needed to continue down toward the deep valley. He was going to the city of the demons, there to rescue his friend.

With one hand on the rough mountain and his eyes on the trail, Klane took his first step toward the evil city and the terrible destiny awaiting him there.

9

Cyrus and Skar ducked low as thunder boomed from the heavens. They hid among boulders near the edge of an incredibly deep and jagged valley.

The valley or canyon reminded Cyrus of the landscape of Mars. This canyon possessed a sheer wall that dropped straight down, possibly two kilometers. Cyrus had spied distant greenery earlier, implying crops. A blue river ran through much of the area, reminding him of the Nile in the Egyptian Sector on Earth. Did Kresh eat grains or vegetables? They looked like strict carnivores to him. In any case, various clusters to the far left showed what might be domed and strangely fluted buildings. Was that a Kresh city or a manufacturing plant, perhaps?

The booms and thunderous noise directed his attention back to the sky. The banded gas giant Pulsar took up half the heavens, while the sun shone off to the right.

"Rockets," Skar shouted.

Cyrus shaded his eyes. He recognized them now. Twin tongues of fire showed two different descending rockets. They must be massive, gargantuan things. Between them they carried a white mountain.

"That's an iceberg," Cyrus said.

"Yes," Skar said. "Ice-hauler pilots bring the bergs from the outer asteroids."

At the far end of the valley, Cyrus could barely make out continuous white vapors billowing into the air. The vapor came from what looked like a vast terraforming machine.

The scale of Kresh tech awed him. The aliens terraformed the planet; they brought life to an otherwise barren world. Did that mean the aliens did something good? Yeah, Cyrus guessed it did mean that. The Kresh weren't inherently evil, he supposed. They were just Sol's enemies, as they had attacked and captured the Earth's colonizing Teleship, *Discovery*.

He wondered how Jasper was doing. The telepath—the Special— had been one of the strongest on Earth and the first to contact a psi-master. Several years ago, Jasper had found Cyrus for Psi Force, and Jasper had helped ensure Cyrus had been on the New Eden mission. The Kresh had captured the Special along with everyone else. They probably ran hideous experiments on the man.

Cyrus knew better than to try to contact Jasper through telepathy. The enemy psi-masters would no doubt like it if he tried that. Why had the psi-masters stopped searching for him? That didn't make sense.

He doubted they'd given up the hunt.

Cyrus forgot about that as he and Skar watched the massive rockets bring the iceberg down to the terraforming machine. How many converters were there on Jassac? It must cost a fortune to terraform a planet.

The Kresh, or perhaps the Chirr, had nuked one Earth-like planet in the star system. The place was a smoldering mass of radioactive ruin. Cyrus recalled observing it through *Discovery's* telescopes when they'd first jumped into the system's outer asteroids. Nuking an entire planet would cost tons of money. The war between the Chirr and the Kresh was nasty and brutish. From what he'd heard, it was also long running.

"I've been meaning to ask you about something," Cyrus asked.

Skar raised an eyebrow.

"Have you ever fought in the tunnels of the Chirr before?"

"No," Skar said in a clipped voice.

What did I say? "Uh, is that a touchy subject?"

Skar stared at him solemnly. Finally, a bleak smile stretched the soldier's lips. "How could you know? Masters always threaten soldiers with transfer to the Chirr War. It is considered bad luck among us to speak about it, about anything concerning the war."

"Oh."

Skar shook his head. "Once I joined the Resisters, I realized the foolishness of the custom. But old habits die hard."

"It's pretty bad in the tunnels, huh?" Cyrus asked.

"Each year, millions of Vomags die fighting the Chirr. It is a depressing and mindless war. The Chirr will never surrender and the Kresh will never stop attacking."

"Hey, look at that," Cyrus said. He pointed into the valley. Skar leaned over and then quickly ducked back down.

Cyrus lowered himself behind a lichen-covered boulder. Four sky vehicles lifted from the shadowy depths. "Do you think they're looking for us?"

"Who else would they seek?" Skar asked.

The two men crouched behind the boulder. They'd seen other sky vehicles these past three days. The vehicles had fanned out over the plains, disappearing. Later they reappeared, heading back for the valley. Were the Kresh capturing more primitives or were those regular sorties doing whatever the raptor-aliens did? Cyrus had no idea.

Fortunately, the sky vehicles were half a kilometer away from their position, heading for the plains. It was hard to tell, but it looked as if the cars carried two Kresh per vehicle.

There was so much Cyrus didn't know about the aliens, and about the star system. So far he had discovered there was a three-way war. The Chirr and the Kresh fought land campaigns against each other on the two Earth-like planets, these days mainly on the second planet, second from its sun. He also knew humanoid cyborgs had attacked the star system at least once.

The Kresh had originally thought *Discovery* was another cyborg military vessel. That the cyborgs had made it out here—two hundred and thirty light years from Sol—indicated they had a type of Teleship, too. It indicated the cyborgs had possessed such a vessel at the end of the Cyborg or Doom Star War one hundred years ago in the solar system.

"So how are we going to reach the other side of the valley?" Cyrus asked.

"There are two choices," Skar said.

Cyrus already knew what they were. Either they had to go around the canyon ends or they had to climb down, walk across the bottom, and climb back up.

"Maybe it would be easier ambushing one of the sky vehicles," Cyrus said, "and using it. We could cover a lot more territory that way."

"Not anymore," Skar said. "The Kresh will be wary after the original loss."

"Yeah . . . you're probably right." He kept thinking about one hundred sleeps. That was a long time to search an alien planet for one man.

They waited to see if any more sky vehicles would show up. None did, although Cyrus noticed a small cloud scudding across the sky. The two humans followed a faint ground trial. Cyrus was hoping there was a way down. One thing was certain: this place was beautiful in a stark way. Too bad aliens had to be in the star system.

New Eden, we called it. What a joke. We should have known such precious territory would have snakes.

A half hour later, they saw what seemed like a cross between a coyote and a spider. It had furry limbs and eight legs, scuttling fast. It chased a smaller creature with large ears.

Cyrus threw himself down with his arms outstretched and the heat gun in his hands. They were almost out of food concentrates. Fortunately, they had found plenty of small streams, drinking their fill each time and refilling their canteens.

Cyrus tracked the strange creature, willing it to come closer. It did, and he could hear something on the ends of its legs clacking against the rocks. Were those claws?

"Now," Skar whispered. "It will sense you soon, and then it will move too fast for you to hit."

Cyrus's stomach growled, and the spider-coyote paused. He squeezed the trigger of his pistol. A blob of heat sizzled from the barrel and it struck the creature in its main body. The thing made an odd wheezing, hissing sound, and it sagged. Belatedly, it scuttled away in slow motion. Cyrus fired again, and this time he killed it. It looked horrid, but as he rose from the rock, Cyrus's mouth had already started watering.

They had a long way to go to get across to the other side. Skar drew his axe. Cyrus holstered his gun and pulled out his knife. A fire was out of the question. That might alert the Kresh. They would have to eat the spider-coyote meat raw.

The two crouched over the dead creature and began to hack it apart. It was messy, and the meat was slimy and bloody. Skar chewed noisily, tearing away chunks of meat with his teeth. Cyrus tried that once, and he gagged, almost throwing up as his stomach heaved.

"Is there a problem?" Skar asked.

"No," Cyrus said. He sliced his meat into tiny portions, held his breath each time, and swallowed them like large pills. Several times he had to wash a hunk down his throat. He never wanted to eat like this again.

Afterward, they wiped their hands on the dirt.

The meat sat heavily in Cyrus's stomach. He tried to think about something else. He didn't want to vomit. He needed the food if he was going to find Klane.

They trudged along the edge of the canyon, seeking a way down. An hour passed, so did a second, and then a third. Finally, thunderous booms alerted them: the two rockets blasted off from the vast converter, minus the iceberg. They headed back into space.

Cyrus watched the heavy lifters and the long, trailing flames. He sat on a rock and shook his head. Who was he fooling? Getting across was going to be murder. After that, they would have to hunt for months, and the Tash-Toi kept shifting their location. What had he expected anyway, another Resister to show up and tell him exactly what to do? There was nothing but desolation out here, vast canyons and the occasional Kresh compound—oh, and don't forget rockets bringing ice down from space. How was he supposed to find a needle in a haystack the size of Earth?

"You know what?" he told Skar.

The soldier turned around.

"This . . ." Cyrus waved his hand. "This is hopeless."

"It was hopeless on High Station 3," Skar said, "but we escaped."

"I'd say we had plenty of help then."

"We are free now, truly free, and know what direction to travel."

"Skar, look around you. Do you see Klane? Do you have any idea where to look other than somewhere on the other side of those mountains?"

"I am not the Tracker," Skar said. "You are the Tracker."

Cyrus laughed. "Well, I've got news for you. I don't have a clue how to go about tracking this hero. It's not as if we have freedom to go wherever we want. The Kresh are hunting us. We're not going to stay out of their sight forever. That means we have an extremely narrow window of opportunity, and Klane could be one hundred sleeps away."

Skar sat erectly on a rock. He put a hand on each knee, and he frowned. "I am a soldier. I fight. You are the thinker, the strategy maker between us. If you don't have a plan, you must make one."

"I do have a plan: find Klane."

"How will you find him?"

"I have no bloody idea other than marching across those mountains and asking whoever we run into."

"Then you do not have a plan, you have a dream or a hope."

"Yeah," Cyrus said. He used to have plans. That had been back in the days of his youth when he'd been on his own and then as a member of the Latin Kings. Later, in Psi Force, Jasper had shared his plan with a young ex-gang member: freedom from the inhibitors in their brains. The Normals of the solar system had chained Specials like animals, putting in the inhibitor so they could turn off the psionic abilities if they wished. During the journey, Jasper had figured out—with psi-master help—how to short the inhibitors. For several weeks now, Cyrus had followed the Resister plan: find the Anointed One. Maybe it was time he made his own plans, lived his life his way.

"I'm not much of a Tracker," Cyrus said. "If I were the real thing, I'd at least know what to do. Wandering this planet, asking the locals if they've seen Klane doesn't seem smart. In the long run, how does that help Earth?"

"I do not know," Skar said.

"I need to think of something practical. This . . . holo-vid drama—Reacher, Tracker, Anointed One—just doesn't seem rational anymore. I'm stuck on a foreign world with raptor-aliens hunting me. Who am I kidding?"

Skar looked away. "If you are not the Tracker, why did the people on High Station 3 die to help us?"

"You mean the Resisters?"

"Them," Skar said, "and the others who died in the blast."

The Resisters had blown up some of the space habitat on High Station 3, helping to cover their escape in the needle-ship.

"Good people have died helping me," Cyrus said, feeling a twinge of guilt. "And I know they're counting on me to save them. I appreciate their help and their dream. But we have to be realistic."

Cyrus made a fist and banged it several times against his knee. "What's the problem? Maybe if I state it in its bald form, something will light up in my head. Okay. The Kresh control humanity here and twist them into all kinds of forms as if they're different breeds of animals."

"We are cattle," Skar agreed.

"No, you're people. I talked to Argon—he was a member of our expedition. Anyway, I talked to him before about some of this stuff.

He believed in the Creator. He told me once that people were made in the Creator's image. That means they had the divine spark in them. Animals don't have that. Therefore, humanity, people have true dignity. The Kresh don't give people dignity, but have made them like animals. The Kresh have tons of Specials in their Bo Taw, in their psi-masters. As crazy as it sounds, as impossible to achieve, instead of finding Klane, I need to find a way back to the solar system so we can really do something to help the people here."

"How would you do that?" Skar asked.

"It seems impossible, but at least I'd have a goal that I know could help those on Earth and possibly here, too. What is a single primitive going to do against the Kresh? Not a whole heck of a lot," Cyrus said. "The solar system is another matter. But before I can think about getting back to Earth, I'd need a spaceship to get off Jassac, right? I need to get back into space and . . ."

Cyrus exhaled. "Suppose I stole a Kresh military vessel. If I could reach the speed of light, it would take me two hundred and thirty years to reach Earth. I need a Teleship, and the Kresh have the only one here."

"Is there a way to take your Earth vessel back from them?" Skar asked.

"I'd need space marines for that, or a whole lot of Vomags."

"The Kresh—"

Cyrus snapped his fingers. "Maybe I'm looking at this the wrong way."

Skar blinked at him.

"There are other Teleships," Cyrus said.

"More have come from your solar system?" Skar asked, hopefully.

"No. I mean the cyborgs must have some."

"You've said before that the cyborgs are your enemy."

"They are," Cyrus said. "But there is also an old Earth saying: 'The enemy of my enemy is my friend.'"

Skar's frown deepened and he spoke quietly to himself, perhaps testing the saying. His eyes brightened and he looked up. "That is a clever saying. How does it apply here?"

"The cyborgs have attacked the star system. The Kresh must have driven them off. I don't know. It doesn't make sense that I could talk to a cyborg and get him to agree to take me home. Everything seems hopeless. I need space marines and a space vessel, but I don't know where to get either."

Skar pointed up at the two rockets leaving the atmosphere. The huge missiles had almost dwindled out of sight.

Cyrus watched them, and the wheels began turning in his mind. "Maybe there is a way off Jassac. We know more rockets are going to land at the converters, right?"

"Yes," Skar said.

"So . . . we head there, wait, and stow aboard one of the rockets, getting back into orbital space. Then what do we do?"

"You have your mental abilities," Skar said. "Can you not twist minds like the psi-masters do?"

"I'm not much of a telepath. My telekinesis is stronger."

"But you have practiced some telepathy, yes?"

"I have," Cyrus admitted. "What's your point?"

"We leave Jassac on a rocket and go to where the ice haulers bring their frozen water. The ice-hauler ships must head back to the outer asteroids. We stow away on a hauler heading out-system. You make them help us."

Cyrus tried to envision that. It was a wild plan, but it was a plan that didn't include Kresh in sky vehicles sweeping the plains for him day in and day out. "Do humans pilot the ice haulers?" he asked.

"Yes," Skar said.

"It's crazy, but that seems more feasible to me than searching for a single man on an Earth-sized moon, especially as I have no idea what to do with Klane once I find him."

It also struck Cyrus as easier than scaling down an impossible canyon wall with Kresh hunting for him.

"Let's go," Cyrus said. "I've rested long enough."

10

Chengal Ras seethed as he stalked back and forth in a home-world atrium. White sand glittered under intense lamps. The sand was warm under his talons and it sparkled from time to time.

Eons ago, the legends said, the Kresh had lived on a perfect world with sand like this. Yes, Zama Dee flaunted her status and her access to great wealth. She—

A large door hissed up, and the 73rd strode into the atrium. Chengal Ras expected a retinue to follow. Instead, the large Kresh entered alone. That was interesting and daring on her part.

Zama Dee was larger than he was. She possessed larger jaws, longer teeth, and a bigger cranium. She had a yellowish hide with black mottling. Metallic streamers tinkled as she stalked toward him. He noticed the steel-shod talons on her feet. Yes, he had heard rumors before that she enjoyed slaying in the old manner. She shredded and, it was rumored, devoured game raw, like a wild beast.

He would be wise to remember that. She ruled Jassac, and her clique wished to terraform as many moons and planets as possible. They opposed intensifying the Chirr-Kresh War, wishing to deal first with the new threat: the cyborgs.

"I welcome you to Jassac, 109th," Zama Dee said. With a hand-talon, she struck the scent maker dangling from her neck. A hiss of powerful odors sprayed outward from it.

"I accept your hospitality, 73rd," Chengal Ras said, following the ancient formula. From his belt, he lifted his own scent maker, squirting acceptable odors into the air.

She bent her large torso, and her nostrils quivered. "Delectable," she said.

"This room," he said. "I am in awe of it."

She raised her large tail and let it swing back and forth in a ritual movement.

These mannerisms were odd to Chengal Ras. He had been born to the Seven Sisters in exile. They had been in rebellion to the old ways, believing in nothing holy, wishing to change to a unified approach where all shared all and did all.

"My latest Attack Talon approaches Jassac," he said.

Her tail thudded onto the white sand, and she faced him with flashing eyes.

He recognized the blunder. He had initiated the topic. He had broken protocol. If he admitted it and sought her recompense—ah, he knew what to do.

"I had wondered if your holy-callers would bless the vessel," he said. "That is why I mention it. I do not wish to repeat the tragic accident of my first Attack Talon."

She continued to regard him. Finally, she asked, "When did Chengal Ras revert to the ancient beliefs?"

That was tantamount to an insult, but he would have to swallow it. He didn't have enough hand to challenge her here.

"If I have misspoken—" he said.

Her tail lashed back and forth, sweeping white sand, throwing some into the air.

Chengal Ras noted that she wore a weapon. Protocol had forced him to surrender his before entering the atrium. Maybe she would attempt to rend him with her steel-shod talons. Yes, she would be practiced in the ancient art of combat. In more than one way, he was at a severe disadvantage. If she wished to harm him . . .

He forced the words through his teeth, expelling them in a hiss. "I have erred."

"You have," she agreed. "How will you repair it?"

Chengal Ras did the only thing he could. He tore a streamer from his arm, and he stalked toward her, handing it to the 73rd. She accepted the streamer, and thus, he gave her ten codex points, weakening his position and strengthening hers.

"You are generous," she said.

"It is an atrium of white sand," he said. "And I am awed to think of ancient times."

She opened her jaws, maybe to spew an insult about the Seven Sisters. With an effort, it seemed, she clicked her deadly teeth together.

Chengal Ras waited in silence, seething inside, hoping that someday soon he could kill her for this indignity.

"It is time for us to speak," she said.

Still he waited.

"You have come to Jassac chasing cattle," she said. "You lost an Attack Talon, and the High Station 3 cattle landed on the surface. Do you realize that they have eluded my investigation teams?"

"I had not realized, no," he said.

She regarded him closely. He wondered at the scrutiny. "Your cattle slew a Kresh," she said.

"Blasphemy against nature," Chengal Ras said, putting horror into his words. This was bad. He had never expected something like this. "I blame you, 109th."

He thought at lightning speed, and he realized he would have to backtrack now. He was in grave peril otherwise.

"I'm afraid I must confess an error," Chengal Ras said. "No. I will be blunt. I have misinformed you of the nature of the chase."

Her tail swished again, throwing up more white sand. The tail and her stance showed her anger. "Logic dictated you would mouth such an obscenity to me," she hissed.

He barely kept his tail from lashing. On all accounts, he couldn't let her goad him into a fight. She was a traditionalist. Therefore, he did not believe she would murder him outright. No. She had honor and she would not take advantage of such an easy kill. But if he gave her an opening . . .

"The records at High Station 3 are exposed for all to view," he said. "One of the cattle in the prey-craft was from out-system."

"Do you mean a metal man?" she asked in outrage.

"No, 73rd," he said. "I would have given a system-wide alert if any metal men were running free. This is something else entirely. The mind extractor has shown us the new cattle speak an old truth. They have come from the original cattle system of Sol."

"This is amazing," she said. "Speak on."

"These cattle have discovered a faster-than-light drive."

"Ah . . . so the rumors are true," she said.

He made a gracious gesture.

"You are free with amazing truths," she said, canting her head and looking at him in a new manner. "Why would you admit this to me?"

Chengal Ras still thought fast, and he came to a decision. He would skate as near to the truth as he could. Zama Dee might be smarter than he was. Likely, she could trap him except for one thing: he would cheat and break every tradition if it helped him achieve his goal. Yet he would have to gauge the use of his cheats very, very carefully if he hoped to defeat her.

"I have stumbled upon a mystery," Chengal Ras said. "The arrival of the new cattle must have unhinged the Humanity Ultimates on High Station 3."

"I do not bother with the cattle cults," she said with a convulsive shake of her tail.

"I believe that is an error on your part," Chengal Ras said.

"You dare attempt to correct me?" she asked, sounding scandalized.

"I correct no one," he said. "Rather, I am letting you know my reasoning for taking the course of action that I have. The needle-ship was not prey-craft. Rather, Humanity Ultimates constructed the vessel in secret perhaps as long as several months ago."

"They did this at High Station 3?" Zama Dee asked.

"Alas, that is so."

"It cost me a Kresh, 109th."

"If you demand blood payment, I suggest you aid me in my quest to uncover the Humanity Ultimate plot. You may then shed their blood in vengeance for the Kresh death."

Zama Dee made rapid hissing noises, Kresh laughter. "Are you expecting me to believe that we here at Jassac are as lax and—I hardly know the right term for the stupidity of letting cattle outwit you. They actually built a spacecraft under your nose?"

"The cattle are clever," Chengal Ras said. Another of his great strengths was his hatred of lying to himself. Kresh were superior to all other life forms, but that didn't mean all other life forms were incapable of clever thought. In this, he saw clearly, he knew.

"These cattle have killed Kresh," Chengal Ras said. "They are dangerous, and they have come to this world for a reason."

"That is absurd," Zama Dee said. "By this world, you mean Jassac?"

"Yes. I am telling you stark truth."

"I had thought you clever and dangerous, Chengal Ras. Instead, I discover you to believe fairy tales and egg-laying fables. This is all utter nonsense."

"If it is nonsense," he said, "do you have any objection to allowing me to inspect your primitives?"

She eyed him, and she glanced at the ten-codex streamer in her talon. "You wish to fly onto the preserve and help in the hunt?"

"No," he said. "I would like to inspect any cattle you happen to have in captivity here."

"You want to interrogate them?"

"If it is permitted, I would like to observe them." At that moment, he caught her eye movement. It was a quick shift up toward the heat lamps. It was an odd flicker, and it indicated—

She's lying to me. She has something to hide. Could it be she, too, believes in cattle fables?

"Yes," she said. "Inspect the cattle. One of my investigation teams has picked up an interesting specimen. Perhaps you can aid me by observing and giving me your opinion."

"Let me be of service, 73rd."

She examined the ten-codex streamer one more time. With a deft twist, she attached it to her arm rack, letting it flutter with her own streamers. "Let it be so," she said, ending the interview with a ritual phrase.

11

Two days later, a downpour nearly caught Cyrus and Skar by surprise. In a matter of minutes, clouds rolled into the sky. They grew ominously, thickening and darkening with black bulges. Soon, flashes of lightning crackled into existence and thunder boomed. It shook Cyrus's teeth the first time, and he instinctively crouched low. The flashes intensified and so did the booms.

"Do you smell that?" Cyrus asked. He meant the ozone. "It's going to rain soon."

Skar shook his head.

"Rain," Cyrus said, "water cascading down from the sky in little droplets."

Skar gazed heavenward.

"As a matter of fact," Cyrus said, looking around, "this area seems unsafe. I bet rainwater will sweep down into the canyon." He'd seen videos of such things while training in Crete.

"Is that a problem?" Skar asked.

"You've never lived on a world, huh? You've been in places like High Station 3 or inside spaceships all your life."

"That is true."

"Quick," Cyrus said. "We have to climb before it starts pouring."

He hurried away from the edge of the canyon. Skar followed, and the two of them soon walked on higher ground.

A big, fat, cold drop plunked against Cyrus's nose. "Here it comes," he said. He looked up and then looked around. He scrambled onto a higher rock. "This will have to do."

After settling onto the rock, Skar scanned upward in wonder as raindrops began spilling onto them. Another flash of lightning slashed down. It struck the ground nearby, splintering a boulder with a boom and a crescendo of stone-raining noises.

Skar huddled beside Cyrus, and cold rain poured onto the weary travelers. The lightning lit up the dark afternoon and the booms hammered right on top of them, shaking them and the ground. Slowly, the flashes and the noise drifted across the canyon. Soon, water raced down from higher ground, and gushing streams poured over the edge of the canyon in an amazing flash flood.

Fortunately for the two of them, Cyrus had had a good eye. They watched as water boiled past them, inching higher and higher. Cyrus spied a spider-coyote bobbing in the waves, thrashing its legs. Pieces of vegetation raced by as everything went over the edge and into the canyon.

"I never knew it could be like this," Skar shouted.

Cyrus had never personally known either, although he had read about it at the institute.

Finally, the rain ended, but the clouds remained. Cyrus shivered, thoroughly soaked.

"We have to keep warm," he told Skar. They huddled closer together, shivering under an extra garment. Soon, water no longer sluiced by, but meandered slowly. That stopped after another half hour, leaving muddy soil.

"Let's start walking," Cyrus said.

Skar nodded as his teeth chattered.

For a time, they trekked farther inland than normal. Skar turned around once and pointed at the muddy footprints they left.

"Yeah, we'd better get back onto the rocks," Cyrus said. "We don't want the Kresh finding those."

It drizzled shortly thereafter, and likely blurred their prints. Too soon, night came. Luckily, their clothes had dried out by the friction and body heat.

The mountain-sized convertor was much closer than two days ago. They heard it in the distance as it chugged vapor into the sky. Large hoses lay on the new iceberg, feeder tubes for the great machine.

"I wonder how often the rockets come," Cyrus said. "We might be in for a long wait."

The clouds dissipated enough so that around midnight the stars reappeared. Skar shook Cyrus awake before taking the extra garment, wrapping himself with it, and lying down. The former Latin King sat up. He rubbed himself around the shoulders and leaned against a rock. He listened for the sounds of a sky vehicle. Later, he wondered about Jana and the primitives. The number of Kresh sorties had lessened, but enough cars still went out that he doubted any Berserker Clan members would dare venture into this area.

Cyrus drew a deep breath and he stared up at the stars. He'd been on Jassac for nearly a week. He'd eaten more bloody spider-coyote meat than he even wanted to think about. He hated the taste of blood. Maybe as bad, killing the creatures had lowered the charge on the heat gun. Skar had shot a spider-coyote once with his gun, but there hadn't been much left to eat after the pellet exploded everything into gore.

Back on Earth at the institute, Cyrus had read a few stories. One of them had been about an explorer who had made a bow and fashioned arrows. The explorer had slain wild game with the arrows, saving his high-tech weaponry for tougher situations. Unfortunately, there weren't any trees out here—at least none that he'd seen. Cyrus had a pocketful of rocks, and he'd hurled a few at the creatures. The spider-coyotes had dodged each one. Skar had done better, had gotten closer, but the soldier had also missed. Successful primitive living clearly took practice.

Cyrus continued to scan the heavens. None of the constellations looked right. It made him feel lonely—stranded far away from the world he'd known. Maybe as bad, the planetary smells were off. He'd noticed it more in the beginning. The sights, smells, sounds, the feel, were all alien. This wasn't Earth and it didn't feel like Earth.

Would he ever see Crete again? Would he ever walk in Milan? He didn't see how. He had joined up for a dangerous quest, and he would likely die on Jassac. He'd hated the Kresh more in the beginning, when he'd been in their ship and the Vomags had kicked Captain Nagasaki to death.

You'd better remember that. The Kresh will kick Earth to death unless you get off-planet and warn your world.

Cyrus drew his knees up to his chest and wrapped his arms around them. He stared at the stars. Later, his eyelids drooped. He heard a scuffling sound—

Cyrus's head snapped up. He dug out his heat gun and scrambled to his feet. Twisting around, he saw that a primitive with smooth legs and a spear stood over him, perched on the rock. A woman grinned down at him. It was Jana. Cyrus brought up the gun. Jana moved faster, snapping her torso and bringing the end of her spear around. The end clipped Cyrus on the side of the jaw and knocked him backward. He slammed down hard, hitting his head on rocky soil, and for a moment, his eyes hurt and blurred.

Jana jumped down onto the ground. He heard her thud.

Cyrus spied his gun lying a few feet away. From on the ground, he lunged for it. With a clatter of noise, Jana kicked it out of range. The two stared at each other in the darkness.

"Skar!" Cyrus shouted.

Jana grinned wider. The primitive had starkly white teeth.

"Skar!" Cyrus said again.

Out of the darkness, Skar appeared. The soldier gripped his short-handled axe. He moved fast, charging Jana. The primitive jumped back.

Even with his head ringing, Cyrus saw it. A net came up from behind the rock he'd been leaning against earlier. The net swished through the air and descended toward Skar. Small rocks weighted down the edges. Other primitives must be hiding behind the rock.

"It's a trap!" Cyrus shouted. He tried to rise, but the back of his head exploded in pain, and he groaned and sank back down.

The net landed on Skar, entangling him. The soldier tripped and went down. Now more primitives appeared, Berserker Clan members, no doubt. They produced clubs and beat the soldier into unconsciousness.

Cyrus waited for the same thing to happen to him.

"No," Jana said, as savages approached with their clubs. "He is not as strong as the demonslayer."

The biggest primitive, a man with a low forehead and huge shoulders, scowled thunderously at Jana. "Are you the hetman?" the man asked in a loud voice.

"Yang is hetman," Jana said.

"Do you try to tell Yang what to do?" the big man shouted.

Under the light of the stars, Jana shook her head. "I tell no one and certainly not Yang. Yet I would remind all of us that the seeker said we must not harm the pale-skinned outlander. He knows strange lore."

"The seeker?" Cyrus asked. "You said the Berserkers don't have a seeker."

The huge primitive—Yang, apparently—stepped up and grabbed Cyrus by the hair, lifting his head. "Who are you to say the Berserkers have no seeker?"

"I am from space," Cyrus said, trying to ignore the man's sweaty odor.

"You are a demon," Yang pronounced.

"The seeker told us—" Jana said.

Yang released Cyrus and whirled on Jana. The beetle-browed hetman used his spear to prod the woman between her breasts.

"The seeker is not here," Yang said. "I am the hetman. I rule the Berserkers."

"These two are a gift from the sky," Jana said. "I saw them slay a demon. They know old lore."

"You lie!" Yang said, with a malicious grin. "I know you lie for you saw me trap your so-called demonslayer just now. He was a fool. He fell to Yang. That proves he could never have slain a demon." The grin grew. "Now that Stone Fist is dead, I say what happens here, and I defy the seeker."

"You are the hetman," Jana said slowly.

"Do any here challenge me?" Yang shouted, looking around, searching faces.

"I challenge you," Cyrus said.

Yang whirled around. "You?" he said. "You are a captive. You are the spawn of the demons. You cannot challenge me."

"Oh, so you're afraid," Cyrus said. "I understand."

"What?" Yang roared. "Afraid of you? I am not afraid of anything, least of all a pale weakling."

"Then prove it and accept my challenge," Cyrus said.

It was hard to tell, but in the starry light, Jana seemed to watched him closely. She cocked her head, and she glanced at Yang. "I could defeat the outlander," she told the others.

Yang's eyes widened. "You told us he killed three Berserkers. He killed Stone Fist with a spell wand."

Jana pointed. "His spell wand is on the ground. He tried to use it against me, but I kicked it away. Yes, he killed three Berserkers, but I could defeat him now that he lacks his wand."

"I am the hetman," Yang said, slapping his chest.

"That is true," Jana said.

"I decide who will fight whom." Yang regarded Cyrus. "Without your wand, you have no more power, demon-spawn."

"That ought to make it a short fight then," Cyrus said. "But if you fear me—"

Yang lowered the spear's point so it rested under Cyrus's chin. "I can kill you here and now."

"I challenge you," Cyrus said again. And even though his telepathy was woefully weak, even though the back of his head throbbed, he attempted to tweak the primitive's mind.

Show everyone here how powerful you are. Accept the demon-spawn's challenge and defeat him before everyone. That will make you the champion of champions, for you know that Jana told the truth and these star men killed demons.

"I should kill you," Yang said.

Cyrus's head hurt, and his eyesight wavered. He sent another thought, another argument, and that was all he could send.

Yang lowered the spear. "What do the rest of you think? Should I thrash the demon-spawn, the murderer of Stone Fist?"

"Accept his challenge," another primitive said.

"I dare you to fight him," Jana added.

"How would you fight me?" Yang asked Cyrus. "What weapon would you choose?"

"A knife," Cyrus said.

A grin spread across Yang's face. "I accept," he said. "Put him on his feet."

Jana came forward, helping Cyrus stand.

"Is there something wrong with me choosing the knife?" Cyrus whispered.

"You have made it a death fight," Jana whispered in his ear. "Yang has a metal knife, and he has killed with it before. He is skilled with the blade. I tried to help you, star man. The seeker . . ." Jana shrugged. "Try to die with honor, at least. Otherwise, I doubt I will be able to keep Yang from killing your friend."

As Jana stepped away, Cyrus blinked several times. He rubbed his eyes, trying to clear the splotches from them. Afterward, he gingerly massaged the back of his head. The blow to the face earlier was going to mess with his reflexes.

"Let us get this over with," Yang said. "We have a long journey ahead of us tonight. Quit delaying."

As he spoke, Yang removed the fur cloak from his shoulders. Then he drew a broad-bladed iron knife from the sheath on his chest. He took several practice slashes before leering at Cyrus.

"I will cut you ten times and watch your blood water the ground," Yang said. "Afterward, I will eat your heart and gain your knowledge, man from the stars. All will acknowledge Yang as the greatest Berserker of all."

Cyrus shook his arms. His face ached, talking hurt, and if he moved too fast, his eyesight wavered. It was a bad combination for a knife fight. He needed nimbleness, and instead it felt as if he were moving through water.

"Hurry," Yang said. "Draw your blade, star man. Face me and die in a death challenge."

It would have been better if Skar fought the monster. Cyrus glanced at the soldier under the net. Now that he thought about it, Yang had clubbed Skar hardest of all. In some manner, it appeared that Jana wanted him to succeed.

The most interesting thing was this: Jana had lied about the Berserker Clan lacking a seeker. Why would she have done something like that?

"Draw your blade," Yang repeated, sounding impatient.

Cyrus licked his dry lips, flexed his knife hand and let it settle on the hilt of his blade. He'd acquired the weapon on High Station 3. A criminal had fought him. He'd gained use of the man's knife and killed with it. He liked its heft. Too bad it wasn't a vibrio-knife.

"Are you afraid?" Yang sneered.

"Yeah," Cyrus said. "I'm afraid you're going to shit your pants once we start and that I'll gag on the stench of it."

Yang stood motionless. Then he howled with rage and charged. He moved like a legendary rhinoceros, an extinct Earth beast, a mass of muscle and heavy bones. The knife thrust and Cyrus twisted aside. He didn't attempt to draw his blade—he tried to avoid death. The enemy knife slid past his chest, slicing fabric and scratching his flesh. Cyrus had been in many knife fights, and he had practiced long and hard. On the voyage to New Eden, he had learned new tricks from the space marines. He wasn't a fancy fighter, but he was gifted in pragmatic tactics and he was exceptionally fast.

Cyrus twisted out of the knife's path again and managed to stretch out his right leg. As Yang continued lunging, moving forward, his right shin crashed against Cyrus's outstretched limb. The big man tripped, and he went flying. The crash of leg against leg nearly crippled Cyrus. He shouted, pulled in his leg, and hobbled in agony. Meanwhile, face-first, Yang thudded onto the stony ground. Like a maddened beast, he surged to his feet, spun around, and snarled with fury.

Cyrus drew his knife, and he knew by the look in Yang's eyes that he should have attacked while the big man lay on the ground.

Spitting with rage, Yang advanced in a knife fighter's crouch. Shame, fury, and blood vengeance seethed in his dark eyes.

"You are quick," Yang muttered. "You are devious."

"You're a clumsy oaf," Cyrus said. "You're cross-eyed and you're stupid."

An evil grin stretched across Yang's face. He rumbled a low-throated laugh.

It chilled Cyrus, and made his spine tingle with unease.

"He is a warrior," Yang shouted to the others. "He tries to goad me to fury. This one thinks. Jana was right about him."

"Kill him," a primitive said.

"Yes, kill him," another called.

"What do you say, Jana?" Yang asked. "Should I kill him?"

"The seeker wishes him alive," Jana said.

"I did not ask you what the seeker thinks," Yang said. "I asked what you say."

"You are the hetman," Jana said. "The decision rests with you."

"I am the hetman." Yang regarded Cyrus. "Do you seek death this night, pale one?"

Cyrus remained silent, waiting for the attack.

"He is devious," Yang told the others. "And the seeker said this one performs magic. Tell me, Jana. Is it the Berserker custom to let a captive challenge the hetman for leadership?"

For a moment, it seemed as if a secret grin twitched across Jana's lips. Then her eyes widened—it seemed overdone. She glanced almost theatrically from Cyrus to Yang. "He cast spells here among us?" Jana asked.

Yang grunted an affirmative.

"He used them against you, my hetman?" Jana asked.

"He is dangerous," Yang said.

The primitives began to murmur among themselves.

Cyrus realized he didn't have much time. If he was going to strike, he had to do so now. Yang was big and strong, with huge bones. Even if he stabbed the man a killing blow, it might not prove fast enough— the hetman could still deliver a deathblow against him. With a quick flip, Cyrus reversed his hold, pinching the blade's tip between his thumb and index finger. Swiftly, he drew back his arm and snapped it forward, hurling the knife. It spun once, and would have struck Yang in the eye, but the hetman was quicker than he looked. He parried the spinning knife. A spark erupted and iron clanged. Then Cyrus's deflected knife flew into the darkness and struck a rock.

"Very devious," Yang said, and it seemed as if the fury no longer shined in his eyes. "But the star man has never fought man-to-man against a Berserker before."

Cyrus wasn't sure what was going on, but suddenly Yang didn't seem to be quite the simpleton he'd appeared to be at first.

"The pale outlander can fight," Yang said, "and he knows mind magic. But his mind powers cannot sweep all of us into his net at once.

Otherwise, he would have cast the spell against all of us, not just me. Therefore, three Berserkers will watch him at all times."

"You're not going to kill me?" Cyrus asked.

Yang snorted. "You are from space. The seeker . . . you will learn about her soon enough. If you try more trickery, I will beat you. If you refuse to learn, I will break your legs so you will never walk again. I will bring you to the seeker, but I will first draw the poison from your fangs."

"What about Skar?" Cyrus asked.

Yang glanced at the entangled soldier. "He is the demonslayer. He is very dangerous. This we know, because Jana told us. But your friend is not a seeker or a wizard. Strong cords will subdue him until the seeker says otherwise."

"Do you know Klane?" Cyrus asked.

Yang's eyes seemed to glitter, and he no longer seemed like a stupid brute. "The less you speak, the better it will be for you. Gag him, tie his hands, and ready the demonslayer. We must be far from here by the time the sun rises."

12

Klane crept past the leafy green fronds of puffer plants. They stood a little taller than his head. The first puffer fruit had started to appear under the widest fronds. They were little brown nodules no bigger than his fingertip. After every few steps, Klane plucked several and deposited the hard fruit into a pouch.

He had seen such fruit before, of course. Puffer fruit didn't grow in the uplands, on the Tash-Toi plains. They were Demon Valley produce. In his time, the seeker had possessed several puffer seeds. When crushed and mixed with gat juice, it made a powerful healing salve. Klane remembered as a child asking the seeker where puffer seeds came from. The wise old man had said, "The Valley of the Demons."

Klane had believed him as a child. These last few years, he had begun to wonder about that, though. Who would dare climb down into the valley to gather seeds? The small fruit in his pouch was proof that the seeker had told the truth.

Klane exhaled sharply. He had aged these past few days since leaving the caves of the singing gods. Wisdom and sadness now mingled in his blue eyes, and his facial skin was no longer as tight as before. That might have been because he had lost considerable weight. Then again, maybe it represented the heaviness in his soul. He wasn't sure.

Klane had rehearsed his magic as he traveled into the Valley of the Demons. He could levitate, move rocks, and far-cast with his mind.

Far-casting was the ability to search ahead. Several times he'd spotted demon sky vehicles before they appeared in the air. He hadn't attempted to probe a demon's mind. A strange sizzling aura protected each one. The sizzling aura did not originate in its mind, but from a device like a junction-stone that it kept on its belt.

One thing Klane had learned: the demons had slaves who practiced magic. He had felt them like feathers on his skin at night. Because of the magic-wielding slaves, he had not dared to mind search for the seeker.

With his magic, Klane had slain several creatures for meat. He had dug up roots and drank water. Each time he ate until his stomach felt bloated, yet still, he had lost weight.

Am I dying?

He didn't think so. Certainly, he had changed. The experience in the caves, the teleporting, the levitating, and the mind healing: he was different from the youth who left the clan.

Now he had reached the valley bottom, and the air was heavier, the days and nights warmer. Sweat remained on his skin longer and the very air smelled of moisture. Crops must surely grow better in such a place.

Klane crept through the field of puffer plants. The demon river gurgled just out of sight. Earlier, he had called river fish to his hands until his thumbs poked through their gills. Who needed a hook and line when his magic could supply him with food?

He came to the edge of the field. Klane paused there, collecting his resolve. He drew back a frond. It had a sticky underside. He'd have to grab them from the top from now on. After pulling the frond back, he peered at the nearby demon city.

There were big domed structures with cellular divisions on the outer surface. Towers had fluted roofs and bridges like spiderwebs connected them together. Squinting, Klane was sure he made out a demon—a speck from here—stalking across a high bridge, moving from one tower to the next.

For some reason that particular sight struck Klane with awe. He froze, with his left hand on the frond. All his life he had heard of this terrible place. Even now, as he breathed the moisture-laden air, he realized that he had descended into the Valley of the Demons. He had expected his spine to shiver and his teeth to chatter.

This was the locus of evil in the world, the abode of the grim demons who haunted humanity. The vile creatures had taken his best friend into the lair of evil. He was about to attempt an impossible feat. His stomach should have curdled at the thought, but it did not.

He wondered why. Did it have anything to do with journeying through the darkness of the singing gods? Had he gone from death to life, and because of that, power filled him as never before? Maybe that was the answer, or maybe doing a thing was less frightening than thinking about it and making himself scared to death.

I am not a warrior, but I have become a man of action. No one else in Clan Tash-Toi has dared such a thing as this. I alone had the courage to come here.

He shook his head. This was a foolish place to make boasts. He had entered, or was about to enter, the foulest lair of evil ever: the demon city. Should he contact the seeker now?

That was a weighty question. If he contacted the old one too soon, the seeker might give away the plan to his captors. Demons were sly and devious. Yet if he waited too long to contact the old man, he might waste time searching in the wrong places.

I will wait, Klane told himself.

He let go of the frond and retreated several paces into the puffer field. He lay down, stretched out, and closed his eyes. He needed the cover of darkness, and he needed to rest. Tonight, he would strike for demon city, and if the dice of fate tumbled the right way, he would contact the seeker of Clan Tash-Toi.

13

Chengal Ras rustled his streamers in agitation. The mentalist looked up at him, and the small creature made a weird grimace.

The 109th stood in a domed chamber filled with medical and mentalist equipment. Machines hummed, gurgled, buzzed, and flashed lights. Tubes, screens, boxes of machinery, illuminated globes, computers, life-support systems—the items cluttered the chamber. It was a mess, and to his way of thinking, it indicated a troubled intellect.

Mentalist Niens was a thin human and wore a long white coat. He reeked of recent sex and pungent foods, and his breath stank abominably. For a human, Niens had narrow features, a beak of a nose, and spidery fingers. He looked devious, but was supposed to be the best at these brain scans.

An even thinner, older, naked human lay on a scanning bed. Mentalist Niens had attached leads, tubes, and other paraphernalia to the ancient, and now lowered a metal dome onto the creature's head.

Chengal Ras had read the information concerning this one. He was a seeker, a psi-able shaman among the human primitives on the game preserve. He had belonged to Clan Tash-Toi. It had been Zama Dee's policy to send failed experimental creatures into the uplands. Chengal Ras wondered about the wisdom of that, but the 73rd had her own schemes and theories she wished to test.

"Do you wish me to explain the procedure, Revered One?" Niens asked.

Chengal Ras swished his tail in annoyance. The creature's offensive breath reached his nostrils. Was this a subtle insult on the 73rd's part? Had she known about the cattle's habits and offensive stenches?

Chengal Ras lifted his scent maker and almost pressed the switch.

"I beg your pardon, Revered One," Niens said. "But your odors may interfere with the scan."

If he had been in High Station 3 or on one of his vessels, Chengal Ras would have struck down the offender. It was inconceivable that a human should attempt to balk any of his actions. Through an effort of will he restrained himself. Mentally, he cataloged the insult to his superiority. After this was over, he would have to bargain with the 73rd for Mentalist Niens. Yes, he would purchase this wretched skunk and run the human in his game room, chasing and killing the man for sport. Blood would wash away the insult.

"What are you hoping to achieve with the scan?" Chengal Ras hissed.

"My predecessor kept the specimen under sedation," Niens said. "During that time, she ran the primitive through routine tests. This one showed a higher than average psionic ability, but little else of note."

"Where is your predecessor now?"

"Scrubbing processing tanks, I believe," Niens said. "She is being punished."

"How were you associated with your predecessor?"

"I was her laboratory assistant," Niens said.

Chengal Ras blinked rapidly. He was sure the creature's stink irritated his eyes. "Did you approve of the sedation?"

"I respect the specimen's abilities," Niens said. "But my personal security isn't at issue. I seek knowledge, data. It is my goal to extract what I can from the specimens in order to broaden my Revered One's fund of raw knowledge."

"You are a dedicated creature," Chengal Ras said.

Niens bowed low.

Chengal Ras knew the signs. This one was a dissembler, a climber, and a possible liar. It must have a keen intellect. Surely, Zama Dee would not otherwise keep climbers among her mentalists. Humans such as these were instrumental in teaching fledging Bo Taw to love their masters, their betters.

"Continue the scan as you explain the procedures," Chengal Ras said.

"As you will, Revered One," Niens said. He lowered the helmet. The outer surface bristled with nodes and leads. Gently, he settled it onto the old human's head. Then Niens slid his narrow hindquarters onto a stool and began to tap controls.

"We have developed a new serum," Niens said. "Some among the mentalists do not believe it is altogether trustworthy, but I approve of it. The serum blocks the majority of the subject's psi process. Psionics is, as I'm sure you are aware, a frontal lobe phenomenon."

It was a talkative creature, this mentalist. That was another strike against it.

Niens made adjustments and tapped the main screen. The old man on the board jerked and groaned.

"Hmm," Niens said. "He's twitchy today. I wonder why."

For the next few minutes the mentalist sat hunched over his controls. The ancient on the table tightened its stringy muscles by slow degrees. Soon, it lay rigid, the otherwise flaccid muscles showing starkly.

"Why is that happening?" Chengal Ras asked.

"That is an excellent question."

"You dare to make an assertion concerning the quality of my question?" Chengal Ras hissed.

Niens looked up in alarm. His tongue flickered into view, sliding across his thin lips. "I beg your pardon, Revered One. I misspoke. Something lies at the edge of the seeker's subconscious. I've been trying to tease it into view. Such was the absorption in my task that I thoughtlessly forgot about your presence."

"Your remarks show an exalted belief in your status."

"I crave your pardon, Revered One. I work too hard, it is true."

"I have not said that."

"Oh. There I go again, Revered One. I—"

"Silence," Chengal Ras said. "Cease this useless rambling. What occurs here? Explain what you suspect and what you're attempting to achieve."

"Do you insist upon hearing my foolish conjectures, Revered One?"

"I am not in the habit of having my orders analyzed or questioned."

Niens lowered his head. "The seeker—as I shall refer to the test subject—appears agitated. I believe he has hope. This hope causes him stress because he doesn't know if the hope is warranted or not."

"That is a convoluted theory," Chengal Ras said.

"I have been told I have chaotic thoughts. Zama Dee approves, however, as I often attempt something new and therefore original."

Clever, very clever, Chengal Ras thought. He saw the utility of it right away. It was also a dangerous practice. The 73rd gave her cattle greater leeway than ordinary. The reason, according to Niens, was to broaden the base of Zama Dee's raw data. That would imply the 73rd thought cattle could uncover information a Kresh could or would not. Yet, didn't the FTL drive—the Faster-Than-Light drive—the Sol humans brought prove the validity of the theory? He would have to consider this in greater depth.

"What causes the seeker's hope?" Chengal Ras asked.

"That is what I'm attempting to discover, Revered One. I wonder . . . maybe we—I—should seek the answer in his memory."

Niens's thin spidery fingers blurred over the touchpads and screens. The ancient one's stiffness remained, but a slow movement of its mouth showed a smile spreading into place.

"Please look at the big screen, Revered One," Niens said.

Chengal Ras twisted around.

"We're viewing the seeker's memory," Niens said.

Chengal Ras instantly recognized the Kresh sky vehicle. It came toward a compound of Jassac natives. He saw a youth sprint into view. The white-skinned native clutched something in its fist. It glared at the sky vehicle, and suddenly, incredibly, the vehicle lurched. A moment later the sky vehicle sailed down and crashed against the ground. Another flash of memory brought a dancing throng of cattle to the broken sky vehicle and to the dead Kresh. The memory showed the grinning youth.

"Is this a dream, or a memory of a true event?" Chengal Ras asked.

"That is an interesting question, Revered One. Certainly, the old one lying on the table believes this to be true. If it in fact happened . . . that is another story. Notice the smile. The memory delights him. I am inclined to believe it happened."

"Why did the investigation team capture this one?" Chengal Ras asked.

"Interesting, interesting," Niens said. He swiveled around on the stool and tapped a computer screen. Data appeared. He read it, and he looked up sharply. "We must assume this is a true memory," the mentalist said. "The specimen was caught due to the Kresh attack, due to Kresh deaths."

"Elaborate."

"It is strict policy to capture and interrogate any human who murders one of the Noble Race."

"This one killed a Kresh?"

"Let us proceed with the interrogation," Niens said, "in an endeavor to find out."

Chengal Ras silently agreed with the analysis. For an hour, two hours, he watched the mentalist at work. This one knew its trade. Perhaps here lay the reason for its arrogance and improper deference.

Finally, Mentalist Niens sat up, and with a tug at his collar, straightened his coat. He peered at Chengal Ras. "A mistake has been made."

Chengal Ras's attention had been wandering as he thought up new axioms involving subterfuge and espionage. Now, he regarded the human. Niens indicated the seeker trembling in exhaustion on the table. "According to the capture report, the investigation team sought the psionic-capable individual who had caused the Kresh deaths. I now realize that this one impersonated the killer."

"You're attempting to perpetrate the notion that cattle can climb to heights of pure altruism?"

"What?" Niens asked. Maybe it took him a moment to untangle the thought behind Chengal Ras's words. "No, Revered One."

"Why would this bag of bones sacrifice its life for another?"

"That is an interesting question. I'm sure it would take extended study to find the root cause."

"Heed my next question carefully, mentalist."

Niens looked up. A second later, he nodded solemnly.

"What or who is the 'Anointed One'?" Chengal Ras asked.

Niens blinked with seeming incomprehension. "Is that a religious term, Revered One?"

"Obviously, yes," Chengal Ras said.

"I ask because I haven't heard it before."

Chengal Ras checked one of the devices attached to his belt. According to this, the creature told the truth. His human operatives on High Station 3 had infiltrated the Resisters. The operatives had returned with several fables, one telling of a being who would lead the humans out of so-called captivity. There were indications that the Anointed One resided on Jassac. Logic dictated such a being would possess unique abilities. That indicated a psi-able human.

"You will probe deeper," Chengal Ras said.

"The seeker is worn out," Niens said. "I suggest—"

"Have I asked for your suggestions?"

"No, Revered One."

"Because you are Zama Dee's creature, I have tolerated your slurs and aspirations to my superiority. I will do so no longer. Approach me."

"Revered One," Niens said, as he remained on the stool. "I hold you in the highest esteem and I worship the floor space you occupy. I would—"

Rage motivated Chengal Ras, as well as the realization that he needed to make the mentalist fear him. Cattle must either love their superiors or fear them. There was no room for middle ground. The 73rd might not approve of this, but she would not be able to press the issue. Custom would restrain her, if nothing else.

In a swift stride, Chengal Ras reached the mentalist and plucked him off the chair. Like all humans, the man was feather light, and Chengal Ras refrained from using his full strength. He threw the yelping man onto the tiles and placed one of his clawed feet on the human's chest. If Chengal Ras pressed down with all his weight, he could easily crack the man's ribs and crush him. He had killed humans like this on several enjoyable occasions. Once, he had done so only for pleasure. Every other time had been to inflict greater obedience from his cattle.

"You have offended me," Chengal Ras hissed.

"I beg your pardon, Revered One," Niens wailed.

The stenches didn't improve, and now the stink of fear radiated from the human filth. Chengal Ras unhooked an agonizer from his belt. Bending low, he touched the cool device to the creature's neck.

Mentalist Niens howled in agony and the creature voided its bowels at the pain. Perhaps he had put the setting too high. Chengal Ras removed the agonizer and saw that it was at the second-highest setting.

Under his clawed talon, he could feel the human tremble and heard the creature weep.

"I have failed you, Revered One," Niens sobbed. "I have grossly failed. Forgive me, please, oh Noble One of Kresh. I am—"

"Silence," Chengal Ras hissed.

The mentalist fell silent.

"I will tolerate no more of your slurs."

Niens nodded quickly.

"You will work efficiently and with due reverence and respect for my rank and my race. Together, we will probe the old one's memories and see what it will uncover."

"I hear and obey, Revered One."

Chengal Ras heard the whining note, and therefore true piety, in the mentalist's words. He removed his foot, and he nodded, indicating the creature could stand.

"You will clean yourself," Chengal Ras said. "You will don fresh garments. No. First, you will shower and use grade-seven solvent on your skin. You stink. You will eat cloves and drink lavender spice. That should mask the foul odors emanating from you. Then you will don fresh clothes and we shall work late into the darkness." He glanced at the pathetic thing lying on the table. "That will also give the seeker time to recover strength for tonight's ordeal."

Niens bowed repeatedly and kept his eyes aimed at the floor.

It was clear to Chengal Ras that Zama Dee did not punish her humans often or hard enough. This was a good lesson for the creature. Maybe one more swift session would be enough to turn the cattle's loyalty to him instead of the 73rd. In any case, something odd was taking place in this chamber. Chengal Ras could sniff it in the air. He needed to find this Anointed One and spirit him or her away.

"Go!" Chengal Ras said in a loud voice. "I have given you commands. Now you will obey with haste or feel the agonizer again."

Niens spun around and nearly stumbled in his hurry to comply. The agonizer, in Chengal Ras's opinion, was the most important tool in teaching humans their proper place in the universe. Yes, finally, he was beginning to enjoy himself on Jassac.

14

Klane slunk through the darkness of the city streets as a riot of emotions filled him. He knew fear. This was the place of evilest legends. But more than fear, he knew an avenging sense of justice and righteousness.

He passed one of the towers with its fluted bridge high above him. He kept in the shadows, and he observed men and women on the demon city streets. They wore strange garments and hurried as if on important business. Ah, there, with the clash of its talons, a demon strode toward a big domed structure.

None paid him the slightest heed. He had borrowed a cloak spun from strange material and he wore a hat over his head. He moved purposefully, trying to mimic how the others acted.

He dared the demon city. He was the Tash-Toi avenger as told in the old tales. He had a knife, and he would slay any who stood in his path. More important, spells seethed in his mind, ready to leap out and do his bidding.

Now he needed to find the seeker. Now he must dare to cast spells in the most magic-filled place on Jassac. He darted into an alcove and peered upward. Windows glistened with artificial light. The smells, the sights—

Klane shook his head. He must focus. He must gather his resolve. The demons had raided the uplands. He now would raid the lowlands and teach the vile ones that men would not lie supine to them forever.

I fight. I strike in the name of justice.

He closed his eyes, steadied his breathing, and roved outward with a Far-Calling Spell.

With the utmost caution, taught to him in the caves of the singing gods, Klane's mind searched for the seeker. He felt the feathery thoughts of other wizards, the demon tools in human guise. He avoided them, acting like a shadow, a whispery ghost seeking . . .

Klane's thoughts whirled around. He sensed an old familiar mind.

Klane.

Seeker?

Klane, you must flee. They are weaving a trap for you. They know. They know you are here.

I have come for you.

You are in the valley?

Caution slowed Klane's answer. Something was amiss. He might not have caught it before, but the laughter of the singing gods had tuned his mind into something much sharper. Others trickled thoughts or invaded the seeker's mind.

Have they drugged you, old friend? Klane asked.

I cannot climb out of slumber.

I sense them.

Klane, you must flee. You must wait for the transfer some other time.

You've spoken about that before, old friend. What is the transfer?

No, no, do not ask me that, Klane. I mustn't let them know.

Who? Let who know?

There is a watcher, a demon with sinister ways. He seeks you, Klane. He waits—

Klane retreated with his Far-Calling Spell. There was trickery abroad tonight. He felt the demons. He felt their devious natures. With a start, he realized that the singing gods had taught him more than he'd realized.

Transfer, the seeker had spoken about a transfer. It was vitally important—to humanity.

Looking up, Klane realized the seeker was near. Should he attack and attempt a rescue? What had the seeker said? That he could not arise from slumber? The demons had drugged him.

Klane grinned. He had plucked many puffer pods earlier. Upon waking tonight, he'd used his thumbnails and pried each one apart. The tiny green seeds had potency. He would trickle three down the seeker's throat. That would wake up the dead.

Yes, he must strike now, and he must strike fast, ruthlessly. The demons might try to stop him. They had demon weapons—

With a flap of his borrowed cloak, Klane strode out of the alcove. He moved purposefully and with speed. He followed a faint mind trail. In a manner of minutes, he crossed several city blocks. It was hard not breaking into a sprint.

He took a deep breath. The air was so moisture rich. It was hard getting used to it. Craning his neck, he looked up. In this tower, near the very top—

Klane had to make a swift decision. How would he ascend the demon tower? If he entered it to climb the stairs, he would have to pass each demon trap. He suspected they knew he had arrived. The seeker had implied as much.

Grinning, Klane decided it was time to use his full powers. Reaching behind him, he gripped the cloak with two hands. He kept searching the windows and their shining night-lights. That window to the left, one down from the top and two over from the skylight: the seeker was in that room.

Klane squeezed his eyes shut, then he opened them wide. His feet lifted off the ground in a Levitation Spell.

"Higher," he whispered.

Just like the time in the caves, he rose. The speed of his ascent quickened the longer he levitated. The cloaked flapped even though he held the edges. He kept his neck craned and his eyes locked on the targeted window. He moved so fast that it almost felt as if he flew. He was the avenger. He was the knife of the Tash-Toi, to cut the heart out of the demons.

Klane reached the window and concentrated, hurling a hard knot of telekinesis. He sank a moment. The glass shattered and shards tinkled onto the inner floor.

Curling himself into a fetal ball, Klane levitated through the broken window and shot down the hall. He landed running on his feet.

His mind pulsed and sweat slicked his ribs. It took great concentration to do this. He didn't realize he'd drawn his knife until he saw it in his hand.

A door opened, and a man in red and blue garments stared at him. He was a tall human, with a long face and high forehead. A metal band encircled his head. The man thought of himself as a Bo Taw, a creature of Zama Dee.

"You are Klane," the tall humanoid said. "We knew you would come here tonight—"

The humanoid quit speaking as he gasped in pain. Klane plunged the metal dagger into the man's belly. He'd aimed the point upward like a crafty Tash-Toi warrior. He shoved the blade and shifted the sharp metal from side to side, slicing organs. Then the tip reached the Bo Taw's heart.

"No," the tall one groaned. "You don't understand."

Klane jerked the knife free. He understood perfectly. He was the Tash-Toi avenger. He had descended into hell in order to free his friend. It was the Bo Taw who didn't understand.

The man sank onto the floor and blood gushed from his mouth.

Klane broke into a sprint. In a raid, one must keep moving. He needed to use the element of surprise. He had listened for years at the war-fires, when the champions and veteran warriors told about their greatest feats.

"I am Tash-Toi," Klane whispered to himself.

Another door opened, this time on the other side of the hall. Another tall human regarded him. "Listen to me," the man said.

The man spoke as if he were a friend. At the same time, the demon-leagued man cast a mental spell at Klane.

Klane laughed. He was primed for anything, and he expected trickery. He deflected the mind bolt and used levitation to gain height. With a slash of his knife, he opened the man's throat. Blood jetted. Some of it splashed against Klane's shoulder. The man toppled, and Klane alighted to the floor, heading straight for the end door.

He didn't wait to see if someone had locked it. The door was thicker and heavier than the others were, with a keyhole instead of a handle. Klane raised his free hand and held his palm toward the door. He cast another Telekinetic Spell. With a splinter of wood along the sides and a crumbling of the metal door, it tore free of its hinges and crashed open. The door thumped onto the floor, and Klane stepped into a large domed chamber.

Several things caught his attention at once. The seeker, naked as a baby, lay strapped to a table. His eyes were closed. He was asleep or drugged. A thin man dressed in white sat near the seeker. The man stared at him in wonder.

"It's him," the man said—his name was Niens. "It's the one who destroyed the sky vehicle. I recognize the face from the old man's memory."

Klane's heart beat faster. The last thing he noticed was a demon. It regarded him. The demon wore metallic streamers and it held a flat device in its clawed hand.

"Are you the Anointed One?" the demon asked.

Klane's eyes narrowed. He released his knife and took hold of it with telekinetic magic. "Fly," he whispered. The knife did exactly that. With a hiss of sound, it shot at the demon and plunged into the creature's leathery hide.

The demon roared with agony, staggering backward.

Klane laughed, and he eyed the man in white. That one backed away. Klane raised his hand. The man fell prostrate on the floor, trembling, pleading for his life through his actions.

In three swift strides, Klane reached the seeker, his old friend. The man's helplessness enraged Klane.

The demon roared again, and it clawed at its belt. Klane concentrated. The blade jerked out of the monster's hide, and blood dripped onto the floor. The knife backed up, backed up, and it plunged at the demon again, sinking into vile flesh another time.

The roar was louder and filled with greater pain.

"As you give us, I give you!" Klane shouted. "Your magic tricks will not help you tonight, demon."

Klane leaped onto the table, and he ripped the leads and tape off his friend's flesh. He removed the iron hat, and with a mental bolt, he forced the old one rudely awake. He had no more time for niceties, and he risked damaging the seeker's mind.

"Klane," the old man whispered, as drool spilled from his mouth. It seemed as if his eyes had trouble focusing. He seemed disoriented. "Klane . . . it's a . . . a trap."

Klane held out his hand. He noticed that the man on the floor—Niens—crawled away. He let him go; good riddance to the mentalist. He waited, and watched the seeker. Understanding struggled against disorientation on the old man's features and in his eyes. Finally, feebly, the seeker reached up and took hold with his dry, leathery fingers. Effortlessly, using a smattering of levitation, Klane lifted the seeker onto his feet.

"You've changed," the seeker whispered.

The demon no longer sagged against a wall. The monster staggered closer, and he aimed a weapon at them. Klane noticed the device, and his eyes tightened. The talon clicked a switch, but nothing happened. Klane had disabled the demon weapon.

With a roar, the demon hurled the useless weapon from him. Then he charged across the room, heavy tail balancing his forward thrust.

Klane jumped down on the other side of the table and pulled the seeker with him. At the same time, the stool Niens had been sitting on moved. With telekinesis, Klane hurled the stool under the demon.

The creature tripped over it, and the demon crashed against the table, breaking it with a splintering sound.

"We're trapped," the seeker wheezed.

Klane felt both exhilarated and tired. He'd never expected it could be like this. He had become something out of legend. He had found his friend, and he had hurt a demon.

I am the demonslayer. It was the hope of every Tash-Toi to slaughter the great enemy.

"Grab my neck," Klane said.

Withered old arms clamped onto him. He felt the tremor of weakened muscles. Klane jumped and levitated once more. He flew up and over the sprawled demon, landing lightly on his feet behind it.

"Let us run," Klane said, as he pried the arms off his neck. He led the way toward the door.

The demon hissed with malice, and it thrashed against the broken table as it freed itself from the wreckage.

"They are very fast on their feet," the seeker wheezed.

Klane glanced back at his friend. The old man had sunken cheeks and feverish eyes. Now that he had a moment, Klane noticed the ribs showing and the frailty of the seeker. He would not last much longer.

Behind them, the demon lurched to its feet. Its arms waved and the talons snapped with anger. The device the creatures usually wore against magic had ripped free. It lay glittering on the floor.

Klane whirled fully around, facing the demon. This was a golden opportunity. He raised his arms and spread his fingers. "Creature of the pit, your time has come."

The nine-foot monster crouched. Its large tail lashed, snapping wood, and it made ready to leap after them.

Klane laughed in a voice he didn't recognize. In the back of his mind, he thought he could hear the singing gods' mockery, their laughter. Could they be guiding him? No. He ran his own thoughts, and he practiced these spells himself.

With his magic, his mind, he pulled the largest table splinters into the air. He made them levitate and back away from the demon.

The creature noticed and its eyes bulged outward. "You cannot do this. I am Kresh. I am your superior. Lie on your face and worship me."

Klane laughed again, in a much uglier way than before.

"I am Chengal Ras the 109th," the demon said. "I am your superior. You will obey me or face the consequences."

"I am the demonslayer," Klane said in an abnormally loud voice. "I am the doom of the Kresh. Prepare to meet the Creator, Chengal Ras. Prepare to die the death of a hundred stabs."

Chengal Ras looked right and left at the wood splinters surrounding him.

"Stab," Klane said, and he brought his arms down.

The circling splinters of table wood hovering around the demon moved. They flashed inward like spears. Some broke apart against the demon's tough hide. Some pierced the leathery skin. Enough slid deeper into the creature, reaching organs and other vitals.

The demon opened its monstrous jaws. It roared in agony, and its arms flailed. How many humans had it slain in its day? How many people had it tormented? The demons plagued the Tash-Toi, tortured all the clans of the uplands.

Klane clenched his hands into fists. With a blast of magic power, he caused the wood inside the demon to explode into tiny particles. It was enough. The monster staggered several lurching steps. It blinked, and blood wept from its eyes. Then Chengal Ras the 109th crashed onto the tiles, dead.

15

"Klane, Klane," the seeker said. The old hands plucked at the youth's garments.

Klane turned around as he touched the bridge of his nose. He felt lightheaded and woozy. He had slain a demon. Yet it had felt as if the singing gods—

"Men come," the seeker wheezed.

Klane cocked his head, listening for the tramp of feet down the hall. He heard nothing but the wind stirring before the broken window at the end of the corridor.

"We must flee," Klane said.

The old man glanced at the demon twitching on the floor. He nodded. "Can you lead us out of here?"

Klane felt mentally winded. He had expended a prodigious amount of magic. He would need time now in order to recuperate. He didn't think he could levitate all the way down to the ground, especially not while carrying the seeker.

"Can you run?" he asked the old man.

"I am Tash-Toi," the seeker said. "You lead, and I will follow."

Klane wondered if he should give the seeker a puffer seed. It might be too much for the old one's weakened body. He would have to trust the man's stubborn pride. Taking a deep breath, holding it, Klane ranged outward with his magic. He wished he still had the junction-stone. The path from this room—he saw the way, and he saw in his mind's eye soldiers racing up the levels of the building.

"This way," Klane said, as his eyes snapped open. "We're going to have to time this perfectly. The demons have soldier-slaves to do their bidding."

After that, neither of them talked as they ran, walked, hid at times, and crawled through the demon building, descending level by level. Men bearing guns tramped past. Tall humanoids with mind magic searched for them, but Klane had learned the art of blending into the surroundings, hiding from magical searches.

After a long descent, Klane eased open a door. He tasted the air, rich with moisture, and spied starry darkness.

"You must walk as I do, with your head erect and in a purposeful manner."

The seeker wore stolen garments they had found in a room. They were woefully baggy on his sparse form. He gripped one of Klane's triceps.

"You have made me proud, slayer. I always knew you had greatness in you, but I didn't realize to what extent."

The praise buoyed Klane. Yes, he had come a long way. But they were far from free of the evil city. He should have slain the demon in an easier manner. As he thought back to his exploits, he realized he had expended too much magic on unneeded flourishes. If he were going to survive to truly become the demon bane, he needed to learn how to kill quickly and with the least amount of effort. Levitating as he had all the way up the building—he had been showing off to himself. He must employ greater guile.

"Now," Klane said. He strode out of the building. The seeker followed. A single glance showed Klane that the old man knew the trick of walking like a demon slave.

They passed several buildings. Then, in the distance, a loud alarm blared with noise.

"Keep walking," Klane said.

"We must hide," the seeker said.

"Not yet," Klane said. "I want to escape the city and hide in the puffer fields."

"No, Klane. You've done the impossible. You're tired and you must regain your strength. I must perform the transfer now while I have time. I've already waited too long. You had to risk everything to reach me. I was foolish, but I cannot take any more chances."

"What is the transfer?" Klane asked.

"You will know soon enough. We need a quiet spot."

Klane heard the urgency in the old man's tone, and he heard a sad remorse.

"Let it wait," Klane said. "We must concentrate."

The seeker clutched his right shoulder, and the old man breathed in his ear. "You have no idea how vital this is. We must transfer. It is everything. I think you're the one, Klane. This is what all of us have been waiting for."

"You're not making sense."

"Find a hiding place." The seeker turned as bright lights began to appear in the buildings. Loud booming noises accompanied the lights. The demon city went from a place of shadows to the full brightness of a sunny day. Behind the blazing lights shined stars. Under the lights—

"This way," Klane said. He dared to run. He heard the seeker breathing hard behind him. He used finesse this time, breaking a lock instead of blowing a door down.

They entered another building, and they took stairs leading down into darkness.

"Perfect, my boy, this is the perfect place." The seeker tugged at him. "Now sit, you must sit."

Klane realized that something extraordinary was taking place. It put a knot in his stomach and tightened his throat. He wasn't sure he wanted to do this.

"Hold my hands," the seeker said. "We must be touching."

Sitting cross-legged on tiles in pitch-blackness, Klane reached out and took the seeker's hands. He realized the old one likewise sat cross-legged on the floor.

"Breathe, my boy. Fill your lungs with air."

Klane breathed deeply. In the distance, sirens wailed and alarms rang with an incessant howl.

The seeker chuckled. "Let them search. We are safe for a few minutes, and that's all we're going to need."

In the darkness, the old man licked chapped lips. He tightened his hold on Klane's fingers. "You must listen carefully, Klane. I'm only going to be able to tell you this once."

"Yes, seeker," Klane said.

"You came to us from the demons," the seeker said. "That was so long ago, so long. But I remember that moment well. Every day I watched you. It hurt to see the stronger boys pick on you. Three times, they broke your nose. Twice, others knocked out a tooth. It had to be that way, Klane. You had to accept the hard knocks of life. If you were too weak—

"Well, never mind that now," the old man said, with hesitation in his voice. "What's done is done. You were a product from the Kresh gene labs."

"Kresh?" asked Klane.

"No, don't ask me questions, my boy. Today, or tonight, you will learn much more than you want to know. You will absorb many lifetimes . . . you must listen to me," the seeker said.

"I'm listening," Klane said, wondering why the old man sounded harsh.

"I have loved you like a son, my boy, loved you more than you can know. I wondered if you would come for me, here in the demon city. Look at what you did. I don't know how you learned so much—"

"The caves," Klane said.

"What?" the seeker asked.

"I went to the caves of the singing gods."

The seeker fell silent.

"Did I do wrong?" Klane asked.

"I should have realized that's what happened," the seeker said, sounding different from before, sounding resigned. "You did what you did. You cannot change that now. Remember one thing, my boy. You are ours. You belong to humanity. Take what the singing gods give you, but do not accept their warped judgments about the universe."

"What are the singing gods?"

The seeker laughed harshly. "Pray you never truly discover that. I shouldn't have taken you there, but I had become worried. You didn't know how to use your powers properly. I thought—

"Listen to me, my boy. It is time for the transfer. Afterward, you must escape. You'll know what to do in a few days. Remember, you must ignore the singing gods. Take the human path. Free us from the Kresh."

"Where are you going?" Klane asked.

"Where I go, you cannot follow, at least not yet."

"I want to follow."

"No, not yet you don't. You have to fulfill your destiny first."

Klane wasn't sure he liked the sound of that.

"The Kresh gene-warp us, seeking to fashion hybrids to serve their alien needs. The two most successful classes are the Vomags and the Bo Taw."

"What are those?" Klane asked.

"You're going to find out soon enough. Occasionally, the Kresh put psi-able genetic rejects into the uplands. The aliens are a strange race. It is hard to understand why they do this or do that. It is enough that they have enslaved humanity under them. We must rise up, Klane, and escape the shackles."

The seeker sighed. "I have rambled long enough. I have sought for the courage to do this, but I am afraid. I'm very afraid. I don't want to die."

"Why would you say that?" Klane asked.

The seeker gripped his hands savagely. "It is time to transfer," the old man whispered. "Remember, you are my son, and I have loved you more than anything in life. You have made me very proud. Now finish the task and free us from the Kresh."

Klane wanted to cry out and tell the seeker to stop. He found himself speechless, and then it hit him. The seeker opened his mind to Klane, and he transferred memories into his brain. They flooded at a terrific rate. Faster and faster, flashes of thought poured from one mind to the other. It was a tidal wave, a tsunami, and it shorted Klane's ability to process.

In that moment, Klane realized there were more than one man's memories. Seekers before the seeker had done the same thing. They had transferred old knowledge to the seeker below him. Sights and unbelievable sounds thundered upon Klane's conscious mind and seeped into his unconscious. Concepts, theories, and knowledge, more knowledge and accumulated wisdom rushed into his mind. He saw stars, oceans, books, buildings, Chirr, Kresh—

What about the singing gods? What are the singing gods?

The memories flooded as from a holo-vid drama at high speed, like a downloading computer.

"What?" Klane whispered in the darkness. "What are these things? I don't understand."

The seeker groaned, and for the first time his grip weakened.

Klane tried to part his lips. He wanted to speak. He wanted this to stop. It was too much. So many thoughts conflicted with each other. Demons, Kresh, magic, psi-power, and on and on it went.

The torrent slowed finally, and the seeker's grip weakened even more. Suddenly, abruptly, it ended as the seeker's hands dropped away. The old man sat still for a second. Then his heart gave way. It stopped beating. He stopped breathing, and he thumped onto the cold tiles.

Klane wanted to bend over him and hear a last word. He wanted to calm his friend. He wanted to weep. He could not. He was frozen, with his mind overloaded.

Time rolled on without meaning. The distant sounds didn't matter anymore. Klane was in his own world, trying to sort things out.

"How . . ."

He found himself on his hands and knees, dry heaving.

"Why . . ."

In the darkness, he bumped into a wall. Only then did he realize that he'd climbed to his feet.

"Where . . ."

A man shouted at Klane, and he found himself on the street. He had come out of the basement, out of the building, and wandered like a fool.

Klane kept walking. The man shouted again and gave chase. Stopping, Klane turned. It was hard to think. He had so many memories, so many different ways of doing things tumbling in his mind.

At the last moment, Klane saw it was a Vomag hailing him. The soldier had a stun gun out, and he approached cautiously.

"What's your name?" the soldier asked.

Klane tried to form a reply. He heard the hovers before he saw them in the air floating. In one of them sat a Kresh.

A grim smile stretched Klane's lips. "What are you?" he asked.

"I'm asking the questions," the soldier said.

"You're a slave to an alien," Klane told the Vomag.

"I'm a soldier, and I'm doing my task."

"You're helping to enslave your race, your people."

The soldier pulled a communicator from his belt. "I've found him," the man said.

Klane raised his hand. He would cause a valve in the soldier's heart to stop, and that would give the Vomag a heart attack. As he tried just that, he felt blocking psi-minds.

Klane snarled, and he charged the Vomag. It didn't do any good. The soldier pressed a stud, and a beam hit Klane. His knees crumpled under him, and he slammed against the ground.

With his mind, he sought to see what the ray had done to his body. Quickly, using bodily chemicals, he counteracted the stun. He let himself go limp, however, and stayed prone on the ground.

Ten different voices sought to give him advice. It was too many memories of doing things many different ways. He needed time to sort the memories into categories. To have all these new thoughts—

A hover—a sky vehicle—grounded nearby. A dome opened and Kresh talons clawed against the walkway. Beside the alien ran a man in a white smock.

"Turn him over," the Kresh said.

Klane decided to wait, to play out the drama.

The Vomag rolled him over, letting Klane witness the new Kresh. He believed this one was called Zama Dee. The human was Mentalist Niens. Klane didn't know how he knew these things.

"He's faking stun paralysis," Niens said.

Klane sat up before one of his memories could warn him in time not to do that.

The Kresh glanced sharply at Niens. "This is the one who slew Chengal Ras?"

"Yes, Revered One," Niens said. "It was astonishing—I mean horrible, horrible, vile sacrilege."

The Kresh's lips peeled back. "Are you the Anointed One?" Zama Dee hissed at Klane.

Klane recognized the name "Anointed One." "Who is to say?" he responded.

"You lack the proper deference," the Kresh told him.

134

Klane could feel the many psi-minds shielding the Kresh from him. He was still tired and weak from the original ordeal. His head hurt and so did his heart. The seeker was dead. The transfer had been made. Now he was trapped in the demon city.

Am I the Anointed One of legend?

Klane lowered his head, and he would have thrown a mind bolt. But the Vomag shot him a second time, with a higher stun setting.

Before he could counteract it, Klane slid unconscious onto the cold ground. He had tried, but they'd caught him nonetheless.

16

Yang of Berserker Clan set a stiff pace every day. They ran single file, one warrior following the next, their callused feet slapping dirt, sand, or rock. Through gorges, uphill, and across the plains they moved.

Cyrus felt their stares, and every time he looked around, he caught one of the warriors watching him. They obviously weren't going to take any risks with him. They were also Kresh-cautious, these Berserkers, and they had marvelous hearing.

Cyrus ran near Jana as she ran behind Yang, who led the way. He caught a sudden shift of her head, as if she heard something odd. As Jana passed a lichen-covered boulder, she halted and raised her spear. The warriors who ran behind her halted. Yang hadn't seen that and he took two more running steps. Then he stopped and whirled around.

"Do you hear demons?" Yang growled at her.

With her spear still raised, Jana cocked her head further. Then she aimed her spear in the direction of the valley. The effect upon the others surprised Cyrus.

"Hide," Yang said. He didn't shout, but it was loud and it was an order. The big hetman glanced right and left, adding, "Blend into the ground."

To Cyrus, the command seemed senseless. They raced across a red wasteland. It was as much rock as sand, and left few footprints that he could see. How was anyone going to hide out here? If sky vehicles showed up, the Kresh had them.

"Jana," Yang said. "Put a knife to the wizard's throat. If he betrays us, kill him."

She grabbed Cyrus's right arm, pushing him away from the lichen-covered boulder. "You must hurry," she said.

The other warriors scattered like mice in every direction. Yang took Skar, with the soldier's arms tightly secured by thick cords.

"Here," Jana said. "Kneel, and curl yourself into a ball."

Cyrus knelt on the hard ground in a shallow depression, but he didn't see how that could help them. She crouched on her hands and knees beside him, leaning her shapely body against his. With a deft move she cast her reddish cloak over them. From underneath it, she adjusted the cloak, tugging down a corner here and straightening a different edge there. Afterward, with a twist of her neck, she faced him, and there was a knife in her hands. It was his knife: the one he'd hurled at Yang.

"If the demons land, I am supposed to kill you," she whispered. Her breath was warm against his skin.

"Why would I want the demons to land?" he whispered back.

She eyed him with something akin to admiration. "You are not sup-posed to talk. Yang said if I let you talk, you would cast a spell on me."

"I won't do that."

"No more talking," she whispered. "Yang might hear, and that would not be good for either of us."

They stayed like that for some time, and finally, Cyrus heard a sharp and steady whine from overhead.

"Is that what you heard earlier?" he whispered, impressed with her hearing.

"I have the best ears of Berserker Clan," she whispered.

"Yes," he said, glancing at one. "Indeed you do."

She smiled. It was a quick twitch of the lips. She must have caught the double meaning. More than once, he had observed her graceful neck and the way her hair curled around her ears. With her so close . . . he wanted to kiss her neck and nibble on those ears.

"Stop that," she whispered. "Remember, one stroke of the knife and your blood will gush onto the sand."

"You would cut a man simply for admiring your beauty?"

"Stop," she whispered, with a hint of desperation in her voice.

The sky vehicle's whine increased. Cyrus felt her tense. What did the Kresh flying the sky vehicle see? Maybe it didn't notice a thing. The alien must have tracking equipment. Then again, no one moved, and maybe the cloaks helped the primitives blend into the surroundings. The Berserkers thought of the Kresh as demons. Over the years the primitives would have worked out a system that kept them hidden while traveling.

Slowly, the sky vehicle's whine began to fade. As it did, Jana relaxed. Long after the last sound stopped, she rose abruptly, yanking the cloak off them, letting their warmth escape.

"You may stand," she said. She turned, put her fingers in her mouth, and whistled. Cyrus was astonished. All over the plain, mounds and flat spots shifted. Berserker Clan warriors rose to their feet. Some dusted their cloaks. Others simply pinned them over their shoulders.

Cyrus had read about Apaches at the institute at Crete. He'd even seen a holo-vid drama about them. Then, their abilities had seemed preposterous. Now he realized the announcer hadn't done the ancient warriors justice.

Without a word, Yang took the lead again, and the trek continued.

As Cyrus put one foot in front of the other, he glanced back at the soldier. He was worried about Skar. They had spoken only once since the capture. That's all Yang had allowed. During that time, Cyrus had noticed lumps on Skar's head and an ugly bruise over his left eye. Skar had gotten those from the beating, from the clubs.

"Are you well?" Cyrus had whispered.

Skar had appeared not to hear the question.

Cyrus had snapped his fingers. Skar's hand had shot out and pressed down the finger-snapping hand. Cyrus opened his mouth to say something. A look in Skar's eyes stopped him. The soldier had a plan, obviously. Very well, that had been good enough for Cyrus.

Skar's eyes still had a glazed look. The Vomag's skin was splotchy. He breathed too hard some of the time. He must have a concussion, or maybe one of the clubs had hurt an organ. Skar was tough, but those clubs had smacked hard and repeatedly. Cyrus was sure that he himself would have been crippled by the beating.

Well, Cyrus's limbs worked fine, and so did his head. He'd been observing the primitives now for several days. It was time to think things through. Yang had Skar's hatchet and pistol. A different warrior carried the heat gun, while Jana had his knife. He'd overheard Jana telling Yang about the pistol. The hetman had hefted the pistol once and thoughtfully eyed Cyrus. He'd debated going to Yang and apologizing for killing the three Berserkers that first day. Then he'd decided he couldn't gain anything by that. They were going to do what they were going to do.

No. He had to think this through. First, Yang wasn't stupid and neither was Jana. They lived out here in the wild, in this thin-air wasteland. They had mastered the harsh surroundings. They didn't eat bloody spider-coyote meat, that's for sure. They fed Cyrus jerky most of the time, plus nuts and some tough fibrous roots. He'd watched them dig with a flat stone until water seeped out of the ground. They had a cloth for purifying the water and they had filled every leathery canteen.

Two things profoundly impressed Cyrus about the Berserkers. First, they hated the Kresh. They fought or avoided the aliens. The other humans in the Fenris System either worshiped the Kresh or did the aliens' bidding. Yeah, High Station 3 had Resisters. Here, *everyone* hated the Kresh and would gladly kill them. Despite their rough ways, the Berserkers were free. In fact, they were the freest people he'd met anywhere. The closest to them in freedom would have been the Latin Kings. Yet in truth, the drug gangs back on Earth had lived like parasites. The primitives on Jassac ran their own lives, and didn't prey on their own kind. That was worth something, even if they possessed freedom at the whim of the aliens.

What did that mean? Cyrus laughed silently as he jogged behind Jana. The barbarian princess had fantastic legs and the shapeliest butt he'd ever seen in person. He'd viewed his share of porn back in Milan, and the ladies had been hot, hot, hot. But Jana was real, not a fantasy on a screen.

Cyrus didn't intend to live the rest of his life out here. Before he made a break, though, he needed to understand the situation. It was why he'd been taking his time, observing and thinking.

What he realized now was that the Berserkers, maybe all the primitives out here, had an extremely precious thing. They had freedom.

Yes, they were free due to Kresh whim. It was critical to remember that. But they thought as free people. That was the most important thing about the Berserkers. The majority of the humans in the Fenris System—at least the ones he'd seen—thought like slaves. Cyrus wondered if he might be able to do more with free primitives than with sophisticated slaves.

"Why do you grin?" Jana asked.

"Huh?" Cyrus asked, looking up.

"You were staring at the mountains," she said. "Your eyes have been glazed as one who is thinking deeply. Then you smiled. It was a cruel smile. Are you thinking of revenge?"

"As a matter of fact, yeah, that's exactly what I'm thinking."

"You are a fool, outlander," she said. "Yang tolerates you. If he believes you are bent on nothing else than revenge—"

"Whoa, whoa," Cyrus said. "Back up."

Jana asked, "You want me to run beside you?"

"Huh?"

"You said back up."

"Oh," he said. "Yeah, back up with your thinking."

"You do not make any sense," she said. "Sometimes I wonder if you are too wise."

What did that mean? Too wise for what? "I make perfect sense," he said. "You asked me if I wanted revenge. I said yes. You assumed I wanted revenge against the Berserkers. But that isn't so. I want revenge against the Kresh."

"Are you boasting?" she asked.

"No," he said. "I'm hoping. That's a completely different thing."

She searched his eyes.

"What are you gazing at, Jana?" Yang shouted from ahead. "Sometimes I think you look at the outlander too much."

Jana turned away from Cyrus.

"Is the outlander plotting an escape?" Yang asked, striding near. Cyrus wasn't sure, but Yang sounded as if he kidded with her. "Is that why you look at him like that?"

"He wants to kill demons," she said, sharply.

Yang glanced at Cyrus. "Bah! He is a dreamer. Kill demons, indeed. Why not ride the wind or fly to the moon? I have seen his kind before. Do not pay any attention to his words. He is cousin to the fool."

Jana nodded, but it wasn't convincing.

The line of warriors ran in silence afterward, their feet rhythmically striking the ground. Later, they rested near an outcropping of stone. The youngest warrior disappeared into the rock formation, and he returned carrying canteens.

Cyrus had seen this before. The Berserkers seemed to know where every trickle of extra water lay. This pool was in a hidden tank of stone. He breathed deeply, sitting alone, resting his back against a rock, gnawing on a piece of jerky. Someone blocked the sunlight then. He looked up, and saw Yang glowering down at him.

With a grunt, Yang rested on one knee. He was even more intimidating up close. He had coarse facial skin and yellowed teeth. In the daylight, his shrewdness was more obvious.

"I have been watching you, outlander," Yang said in a rough but quiet voice. Maybe he thought this was whispering. "I know you are watching us, studying everyone, but most of all studying Jana."

Cyrus continued to gnaw the jerky, but he became tense. Years in the Latin Kings had made him sensitive to these kinds of conversations. The hetman was going to warn him about something. Since he'd spoken about Jana, Cyrus wondered if that was the sore point. Maybe Yang wanted the girl for himself. Maybe Yang was going to warn him Jana had a boyfriend who would carve the flesh out of him for even eyeing the shapely barbarian princess.

"I want to live," Cyrus said.

Yang shook his head. "No. You are not a slave."

Cyrus raised an eyebrow, wondering where Yang had gotten the idea to say such a thing. Maybe the clans kept slaves of captured enemies.

"Those are slave words," Yang said, as if reading his thoughts. "A warrior does not speak like that. You are a warrior. You risked everything on the single cast of a knife throw. That took courage." Yang showed his yellowed teeth in a grin like a wolf. "You dared to fight me because you sought to rule the Berserkers, even though you are an outlander, a man from space who knows nothing about us. When you say, 'I want to live,' you imply that you will bear any degradation to remain living. I do not believe that about you."

"Yeah?" Cyrus asked.

"There—you have a sharp tongue, not a slave tongue. You itch to insult me. You desire a rematch. It oozes out of you, outlander."

Cyrus's estimation of Yang's intelligence climbed yet another notch. How could he ever have believed the man was stupid, an oaf?

"So what happens next?" Cyrus asked.

"The seeker wishes to speak with you. Yet you should not believe that is a good thing. We of the Berserkers have a law. A clan can have only one seeker. More, and the warriors begin to lose respect in the eyes of the women and children."

"Uh, you're telling me that you plan to kill me?"

"Maybe, but maybe the seeker knows a way to burn the magic out of your mind so you may live as a warrior."

Cyrus went cold inside. These bastards wanted to take away his psi-power, as limited as it was?

Yang's eyes shone. "Yes . . . not so willing to live at any cost, are you? I see the fight rise up in you. You are a warrior born."

Cyrus held himself still. Now wasn't the time to strike. What could he do anyway to change his position? If he wanted freedom, he'd have to kill all the Berserkers or chase them off. Then he'd be back to living off the land, but without primitive know-how. Unless he stole Skar's gun, he couldn't kill them all, and Yang must know that. No, this was like his earliest days in Milan. He was on the bottom rung, facing dangers many times more powerful than he was. He needed to use cunning and daring at the right moment.

"Magic is a two-edged knife," Cyrus said.

"What does that mean?"

"It's a curse as much as a gift."

Yang chuckled in a nasty way. "If you feel that way, let us burn out the magic now."

"Sure," Cyrus said. "I'm sick of it anyway."

Yang's gaze bored into him. "No. You must realize that only a seeker could do such a thing. You have gambled again, just like in the dark with your knife cast. You are dangerous, star man. Maybe you are even more dangerous than the demonslayer."

"How about you take the ropes off his arms," Cyrus said. "Have you noticed he doesn't talk much lately?"

"He waits," Yang said. "I have also watched him closely. He playacts his hurts. No. He will remain bound until such a time as I trust him."

"And if that never happens?"

"Then I will kill him with the spell wand. I will explode his chest as you slew Stone Fist."

"They tried to kill us first," Cyrus said. "Doesn't a man have a right to defend himself?"

"You do not know it, but you act at times more like a seeker than a warrior. You use words like knives. I do not trust you, but I haven't yet made up my mind about you. Still, I feel honor-bound to tell you this. Though you are my enemy, we shall speak man-to-man now."

"Okay."

"Jana is a special woman. I have seen how you watch her. So it is time you know the truth about her."

Here it comes. This is why he's talking to me. He's going to warn me off.

"By special," Cyrus said, "you mean you're going to make her your mate?"

Yang chuckled. "No. I am not such a fool. I do not want a warrior for a mate. I want a regular woman who cooks and cleans, who obeys my commands. Jana is a hunter, a spear carrier. She speaks like a man and slings stones with uncanny skill, better than any man. None in Berserker Clan would take her for a mate. She is uncommon and special. No, Jana's only hope for a mate is if a warrior from another clan catches and subdues her. That would not be easy for the warrior, and he would always have to beware of her, lest she knife him in his sleep."

"She sure looks like a woman to me," Cyrus said.

"As I said, I have noticed the way you watch her. You think because she has smooth legs and a pretty face that you can tame her. I do not trust you, but I do not fully distrust you, nor do I hate you. Thus, I have come to warn you about Jana. She is a warrior, and she would as soon devour you as let you subdue her and take her as a mate."

"Yang, just when I think I know you, you go and surprise me. You are much more devious than you let on."

"It is as I said. Though you have the heart of a warrior, you have the shrewdness of a seeker."

"And you don't?" Cyrus said.

Yang's grin departed. "You do not know our ways, star man. So I will let this insult pass. Until the seeker decides what we should do with you, I will withhold my judgment."

The hetman grunted as he stood, and his right knee popped. Without another word, he walked away.

Cyrus's appetite had fled—they were thinking about burning out his psi-ability. He pocketed the jerky. These primitives with their harsh ways were going to mind cripple him. He couldn't believe it. He didn't know what to do on this wasteland of an alien planetoid.

17

Cyrus should have known the journey was almost over. Yang wouldn't have told him all those things so he could make plans to escape. From the evidence of the past few days, Cyrus could see that the hetman ruled justly. He must have told Cyrus what he did in order to play fair with him.

They reached the Berserker encampment with its skin tents and campfires. Cyrus spied children and women and a very few old people. They hid the camp among thin trees with triangular leaves.

Yang ordered Cyrus into one tent, and he didn't see what they did with Skar. Before Cyrus could decide what he should do, two warriors he'd never seen entered the tent, sat cross-legged, and watched him.

Cyrus tried to engage the two in conversation, but they refused to answer any questions. Finally, he lay down and slept, and he did so hard. Maybe he felt safer in a tent than sleeping under the stars. He slept until a rough hand shook him awake.

Cyrus looked up. Yang knelt beside him. A pan of cooked meat with green pepper roots sat nearby, together with a wooden cup of water.

"Eat, drink," Yang said. "The seeker will judge you afterward."

"And then you castrate my mind?" Cyrus asked bitterly.

"These are strange times," Yang said. "Who knows how the seeker will judge?"

Cyrus sat up, and he began to eat and drink. Then it penetrated, what Yang had just said.

"So what's going on, exactly?" Cyrus asked.

"Your words are odd," Yang said.

"Why are these strange times?" Cyrus asked.

"You two have come down from space. Stone Fist and the others perished at your hand. A demon died in its sky vehicle. The seeker listened as I told her these things. Then I told her you had asked about Klane. She became very agitated and demanded to see you at once."

"The seeker has heard of Klane?"

"I will be with you in the seeker's tent," Yang said. "Jana will join me. She has witnessed several marvels. The seeker is excited about you. She should have waited a week before you entered her tent. You haven't even undergone purification for slaying Stone Fist and the others." Yang shook his head. "Times are strange. Now eat up, hurry. The seeker wants to hear your tale."

Cyrus did exactly that, and he became excited himself. Soon enough, he wiped his hands and told Yang he was done. They went outside the tent. No one else was outside. Cyrus wasn't sure he liked that.

Yang escorted him to a larger tent where Jana waited by the flap entrance.

"Is there a ceremony to follow before we do this?" Cyrus asked.

"She is the seeker," Yang said. "She is not the speaker to the gods."

"Oh."

Jana stepped back as Yang approached. The hetman pulled back the tent flap and indicated Cyrus should enter first.

He did. He wasn't sure what he'd expected; maybe a hundred skulls or burning incense. There were furs, a sleeping mat, a small hanging stone, a flickering oil flame, and a stand with several glistening stones on it. A young woman with long, dark hair and a curious symbol painted on her forehead sat cross-legged on a mat. She had frank and pleasing features.

The seeker smiled in a friendly manner.

Cyrus glanced back at Yang.

"This is the Berserker Clan seeker," Yang said.

For a moment, Cyrus wondered if Yang had tricked him. Was this all an elaborate charade?

No. I am the Berserker seeker, the woman told Cyrus through telepathy.

Cyrus's eyes widened. *You're so young. I expected someone old.*

The seeker nodded, and she indicated a mat near hers. "We will speak aloud," she told Cyrus.

"Sure," Cyrus said.

Jana and Yang sat behind Cyrus.

"You have eaten?" the seeker asked.

"I have," Cyrus said.

"And you are well rested?"

"Yes."

"Then it is time for you to tell me your tale," the seeker said.

"And afterward you burn out my psi-power?" Cyrus asked.

The seeker frowned, and she fidgeted with an oily stone. "The clan laws are firm," she said, finally. "There can be only one seeker and no other magic user in the clan. If you were young enough, you might have become my apprentice. But that will not work now. Let us consider that later. For now, I must hear your tale."

"Okay," Cyrus said. "I'm glad to tell it. First, do you know anything about Klane?"

The seeker's right hand tightened around the oily stone and her features grew taut. "We must take one careful step at a time. It appears as if the days of prophecy are upon us, but one must not rush to judgment. The ancient ways tell us to consider wisely. That is what I plan to do. Cyrus Gant of Earth, I want to hear your tale. Do not leave out anything. Do not fear that I cannot understand you. I understand much more than you realize. I want you to begin by telling us how you came to Fenris."

"How I came to the Fenris System, not just Jassac?" Cyrus asked.

"That is correct," the seeker said.

Cyrus glanced back at Jana. She gave him a tremulous smile of encouragement. Warrior princess or not, Cyrus believed he could get used to looking at her every day of his life.

"Okay," Cyrus said, facing the seeker. "This is how it began . . ." He told her about underground Milan with its forty levels, about the institute and Specials. He talked about the inhibitor put in his mind and how Jasper had spoken to a clairvoyant about New Eden—the Fenris System. Cyrus told the young seeker about discontinuity windows, how it took AI technology and Specials melded together. The seeker nodded from time to time as if she understood the concepts. When Cyrus twisted around, Yang looked sleepy and Jana was absorbed with his words, staring at him with shining eyes. He faced the seeker again.

"Please," the seeker said, "continue with your tale. I find this fascinating."

Cyrus did exactly that. He explained how a psi-master—one of the Kresh's slaves—tricked Jasper during the space journey. He told the seeker about the mutiny aboard *Discovery*, and how he had saved the Teleship during the first battle. He talked about the ship's boarding. He spoke about the flight to High Station 3, and how he'd made his escape during the docking ceremony. Lastly, he talked about the Reacher, the Anointed One, and Skar's and his escape to the needle-ship and the battle three weeks later in Jassac orbit.

It was a long story, and Cyrus drained a stone cup of water at its ending. He discovered that Yang and Jana had departed. The seeker frowned and stared at the ground, with lines in her forehead.

Cyrus felt purged. He was lost on an alien world, but at last he'd found someone similar to himself, or more so than the Reacher and Vomag soldiers. The seeker felt like a fellow Special, someone who would have gone to classes with him in the institute on Crete.

The seeker sighed loudly.

Cyrus looked up to find the young woman studying him.

"I do not want to burn out your psi-power," the seeker said. "That would be foolish. We'll have to think of a way around that."

"I already have one."

"Yes?"

"Release Skar and give us back our weaponry. We're visitors, not Berserker Clan members."

"There is a certain elegance to that," the seeker said. "Unfortunately, Yang and the other warriors might not agree. There is the matter of you slaying three of our warriors."

"They attacked us first."

The seeker shook her head. "That has no bearing on blood vengeance. The relatives of the slain warriors will want to kill you. In fact, they await our verdict."

"So . . . if I become a member of the clan . . . ?" Cyrus asked.

"You would have to pay blood guilt for the three slain warriors," the seeker said. "Jana would have to return your metal knife, but then you would have to give it up in payment. The same thing would be true for your heat gun. I'm not sure how you would appease the third family."

"And if I'm part of the clan and can pay blood guilt with valuable items, I would also have to burn out my psi-power, right?"

"Or I have to allow mine to be expunged," the seeker said.

"What?"

"You would have to become the clan's seeker in my stead."

Cyrus stared at her. The woman was serious. It amazed him. He cleared his throat, saying, "I don't plan on living on Jassac for the rest of my life."

"You would desert your post as seeker?"

"Look—" Cyrus chopped his hand through the air. "Do you have a first name? I don't want to call you 'seeker' all the time."

"Seekers forgo a name when they accept the position."

"Okay. Look, seeker, do you know anything about Klane?"

"Yes."

"Then why are we talking about burning out psi-powers? Where is he?"

"He has gone to the Valley of the Demons."

"Come again?" Cyrus said.

"He is in the valley."

"The valley that has the terraforming convertor on the nearby mountain?" asked Cyrus.

"Yes."

"The Kresh live down there in the valley, right?"

"Klane went to free his seeker in the Kresh city."

"How about you start from the beginning," Cyrus said. "Tell me what's going on."

"I do not know the entire tale, but I know the Kresh captured the Tash-Toi seeker in the uplands. Klane killed a demon earlier—one of the Kresh. In retaliation—or for whatever reason they have—the Kresh came back from their valley, likely to capture Klane. The seeker sacrificed himself in Klane's place."

"Wait, wait," Cyrus said, as he massaged his forehead. "So . . . you seekers keep linked together?"

The Berserker seeker pursed her lips thoughtfully. "These are abnormal times. I do not pretend to understand everything that you told me. But I do understand the majority of it."

"Yeah, that's been troubling me. How do you know so much about technological things? The others don't," he said.

The seeker stiffened. "Do not attempt to discern all our secrets, Earth man."

"I'm not asking as an Earth man," Cyrus said. "I'm asking as the Tracker. Or don't you know about that part of the prophecy?"

"I know it."

"Good. That saves time. The Reacher on High Station 3 named me as the Tracker. He said I'm supposed to find Klane."

"No. You're supposed to *free* Klane. The prophecy tells of his capture and his time under Kresh evil. He will learn a secret, something incredibly important to humanity's freedom. Afterward, he will need your help escaping from the demons, the Kresh, I mean."

Cyrus laughed. "I'm supposed to free him from the aliens?"

"You're supposed to free him from captivity," the seeker said. "That is a subtle difference. Your question implies that you're supposed to free him from all the Kresh. But in reality, you're just supposed to free him from their clutches down in the city."

"That's a pretty elaborate prophecy," Cyrus said.

"I have interpreted some of the signs differently than others have," the seeker admitted. "It is also true that I hold to the First Form interpretation. Second Form people would undoubtedly tell you something else. There are, of course, subtle variations between each form—"

"Forget about that," Cyrus said. "I'm not interested in theological niceties concerning this prophecy. Klane is in the valley, right?"

"The last I know, yes. It has become too dangerous now to far-cast for him. The Bo Taw would perceive me, and that could possibly ruin everything."

"Do the Kresh know about the prophecy?"

"It is possible. Luckily for us the aliens are incredibly arrogant. It has been one of our greatest shields. They may know of it and discount it as human superstition."

"Listen, seeker, I have to know as much as possible about everything. I don't see how Skar and I could sneak down into the valley city. Some of the Berserker warriors would have to help us."

"None here except for me would dare to attempt such a dangerous feat. The evil legends of the valley—"

"The others would be too frightened to go?" Cyrus asked.

"People like Yang and Jana are very brave, but they are also fiercely superstitious."

"So we're back to square one."

The seeker drummed her fingers on the hard-packed dirt. She had bitten her nails to the quick. "This is a terrible time. The prophecy is upon us, and we cannot change clan custom. One of us must lose our psi-powers. Equally troubling, I cannot break my solemn word without damning myself."

"Now what? Is there something else you're not telling me?"

The seeker slammed a fist on the ground. "I must tell you. As you've said, you are the Tracker. You will have to risk everything to save the Anointed One. From what you've told me, there is more at risk here than the Berserkers, the Tash-Toi, and the other peoples of the uplands. All of humanity's enslavement and genetic manipulation possibly rests on my choices—not just the Fenris humans, but the homeworld humans of Earth's solar system as well. I agree with your idea that the Kresh will copy DW technology and send a fleet to enslave the humans of the solar system. The Kresh are an aggressive species. Their millennia-long war against the Chirr proves it. By your words, you have implied that Earth has only a handful of psi-able people."

"You're not primitive at all," Cyrus said. "How is that possible?"

"We'll get to that. First, I need to know how many psionics Earth possesses."

"At last count, including Jasper, Venice, and me, fewer than one hundred and fifty."

The seeker shook her head. "The Kresh could send a vast fleet against the solar system."

"That's what I've been thinking," Cyrus said. "But one thing about all this troubles me. How can the Anointed One defeat the Kresh?"

"Alas, the prophecy does not say."

"What good is the prophecy if it doesn't tell me anything useful?" Cyrus asked.

"The prophecy gives us hope," the seeker said. "I refuse to believe it is useless."

Cyrus almost told her that it didn't matter what anyone believed, but what was real. What was the point of saying that, though? He needed the seeker as his ally, not as his enemy. Getting smart-mouthed with her wasn't going to help any.

"I must damn myself for the betterment of humanity," the seeker said quietly. "I must tell you everything I can."

"Tell me what?"

The seeker licked her lips, and she wouldn't meet Cyrus's eyes. In a deathly quiet voice, she said, "I can tell you about the transfer, the method we've devised to keep our knowledge alive throughout the long years of our subjection."

18

Mentalist Niens picked up a cloth and blotted his forehead. He couldn't believe his luck, and his swift elevation in rank.

That had gone against protocol on two counts: he had witnessed a Kresh's murder by a man, and he had not attempted to protect or help Chengal Ras. Normally, on general principle, the Kresh would destroy such a person. Bo Taw had interrogated Niens through psionic probing. He disliked and feared that, but it didn't matter. It never did with the Kresh. He'd wondered why Zama Dee bothered, and had expected death.

Instead, he lived, and he gained rank. That sent his curiosity spinning like a rodent on a wheel. Ever since youth, he had an insatiable desire to know why. In his secret thoughts, he believed it made him like a Kresh. Perhaps the intense self-training to keep that assumption hidden from the thought police—the Bo Taw—had set him on his present path. He realized his curiosity inevitably led him into modes of illegal thought. That in turn had long ago put him on the road of enjoying life while he could. He had these few precious moments of life and planned to wring from them every ounce of pleasure that he could. He'd better enjoy them before he was worm food. Then his damned curiosity would lift its simian head and he'd tinker with a thing, probing, wondering, and bringing himself nearer the edge of destruction.

Several incidents in quick succession now threatened his existence, because he couldn't erase them from his thoughts. He didn't know how the Bo Taw hadn't detected them.

First, Klane had killed Chengal Ras, the giver of pain. After the agonizer, Niens hated the 109th. He also dreaded the Kresh. The human had slaughtered Chengal Ras, and Niens secretly approved. He tried not to, but he couldn't help it. Klane had killed a Kresh and he had shown Niens mercy.

Why had Klane done that? Why had the man let him live? It was inconceivable. The more Niens thought about it, the more he wanted to know the answer, *had* to know the answer.

Niens knew he should be dead. Yet he lived and he had gained rewards. Zama Dee wanted something from the amazing Kresh killer. Was that why he lived? Did Zama Dee believe he had a novel perspective on Klane? Niens didn't know the reason, but he would find out.

One thing was clear: the new rank had brought about commensurate rewards, and it had brought greater responsibility.

"Test the calibration, Niens," the head mentalist said in a harsh voice.

Niens swallowed uneasily. He had a task to perform and he'd better concentrate on the here and now. He adjusted the setting a tap at a time. It was delicate work. They planned to go deep into Klane's ego and begin to adjust his view of reality.

On Niens's screen, a red dot blossomed into a larger green circle. The dot shifted, heading up toward the circle's northeast quadrant. Carefully, he brought the red dot back to the center and enlarged it, attempting to fill the green with the red.

On the table, Klane began to twitch.

"You're going too quickly," the head mentalist said.

Niens paused, with one of his fingers hovering over the tap pad.

Five mentalists ranged around various pieces of equipment. In their center lay Klane, strapped down on the table. Assorted leads and pads had been attached to his naked flesh. More ominous, a cutter had opened the top of Klane's skull. The sliced-off bone lay in a blue solution to the side. Precise glass splinters stuck into the gray matter of his exposed brain. They worked directly, with tiny dots of light on top of the splinters indicating the connections with the machines.

The chamber was larger than the one they had used for the seeker. A glass dome protected the air from germs. Looking down through the glass were two masters, two Revered Ones, one of whom was Zama Dee the 73rd.

"Slowly," the head mentalist said.

Niens swallowed audibly, and tapped his pad. He enjoyed his new privileges, having used a pay girl last night for several hours. Because of his new rank, he had finally rid himself of his harridan of a wife. She'd packed her few belongings and left for one of the stations in orbit around Pulsar. *Good riddance to her,* Niens thought to himself. With his rank, he would be able to afford pay girls every night of the week. The things the girl had been able to do to him sexually . . . simply marvelous.

Niens almost grinned at the memory. The head mentalist might see that, however, and it would show poor form here under the Revered Ones.

"Hold, Niens," the head mentalist said. "Proctor, make your adjustments."

Niens exhaled. A lean vulture of a mentalist now worked a station, with the head mentalist and Zama Dee watching.

I need to see the pay girl again. I need some release. Maybe I can be allowed two at once. That would be something special.

"Niens!" the head mentalist shouted. "Do you hear me?"

"I hear and obey," Niens said, feeling panic, but gratified at his calm voice.

"Then make the adjustment," the head mentalist said.

Niens tapped the pad, with his gaze on the screen.

"There," the head mentalist said.

Niens locked the sequence.

"Proctor," the head mentalist said. "Begin the tertiary maneuver."

Niens watched the other, absorbed with the mechanics of the operation. No one had ever attempted this directly before, although theoretically, it should work. The Revered Ones wanted full control of Klane. Why did they want that instead of simply destroying him?

Niens dared to glance upward. Both Revered Ones gazed down into the chamber. The masters watched with Kresh avidness.

I love all of you, Niens told himself, before his true feelings flared into thought. *I want every Kresh on Jassac to bathe in acid and bubble into extinction.*

A beep sounded—a loud, alarming sound.

No! A Bo Taw has discovered me. I love the Kresh. I love the Kresh.

Then Niens realized the alarm didn't have to do with his thoughts. On the central table, Klane's body thrashed and it began to convulse.

"Proctor!" the head mentalist shouted. "Dampen the rods. Hurry, before we lose him."

Niens focused on his equipment. If Klane died, or if his mind blew, they would all face horrible punishment. The masters watched. The mentalist team could not afford any mistakes today.

"Proctor!" the head mentalist shouted.

A glass splinter slid out of Klane's exposed brain matter. The tops of the rest of the splinters blinked with bright lights.

"Dampen, dampen!" the head mentalist screamed, his face red with panic.

Niens wasn't sure what possessed him. In a flash of certainty, he saw what to do. With a sure stride he left his station, used his shoulder to shove Proctor aside, and began manipulating furiously.

The others watched him in frozen wonder. The masters gazed downward.

In seconds, the thrashing ceased. Klane lay supine on the table as he breathed evenly.

One of the other mentalists seemed to awaken as if from a drugged sleep. He stared at his screen. Then the man looked up. "I've lost his brain rhythm," the man said in a high-pitched voice.

"What?" the head mentalist said.

"I cannot find his consciousness," the other mentalist said. "I think the subject's consciousness may have escaped us."

Every mentalist in the chamber stared at Niens.

Zama Dee pressed a switch, and an intercom crackled to life. "Arrest Mentalist Niens and take him into an isolation chamber. Then replace the subject's skull and put him under full sedation."

Niens wanted to shriek. He had just saved the situation. Couldn't the others see that he had saved the subject? Apparently they could not, for doors slid open and three Vomags entered the room, heading straight for him.

He knew this day would come. *At least I enjoyed the pay girl last night. That was nice.*

As a Vomag grabbed an arm, Niens swallowed in a dry throat. He wanted to live, and he dreaded Kresh torture. The day of reckoning had finally come.

19

The transfer with the seeker changed Klane. He now experienced thoughts and ideas of bewildering complexity. It had taken him time to come to grips with the idea that the demons were Kresh aliens. The true history of humanity and the place the Tash-Toi held in it had been humiliating to accept.

He had sorted and cataloged millions of bits of new and incredibly old data. Then stern-faced men had wheeled him into a mentalist operating chamber. They had cut away some of his skull. With the transfer, with the hidden knowledge of the singing gods, he had new levels of awareness. He had used his psi-powers to see, even though he had been drugged into seeming unconsciousness. It still didn't make sense to him how he did it.

The transfer memories or the singing god . . . alien—ah. That made sense. They were not singing gods. They were aliens, or an alien machine. He wasn't sure about that yet. In any case, with his new awareness, a part of Klane recognized the danger the mentalist and their glass slivers represented. The Kresh were trying to reprogram his brain.

It would take weeks for them to accomplish it. He understood the complexity of the operation. He also knew it would take one of the arrogant Kresh—a higher-ranked individual—to believe such a procedure would work. More likely it would sear his mind and leave him a blithering imbecile.

Klane had decided on harsh countertactics. During the first phase of the operation he had brought about his near death, used one of the mentalists for several seconds, and had forced that one to give his consciousness a rocket boost to a safer clime.

It was like a Far-Calling Spell, but even more so and with more than just his thoughts leaving. His consciousness had fled his body. The most tenuous of threads would allow him to return someday. For now, he sped from Jassac, fled past several planets at the speed of thought, and slid away from occupied spacecraft traveling through the void.

He had a vague understanding of the psi-mechanics of this, but didn't worry about it unduly. As his consciousness flew past the planets, heading inward toward the Fenris sun, he sensed various intellects. Some had high psionic strength that produced a screeching sensation in him. Those congregated on the third planet from the sun.

The smoldering, radioactive surface had once been pristine, full of life. Underneath the seething soil, the Chirr waited. He sensed alien intelligences many degrees removed from Kresh intellect and much different from human minds. One of those intelligences reached out for him.

Klane fled from it, as the alien psionic intelligence dwarfed his own. *What are you?* it asked. *Tell me. I have never sensed one like you before.*

The thought pulsed into Klane's consciousness. But he slid away from it, and he moved faster toward the second Fenris planet.

A ring of Kresh-fashioned satellites orbited the second planet. Sitting in each armored station, heavy lasers aimed planetward. Klane also sensed Bo Taw psi-adepts and machines of deep complexity. He sensed the human adepts and their amplifiers as his consciousness whipped past a satellite. The Bo Taw manned the core of the station, and they kept Chirr psionic probes from reaching past them into space or coming from the third planet and going down. In fact, the questing alien mind that had questioned Klane failed to penetrate the Kresh-instituted psi-shield.

In those seconds, Klane realized the Kresh blocked the two Chirr-held planets from communicating with each other. He realized it, and he blazed downward toward an intensely bright point of thought.

Klane's free-form consciousness didn't view reality from a visual perspective, nor was it limited by the speed of light, meaning it didn't rely on luminar mechanics in any way.

Thus, the sun didn't seem to be the brightest object. Those possessing psionic abilities radiated the greatest glare—except for the one mind down there on Fenris II. That mind was ordinary enough—it lacked any extrasensory ability at all. Nevertheless, the mind beckoned Klane's consciousness for one critical reason: the mind was similar in structure and thought pattern to Klane's own.

In a brief span of time, Klane's consciousness leapt from Jassac to Fenris II. It invaded a Vomag soldier's mind, one named Timor Malik of Cohort Invincible. The mind had drawn him like a magnet. There must be something here he was supposed to see. Was this clairvoyant knowledge? He wasn't sure.

The soldier resisted. It was an automatic response. As Klane attempted to merge with the man, he lost the interplanetary-spanning ability. Klane's consciousness became anchored in . . . in . . . Timor Malik.

In those first wild seconds, bewildering memories and ideas smashed against Klane's consciousness. He saw Timor Malik's life in a blast of data. Without the experience of the previous transfer, Klane's consciousness might have wilted under the torrent of information.

Timor's resistance threatened to overwhelm Klane's unattached consciousness. Klane became aware of a real threat of merging with the man without maintaining his own identity.

I must make my own foothold and take over completely later—first things first.

Klane recalibrated masses of new information. He'd done so once already. His consciousness cataloged and sorted at blinding speed. He watched the soldier's thoughts while remaining outside the man. Klane consumed things in broad swipes: birth, childhood, soldier training, cadet school, and tunnel tactics. He observed Malik's first spark of rebellion—it had happened in the tunnel collapse of 44-C-33, resulting in twelve days of black entrapment. Later, freed due to a lucky break, Malik had begun to secretly oppose the Kresh. Soon, a religious officer—a member of the formal, alien-instituted religion promoting Kresh love—had discovered Malik's baleful thoughts. Klane followed Malik's subsequent reeducation and his entry into a suicide squad.

Malik's memories were fresh and bitter in the extreme. He was the squad leader of twenty selected suicide soldiers. The Kresh wanted a Chirr Nest Intelligence, but not just any one. They wanted a big jungle intelligence, one of the old ones protected by planetary-level defenses.

Klane's consciousness took a metaphorical breath. The concepts would have bewildered his senses without the transfer memories from the seeker. He had integrated those memories barely long enough to both accept and understand what he learned from Malik's mind.

Timor Malik's cohort was part of the jungle raid, an *equatorial* jungle raid.

The extent of what they meant flooded into Klane as he examined the bigger picture. The Kresh had fought a fifty-six-year campaign in the northern polar region. It had taken one hundred and seventy-five million soldier deaths to secure it. Presently, a southern polar conquest of similar scope took place. Timor Malik had fought and rebelled there. The equatorial raid was tiny in comparison, a mere five hundred thousand Vomags.

First, space lasers had scoured the dense, targeted jungle growth. Afterward, bombers had raced down into the atmosphere and sprayed a one-hundred-kilometer circumference with herbicides. Another wave dropped inferno-bombs, and fires raged for days, devouring the dense jungle and slaughtering every living thing on the surface.

Later, Vomag soldiers in powered armor landed and set up kill zones. Chirr warriors boiled out of the ground and attacked, and gore ran green and black for weeks. Space lasers, bombers, tanks, and powered armor: the Kresh threw everything against the Chirr, whose numbers seemed never to end.

Eventually, the insects stopped attacking. The soldiers on the ground had no idea if it meant a lack of Chirr numbers or a new strategy on their part.

This was a raid against an equatorial nest. Phase two was the underground assault, where the real fun began. The Kresh knew—and so did the genetic soldiers—that there weren't enough humans in the Fenris System to battle their way down to a deep nest using regular warfare. Thus, this was a snatch and grab, a commando operation on a vast scale: five hundred thousand soldiers. Instead of securing a level before advancing to the next one, the Vomags battled down like a drill, narrow and straight. If they couldn't reach the Nest Intelligence in nine days, they weren't going to do it at all. If they failed, it meant everyone would die down here in the Chirr tunnels.

If Timor Malik's body died, would Klane's consciousness die with it? That seemed most likely. It was a problem, a grave one. Realizing that, Klane tried to depart the body and failed. He concentrated, willing himself away. That didn't work, either. After an hour of attempts, Klane realized he didn't have enough psionic strength of mind to leave. That sobered him, and focused his thoughts. He was stuck here, or his consciousness was, until he could figure out something different. That meant he had to help keep the soldier alive.

Klane started paying greater attention to details, and he tried to take over control of Malik's eyes, ears, nose, and bodily functions. Eventually, Klane hoped to take over the man's entire identity.

Klane realized that he'd joined Timor Malik on day three of the nest invasion. Malik and his squad had traveled from the southern pole region. Several hundred supply barges arrived each day, bringing ammo and material and taking away the lightly wounded.

On day three, Malik and his suicide squad, the entirety of Cohort Invincible, traveled through surface tunnels to the lower levels. They marched deeper still and soon arrived at their battle zone. They were here to breach a tunnel strongpoint that was halfway to the Nest Intelligence. It was a nexus node, and Chirr warriors would heavily defend it.

Klane struck at Malik's identity fast and hard. He smothered the other's mind, and in the tunnels, squat Timor Malik, a soldier known for his stubbornness, seemed to faint. In those seconds, two wills fought for control of the body.

What are you?

Trust me, Klane said.

No, no, you're a Chirr.

Malik tried to roar a warning to his comrades. Klane couldn't afford that. He clamped down on the speech center.

In the tunnels, as worried soldiers gathered around Malik's body, the internal war continued.

I'm human, and I've come . . .

Klane wasn't sure why he'd come. He'd needed to escape the Kresh, the mentalists on Jassac. He had roved outward with his consciousness, and for some reason Timor Malik's mind had drawn him like a magnet.

There's something here I need to see. Was that clairvoyant knowledge? Maybe this was a way to free humanity from the Kresh. They needed Chirr allies and he'd come to bargain with them.

I hate the Chirr. I want to kill the Chirr, Malik thought.

The Kresh have conditioned you to hate the Chirr, Klane told Malik.

I don't care why. I hate them. I hate them.

The struggle of wills turned savage. Klane's consciousness weakened. If he went under, then everything he'd done so far would mean nothing. His life, the spark of him, would flicker out and that would be the end of the story for Klane the demonslayer. *I must use my wits. I must think like a seeker.* What did that mean? How could he—

It came to Klane. He needed to use Malik's memories. He needed to convince the soldier, not just batter at his extremely stubborn will.

He saw how Timor Malik had waited twelve days on the other side of a tunnel collapse. The trapped soldiers had fought off Chirr wave attacks, waiting for the Kresh to drill through to them. Twelve days in the dark had strengthened Malik's rebellious thoughts into hatred for the Revered Ones.

I can show you how to defeat the Kresh, Klane told Malik. And he showed the soldier what had happened in the demon city on Jassac.

You lie! This is simply another Chirr trick. Get out of my mind!

They fought for control, and both grew weary. Malik proposed a bargain: they would have joint control of the body and mind.

Klane accepted even as he took over the citadel of the mind.

The soldier, however, had fought all his life. He was a master of tactics and fighting retreats. He grabbed eyes, ears, and bodily functions.

And Timor Malik sat up in the tunnel. He snarled at his friends and underlings hovering over him. He told them nothing was wrong with him.

Weary from the flight from Jassac and the battle of wills here, Klane waited and watched in the citadel of the ego. He sat like a man besieged in a castle, in control of his patch of ground behind the stone walls, but unable to go outside. He saw what Malik saw and heard the same sights, but for the moment, he could not control the soldier's body.

The veteran Vomags now gathered on a ridge, with dark tunnel openings before them. The damp dirt ceiling was high here, as far as Malik could hurl a grenade. Like the others, Timor Malik wore a helmet with a shining lamp, a breathing mask, and body armor. For the tight confines of the tunnels, the soldiers carried steel hatchets and pistols with exploding pellets. They were the suicide teams, there to create breaches in difficult spots.

The order came down from cohort HQ. The battle chief ordered them to attack.

With Timor Malik leading, and with Klane's consciousness watching and learning, the suicide squad slipped and slid down from the ridge. Their booted feet dislodged quarry rock and kicked up dust. Muffled alarms clanged from the Chirr strongpoint, but no warriors appeared. As they charged, the Vomags chanted an attack paean. Fighting in the tunnels took fantastic courage and resolve. Klane noticed how fierce elation seized Malik.

It was more than simply conditioning. The soldier liked to fight.

As Malik/Klane neared the strongpoint—pink, crystal-like walls in a fused, jigsaw-puzzle pattern—an odor like sour milk drifted up from the soil. It was a mist, a chemical attack.

One soldier must not have secured his breathing mask well enough. He exploded into a coughing fit and stumbled onto the ground, quivering. Malik twisted his head so the helmet-light washed over the soldier. The Vomag was still, already dead.

The rest of the squad trampled across something like moss. Malik's boots sank into the substance. In places, the mossy soil opened up and soldiers plunged out of sight. Wet sounds and painful grunts told of traps. From experience, Malik knew the Vomags had fallen onto poisoned spikes. A single scratch killed. A few soldiers veered into brittle vetch. Maybe they thought to avoid the moss traps. Loud snaps and accompanying groans told of whip spikes that impaled the men through body armor and into chests or stomachs.

Malik roared orders at the others, "Break into the strongpoint!"

The soldiers took out their steel hatchets. The first to reach the crystal wall hacked at it, causing glassy chips to fly. Malik knew and Klane learned that the crystal was really dirt fused with Chirr spit. Even so, it was hardly softer than asphalt.

The defense became active as portals opened above and toxic liquid sprayed out in hosing arcs. Malik leaped out of the way. Others weren't as fast. They screamed as flesh boiled away. Some had dislodged their masks and coughed black gouts of liquefied flesh and blood. Sickened, Klane had his first true taste of what it was like battling in the tunnels of the Chirr.

More soldiers rushed to the attack. Only a few of the vanguard survived. Malik was among them. With their hatchets, the soldiers hacked out handholds and scaled the crystal wall. Another portal opened. Malik was near enough and scrambled for a grip. He drew himself within and surprised a Chirr worker. With a roar behind his breathing mask, Malik lay about him, slaying the creature with three crunches of his axe. The head fell from the body, with black ichor squirting from it. The worker was a small thing like a dog, with mandibles for a mouth and brittle tentacles instead of arms and legs.

More soldiers squirmed through the portal and into the chamber.

"Slay them all!" Malik shouted.

With helmet lamps, pistols, and hatchets, the soldiers ran amok throughout this portion of the strongpoint. Battle madness took hold. They kicked down partitions, slaughtered workers, and broke the sprayer pumps.

Then Chirr warriors arrived. They towered over the squat Vomags. The beams of the helmet lamps washed over red things with black eyes like charcoal. They stabbed with lethal braches and spit acid with uncanny accuracy. In the confines of the narrow chamber, the Chirr warriors boiled at them, slashing hatchets, firing exploding pellets, and laughing madly.

"Blow them up!" Malik bellowed. "Avenge our fellow soldiers!"

In fury, the Vomags demolished the first Chirr wave. Then they broke into the many chambers and massacred imps and bantlings. They cut down fecund genetrices with swollen bellies. The Chirr queens were sluggish, monstrous things, surrounded by molds and fungus, likely their food.

Despite the depth underground, fires raged here, making the air smoggy. Anyone without a breather soon sank to the ground, exhausted.

It was a nightmarish battle fought with desperate courage and admirable skill. Klane had Malik's memories and understanding, but even so, everything around him seemed grossly alien. The sickening reeks, the high-pitched squeals, and the black gore that poured out of the creatures nauseated Klane's consciousness.

Finally, the vanguard broke into a grand chamber. Malik panted; his limbs ached and the notched hatchet looked more like a saw blade. More soldiers poured in behind him. A barker joined the throng.

"Charge!" the barker roared.

They did, but halfway across the grand chamber a strange lassitude slowed Malik's step. He found it nearly impossible to keep his axe up. He wanted to look back, but was too tired now. He fought to keep his eyes open.

"What's wrong with me?" muttered a soldier beside him.

Klane knew with a sudden, grim understanding. The soldiers weren't suicide fighters because of the bleak tactical situation, but because they fought beyond the protective psi-shield of army Bo Taw. With his heightened senses, he felt the Chirr psionic presence. By then it was too late and he couldn't keep the body awake.

As Timor Malik attempted to answer the soldier's question, he—and Klane's consciousness—went blank.

|||||||||

Malik/Klane awoke with hundreds of other soldiers. They stood in a different chamber. Malik still gripped his notched axe and he wore Chirr-bloodied armor. He couldn't turn his head, but he heard the breathing and rustle of many cohorts of soldiers. With some of the same lassitude as before, he halfheartedly examined his surroundings.

A shimmering pool of some inky substance lay ahead. A few feet above his head was the ceiling, an odd wattle-and-daub construction. Then he noticed the new Chirr. In ways they resembled the red-skinned warriors. They were thin like praying mantises, holding their sticklike arms in a similar manner. They had long insectile heads with small mandibles and horrid eyes like gigantic flies. Their mandibles moved, but not vertically like a man's; theirs worked side to side. They chanted, but Malik couldn't understand the words.

More than anything, he wanted to attack them. He realized with a numb horror that their chants had immobilized him and the others. The Chirr held everyone captive with words. Malik's eyes widened with true revulsion.

At that moment Klane rushed from the citadel of Malik's mind to the forefront. He took over eyes, ears, and bodily control, and he discovered that with the takeover came the ability to use Malik's mind in a limited psionic manner. His consciousness must have altered Malik's mind patterns just enough.

Klane grew aware that something vast shuffled behind the psionic Chirrs.

Before Klane could investigate that, a new type of Chirr warrior approached. It was tall, red, and massive. Between its pincers it held a metal rod with an electronic device on the end. It raised the rod and spoke in the language of the Kresh. It was an interpreter.

"Men of the Kresh, you have invaded our home-hive. You have killed Chirrs. Now, to your dismay, you have witnessed our newest modification, the magus-Chirr. In olden times, your flesh and blood would have fertilized the hatcheries. Now we have devised a greater use for your flesh. You shall feed the Great One and he shall empower our magus-Chirr. It is a terrible doom, for it will strip your minds in the most agonizing manner possible. I bid you to know terror, men of the Kresh. And know that the greater your terror, the more it delights the Great One. If his delight is great enough, he will teach the Nest Intelligence more and marvelous magic techniques. So, men of the Kresh, the magus-Chirr will force you into the pool in order to extract your combined essences. Think upon your doom. Think upon your helplessness, and let your terrors mature for the benefit of the hive."

The interpreter scuttled back toward the vast and shadowy shape behind the chanting magus-Chirr. The interpreter chittered in the language of the Chirr to the Great One.

Klane struggled against the psi-induced lassitude. The clatter of body armor told him the others likewise sought greater movement. The mandible chants of the magus-Chirr grew louder and more earnest.

Klane exerted his considerable power, and the lassitude fell away. At that moment, Malik strove to regain control of his own body, but Klane held him down.

After the swift victory, Klane finally felt what it meant to be deep underground the surface. The stench was like rancid water and the psychic weight of the depth pressing against him was crushing to his ego. He found it hard to breathe. He might have shouted with fear, but he didn't want to give away his ability to control his body.

All around him, the soldiers began to move in a mechanical, puppetlike fashion. Klane glanced at the nearest Vomag. Fear, loathing, and terror twisted the soldier's features. Maybe because he hated being so deep underground, Klane felt compassion for the man. He needed a friend in this place of horror, because it was easier to deal with horror with a friend beside him. Klane grabbed the soldier's arm, breaking the Chirr psionic paralysis.

With the touch came knowledge about the Vomag. His name was Turk, and this was his first battle. Ah . . . Turk was Timor's friend, a third cousin, it seemed.

The rest of the soldiers shuffled toward the shimmering pool. It changed colors, from black to green, to red, and then to an inky color of doom. Within the blackness Klane spied a grotesque creature of vast bulk with many tentacles moving at once.

With a start, Klane realized several things. The creature wasn't in the liquid. It projected its image onto the liquid. Soon, it would *use* the liquid to drown the Vomags and extract what it considered their essence from them. The creature was a Nest Intelligence, the highest level of Chirr, and a powerful psionic being. It was the Great One.

Magus-Chirr chittered, and the mass of Vomags halted, some already in the pool up to their hips.

The interpreter scuttled forward with its rod and electronic device held up. It neared Klane and the trembling Turk.

"What are you?" the interpreter asked.

"I am a soldier," Klane said with Malik's mouth and tongue.

The interpreter turned back to the tallest magus-Chirr. A fast sequence of chitters and clacks passed between them. The interpreter faced Klane again.

"Who are you?" the creature asked.

Klane could feel psionic fluttering against Malik's mind. He raised a psi-wall, blocking the Chirr.

"There is another mind inhabiting the shell of the soldier," the creature said. "We want to know who the other mind is."

"I am Klane."

"What is a Klane?"

"That is my name. I am an enemy of the Kresh."

The interpreter stood motionlessly, staring at him. Finally, it turned to the magus-Chirr. They seemed to speak to the Great One.

"Tell us more," the interpreter said.

"Release these men first," Klane said.

The interpreter lifted its rod high, and noises emanated from the device.

Klane clapped Malik's hands over Malik's ears. At the same moment, magus-Chirr mentally attacked him much more powerfully than earlier. Klane strove to shield himself and his host. He felt the alien Chirrs pressing in, and then Klane's mental strength failed. Deep in the equatorial nest on Fenris II, Klane lost consciousness and he lost control of Timor Malik's body.

20

Cyrus Gant sat on a fallen branch, a thick one. He tapped the dirt with a much thinner stick.

Around him, triangular leaves rustled in the cool breeze. He sat alone, the Berserker compound hidden by the forest. Every so often, usually with a shift of wind, he heard a child shout in play or a woman telling the children to stay away from the seeker's tent. Otherwise, the leaves and whispering wind were his only sounds.

He'd been doing some hard thinking. The seeker's revelation concerning the transfer was interesting, but he didn't see how it could help their situation any. It let him know why the seeker understood star mechanics and other technological concepts. The seeker had never seen such things herself, but she had sharp memories concerning them.

Cyrus snorted to himself. What would that be like, knowing things that had never actually happened to you? It struck him as odd.

He rested the stick on his knees and wondered what in the world was going to happen to him next. The clan had debated the critical issue for Skar and him. After the initiation yesterday, they were Berserker Clan members. It seemed silly to force them into clan membership, but the Berserkers either killed "others" or made them slaves. Now, as clan members, they were safe, in a sense. However, because he was a Berserker, Cyrus only had three days left with his mind intact. After that, the seeker or he would have to submit to the psi-burning medicine.

Cyrus took a deep breath. Could he accept the clan verdict? It didn't matter that it didn't make sense. He had to abide by the custom or run away. If he ran, he was out of the clan. He would be an outcast. Yang would hunt and kill him. Not only Yang; all the warriors would have to give chase.

Cyrus picked up the stick again and tapped the tip against the ground. He'd set up stones to represent Fenris System's planets and moons. There were Jassac, Pulsar, and High Station 3. There were the Fenris sun and the outer asteroids. Then he'd put in the other planets from memory, the inner ones and the outer ones, the gas giants.

He'd scratched a *C* by Fenris II and one by Fenris III. From what he knew, the Chirr held those planets. The Kresh held everything else. He'd written "CYBORGS" beyond the outer asteroids. The cyborgs were the X factor, the unknown in all this.

Cyrus was piecing together what he knew to see if he could come up with a better plan. The Kresh had *Discovery* and were likely reverse engineering it. They, therefore, had a Teleship. By logical deduction, the cyborgs must have Teleships. Those were the only spacecraft in the Fenris System able to travel back and forth in a matter of a year or two from Sol to Fenris. If he wanted to see Earth again, he had to acquire a Teleship from either the Kresh or the cyborgs.

Yet how logical was it to expect that? Suppose he never did get a Teleship. What had been his original plan on Earth? After reaching what was supposedly the New Eden system, he'd wanted to skip out of *Discovery*, with a pretty woman preferably, and start a family on the surface of an Earth-like planet.

Okay, he was on an Earth-like planet and there was a pretty girl to win, a barbarian princess named Jana. If he couldn't get back to Earth, would it be the worst thing in the world to live here the rest of his life?

It wouldn't be so bad except for the Kresh. They might always hunt for him. Then again, maybe they would stop after a time. Yet even if they stopped hunting for him personally, the humans here were always at the mercy of the aliens.

He didn't want to raise a family and have the Kresh stomp them out on a whim. So, if getting back to Earth was impossible, or nearly so, what was the next best option?

With his stick, Cyrus tapped the dirt in thought. Maybe he should join the Resisters all the way. It was a good fight, a worthy one, and it might be the only hope for his children, provided he ever lived that long. Yet if the Kresh built a fleet of Teleships—

"Yeah," Cyrus said aloud. That meant getting back to Earth wasn't quite as impossible as it sounded. The Kresh wouldn't attack the solar system right away. They'd first build a fleet. That took time. Years. During those years, he might pirate one of the new Teleships.

He needed to think a little more long-term. The needle-ship showed it was possible to use a space vessel here provided one was stealthy enough. That meant a possible plan would be to storm a Kresh ship, capture it, and head to the outer asteroids. How long could he wait for that scenario? Years?

"Maybe," he muttered.

Okay. Suppose that was the goal: capturing a Kresh ship. How did one go about doing that? The Anointed One was supposed to be able to do incredible things, right? And a whole host of Resisters were out there ready to lend a hand.

With the tip of the branch, Cyrus scratched the dirt, making tight swirls. He didn't see a way to getting onto a spaceship. Well, he might hijack one of the ice-hauler rockets and go . . . where? He didn't know exactly where they went. Skar had an idea, but the soldier didn't know for sure. He didn't really see a way for two men to free Klane from the Kresh down in the alien city.

Could he do it with Argon? Having the chief monitor along might make a commando raid more possible. Cyrus snorted. He'd rather have the Teleship's space marines. Now that would be something.

Sneaking down into the alien city with the colonel leading the Earth marines. Yeah, he could think about rescuing Klane then. Modern soldiers against the technologically advanced Kresh would give him a chance. Instead, all he had were the primitive Berserkers.

"They aren't space marines, that's for sure."

"What?"

Cyrus spun around as he shot to his feet. Jana stepped out from behind a tree, smiling at him. He wondered how long she'd been hiding there.

"I heard you talking to yourself," she said.

After getting over his start, Cyrus grinned. She looked better than ever with her water-scrubbed flesh and soap-cleaned furs and leathers. The way she walked . . .

"There," she said. "That's what I've been meaning to talk to you about."

"What's that?" he asked.

"Your eyes follow me when I walk," she said. "Why is that?"

Cyrus raised an eyebrow. "Don't others watch you the way I do?"

She seemed to consider the question. "Yang does sometimes, but he always turns away when I notice."

"Sure," Cyrus said. "The hetman fears you."

"That's foolish. Yang fears no one."

"Maybe fear is the wrong word."

"You do not fear me," Jana said. "You watch me. I see the hunger in your eyes."

Cyrus's heart beat faster. This was getting interesting quickly. He'd never been truly alone with her before. If he was going to be spending the rest of his life on Jassac, the sooner he found his woman, the better. With that thought in mind, he took several steps closer.

Suddenly, Jana drew his stolen dagger, pointing the blade at him. "I do not permit any to touch me," she said.

He stopped, and he couldn't help but notice that the way she was poised made her look even better. "Maybe it's time to change that," he said.

She brought the knife a little higher into an attack position.

Despite that, he stepped closer. He couldn't believe what happened next—she made a stab at him. He barely twisted aside in time.

She laughed, and said, "If you continue to watch me, I will attack you at my choosing when you least expect it."

He studied her, and he saw her lips twitch. Did she mock him or did she goad him to do more? Maybe it didn't matter which it was: he was going to hug and kiss her.

She clutched a knife, though, a good one, and it looked like she knew how to use it. He knew it was hard to disarm someone with a knife. Moreover, Jana was a warrior, and she had good reflexes. He needed to trick or lull her.

"If you continue to watch me, I'm going to do something about it," she said.

"Oh," he said, letting his shoulders slump and looking away.

She frowned in what might have been disappointment. But she said, "Good. Now we understand each other."

At that moment, he decided on his game plan. She had a knife, but he had telekinesis. Cyrus moved in. She sliced at him. It was as if someone held her wrist—that was his psi-power—slowing her speed. Despite that, she cut him along the forearm enough to draw blood. Then his fingers curled around her wrist. Cyrus twisted. Her hand opened and the knife fell onto the ground.

"No one can outwrestle me," she said.

Her eyes told him to try. Even though he bled, he held her. A moment later, his lips sought hers. Jana kissed him hungrily in return.

Branches rustled then. A hidden girl or a younger boy giggled.

Jana gasped with shock, and she kneed Cyrus, breaking free. Whoever was watching yelled and took off running.

Jana stepped away from Cyrus and shook her head, flinging her hair back. "Never do that to me again," she said.

He stepped toward her, and she skipped back. He stared into her eyes and saw fear in hers. Would she be in trouble for what had just happened? Would he be in trouble?

On impulse, he scooped up the fallen knife.

"That's mine," she said.

"Nope, I claim it."

"On what grounds?" she demanded.

He showed her a cut on his forearm. "Blood guilt ought to work," he said.

The fear oozed away from her, and she nodded. "Are you always so clever, star man?"

Instead of answering, he flipped the knife before tucking it in his belt.

"I must go," she said. "Others . . ."

"I understand," he said.

She smiled then. It was a shy thing. A moment later, she dashed away.

He decided he'd better get the cut on his forearm looked after. There were going to be questions, but the barbarian princess had come to him to get the ball rolling. How about that, eh? With a grin, he headed back for the encampment.

||||||||||

Yang ruled that the knife belonged to Cyrus. Jana had cut him and she refused to tell anyone why, nor had Cyrus given the reason.

Most of the warriors of the council grinned upon hearing the tale. Yang even grinned once, although he remained solemn the rest of the time.

One warrior didn't grin. He was the brother of Stone Fist, a big man called Grinder due to the strength of his grip. He had spoken against accepting either Skar or Cyrus into the clan.

A meeting took place at noon, with the small sun shining in the heavens. The warriors sat around a fire, with bosk meat dripping fat that sizzled in the flames. Each warrior, including Jana, sat cross-legged in a circle around the fire. The High Station 3 knife lay on a leather cloth before Yang.

"This is Cyrus's knife," Yang pronounced. It had taken lengthy discussion to reach the verdict. The hetman turned to Grinder. "The former outlander owes you a blood debt. Will you accept the knife as payment for your brother's death?"

Grinder had thick slabs for shoulders and rough features. He was good at scowling. He glared at Cyrus now, saying, "I want to fight the outlander."

"No!" Yang said, banging a fist against the dirt. "He is a Berserker. You may wrestle with him for rank, but you may not fight to kill. Do you dispute my word?"

Grinder glared at Yang. "Have you forgotten that they killed three of ours?"

"They also killed a demon," Yang said.

"Does that wash out Stone Fist's death?"

"Stone Fist attacked them. Jana—"

"Don't talk to me about Jana," Grinder spat. "She likes the outlander. She wants the outlander's babies. She—"

Jana leaped to her feet, and she kicked dirt, spraying a sandy cloud into Grinder's face. "You filthy monger—"

"Hold!" Yang shouted.

Jana whirled toward the hetman while pointing at Grinder. "He insults me."

"Do you wish to wrestle him?" Yang asked Jana.

"I do," Cyrus said, answering for her.

"No," Skar said. "That right is mine."

"I will wrestle no one!" Grinder shouted. He put a big hand onto the hilt of his flint knife. The scabbard dangled on his chest. "But I will kill outlanders and I will kill those who kick dirt into my face."

"Do you challenge me as hetman?" Yang asked ominously.

Before Grinder could answer, Cyrus stood. "There's something I want to say."

Yang and Grinder continued to glare at each other.

"Hey!" Cyrus shouted. "I said there's something I want to say."

Yang scowled, and he turned to Cyrus. So did Grinder. Quietly, Jana sat back down.

"By standing, it means you challenge me to rule," Yang said. "Are you challenging me, Earth man?"

"No," Cyrus said, sitting. "But I do have something important to say." He'd been thinking about the Kresh, the crew of *Discovery* at High Station 3, and Klane. He'd been thinking about strategy and tactics, and he'd interspaced that thinking with thoughts about Jana and him. He also knew that he had one day left before the clan ordered his psi-ability burned out.

"Is this about Jana or about Grinder?" Yang asked.

"Neither," Cyrus said. "This is about the demons and the Anointed One in their grasp."

The seeker hadn't joined the warriors in council, but she must have been listening from a nearby tent. A flap opened and the seeker strode out angrily as she brushed her long hair with a flick of her hand. She wore a bone ring on her middle finger.

"You cannot speak about hidden things," the seeker said. "This is blasphemy."

Grinder cried out, and he pointed at Cyrus. "The outlander mocks us at every turn. You saw what he just did. The warrior leaped up in a challenge. Yang should have accepted and slain him, breaking his back. The outlander steals Jana's knife, and Yang agrees he can keep it. The outlander slays our warriors, and we do nothing about it."

"No, no," the seeker said, with her hands in the air.

"Do not interrupt me while I am in the Warrior Circle," Grinder said in an ugly voice. "You have no say here, seeker."

The seeker turned from Grinder and pointed at Cyrus. "You mustn't reveal the deep truths."

Grinder drew his knife and stabbed it into the dirt.

Silence fell, and no one moved. Finally, the seeker hung her head, and she took several steps back.

"Okay," Cyrus said. "This is crazy. We have a war to the death going on with the Kresh and—"

"Demons!" Grinder shouted. "They are demons, and you are a filthy outlander!"

"I am in the Warrior Circle," Cyrus said. "I demand my say."

"Yes," Yang said. "Speak."

"He interrupted me," Grinder said.

"Let the outlander—let Cyrus of Berserker Clan speak," Yang said. "Afterward, you can challenge him to a wrestling match if you desire."

Cyrus tried to steady his nerves. He'd been doing some deep thinking on these issues. The Berserker Clan would never accept him, not really. He was too odd, and there wasn't any way he was going to let them burn out his psi-powers. Could he stand by while they burned out the seeker's powers? What would happen to the many transfers' worth of knowledge in the woman's memories? Could the seeker teach him how to transfer someday? Would he someday give a primitive man the knowledge of Milan, Teleships, space war—?

Cyrus's jaw dropped. He blinked several times, and he glanced at the seeker. The woman stood back, with her shoulders hunched, but she was listening. With a glance, Cyrus saw the warriors were watching and listening. Grinder breathed heavily, with his nostrils flaring.

The answer came to Cyrus. He knew what he had to do. The question was whether he could get any of these primitives to agree. It seemed doubtful—

Then you'd better persuade better than you ever have in your entire life.

He switched his gaze to the fire. A drop of fat fell from the bosk carcass, sizzling with a delightful aroma. He needed to think this through.

No, you need to go for it. This is a verbal knife fight. You win those by acting fast.

"I know how to defeat the demons," Cyrus said.

Grinder snorted rudely. "Boastful words, outlander."

"Maybe Grinder is right," Cyrus said. "Or at least he would be right if we did this the old way. I know how to do this the new way that will give us certain victory. We can throw off the demons and take our rightful place as men."

"If you could do this, you would have already done so," Yang said. "I think Grinder is right. These are boastful words."

"No. I couldn't have done this on my own," Cyrus said. "That's just it. The seeker has the knowledge I need and you have the warriors."

The seeker's head whipped up, and she looked at Cyrus with curiosity.

"The demons are too powerful to defeat," Yang said. "That has always been so and will always be so."

"He's killed one before," Cyrus said, pointing at Skar.

"Yes," Yang said. "Jana told us. He also wielded a magic weapon."

"No," Cyrus said. "It's not magic, it's a gun. It's as simple in its own way as your spears."

"You spout nonsense," Yang said, as he banged a fist against his right knee.

"I don't," Cyrus said. "You, Jana, Grinder, everyone here but for the seeker—is too ignorant to understand high technology. But that doesn't make anything magic."

Some of the warriors grumbled angrily.

"Do we have to sit and listen to these insults?" Grinder demanded of Yang.

"I'm not insulting you," Cyrus said.

"I just heard you with my two ears," Grinder said. "You called me ignorant."

"Is a child wise like a warrior?" Cyrus asked.

Grinder scowled, clearly refusing to answer.

Cyrus turned to Yang. "Does a child know the same things as a warrior?"

"You are calling us children?" Yang asked.

"Do you know about guns?" Cyrus asked.

"Magic—"

"No," Cyrus said. "We came down from space. We know how to use basic weapons. You don't. In that way, you are like children. The demons—the Kresh aliens—stole the knowledge from you long ago. Your parents' parents' parents knew about guns and spaceships. The demons must have scrubbed that knowledge out of you, or it died out."

"You said the seeker understands high technology," Jana said. "How can that be?"

"Jana is listening to me," Cyrus said. "She's used to using her wits."

"We are Berserkers," Yang said in a low rumble. "We may have lost ancient knowledge, high knowledge. But that doesn't make us children."

"You're right about that," Cyrus said. "I didn't call you children. I said in terms of knowledge you're *like* children. If you think about it, there's a difference, a big one."

"How does any of that help us against the demons—against the Kresh?" Yang asked.

"Very simply," Cyrus said. "Your seeker remembers the old knowledge."

"No!" the seeker said. "You mustn't speak about that."

Cyrus looked up at the woman. "You and your fellow seekers have held onto the old knowledge for a long time. There was a reason for that. It was to keep it intact or alive until the Anointed One was born and made his move. Klane has made his move. We must, or I must, free the Anointed One. I can't do that on my own. Skar and I together probably can't do that. I need your help."

"You want us to go into the Valley of the Demons?" Grinder asked in a mocking tone.

"I want you to grow up and remember how to use high technology," Cyrus said. "You can fight. If you knew about the old ways, why, you'd be as good or maybe even better than space marines. I need them about now, and with the seeker's help at transfer, I can get it."

"You speak blasphemy," the seeker whispered.

"With my help, with my psi-power aiding the seeker," Cyrus said, "I think we can focus the old knowledge. I think there's a way to do it without the transferring one dying. Imagine it for a moment. If all the Berserkers remember about spacecraft, guns—"

"You don't have enough guns," the seeker said. "Yang has the pistol and a nearly empty heat gun."

"Yeah, I've thought about that," Cyrus said. "We have spears, slings, and stone knives. If I had a bunch of marines helping me, though, we could sneak down into the valley and help ourselves to some of the Kresh weapons. Even better, we'd get hold of Kresh rockets or sky vehicles, and find ourselves a way to capture a spaceship. Best of all, with armed marines, I'd be able to free the Anointed One and give him a platform to defeat the Kresh."

The seeker stood blinking at Cyrus. "What you suggest has never been done before," she finally said.

"Yeah, I bet," Cyrus said. "This is a new age, though, right? This is the era of the Anointed One."

"Who or what is the Anointed One?" Yang said. "As the Berserker hetman, I have a right to know."

"It is magical knowledge," the seeker said.

Cyrus grinned fiercely. "The seeker and I are offering you the magical knowledge needed to defeat the demons. Humanity's greatest wizard went down to the Valley of the Demons. If we can free him, we can destroy the Kresh forever. But it's going to take more courage than most clan warriors possess. I want only the bravest and best warriors. Jana, will you go with me, if I promise to give you this magical knowledge?"

She became pale, but at last, in a quiet voice, she said, "Yes. I will go. I hate the demons. I want to kill them, all of them."

Cyrus scanned the throng. "What about the rest of you? Is Jana the bravest here? Isn't there another warrior who wants to boast and perform great feats?"

"Madness isn't courage," Grinder said.

"Then sit home in your tent," Cyrus said. "Let the mad warriors destroy the demons. Cower from them the rest of your lives. I've seen them killed before. He did it." Cyrus pointed at Skar. "He can do it again. If you gain the magic knowledge, you can do it, too."

"You give us much to ponder," Yang said slowly.

Cyrus laughed. "Why do you think there are two here with seeker powers? Have there ever been two seekers before?"

"Never," Yang said.

"That's because there's never been an Anointed One before. Today is the day, and there are two here to wield the great spell. If you dare, you can slay demons. If you're afraid, then live like mice the rest of your days."

"I will go," Skar said.

"And I," a young warrior said. "I hate the demons. I want to destroy them."

Silence fell over the circle. Warriors stared at each other. Cyrus wondered what else he could say to persuade them. He couldn't think of anything more.

Then Yang rumbled, "I believe the demonslayer. I believe the man who floated down from the heavens. The demons have hunted us for too long. If there is a chance we can slay them, then we must take it."

Another pause fell over the group. Then, one by one, all the warriors raised their spear arms, agreeing with Yang and with the man who had floated down from space.

21

Mentalist Niens sat on an iron bench in his isolation cell. He was naked, with skinny shanks, and wrapped in despair. Despite that, he retained a modicum of cunning and curiosity.

For an unknown span, he had endured in the chilly cell. As a mentalist, he was aware that subjects isolated without time references turned minutes into hours, and hours into days. He did not know how long he had spent here. He consoled himself with the hope that it had in fact only been a few days, not the weeks that it seemed to be.

I love the Kresh. I hope to work my way out of disfavor. I completely deserve this punishment.

He wouldn't allow himself any other thoughts. Upon lying down and immediately upon waking, he continued the endless litany. Niens had forced himself into a draconian regimen, without letup, silently reciting his loyalty mantra again, and again, and again.

Anytime he felt his mind slipping or an anti-Kresh thought stirring, he allowed himself the hideous mental picture of a Vomag throttling him with a cord. Twice, Niens had lain on the cold floor, imagining a Vomag had thrown him down and pressed a steel-armored knee into his back, the better to leverage the throttling cord.

That end could become reality all too easily. With his vivid imagination, Niens could feel the cord digging into his throat. Breathing became difficult and ugly. The last time, he had even fingered his throat.

I love the Kresh. I deserve this punishment. I should have worked harder for the masters' betterment.

Likely, he embraced futility—

I love the Kresh. I love the Kresh with all my being. If I have failed the masters in any way, let them boil me in machine oil and eviscerate every organ.

Niens paced back and forth. Tears dribbled from his eyes. He would love the Kresh supremely if he could only see a master one more time. He was aware that he practiced a form a self-hypnosis, but that did nothing to stop him. His dread of death gave him relentless zeal.

After a seeming eternity, the moment arrived when the cell door swished up. By that time, Niens had become like a drugged zombie, sluggish and indifferent.

Two Vomags in uniform regarded him from under the short bills of their military caps. Niens towered over them, although they had the greater mass and physically were many times more dangerous.

Niens's mouth opened, and he attempted to speak, managing a croak instead. He expected them to lunge and encircle his wrists with their unbreakable grips.

Instead, the senior soldier beckoned him to follow them outside the cell.

"Where . . . ?" Niens managed to whisper.

"You must maintain correct decorum," the senior soldier said in a low voice, the sound seeming to go right through Niens's torso.

At the moment, the idea of decorum didn't mean anything to Niens.

I love the Kresh. They are masters of life. They guide our brutish natures into pure serenity and bliss.

"Come," said the senior soldier.

The junior Vomag reached into the cell. He grasped Niens's upper left arm and tugged him into the corridor, propelling him into motion down the hall.

Walking seemed to numb Niens's senses. He glanced back. The two soldiers marched behind. "Where . . . ?" he tried to ask again.

The senior soldier shook his head and put a blunt index finger before his lips, indicating silence.

Finally, Niens understood. He must remain quiet, as he was likely under sanction. His step faltered and fear boiled in his stomach.

I love the Kresh. I love the Kresh. I love, love, love them.

Niens's breathing became raspy and his eyesight wavered. Soon enough he reached scrubbers and entered a stall. With a hiss, warm water gushed over his head and cascaded down his torso.

The soldiers picked up stiff brushes and went to work as if they washed a vehicle or a large animal. Niens had to raise his hands and brace himself against the tiled walls so the two didn't knock him down with the bristles scratching across his skin. The soldiers squirted disinfectant on him and later scrubbed him with soap, once more applying the brushes. A glance down showed him that his skin shone red from overstimulation.

They dried him, propelled him into another room, and pointed out mentalist garments on a chair.

"Why are they here?" Niens asked in bewilderment. Wasn't he under sanction?

"Put them on," the senior soldier said.

"But . . . I'm under arrest."

"Do you question orders?" the senior soldier asked.

In a daze, Niens put on underwear, pants, shirt, socks, shoes, and the white mentalist jacket that reached down to his knees. It transformed his self-image, causing him to lift his chin. Confidence and hope flooded him, and he quit humming the mental litany.

I did it!

His sense of well-being grew at a phenomenal rate. He breathed deeper, and readied himself to face the two soldiers and quiz them anew.

What if this is a trap?

A frightening moment of clarity struck. Perhaps the litany of love had shielded him from Bo Taw mind spies. He had donned a few clothes. Did that change anything fundamental about his dangerous position?

I love the Kresh. I love the Kresh.

The litany wasn't as strong or thorough as before. The clothes gave him hope. The hope made him feel better. He had lost the feeling of despair, and that seemed to lessen the intensity of the litany.

Don't be a fool, Niens. You're in for the fight of your life.

I love the Kresh. I hope I can repay for my mistakes. I want to work my way out of trouble.

Niens nodded once, to himself. Then he faced the soldiers. He did not do so as he once would have, with mentalist haughtiness. Instead, he gave them a measured glance, knowing these two could be the ones to throttle him to death, with their knees on his back.

"Follow me," the senior soldier said.

As Niens did, the second Vomag fell in step behind him. Emptiness made Niens's stomach cold. They guarded him, clearly. What could it mean? He didn't know. At least this was better than sitting naked in his cell.

No! Life is better. If they're taking me to my death . . .

The faintest of sneers touched the left corner of his mouth. If the Vomags took him to his death, then he most assuredly deserved death.

I am at the master's service. Whatever she decides for me is good and just. I know that, and I approve of it 100 percent.

The three of them exited the detention center and walked outside in the city. It was brisk today, with a breeze. A hover floated toward the great canyon wall. The vehicle began to lift, and would likely slide onto the plateau uplands where the primitives dwelled.

Before Niens could think about the old seeker and Klane, the senior soldier turned sharply. He headed toward a plaza. To Niens's astonishment, he saw an atmospheric vessel waiting there with an open port.

Curiosity turned to fear. What did it mean? This was a Kresh vessel, an antigrav vehicle to transport personnel to an orbital Attack Talon or other spaceship. Niens wanted to ask the soldiers but knew better. Likely, higher-ranked personnel and maybe even masters watched him.

He entered the vessel, listening to the Vomags' boots ring against the metallic flooring. Humans scurried about carrying equipment and baggage, stowing it or hurrying with it elsewhere.

The senior soldier headed unerringly for the Kresh-only compartments. That amazed Niens. It made no sense.

The three of them soon strode down a wide, empty hall. The Vomags stopped and whirled around. Niens stopped, and a door appeared to his left. He turned, feeling the dry, hot air and smelling the musky Kresh odor before facing Zama Dee the 73rd.

To most humans, Kresh looked alike, but Niens was a mentalist, trained to notice details, thus he recognized her easily.

Zama Dee wore metallic streamers, and she possessed more authority than any Kresh he'd ever met. Behind her stood computer consoles, screens, and ancient folios behind glass barriers.

"Enter, Mentalist Niens," Zama Dee hissed.

His knees almost unhinged, and he would have collapsed in shame. Woodenly, Niens entered the chamber, and the door solidified behind him. It felt as if he had been transported elsewhere, with a towering monster—

Kresh! I love the Kresh. They are humanity's life and reason for existence.

"You intrigue me, Niens," Zama Dee said. "It is the reason you are here instead of expiring in a painful manner before the gathered mentalists."

Niens's throat went dry. Yet he managed to croak, "You honor me, Revered One."

"No. That is imprecise, Niens. I use you because I wonder if you can succeed where another would flounder."

"Your wisdom precedes—"

"Silence, mentalist. Your bombast and animal scraping and mewling does not impress me in the slightest. I understand your native cunning. You are sly and nefarious, without a shred of honor or proper piety toward me or any of the Kresh."

"Master," Niens protested. "I assure you—"

Zama Dee turned her carnivorous head and spoke a harsh, Kresh syllable.

A high-pitched sound directed at Niens dropped him with uncanny speed. He writhed on the sandy floor, stiffening, with his mouth open and his eyes bulging. The horrible, pulsating pitch—

The Kresh uttered another harsh syllable.

The torment stopped, leaving Niens panting on the floor with his ears ringing.

"Stand, Niens. Dust off your garments and remain silent until I give such an order otherwise."

Sluggishly, Niens climbed to his feet. He brushed his coat and he found himself trembling. With an effort, he forced himself into loving thoughts.

If she meant to kill me, she would have said so. Something else occurs, and I believe it is in my favor. I must relax—relax in the presence of such noble greatness.

"I will rephrase," Zama Dee told him. "You have useful qualities, particularly during this odd sequence of events. I do not waste materials or animals. It is true that you lack the proper deference toward us. Perhaps you can imagine my astonishment to realize I had a nascent Humanity Ultimate among my mentalists. It is clear you do not yet understand that you possess such features within your thinking. You quiver with negatives, to assure me I am wrong in my assessment. In other words, you are insulting me in your thoughts even after I have spoken the truth to you."

Was that the truth? Ah . . . he knew what must have happened. The Bo Taw must have sensed or read his deepest belief. With his curiosity, he thought of himself as Kresh-like. To the Revered Ones that would be a gross insult. In fact, they thought of it as Humanity Ultimate. The Kresh were mistaken, though. Somehow, he must convince Zama Dee of that.

Niens hung his head and tried to ooze contriteness.

"Some Humanity Ultimates are filled with noble sentiments concerning their race," Zama Dee said. "I am one of the few Kresh to realize this. You lack these noble thought qualities, however. Yours is a self-absorbed personality, filled with impulses toward sexual gratification, ease, and fullness of food. Despite these black marks, you have a clever mind, nimble in many ways and full of curiosity. This is what I seek."

I love the Kresh. You are totally correct, Revered One, even though I would rather have you believe I am good and upright, fully brave.

"I now realize that Chengal Ras must have sensed or discovered these qualities in you," Zama Dee said. "It was no doubt why he chose to work in your company. The 109th met a strange end, and you were there."

"I tried to defend him, Revered One," Niens whispered.

Zama Dee froze.

Niens fell on his face before the Kresh. He had spoken after she had warned him about that.

"I can use you, mentalist, but not if you disregard my commands. I give you this one lapse, but no others. Disobey me again and I will destroy you. Now stand at attention where I can see you."

Niens scrambled to his feet, wondering at this stay of execution. Normally, when a Kresh said he or she would do this or that given a circumstance, they did it without a thought.

How badly does the 73rd need me? This is interesting. No! This is unprecedented. I must have more value than I realize.

Niens forced his thoughts blank, and he held himself in readiness.

Zama Dee's heavy tail lashed. That almost made Niens quail. He knew some of the signs. The tail lashing usually meant a Kresh readied herself to kill in the primitive way.

"I have a task for you, mentalist," Zama Dee hissed.

Niens waited. What had happened while he'd been in the cell? The Kresh hunted for something and she needed him.

Incredibly, Zama Dee moved leftward, stalking in the Kresh manner, with her tail lashing. She went to the edge of the bulkhead, turned around, and stalked the other way, passing before Niens.

She's agitated. I've never seen a Kresh like this. What can it mean?

The nine-foot Kresh halted before him. One tilt of her bulk would bring her massive teeth into play. She could bite off his head with ease.

"Chengal Ras discovered a hidden truth," Zama Dee said. "He is dead, and I realize that is unfortunate. I could use his insights. Yes. I will journey to High Station 3 and retrace his mental journey. I will discover what brought him here in such haste for the cattle. No doubt you wonder why I would tell someone like you any of this. I have my reasons. I understand your love of comfort and love of ease. Mentalist Niens, I will install you in your own pleasure palace with as many sex objects as you desire. I will reward you for the rest of your natural life. For this, you must do one thing for me."

Niens waited. Could he have heard correctly?

"I must have the subject's consciousness. The body is under a reality field. You will study the subject and devise a method to entice the consciousness to return. If the consciousness returns, you must put him under the reality field. That is assuming you release the field to permit the consciousness to slip back."

Zama Dee hissed in seeming frustration, and said, "You have questions."

Indeed, Niens had many. He couldn't believe they were using a reality field. He knew about them. They were experimental. The reality field did the opposite of its name. While under the field, it was impossible to tell fact from fiction. Psionics couldn't read a mind under a reality field because the field began to conflict the Bo Taw searcher. The field could even affect those standing too close. The reality field was an excellent place to put dangerously powerful psi-able individuals, as it rendered their ability inert.

"Revered One, I am obviously slow-witted compared to you. Are you saying that you're placing me in charge of the test subject?"

"Yes. Next question."

Niens frowned. "Why . . . why do you think I can do any better than your chief mentalists?"

"That is an astute question, but the answer should be obvious. You have a clever mind. Hmm. Let me rephrase. You are devious and filled with greater zeal than the rest of my mentalists. You can probably trick the subject better than the others could. Naturally, I shall watch you closer than ever. The Bo Taw will catalog your seditious and heretical thoughts, even as they're doing so now."

Niens licked his lips. "May I make a statement?"

"Yes," Zama Dee said.

"I do not find in myself any desire to think or act like a Humanity Ultimate. I am satisfied with my lot in life."

"You are incorrect. You are not satisfied. You strive in many areas. You sought to rid yourself of your mate, and you did. You sought younger and more numerous sex objects—and you have them. You used guile to survive during the attack that slew Chengal Ras. Other mentalists would have aided the 109th, helping him to defeat the intruder. You merely sought to preserve your own life. Those are actions of Humanity Ultimates."

"The actions shame me."

"On one level that is true," Zama Dee said. "However, Klane would have slain you and Chengal Ras. Through that, I might have lost the clue that has put me on the present path. Therefore, your guile has aided me. I will give you the rewards you desire, but I will also cage you out of the way. I will gain from new knowledge and I will protect the Kresh from a random element such as you."

"Your logic—"

"Stop," Zama Dee said, with her tail lashing. "Your praise leaves me cold. It is also self-serving and improper for one of the lower forms. You are not Kresh, but one of the cattle."

Niens bowed his head.

"You will bend your intellect and curiosity toward solving the mystery of Klane's consciousness," Zama Dee said. "In order to invest you with greater zeal, I now tell you that failure in your task will bring about a hideous and shameful death. You are a Humanity Ultimate. You seek your own good above the good of the Kresh. That is intolerable unless you give me a greater good: the so-called savior of humanity. On those conditions, I can allow a worm like you to exist. Any other conditions are too distasteful. Do you understand me, Mentalist Niens?"

"I do," Niens said.

"Revered One," Zama Dee reminded him.

"Revered One," Niens hurried to say.

Her tail lashed one more time, striking a wall with a thud. Then Zama Dee pointed at the bulkhead. Niens turned. The way appeared, as did the two Vomags.

"Trap him, Niens, and all will be well. Fail in this, and your existence will end sooner than you can believe."

22

Cyrus hunkered low in the seeker's tent, trying to get it straight in his head how the transfer actually worked. She'd been explaining it to him for quite some time now.

The gat-hide tent rippled in the powerful gusts of wind sweeping through the forest. Outside, branches swayed and creaked, and leaves rustled by the tens of thousands. The tent motions and outer sounds intimidated Cyrus. He'd lived on Crete for a few years. Otherwise, he'd been in controlled city and spaceship environments. The sudden thrust of the hide and the flapping unnerved him.

The insides here also unnerved him more than he cared to admit. There were far too many bones and slick things called junction-stones. He'd picked one up yesterday, and had felt it quiver in his mind.

The seeker had berated him, telling him the stone could have put a curse on him, might have even killed him.

"How can a stone do that?"

"Through magic, psionics," she said.

Cyrus didn't see how, but he didn't pick up any more of the oiled stones. The bones disturbed him more, though. There were big ones—thigh bones—middle-sized ones, and tiny ratlike bones. The seeker had clay jars full of crushed substances and leather bags filled with more stuff.

It felt like a witch's tent in here. Even with his psi-training, the feel in this tent, the way the others treated it, made him uneasy.

The howling wind seemed to reverse course, shoving the nearest tent wall toward Cyrus and blowing the one near the seeker outward.

"What are you doing?" Cyrus asked.

The seeker had been chopping roots and grinding bones. Now, she mixed stuff in the biggest clay container of all, gathering saliva and spitting into it.

"I'm gambling," she told him.

"You mean with the transfer? I've already told you I can help you with that."

She moistened her lips. "What you've been suggesting . . ." She shook her head. "I don't think it's possible. There is only one way to make a transfer. At the end of the ceremony, the giver of memories must die."

"Why? I don't get that part."

"I've already explained it two times," she said.

"And I've told you what Jasper did with me in the Teleship. I think I can anchor you right there at the end. I can draw you back, stop you from giving everything."

"That might foil the transfer. It's more than mere memories we're giving."

"I hope you're not suggesting a transfer of souls," Cyrus said.

"No, nothing like that," she said. "I don't think something like that is even possible."

"Okay." He didn't like the subject, not in this tent and not during the storm outside.

"The others must be ready to accept what I'm going to give," the seeker said. "I don't see how more than one person can receive the memories."

"I've been thinking about that," Cyrus said. "It's groupthink. We had to do that sometimes during training in Crete."

"Can you show me how it was done?"

"I'll try," he said.

They sat across from each other holding hands, and Cyrus used his limited ability. Soon, his head hurt, making his eyes watery. He detested the fact that he had such a weak talent.

The tent flap opened, surprising them. Cyrus looked up and spied Jana staring at him. She'd been grinning, but when her gaze fell upon their hands—

"I can't believe it," Jana said. She darted out of the tent, letting the flap drop down.

"Jana," Cyrus said.

"Let her go," the seeker said. "Your talent is weak. You need rest now from your mental efforts."

Cyrus shot the seeker a glance.

"Am I supposed to hide the truth in order to shield your soft ego?" she asked.

With a heave upward and a grunt, Cyrus stood unsteadily. He swayed, and vomit burned the back of his throat. He *was* a weak talent. He'd always known that. Was he too weak to anchor the seeker during the transfer ceremony?

Grinding his teeth together, Cyrus staggered out of the tent. He saw Jana race into the forest. He looked up at the swaying trees with their billowing and wet leaves. Drops fell from them, and the ground was muddy, slippery.

"Jana!" Cyrus shouted. He staggered after her. Yeah, it was probably stupid. The way to deal with something like this was to ignore it. She'd get over what she saw. Besides, she didn't see anything. The seeker and he had been holding hands to strengthen the psi-connection. Surely Jana could understand that.

Cyrus's steps grew steadier as he ran past wet trees. Branches bent low and groaned ominously. Rain flew into his face. He wiped his eyes and caught another flash of Jana. This was crazy . . . but what the heck. It was a whole lot better than sitting in the tent and getting a splitting headache.

Cyrus put on a burst of speed, and he began to enjoy himself. Then he ran between some bushes and yelped. Jana stood before him, with a spear in her hands. She thrust the flint tip at his belly. Cyrus dove low, and he used his power, deflecting her thrust. It made his mind throb painfully and wiped away the good mood. Why did she have to go and do that?

He slid on mud, and he tackled her, bringing her down. She yelled as her head thudded into a puddle. Then Cyrus clambered up her prone body.

"Listen," he said, angrily.

He never had a chance to say more. Jana grabbed his face with her cold, wet hands, and she yanked his face down, pressing his lips against hers.

Some of the headache went away. She had a tasty tongue. Then she pushed him, and with an oath, she tried to hurl him away.

"What's wrong with you?" he shouted. "You're hot and cold."

"You were holding her hands," Jana said.

"Yeah," he said, "because we used psionics."

"Magic," she said, managing to make it a superstitious word.

"We're getting ready for the transfer."

She peered into his eyes. "I don't think I can do it, Cyrus."

He knew what she meant. Jana wanted to back out of the group transfer, the mind teaching to the warriors. She didn't want to receive the seeker's many memories.

"Of course you can do it," he said. "You're coming with me into the valley."

"You've never asked me to come with you."

"Of course I did," he said. "I asked you at the meeting around the fire when I first proposed the plan."

"Why?" she asked, while searching his face. "Why do you want me to come with you?"

"Because you're a good warrior," he said, lamely.

"That isn't the reason."

"Uhhh . . . you're smarter and cleverer than the other Berserkers," he said.

"Is that it?"

"Yeah. What other reason could I have?"

Her eyes hardened.

"And I like you," he added.

She searched his eyes.

"I want you to stay with me," he said.

"As a pet for the star man?" she asked.

"No," he said.

"Stay how?"

"You know," he said.

"The great Cyrus cannot speak his heart. I've seen how you look at me. Are you strong or are you weak, star man?"

He took her face in his hands. He stared down at this beautiful primitive. He'd known pretty girls in Milan and good-looking women in Crete. None of them had Jana's vitality. None of them had her eyes. He wanted Jana. He wanted her to stay with him no matter where he went.

"I want you to be my wife," Cyrus said.

"Oh. That is what the great star man wants. Maybe Jana wants something else."

He knew then what she wanted from him. Wow. He couldn't believe it. This was crazy, really. This was humanity on the edge of existence. He was marooned way out here, far from the solar system. Yet . . .

"Jana," Cyrus said, as he lay on her in the rain. "If I asked you . . . no. I'll do this straight up. Jana. Will you marry me?"

Cyrus wasn't sure what he expected, but it wasn't what happened.

"Yes," she said in a small, soft voice.

He couldn't believe it. His heart melted. Some of the dross burned away in that melting. Something tender and something fierce welled up in its place. If anyone ever tried to hurt Jana . . .

He bent his head, and he kissed her tenderly. After he raised his head, she said, "Now I know you really want me for me, and not just to use my body. We Berserkers believe a man should stay faithful to one woman his entire life."

"Yeah?" he said.

"Do you believe that?"

"I do," he said, kissing her again, and he did believe that. He didn't want anyone else but her. He wanted this woman for his wife.

"You've made me very happy, Jana."

"Yeah," she said, mimicking his way of talking.

The two of them burst out laughing. Life was good. It was very good.

IIIIIIIII

The rain had stopped as night fell. Jana wore dry furs and Cyrus, Berserker leathers.

Eight warriors, including Yang and Grinder, stood around a crackling fire. Skar was present, together with the downcast seeker. Cyrus had wanted to wait to attempt the transfer. He felt terrific, but his mind was fuzzy. That wasn't due to Jana's acceptance of his proposal—well, the terrific part was. The psi-practice earlier had worn him down.

Cyrus pulled the seeker aside, saying, "We should do this later, after we rest."

"No," she whispered. "We have already run out of time."

"Why do you say that?"

"I have sought the future," she intoned.

"You're a clairvoyant?"

She looked up with haunted eyes, whispering, "Enough of one to know that I do not belong in it."

Cyrus clutched her arm, and he opened his mouth to assure her that everything was going to be fine. Yet how did he know? What if she did die tonight? Wouldn't he have talked her into doing this? Did that mean he was killing her?

He closed his mouth and released her arm, indecisive. Maybe he didn't need the primitives to understand high technology. Yet even as he considered it, he rejected the idea. He needed competent allies; space marine equivalents would be optimum. So what should he do?

"It is time," she whispered.

Cyrus frowned. He couldn't let the seeker kill herself just so the rest of them would survive. Well, it wasn't going to be easy on their end. They merely wanted the *chance* to fight on better terms. This wouldn't help them fight on equal terms, because they lacked modern weapons and spacecraft. They needed the seeker's knowledge. She had to do this for them. Therefore, he had to ensure her survival tonight.

"I told you I'm going to anchor you," he said. "You know that, right?"

"Yes," she said, and she avoided his gaze, heading toward her belongings stashed in the shadows.

"I promise you, seeker—"

She whirled around, and her eyes flashed. Maybe that was the firelight reflecting in her orbs. In that moment, she seemed powerful and stern, uncompromising, a cobra rising up from the grass to confront him. He set himself, and he readied his mind. He realized he hadn't been practicing his psi-exercises lately. No wonder his mind felt fuzzy. Then her features softened. She stepped near and pressed a hand over his mouth.

Cyrus sensed instead of saw Jana inching toward him. He hoped his fiancée had the presence of mind to give the seeker room.

Before anyone could discover the extent of Jana's self-control, the seeker removed her hand. Sadness filled her. "I do not do this for you, Earth man. You are not talking me into anything."

His eyebrows rose. Could she read his mind? Was the seeker that much more powerful than he was?

"I love the Berserkers," the seeker said. "I am a link in a long chain of events leading up to this day. The memories in me push me toward your path. The voices can see the wisdom of your words, of your plan. The hour approaches where the Anointed One will reveal to us the final path. The demons crush our spirit, Earth man." She gestured around her. "The demons have twisted humanity through their perverted genetics. We here on Jassac, on these bleak highlands . . ."

The seeker turned away, and she hugged herself. "The weak will rise up tonight in order to help defeat the strong. We are but slaves to, to . . ."

I am Spartacus, Cyrus told himself. *The greatest gladiator in Earth's history rose up and fought for a time. He must have seen many of his friends die. Can I do less?*

"I will pass so that you may become greater," the seeker whispered. "But it is hard, Earth man, very hard. I did not realize how much I love life."

"I'll anchor you," Cyrus said. "I promise—"

She put a soft hand on his cheek. "Don't promise me, Cyrus Gant."

"I do," he said, the words gushing out of him. "I promise to anchor you and keep you here with us. We're going to need your wisdom."

She smiled sadly. "You promise and I will forgive," she said in the quietest voice so far. "I absolve you from your promise."

"No!" he said, becoming stubborn.

"Remember, I have seen the future." She removed her hand from his cheek, lifted a shawl over her head, and walked toward the fire. She raised frail arms and regarded the assembled. "You must sit around the fire," she said in a strong voice. "You must stare at the flames and do exactly as I tell you. No," she told Skar, who went to sit. "You are not a Berserker, nor is Cyrus Gant one. You are outlanders. Grinder spoke the truth about that."

Grinder grinned, showing off his teeth, his manner saying, *I knew it!*

"My knowledge is for you eight alone," she told the warriors settling around the fire.

"But if they do not belong to the clan—" Grinder said.

"The Great War is upon us, warrior," the seeker said in a loud voice. "They are in the clan, but not of the clan. They are the allies that the dreams foretold. We need them and they need us. Can you not feel the sacredness of the moment? The Earth man has told us the chosen path. You must walk it and obey his words."

"I would rather kill him," Grinder said.

"I know," the seeker said. "But you must open your mind tonight. You must drink from my memories. Then, and only then, can you make an informed decision." She shrugged. "Maybe you are too angry to understand, but I don't believe that about you, Grinder. You are a warrior of the clan. You will fight the true enemy, the one that condemns humanity to slavery and servitude."

Grinder looked down, troubled.

The seeker clapped her hands twice. "We will prepare."

Cyrus retreated to the shadows where Skar joined him. *I will save her. She isn't going to die. I don't want her death on my conscience.*

Yang, Jana, Grinder, and the other candidates sat around the fire, the play of light and shadows dancing on their faces. Logs cackled as flames leaped. Wood popped and sparks showered, one carried upward and away. The rain had stopped several hours ago, but the wind blew harder than normal, although less than earlier. The seeker spoke to them in a soothing voice. It was clear they were afraid.

"Watch the flames," she said. "See how they dance and writhe with life. We are alive and we are like fire, existent for a moment in time. You must soar and flicker with everything in you. Yes, I bid you to fly as high as you can. Soak up memories tonight and learn the true secrets of the universe."

Despite the gravity of the evening and the seeker's words, Cyrus found himself focusing on Jana. She sat cross-legged, and she kept brushing her hair nervously. How long would he have to wait to make her his wife? He wanted to do it tonight. Her legs, her breasts, her long hair—

"The time approaches," he heard the seeker say in a crooning voice.

With a start, Cyrus realized he'd been lost in a daze. The seeker's words had lulled him. Jana had merely been the easiest subject for him to fixate upon. For the others, for the way they sat transfixed, it must have been the flames.

"You must open yourselves," the seeker crooned. "You must release your old ideas and accept these. You must—"

The seeker reached into a pouch slung at her side, grabbing fistfuls of the substances she'd mixed earlier. She threw each into the fire. It didn't burn, but settled heavily upon the wood like a fire retardant. Gray, vile-looking smoke billowed.

"Breathe deeply," the seeker said. She walked around the circle and examined the eight warriors in turn. She struck one on the back of his head. "Get up," she said.

It took two tries, but finally the man stood.

"Face me," she said.

The warrior found that even harder to do. He swayed, still facing the weakened flames.

"Are you afraid?" the seeker whispered.

"Yes," he slurred.

"Do you wish to scurry away to safety?"

It seemed as if the man wanted to say yes. Cyrus expected the seeker to touch him and tell him to go, to leave, that he was unworthy of this.

"Everyone fears," the seeker told him. "It is the way of those who want to live. Are you a warrior?"

"You know I am," he said.

"That isn't a direct answer. So I say again. Are you a warrior?"

It took him two attempts, but he said, "Yes."

"Then sit down and stop being afraid."

Finally, the warrior looked at her. He nodded, and sat with a seeming greater ease of spirit.

She spoke to several others in a similar manner. But she did not speak to Yang, Jana, or Grinder.

"It is time," the seeker said. She threw back her head, lifted her arms, and screamed into the darkness. None of those seated around the fire flinched or seemed to hear.

Skar's shoulders twitched, while Cyrus blinked himself out of a stupor.

What's wrong with me? Why can't I stay awake? Why is she screaming?

With a start, Cyrus realized he should have already begun to anchor her. He composed himself, and suddenly her shrieks quit. He could feel her mind open, and he wanted to shout at her to wait, to stop. A small, deep part within him realized she had lulled him. Didn't she think him strong enough?

"Wait," he whispered.

The seeker didn't wait. She opened her mind, and she began to pierce each of the eight minds around the fire. Memories began to tumble from her and into them.

Cyrus reached out with his psi-power. Something baffled him. It was like walking into a hurricane. He fought the onrushing memories. He had to reach her. He had to close her mind for her. She would simply let every memory leave her and enter the warriors, and then she would perish.

Cyrus realized that more than just memories left her. He wondered about that, and then it came to him. To seal the thoughts and patterns, the visions of other times and places, she had to expend part of her being. It was half psi-power and half a surrendering of life force.

"Let me help you," he whispered. He tried, but the battle against the memory/life force torrent weakened him. He struggled on, concentrating, refusing to let her expire. This one time he would prove to others that he was stronger than anyone believed.

He wasn't sure if he tapped a life force of his own, burning it up in an effort to reach her mind. Suddenly, his legs gave out and he struck his chin against the ground. Losing concentration, he had to begin anew, battling now from the dirt. He couldn't let her die. He refused.

"These are true things!" the seeker shouted, sounding winded. "I give you the gift of many minds from many different times. Now you know who and what the demons really are. They are aliens from another star system. They have used us in their genetic experiments. Now, you must rise up and help Cyrus Gant the Earth man save the greatest Fenris human of them all: the Anointed One known as Klane."

With that, the seeker collapsed.

The torrent of memories and life force ceased. Cyrus's eyelids quivered and his breath came in short gasps.

"Help . . ." he slurred. "We must . . . help her." He tried to rise. He could not. He'd already used up everything. "Please," he whispered. He tried to turn his head and implore Skar to do something.

Unconscious on the ground, the soldier did nothing.

Cyrus was the last to pass out. He wanted to save the seeker. He fought with the last dregs of his psi-power, but then he, too, closed his eyes.

23

Klane's consciousness on Fenris II struggled for identity and existence. For an unknown time, he had fought off Chirr psionics as he held the citadel of Malik's mind. During that time the Chirr had tormented Timor Malik in order to make him reveal what he knew.

The torments had weakened the mulishly stubborn soldier and brought him closer and closer to death. Finally, because his battered will could no longer suppress Klane, the youthful consciousness burst out of the ego citadel and once more took full control of the soldier's body.

It happened at a grim time. A Chirr warrior prodded a sweat-drenched, naked, and stumbling Klane, or a Klane in charge of the Vomag soldier. Awful bruises covered the body. It had lost weight, while horror and pain stamped its features. The sour-smelling Chirr shoved the tip of its pincers between Klane's shoulder blades, making the soldier stagger faster. The two of them traversed a narrow underground passage, the floor, ceiling, and walls made of Fenris II dirt and Chirr-spittle mix.

The warrior was immensely strong and stood head and shoulders taller than the soldier. The creature had a coppery-red carapace and scuttled on four of its six legs. It wore a harness around its bulk. On the harness rattled a hazy bulb where several glow-moths fluttered. They provided the dim lighting. On the harness also rattled manacles and several sharp implements.

On two different occasions when Malik had been in charge of the body, he had spoken through an interpreter to vizier-Chirr. Because of the memory, Klane now learned that the vizier-Chirr were the decision makers, along with the Nest Intelligence.

Klane didn't know how they all interacted with each other and hardly cared. The earlier bargaining sessions had gone poorly. Malik had little to tell, and that little he'd refused to speak. The interpreter had informed him that the Chirr knew that torture induced humans to reconsider their actions. He would thus continue to undergo torture sessions to help clarify his thinking concerning a revelation about the Kresh.

During Malik's stay down here, he and Klane had learned a few things about the Chirr. Their self-awareness wasn't like that of the Kresh with their stiff rationality. The Chirr, it seemed, viewed psionic power as supernatural, just as Klane once had. Yet the insects also had high technology.

Klane wondered if he understood their worldview properly. The Kresh were alien. The Chirr seemed otherworldly.

In any case, Klane, in Malik's body, now shuffled from the latest torture cell. He hobbled as a bent wreck. Sweat drenched him. Every step was agony to his sore hip sockets, to his aching knees, and to his twisted ankles.

The last torture had been primitive in the extreme. They'd strapped Malik's body to a rack and had brought their alien science into play. A scuttling Chirr like a giant crab had injected its proboscis into his hip. That's when the pain had become an exquisite thing. The Chirr had added a pain heightener so even the manacles around his ankles and wrists had hurt, and that had been before they'd begun to stretch Malik on an insect-fashioned rack.

Some of the drug still lingered in the soldier's body. The ground felt like fiery sandpaper against his feet. Klane shivered with fever. He would have hugged himself, but his half-dislocated arms dangled from his shoulders. Despite the fever and the agony of moving, he was desperately grateful to be off the rack, to be out of the torture cell. The Chirr were as much demons as the Kresh had been.

"No," Klane whispered.

He had to forget about that and marshal his thoughts. It didn't matter if his thoughts were blurred. He could not return to a torture cell. The body couldn't take any more pain. The proboscis in his hip had finally done it. Malik had sobbed *yes, yes, yes.* He would give them knowledge of the Kresh and ways to practice new magic—if he had possessed such knowledge.

Klane smacked his lips. He was so thirsty. It was just like Jassac in that way. No. On Jassac, he had been able to move from place to place. Here, he was trapped inside a hive full of truly alien beings. The Chirr had all the power here. The only way to escape this hell would be to die.

What have they done to Turk?

Klane hoped the Chirr hadn't used the tough soldier as fodder for imps and bantlings. Still, that would have been better than torturing him.

Klane began to gingerly shuffle toward a side tunnel where light pulsated as if illuminated by a fire.

The warrior shoved him between his shoulder blades. The Chirr made him stagger past the side tunnel.

Klane breathed hard as sweat dripped from him. Horror twisted his thinned face. Any deviation here in the nest always led to greater pain and agony. He didn't want to mewl, to crawl or beg.

A sick knot tightened in his gut. The present tunnel led deeper underground. Was the Chirr taking him to a worse torture chamber? He wished an interpreter were here so he could ask.

Maybe because of the fear, Klane's shuffle slowed even more. The Chirr pushed again. Klane reeled, almost collapsed, but managed to keep his balance and to keep from groaning. The air stank worse than ever. His gut roiled in rebellion. It was too much. His gut heaved, and he spewed a thin stream of bile. He coughed, which wracked the poor, misused body.

Where is it taking me?

The insects would surely kill him after he gave them whatever it was they wanted. Maybe that didn't matter anymore. It would end the pain. It would stop the horror.

It was too bad Malik and the Vomags hadn't slain every Chirr in the nest. The Chirr weren't just different. They were hideously evil, vile, inhuman, and cruel, like insects.

Klane shivered, and the idea that he would give such alien creatures any help troubled him. He didn't want to add anything to their power. Yet he had to keep out of the torture cells.

Klane blinked gritty eyeballs. Something odd impinged on his senses. It was . . . a thrum. He might have cocked his head, but his neck muscles were too tight, too misused for that. He shuffled, sweated feverishly, and listened.

Thrum-thrum-thrum; it was like a drumbeat, but not to his ears. Behind him, the warrior made clicking noises with each step. It had horn-covered talons, not flesh like a man's foot. Things rattled on the Chirr's harness. From side tunnels came hissing, shushing sounds and the clunk of things being stacked.

Thrum-thrum-thrum. The drumbeat grew. It pulsated through Klane. The pulse should have shaken his bones. It should have vibrated his bruised flesh and created more pain. The thrumming did neither. It warmed him somehow, and he didn't understand that. Everything in the nest had hurt so far.

Once more, the warrior shoved him, this time toward a new side tunnel.

Klane staggered through it and gobbled down the whimper in his throat.

The tunnel led into a low, long chamber with glowing pits to the sides. The pits warmed the chamber and revealed ranks of vizier-Chirr.

Each was like a giant spider with a huge, vein-ravaged bulk on its back. The veins surged and shrank, likely the blood pumping through them.

The dark bulk on the spidery back shifted occasionally and hideously, reminding Klane of a Tash-Toi he'd seen once, half-dead from a gat's attack. The gat had bitten away part of the man's skull to reveal the pink-white matter underneath. Klane imagined that's exactly what the bulk was here: a vizier-Chirr's brain.

There were more viziers here than he'd seen previously. There were dozens, too many for him to count. They scuttled like bugs and continuously chittered to each other. Among them prowled small, dog-sized Chirr. Frog-like tongues flicked from them and licked the vizier-Chirr. The tongues left a sticky substance, and then they smeared it all about. Whenever the small Chirr licked them, the viziers stood very still as if they enjoyed the process.

The idea sickened Klane. Were they pleasure-Chirr, perhaps?

An interpreter scuttled up.

The chittering from the others quieted but didn't altogether stop. The pleasure-Chirr lay down and nibbled on their tentacles.

Klane had forgotten about the warrior. It gave him a shove. The strength of the shove surprised him, made Klane stagger, trip, and sprawl before the red-skinned interpreter. Its talons tightened so the tips dug into the hive floor.

"You are here to talk of magic," the interpreter said.

Despite his pain and weakness, Klane climbed to his feet. He gazed at the ranks of minutely scuttling, quietly chittering vizier-Chirr. If he were alone with one, he'd stomp it to death.

"Human," the interpreter said.

Klane swallowed, and his gut churned. Fever dulled his wits. He shivered and knew he needed to bargain for some advantage.

Maybe the hidden thrum-thrum-thrum aided him. What was that noise anyway?

The interpreter half turned toward the vizier-Chirr. Soon it faced Klane again.

"You will return to the torture cell," it said.

"Wait!" Klane shouted.

From behind, the warrior grasped his arm. It began to drag him.

"Wait!" Klane said in a loud voice. "Why don't you wait so I can give you what you want?"

The warrior released him.

"You are ready to tell us your magic?" the interpreter asked. "You will show us how to leap across space and gain entry into another person?"

"Yes, I want to tell you everything," Klane said. *I need help. I need a companion.* Men weren't fashioned to stand alone down here deep under the surface. "But I'll need Turk," Klane added.

"What is Turk?"

"The soldier—" Klane began. "He's the other man you took with me from the pool."

The interpreter stared through him.

Klane lacked the will to stare back into those emotionless eyes. He dropped his gaze.

"Is this certain?" the interpreter asked.

"I need him, yes," Klane mumbled.

"Clarify 'need.'"

Before he could answer, vizier-Chirr began to chirp and chitter in greater volume. The interpreter chittered back. The interplay continued for a time. Finally, the interpreter regarded Klane.

"Clarify 'need,'" it repeated.

"I cannot perform magic without the other," Klane said, hoping they would believe that. He was too sick to think up slick lies.

"You will do nothing," the interpreter said. "You will explain your magic in detail and how you came from the Kresh stronghold moon all the way here."

"That's what I meant," Klane said. "Only the other can give me permission, though. And it must be in person," he added.

"You are falsifying," the interpreter said.

Klane shook his head. "I fear the Chirr too much to lie."

"The other is a soldier. He lacks knowledge of magic, what you call . . . psionic ability. You falsify and thus waste time. You will return to the torture cells."

The threat made Klane tremble—he'd have to ignore that for now. He needed to concentrate on weaving lies and half-truths into—he didn't know. Yes! Into a Chirr miscalculation.

"You're correct," Klane said. "He's a soldier. But the ordeal changed him."

"Soldiers have never used magic," the interpreter said. "The Kresh-trained magicians have always remained hidden in the rearward zones. We know. Otherwise, the hive would have devoured them."

"The nest sacrificed soldiers in the pool," Klane pointed out. "The exchange granted magical power to you, yes?"

"Man, you equivocate. Detail your magic or return to the torture cells now."

"Yes, I want to tell. That's what I'm saying. But I'm also trying to explain to you that I need the former soldier. He has learned magic. We learned together, practiced it together, and can only show you together."

"You said he grants or withholds permission."

"Talking with Chirr confuses me," Klane said. "I used the wrong word to express my meaning."

The interpreter chittered and chirped with the vizier-Chirr. Their conversation lasted longer than before. That agitated the pleasure-Chirr. They hurried to various viziers and began licking them.

Klane found the spectacle revolting, a dark sea of surging, scuttling, clacking Chirr. That, along with the talk, wearied him so his head began to pound. In this hive of horrors, he desperately needed another human.

214

"Man," the interpreter said.

Klane jerked in surprise.

"The other is sick, near death," the interpreter said.

"Then I must see him at once," Klane said.

"You will give us the magic then?"

"Gladly," Klane said. "I would have given them to you already if I'd only understood you before. My ignorance of your ways is nearly total. Only now have I realized what you asked. Please, let me see the other so he and I may give the magic you desire."

The interpreter turned to the viziers.

Exhausted, feverish, and with a pounding headache, Klane lay down.

"Man," the interpreter soon said.

"I can't think anymore," Klane groaned.

"You need nourishment?"

"And rest," Klane said. "I'm very sick."

Klane faded until someone set a bowl of water before him. He stirred enough to slurp it. Someone set down gruel. He sniffed it and groaned. The interpreter spoke and the warrior grabbed a fistful of Klane's hair and shoved his mouth into the gruel. Rather than fighting them, Klane ate the bitter slop. Surprisingly, he kept it down. A little later, the fever seemed to recede.

Had the Chirr medicated his gruel?

Thrum-thrum-thrum beat that intrusive sound or—

Klane pushed himself to a sitting position. Viziers watched him and chittered quietly among themselves. The pleasure-Chirr licked them vigorously. The interpreter stood motionless like an idol.

Klane tried to concentrate on the thrum. There was something about it—something that could work in his favor. He glanced back. The warrior waited, and it watched him. Klane shuddered. There was motion to one side that drew his attention.

Two warriors carried a litter. On it lay a naked, scarlet-spotted soldier. The spots dotted Turk from crown to heel. The soldier was thinner, although still muscled. His eyes were filmed over and drool spilled out of his mouth.

Something tore deep in Klane's chest. This was awful.

While carrying Turk's litter, the warrior-Chirr marched to Klane.

"Ask for his permission," the interpreter commanded.

Klane struggled to his knees. "Turk," he said.

With infinite slowness, the soldier turned his dotted face.

Klane wiped the filmy gunk out of Turk's eyes. Heat radiated off the soldier.

"Turk, right armguard to the senior drummer, the Ninth Maniple, Tenth Cohort Invincible, at attention," the soldier mumbled.

"Turk," Klane whispered. He touched the soldier's cheek. The dots were hard raised bumps, growths.

Turk blinked several times, but without seeing.

"He's dying," Klane accused the interpreter. "What have you done to him?"

"Clarify your statement," the interpreter said.

"What are these red spots?"

"We tested new spore," the interpreter said.

The tearing within Klane changed into a terrible hardening of resolve. He would never return to the torture cell. Bravery was beyond him here, deep in the hive. But—

"You must heal him." Klane said.

"Clarify 'heal.'"

"Fix him as before," Klane said.

"He must give you permission," the interpreter said.

Turk's left hand lifted and he groped toward Klane. Klane grabbed the soldier's heated hand.

"I expire," whispered Turk.

"Hang on," Klane said. "Don't quit yet."

"I will find out soon what waits on the other side of death," Turk whispered.

"Don't leave me here alone," Klane pleaded.

"I have never deserted my post," Turk whispered.

"Tell us your magic," the interpreter said.

"What?" Klane asked.

"He has given permission," the interpreter said. "We heard him speak."

"He's too sick to give his permission," Klane said. "You must fix him so I can get permission."

Vizier-Chirr interrupted the interpreter before it could reply. Their movements were like crickets rustling.

Soon the interpreter said, "It is too late to counteract the spores."

"Can you try?" Klane asked.

"Clarify—"

"Give him the counterspore and find out if it's too late or not!" Klane shouted.

"You speak futility," the interpreter said.

"I want his permission for the good of the nest," Klane said. "He must help me remember the magic."

The interpreter blinked its eyes and spoke to the viziers. The exchange was faster than before.

"You want his permission so you can forgo more torture," the interpreter said.

"Wouldn't it be quicker to give him the counterspore than to torture me?" Klane asked.

At that moment, a warrior marched toward Turk. The Chirr held a flask.

"Stand back," the interpreter told Klane.

"Fight it," Klane told Turk. "Fight the sickness and help me."

"Stand back," the interpreter repeated.

Klane shuffled away, horrified.

The warrior-Chirr uncorked the flask, pried open Turk's mouth, and poured a substance with the thickness of blood into the soldier's throat. Turk began to thrash and jerk. The Chirr set him down, and each clutched part of his body. Turk humped, screamed, and spewed a globule spray. He began to tremble.

Klane's features had hardened, and his heart thudded painfully. If only he had more power. If only there was—

Shocked, Klane looked over his shoulder. The thrum-thrum-thrum—he finally recognized it. If a fever hadn't raged through him, if he wasn't tormented by pain and fear, he would have surely realized before now. The thrum was like a giant junction-stone. But it was more than that. It thrummed and buzzed in a similar way his mind did whenever he used his psionic abilities. Something decidedly strange occurred here, something alien beyond his understanding.

As Turk humped and twisted, as the soldier trembled and cried out, Klane attempted to tap the alien junction-stone. His mind sought to use the alien power. With a shock, he realized he psi-touched a living thing, a dumb thing without intellect that yet held onto churning psi-ability of an incalculable nature. He couldn't breach the main stores of power, but like condensate on a barrel, he sampled the dribbles of power from the weird living storage.

Psionic energy trickled into his being. It strengthened his mind, and he wondered if he could help Turk as he'd once repaired his own flesh on Jassac. With psionic concentration, he attempted to heal.

Unfortunately, the warrior from earlier shoved Klane from behind. It broke his concentration as he sprawled onto the floor.

"The soldier is too sick," the interpreter said.

With inspiration, Klane said, "Touching him has helped me recall magic."

"Explain it," the interpreter said.

Klane began to explain how he used psionic telekinesis to repair damaged tissues.

As Klane spoke, the interpreter chittered to the vizier-Chirr. None wrote on parchment that Klane could see. He concluded that vizier memory must be excellent.

"That is all?" the interpreter asked.

"That is one technique," Klane said. "I remember more now. His presence helps me," he said, pointing at Turk. "If the soldier lives long enough, I'll be able to tell you all I know."

"How many do you know?"

"Several hundred," Klane said.

"You falsify. We of the hive only know of six spell techniques."

"With my new technique, you now know seven," Klane said. "And if he lives long enough, I'll be able to tell you everything I know."

The interpreter chittered and chirped furiously to the viziers. As they communicated, two warriors picked up Turk's litter.

"Where are you taking him?" Klane asked in alarm.

"We go to the magus-Chirr," the interpreter said. "They will use your new knowledge and heal him, and you will begin to explain your other techniques. We particularly want to know how your consciousness can cross space as it has."

"Yes, I'll gladly tell the magus-Chirr," Klane said.

"But if you have falsified, you will return to the torture cells."

"I've learned the power of the Chirr. I fear you. I will tell you only the truth."

"The power of the hive is only matched by our wisdom," the interpreter said. "Unmodified humans always succumb to the persuasion of the torture cells. We knew it would be so with you. Now go, follow the other."

The journey lasted longer than Klane expected, and it showed him several incredible sights.

The interpreter led the way, while warriors carried Turk and another followed Klane. They entered a new area with steel walls, a steel ceiling, and electrical lighting. It was unlike anything Klane had seen in the hive before. They entered a lift with a glass front, and it immediately sank with speed.

Klane's stomach lurched, and the window passed steel banks, pink crystal walls, and suddenly a cavernous open area. The extent of the cave boggled Klane's senses. How far were they underground anyway? How much labor had this taken? The need for the vast lair became evident a moment later.

What are those?

Shoving past the Chirr holding Turk's litter, Klane stepped up to the glass. His mouth opened in shock. The cavern rivaled the Valley of the Demons in extent. It was huge and lit, and it contained hundreds of thousands of Chirr. They swarmed what looked like rockets. Some were vast, others small.

"Are those missiles? Or spacecraft?" Klane asked.

"Step away from the glass," the interpreter said.

Klane took a last look as the lift sped down. In that look, he realized he hadn't understood the gargantuan nature of the rockets. Those weren't missiles. Those were indeed spacecraft. They had to be.

Had the Chirr built a secret space fleet under the surface? If so, how long had they been building it? Years, decades, centuries?

"Step back from the glass," the interpreter repeated.

Klane did, and he marveled at what the Chirr had accomplished. They must mean to challenge the Kresh in a new realm, not just on the planets. It made strategic sense. Until the Chirr won space, they would always be on the defensive on and in the planets.

Did the Kresh know about the secret Chirr fleet? He doubted it.

They passed the cavern and continued to sink into the ground. The ride down lasted longer than Klane expected. It depressed him. He looked up at the lift ceiling. Would he ever see the sun again? Would he ever leave Malik's beaten body?

Eventually, the lift came to a halt. They exited and marched through steel corridors and soon reentered dirt tunnels. In time, they trekked through a low chamber. The warrior-Chirr carrying Turk led now and the interpreter brought up the rear. They marched through narrow lanes.

On either side, lumbering genetrices fifteen feet long twitched and squirted eggs. Scuttling, crablike Chirr hefted the eggs, carting them toward glowing domes. Thousands of eggs lay under each heated dome. This must be a hatchery. It also must be one of the more protected places in the hive.

They exited the hatchery and hurried down a steep tunnel. The entire time the thrum-thrum-thrum grew in strength.

Finally, they entered another large chamber. Although they were extremely deep underground, the chamber had a high vaulted ceiling. Klane might have examined the ceiling in detail, but another marvel had his attention.

A mighty, swirling, seething, ghostly ball radiated over a dark pit. The immense ball heaved one way and coils of sizzling power jagged into the air, only to sizzle back into the ball. The sight staggered Klane. It awed him. One didn't see psionic power. The idea didn't make sense, did it? What was that thing anyway?

Several dozen magus-Chirr circled the giant pit. Klane recognized them. Thin, with skinny braches folded inward like a half-open flick-knife. They had elongated insect skulls and horizontal mouths. They chanted, or sang, or chirped in unison. It was obvious to Klane that they balanced the seething ball of psionic power. In some alien manner, the psi-able among them must have transferred psionic strength into the sizzling, ghostly ball of power.

It was a hive psionic bank.

"Man," the interpreter said.

Klane twisted around.

"Explain to the master magus your healing magic." The interpreter pointed at the thinnest, tallest Chirr present. It was half again as tall as a man was and it seemed old and brittle.

Klane spoke, and the interpreter and the master magus chittered together. Soon, a loud whistling chirp emanated from the master magus. More magus-Chirr appeared. They each held a buzzing instrument.

To Klane, the Chirr seemed like worshippers. What would magus-Chirr worship? Klane wasn't sure he wanted to know.

The magus-Chirr towered over Turk. They waved their buzzing instruments in seeming magical passes and chittered in unison.

For an instant, Klane felt he almost understood the words. He stood transfixed, and he noticed that the red spots dotting Turk's skin began to fade.

Klane took several slow steps back. The magus-Chirr continued their healing psionics. Klane didn't dare twist around to see if the warrior from earlier still watched him. Instead, as if stretching, Klane lifted his aching arms. That hurt. He almost lacked the strength and will to force his puffy joints to move.

He attempted to settle his mind. A plan had been forming during the journey down. He hadn't let himself think about it, lest he give himself away. This was a horrifying world, a nightmare beyond what any man should have to face. He wanted to get back to his body on Jassac. He hated the Kresh, but he loathed and abhorred the Chirr even more. He could half fathom the Kresh. They had enough similarities with men that one could bargain with the other. The Chirr were just too alien, too strange for him.

Klane was going to take what he foresaw as his lone chance for life. He opened himself and began to drink from the seething ball of stored psionic power. Unfortunately, only trickles of psi-energy entered him, no more. Something inhibited him. Klane had an idea what might be wrong. The magus-Chirr circling the pit balanced the psi-power. Their balancing must help keep the power in place. They also kept the psi-power from entering him in any large amount.

The warrior from earlier shoved him, making Klane stagger. But it didn't stop Klane from doing what he'd done before on Jassac. He gave himself strength, even though this time he wasn't able to heal his joints and smother the aches. With the physical strength came the ability to ignore the bodily pain.

Then an idea struck. He couldn't pull the power to him. Maybe he thought of this the wrong way. Instead, he willed a void in his being, and that void he increased in size.

The warrior neared again. Maybe it sensed something wrong. It chirped angrily and raised its pincers.

Klane shuffled toward Turk, guessing the warrior would fear to upset the magus-Chirr. Indeed, the warrior-Chirr hung back, but its pincers jerked as if in agitation.

The master magus glanced at the warrior.

Klane knelt beside Turk. He knelt even as he increased the void in himself, and as more trickles of psionic power siphoned into him. It felt oily and alien, but useable nonetheless.

The magus-Chirr completed their mind weaving. The spots were only vague marks on Turk's skin. The soldier breathed evenly now.

The magus-Chirr circling the pit began chittering loudly amongst themselves. To Klane's ear, they seemed concerned.

The master magus turned toward them.

The interpreter told Klane, "The soldier is healed. Explain how you transferred your consciousness to this body."

Fear and elation battled in Klane. He wondered if the magus-Chirr had to act in unison to use their psionic power. Fear filled him because he would have liked to plan better. He needed more time for this. Yet he knew this was all the time he was going to get. He had to strike now before the Chirr grew aware that they'd clutched a gat to their bosom.

Klane stood over Turk. He built a shield over the soldier and himself, a half-visible telekinetic force that would stop physical objects and mental thought. Then he attempted a technique of psionic ability that the seeker had once spoken to him about: spontaneous combustion.

The others drifted toward the master magus. That allowed the warrior to lunge near Klane. It raised its pincers and chittered a command.

Klane pointed at the warrior. It squealed like a stuck gat. It howled as it burst into a fiery blaze of fire, the base around its body an intense blue color.

Then time seemed to stand still for Klane. The magus-Chirr circling the pit stared at him. The master magus made a high-pitched, twittering sound. The ones holding the buzzing objects opened their mandibles, perhaps in stunned amazement. In the frozen moment and in rapid succession, Klane pointed at various magus-Chirr circling the pit. Like some horrible musical instrument, the squeals increased in number and pitch as one magus after another burst into a flaming blaze.

Whether it was surprise or because too many psi-balancing Chirrs blazed like living torches, a coil from the seething, ghostly ball jagged toward Klane, seeking a place to go. It zigzagged like a slow-moving lightning bolt and thrust into the void in Klane's being as a knife shoves into a scabbard. Klane screamed, and his eyesight wavered and his ears filled with a roaring sound. He'd never felt so much psionic power roiling within him at once. If he lived twenty lifetimes, he could never have attained so much strength. It was beyond human capacity and he glowed so his bones showed through his now translucent skin. Instinct took over, and unconsciously he strengthened his telekinetic shield, which also continued to protect Turk.

In a wavering blur, Klane saw images around him. The master magus raised its thin braches. Around the master chirped smaller magus-Chirr. They tried to counter Klane. Other magi scuttled toward the group, chirping their chants. The seething ball seemed more settled. The coils had submerged into the whole. They had become humps circling the ball at high speed.

Klane screamed his thoughts. Everything seemed distant and surreal. He thrust an arm at the interpreter as it lunged at him. The Chirr squealed, burst into a blaze, and rebounded off the telekinetic barrier Klane had erected.

Fear boiled with the exaltation. Klane realized this wasn't a time for niceties. His new body had spent far too long in the torture cells.

The Chirr had tormented Malik and him for the last time. Now, now was the time for his revenge and for revenge against what the Chirr had done to Turk.

Oily, seething, alien psionic power filled him. Who knew how many generations the Chirr had been adding to the sphere of power? Klane was beyond caring. He screamed in terror at his own daring. He'd endured too much. The torturing Chirr had stung his pride to the depths of his being. And there was too much power in him.

One after another, Chirr burst and exploded into fiery pillars. The floor smoldered and exuded a vile stench. Chirr psi-masters died. The master magus made the tallest blaze. The wave of heat reached the Chirr encircling the sphere of power. They, too, burst into fire. Their squeals were music to Klane's ears.

Now great gouts of psi-power leaped from the sphere and jolted into Klane. He laughed insanely. He howled, and aimed his two arms at an upward angle. Fiery spontaneous combustion like lava poured from his clenched fists. As the sizzling jolts of psionics entered him, they poured into the pillar of superheated plasma. Like a volcano, the force spewed against the asphalt tunnel walls and burned through. Everything in the subsequent chamber exploded into flame. The pillar licking from Klane's arms smashed into the next wall and blew it down. The irresistible fire—powered beyond anything Klane knew—blasted like magma against level after level.

Klane felt like a god, yet he howled in agony. Fires raged in the equatorial jungle nest. Chirr by the tens of thousands, hundreds of thousands, exploded into flame. Imps and bantlings perished. Genetrices shriveled. Warriors, interpreters, workers, and eggs blazed. It was a holocaust. It was disaster. And it came from the heart of the hive. The fiery pillars melted spacecraft alloys and continued to blaze upward. Incredibly, they smashed through to the Kresh-held tunnels, and they finally shot out of the nest's outer shell. The lavalike columns raged into the air like a volcano, as if hell itself spewed its hatred.

The torrent of psionic power from the seething sphere would soon kill him. Klane was incapable of funneling so much pure power through this body. He could not expel it fast enough. So he reversed the void in him. He did it even as the power poured out of his fists. The coils of alien psionics no longer writhed into Klane. Like wounded snakes, they lashed and sizzled into the heated air of the burning hive. In almost the same instant, Klane stopped shooting the fiery pillars out of his clenched fists. Lastly, realizing this was the moment he needed, Klane's consciousness shot out of Timor Malik's body.

He used the teleport capacity then, transporting Timor Malik and Turk to the surface. He couldn't do any more for them. They would have to explain their presence there as best they could.

After that, Klane's consciousness roared out of the equatorial nest and shot heavenward. He reached a Kresh satellite, and the Bo Taw there tried to stop him. As powerful as Klane had become, they didn't have a chance, and three of them screamed in pain, bursting into fire and howling on the floor of the Fenris II satellite.

Klane's consciousness continued to speed into the void, heading back for Jassac and to whatever state in which the Kresh had his body. He believed he could bargain with the Kresh now. He had information he was sure they didn't have. The ambitious Chirr had built a space fleet, and they had stored psionic power such as the Fenris System had never seen.

This was about to get very interesting, indeed.

24

Mentalist Niens paced back and forth before the test subject. He had a decision to make, and it frightened him to the core of his being.

The huge chamber hummed with equipment. Several brown-skinned techs monitored the banks of machines, computers, and reality enhancers. They were a self-contained group and wore dark uniforms with various markings on their shoulder boards. Each of the techs wore a cap, some with one stripe, some with two, and only one with three. That last was the chief technician, and he was the only one who had spoken to Niens.

The machines kept the test subject alive, and they kept the reality field shimmering with electrical and psionic-laced substance.

At a distance, Niens circled the reality field. It was difficult to marshal his thoughts while he stood beside it. Worse, fantasies began to coalesce into reality, or seemed to. He had debated recording the various sequences. Then he had wondered what would happen to him if he were trapped in a "real" fantasy. The recurring imagery had been of exquisitely beautiful pay girls engaging him in his dearest desires. The conversations with them had nearly lulled him. Only at the last minute had he staggered away from the reality field. What had made it worse had been the pay girl pleading with him to make her real.

The reality field confused those under or too near it by creating believable fantasies in a person's mind. It was one of the best ways of nullifying a powerful psionic individual. Those near the field were also shielded from Bo Taw psionic spying.

Niens exhaled sharply. It was clear that Zama Dee had a hunch, or whatever a Kresh called such a thing. The 73rd believed he could achieve a miracle by enticing Klane's consciousness back into his body and then trapping it behind the reality field. If Niens did this thing, she promised to cage him with beautiful pay girls and let him marinate with pleasure for the rest of his life.

There were two problems with that. Firstly, could he trust Zama Dee to keep her word? He believed so, but there was a possibility she lied to him. The second problem was more devious. If the 73rd kept her word, he would be trapped in a hedonistic but potentially dull world. Yes, for a time gluttony and fantastic sex would satiate him. Yet he knew himself: boredom in such a place would drive him mad. The cage would cut him off from new insights and new curiosities. Besides, the episode with Klane had opened new thoughts.

What was the origin of human life in the Fenris System? The idea of an Anointed One led to the conclusion that once, men had been free to think and act for themselves. Was there truth then to the Resister ideas? It hardly seemed conceivable. Yet Zama Dee had called him a nascent Humanity Ultimate. That meant the Kresh would never trust him. He was living on borrowed time with no good options for his future.

Another thing bothered Niens. Klane had shown him mercy. Klane had slain Chengal Ras, but let him live. He owed the test subject his life. It was an odd idea, yet Niens found it strangely compelling.

Did that mean he should consider Resister ideas because they might be his only salvation?

He glanced about the chamber as fear compelled him to drown the thought. Was he insane? The Resisters lacked the strength to challenge the Kresh. And yet, Klane had slain Chengal Ras. What would happen if Klane's consciousness returned to his body? Was it conceivable the Anointed One could achieve a Humanity Ultimate miracle?

Niens didn't see how. But in the interests of self-preservation and more than idle curiosity, he wanted to know.

Very well. *How do I entice Klane's consciousness to return? Can it return and pass through the reality field? If not, then why do we still have it up?*

Clasping his long-fingered hands behind his back, Niens began to pace around the reality field and the test subject underneath it. Niens had been reading the data the 73rd had left behind for him. For the most part, it was Resister literature. It was mainly about a psionic savior helping to free humanity from the scourge of the Kresh. It other words, it was Humanity Ultimate heresy.

Why didn't Zama Dee simply firebomb the game-preserve primitives and destroy the test subject, Klane? Niens had a theory about that, and he knew he was right because it was his own problem. The Kresh had a curiosity failing. They wanted knowledge. To gain new knowledge they would go to just about any length and risk any danger. New knowledge had the potential to give the Kresh insights that would help them gain codex points. If they could increase the *Codex of All Knowledge* . . .

Niens nodded somberly. In his opinion, Zama Dee hadn't destroyed Klane because she saw a benefit to herself through him. She wanted to know how Klane had evolved such psi-powers. Yet the Kresh rightly feared the man.

Tapping a middle finger against the palm of the other hand, all while keeping them behind his back, Niens continued to pace. Zama Dee had given him this task because of his curiosity and cleverness. Given that, he should attempt experiments that a regular, staid mentalist would avoid.

He would do so for three reasons. The first was to continue his existence a little longer. The second reason was his desire for knowledge.

He needed to know. The last reason was self-preservation. He was beginning to believe the Resisters had a point. He didn't know how it could be that they could successfully challenge the Kresh, but it seemed to him he ultimately had no other reasonable option. He needed a miracle in order to survive more than a few extra weeks. By naming him a Humanity Ultimate, the 73rd had pushed him into a corner.

Niens now turned toward the fuzzy field. He had to do something radical.

Mentalist Niens cleared his throat in an authoritative manner. Reluctantly, it seemed, the chief tech faced him, although keeping his gaze downcast.

"Lower the reality field," Niens said, crisply.

The chief technician looked up. The man had dots for eyes and leathery features, with lines around his mouth. "That would be against regulations," he said.

"You surprise me," Niens told him. "I have full authority over the test subject."

"I hesitate to correct you."

"Then don't," Niens said. "Get on with your task."

"But you lack anything approaching full authority. For instance, you cannot order me to move the test subject."

"I have authority to turn the reality field on or off. Check if you must, but be quick about it."

The chief tech pulled at the bill of his cap. "Very well, if you insist." The man palmed a small device. He read the tiny screen while clicking it with his thumb. At last, his head darted up.

"I beg your pardon, mentalist," the chief tech said. "I will turn off the field."

"You will remain at your stations ready to snap the reality field back into existence."

"I will remain. But may I point out that one doesn't *snap* such a field on and off. It takes time to calibrate and—"

"I'm not interested in the technical side of your equipment." Niens knew the limitations of the reality field. He didn't want the others to know that he knew, though. "You will keep the machines in prime readiness as I . . . you will remain ready."

"Yes, mentalist," the chief tech said.

"Good," Niens said. "Now begin."

The chief tech hurried to his fellows.

Niens faced the test subject. What had happened to the consciousness? The Kresh's data hadn't given any suggestions. How could a consciousness survive without its body? It was very interesting.

Keep thinking about that instead of—I love the Kresh. I love them with all my heart.

He didn't know how, but he had to survive long enough to bring Klane back and win himself extended life.

25

Cyrus lay in the seeker's tent, surrounded by the strange junction-stones. He had just come back from the funeral, and he couldn't stand his own company. He wanted to get drunk or high, do something other than think about his failure.

He'd told the seeker he would anchor her. She'd known he would fail. She'd tried to soften the blow, in fact. That only made it worse.

"I killed her," he said. "It was my insistence."

The tent flap drew back, and Jana bent down, stepping within.

Cyrus closed his eyes. He didn't want to see or speak to anyone. He had failed. He was forsworn.

"It's time," she said.

He exhaled, sat up abruptly, and regarded her. Jana had changed. There was a new awareness in her. She didn't smile as much, and she looked at him differently.

"Time for what?" he said.

"To leave," she said. "The rest of the clan has grown wary of us, and they hate you."

"They should," he said.

Jana frowned. "You told us what happened—"

"Bah," he said, looking away.

"The seeker is dead," Jana said. "By sacrificing her life she gave us knowledge. Yesterday I was a Stone Age tribesman. Now—I don't know who I am."

He hadn't thought of that. He'd been so absorbed with his failure he hadn't thought about her. "How are you feeling?" he asked.

Jana shook her head.

He wanted to ask her if she was still willing to be his wife, but this didn't seem like the time. *What's wrong with me?* This faintheartedness wasn't like him. He was the man from the slums. He'd killed as a kid. He'd done it without mercy. So why should he become soft all of a sudden?

His eyes widened.

"What is it?" Jana asked.

Had some of the seeker's memories or personality transferred to him last night? Had they lodged in him? Did he now carry some of the seeker? Those seemed like crazy questions at a time like this. He regarded Jana. Maybe she didn't smile as she used to because similar questions rattled around inside her head. He should be helping the eight, not moping around. He was a knife man, a killer. He—

"I'm the Tracker," Cyrus told her.

Jana smiled, and it made her seem like the woman he'd asked to marry. He stepped beside her and took one of her hands. Then he leaned over and kissed her on the lips.

"It took you long enough," she said.

"Yeah, I've been busy thinking."

"So have I."

"We'll talk about it later," he said. "Tell them I'm coming. I want to look around in here, see what we can use."

"Maybe I should do that. I have her memories and will know what will come in handy."

"Good thinking," he said. He stepped outside.

Clan members quit talking and quit moving. Everyone stared at him. A warning crawled up and down his spine. They wanted to kill him. He was evil in their eyes. He couldn't blame them for thinking that, either. They still thought like primitives, and now some of their best people had become strangers and were heading off on an impossible quest to slay the demons in the valley.

Cyrus knew better than to hurry. Running or moving fast only encouraged primitives to give chase like dogs. He put a sneer on his lips, one that he'd used in Bottom Milan many times. With the sneer, he reached the other end of the tents. Then he saw Grinder, and he hailed the man.

Grinder scowled and hesitated, but finally he motioned with a thick arm. When Cyrus reached him, the man said, "I still think you're a bastard for gunning down Stone Fist. Now that I know more . . . I see it was—"

"The only thing I could have done to survive," Cyrus said. "It wasn't fair, but neither were the five-to-two odds coming against us."

Grinder didn't say anything more. He took Cyrus to where Yang and the others fashioned bows. So far there had never been any bows and arrows on the uplands of Jassac. There had been only knives, spears, and shields. Bows against blasters weren't good, but at least bows were better as ranged weapons than hurled spears.

The ten of them worked hard on the implements. As they worked, Cyrus began to explain about space marines and their tactics. Skar added information concerning Vomag practices. The others asked plenty of questions. It reminded Cyrus of his time among *Discovery*'s marines during the journey to the Fenris System. He wondered how many of the marines were still alive on High Station 3. Would he ever see them again?

Jana joined them later. She handed Cyrus a leather bag. Whatever it held rattled.

"Junction-stones," she whispered.

"I'm not sure I want those along," he whispered back.

"You're the only one with psionics who can handle them with any degree of safety," she said.

"You're not calling it magic anymore, are you?"

"Psionics," she said. "I know what's going on. Maybe Klane will want them."

"Okay . . ." he said, reluctantly. "I hadn't thought of that."

After everyone had fashioned at least ten arrows with fire-hardened tips, Yang suggested they leave.

"The rest of the clan is getting antsy," Yang told them. "If we stay too long, they might decide we're possessed and try to stone us."

Cyrus wanted to ask the others about the transfer. Memories—the seeker had given each of them several lifetimes' worth of memories. What was it like to go from being primitive one minute to high-tech the next? Maybe a little bit like what he'd gone through when he'd gone from Bottom Milan to the institute at Crete.

An hour later, they left the last trees behind, skinny, twisted things with shriveled leaves. Yang led them, moving onto what seemed like a trackless red desert full of half-buried boulders. The former hetman broke into a trot, one that Cyrus had learned a Berserker could hold mile after mile after mile.

Cyrus followed Skar, breathing the thin air, knowing he'd have trouble keeping the stiff pace. Even so, it felt good to be on the move again. Yeah, the guilt still haunted him. He wished he could have saved the seeker. But she'd had no illusions about what she'd been doing. Jana had spoken to him, explaining how the seeker had realized and been glad that this was the long-sought day when humans could finally turn the tables on the aliens.

As he thought about that, a sad grin spread across Cyrus's face. Including Skar and him, ten puny humans crossed a desert on foot. They were off to challenge a star system filled with space-faring aliens. It was crazy. It was a holo-vid drama come to life, and it was the stuff of legends like Spartacus.

As he ran, breathing deeply to get all the air he could, Cyrus recalled waking up inside a Kresh spaceship that first time. It had been after the lost space battle. The Vomags had kicked Captain Nagasaki to death and everything had felt hopeless then. But maybe as long as men and women had breath in their bodies, they had a chance to turn things around. This was payback—he hoped.

Before evening fell, Yang called a halt. Grinder dug with a stone, finding water. Cyrus and Jana strained the water through a special cloth, filling up everyone's canteen. Skar and Yang brought back three long-eared pas. The fresh meat would supplement their jerky.

"It's time we started thinking about our actual strategy," Cyrus said later. The stars had begun to appear and it would be fully dark soon. "Originally, Skar and I thought about boarding a rocket, one of those massive things that brings the ice down to the convertor."

"What would you have done then?" Yang asked.

"Try to storm an ice-hauler ship up there," Cyrus said, while looking at Skar.

"It was a long shot," Skar said.

"What do you call what we're attempting?" Yang asked.

The soldier sat on the ground with his knees raised. Like a robot, he turned toward Yang. "This is suicide," Skar said.

"No, seriously," Yang said.

"I am always serious," Skar said.

Cyrus glanced at his soldier friend. "Do you care to explain why you think it's suicide?"

"Before, you and I were going to attack ice haulers," Skar said. "All of us here are talking about taking on soldiers like me. For there will be soldiers in the valley. And *that* will be suicide."

The Berserkers stared at Skar before they glanced at each other.

Cyrus knew the soldier better than the others did, and he'd seen Skar's wink. He finally burst out laughing.

"What is funny?" Yang asked. "We are dead men, and one dead woman."

"Don't you know when a fellow marine is pulling your leg?" Cyrus asked.

"I thought you said you were serious," Yang told Skar.

"I did say that," Skar said.

"And?"

A tight grin spread across Skar's face. It was one of the first Cyrus had seen.

Jana scooped up sand and hurled it at Skar.

Yang stared at her in wonder, and then the realization must have sunk in. He didn't chuckle, but a grim smile appeared before disappearing.

"I will remember that," Yang told Skar.

"Just as I remember the beating I first received at Berserker hands," Skar said.

"This is not a game," Grinder told them. "This is a war of extinction, either theirs or ours."

The word sounded strange coming out of Grinder's mouth, but Cyrus knew the man was right. The word also showed him how much the former primitives had changed.

"I have a question," Cyrus said. "It's for any of you who can remember. Did the seeker know, or did any of those before her know, what Klane or the Anointed One was supposed to be able to do to throw off the Kresh yoke?"

"No," Jana said.

"How can you say that with such certainty?" Yang asked. "The seeker's thoughts or memories . . . I still have trouble with them. It's like a second voice in my head. But if I listen too closely, I lose the train of thought."

"Maybe because she was a woman, her thoughts soaked more easily into me," Jana said.

Yang pursed his lips, soon nodding in agreement.

They spoke awhile longer, agreeing their first priority was to gain modern weapons. Skar had received his Vomag pistol back. It had one clip left, twelve pellets. Grinder had gotten hold of the heat gun, and it had three shots, maybe four, left. If they found a source, they could recharge the gun.

"We have to get to the valley and ambush someone bearing arms," Yang said. "It's a risky plan, and even riskier entering the demon—the Kresh city."

"We'll have to wear disguises," Jana said. "I have a memory of a seeker long ago passing through the city."

That was something Cyrus found interesting. They didn't all seem to have the same memories, as if the seeker had parceled them out.

"Why don't we ambush a floater like the three of you once did?" Grinder suggested. "Then we could swoop down in it in a surprise raid."

"If the opportunity arises or we're forced into it, possibly," Yang said. "For now, we must sleep, and trek hard and far tomorrow. We must let our new memories soak into us. Then, as we close upon the valley, we will understand better and be able to formulate a cunning strategy for freeing Klane."

Jana had told them about the seeker's urgency. She didn't have any clairvoyant memories, but she felt they should go as fast as they could.

"Now is the time," Jana said.

"Yes," Yang agreed, as he slapped his leg. "After all these years, these decades, now is the time to free our world of the Kresh."

26

Klane's baffled consciousness had left Jassac far behind. He'd attempted to reenter his inert form lying on a mentalist table. Something had hindered him from reaching his body, his mind and ego citadel. Angry and afraid, he'd leaped away in the opposite direction from before. This time he went out-system instead of in.

His consciousness roamed past the outer asteroid belt with its lonely ice-hauler teams attaching rockets to dirty snowballs. Once, there had been a silvery Bo Taw station out here, radiating thought waves into interstellar space. Klane's consciousness didn't even notice the wreckage created by *Discovery*'s heavy beams several months ago. His consciousness flashed toward a distant point an unimaginable distance—light years—away. Even at the speed of thought, it took time to cross.

Loneliness filled him, a sense of futility. Would he ever return to his body? Would he smell again, taste, touch . . . or hear? He longed for those things. The sense of disembodied wrongness grew stronger and harder to bear the farther he traveled. He recalled the savage destruction of the hive, and he wanted to smile and laugh about it. He hated the Chirr. Nothing in existence was worse than them. The Kresh should develop planet busters and use them on Fenris II and III. Annihilate the Chirr. Kill the insects. Without the Kresh, the Chirr would have likely long ago sent sub-light-speed craft to humanity's home system and demolished every living thing there.

The beacon he'd been traveling toward now splintered into several distinct points. Vaguely, Klane was aware he must have voyaged twenty or thirty light years.

The distinct points turned into five vast spaceships. They could have been minimoons or large asteroids, but each was a metallic spheroid. Each pulsed with interior life. Messages zipped between vessels. He sensed limited psionics among them. The strongest sensation came from the last ship, and within it burned the brightest point of all.

It was another compatible mind, although there was something highly regimented about it. Klane hesitated. He didn't want to go through another hive experience. Should he turn around and try to reenter his body again? What if he couldn't break in? What if the strength of his consciousness weakened after prolonged traveling? He had to make a decision.

A moment later Klane's consciousness moved through the last craft's metallic skin. It sped past machinelike humans with biological brains. Klane noticed, wondering about them, and then his consciousness fell toward the compatible mind.

He saw it for a moment, and he knew greater fear than ever. He received psionic data concerning a thing boasting the name of Prime Web-Mind of the Fleet. It was a complex cyborg, a thing or meld of man and machine. There were rows and rows of clear biodomes. In the dozens upon dozens of domes were sheets of brain mass, many thousands of kilos of brain cells from as many unwilling donors from a war fought over one hundred years ago.

Green computing gel surrounded the pink-white mass. Cables, biotubes, and tight-beam links connected the endless domes to computers and life-support systems. The combination made a seething whole. It was an empire of mind. The biotubes gurgled as warm liquids pulsed through them. Backup computers made whirring sounds as lights indicated ten thousand things.

Then Klane's consciousness entered a section of brain mass. He expected to breath, smell, see, and hear again. Instead, a strange, bewildering complex of thoughts drowned him in an avalanche of me, me, me, me.

"Attention, attention."

"What?" Klane asked.

He didn't articulate anything more. Chemicals sprayed his brain mass, his particular dome. It drugged him, made his thoughts sluggish.

Despite that, waves of data flowed through him. The Prime Web-Mind—the combination of the many biodomes—felt fear and tried to soothe itself. By degrees, and due to demanding interrogation, Klane released information. He didn't do so with words or with psionic thoughts. He communicated with chemical and neurological reactions, a vast and mighty brain—perhaps the mightiest in the universe—that had an interior split personality.

By degrees, Klane divested himself of the hive experience to the greater Prime.

There are other life forms in the Fenris System, more than just the dinosaur aliens?

Sluggishly, Klane assured the Prime Web-Mind that was so. There were the Kresh, the Chirr, and humans—

Warning! Warning! Are you depicting solar system humans?

Yes. My ancestors originated in the solar system.

Klane received his greatest download of data yet, as the Prime knew panic. The solar-wide war over one hundred years ago between the Social Unity Party, the Highborn, and the cyborgs replayed at fantastic speed. Klane learned about Marten Kluge, Neptune, and the last desperate days of the cyborgs. One cyborg starship had escaped destruction, limping into the galaxy and painfully rebuilding these last one hundred years in a new system.

The Prime Web-Mind had begun as a backup to the original

Prime of Neptune, and attempted to learn from the old one's mistakes. The new cyborg empire had found a dead system forty light years from Fenris. There, the cyborgs had built automated factories and thousands of robots. Slowly, the automated factories built new ones, more and more and more. In the last ten years, the vastly increased Prime received telemetry data from probes launched eighty years earlier at the Fenris System.

The first raid into the Fenris System had shown the empire much. This was the second attack. The Cyborg Empire needed biomaterial, hundreds of thousands of tons of brain tissue. The Prime Web-Mind dreamed of conquering the solar system and creating the greatest political unit in existence.

Why must you grow? Klane managed to ask.

Expand! That is the only true directive.

Klane struggled to understand. According to the Prime, these five vessels could have destroyed the original Doom Stars, whatever they were. These five warships were the ultimate in design and destructiveness.

Open yourself, the Prime said. *Do not resist the data intake.*

Klane resisted as more chemicals and neuron charges attempted to tame the biomatter he inhabited. Once he took over a brain, he was affected by "material" attacks. A wealth of information smashed down on him now. The cyborgs would rip men and women, Kresh and Chirr, anything with brain tissue, putting the biomatter into layered mats and then inserting that into robotic bodies. Many humans, Vomags, Bo Taw, Tash-Toi—it didn't matter—would enter conveyor systems. Spines, nervous systems, and brains would be torn from flesh and married to plastics and metal, creating fighting cyborgs, throw-away assault troops as the melded society grew exponentially with each conquest. Alien concepts—stealth campaigns, Lurkers, webbies—flooded Klane, bewildering him anew.

What are you? the Prime demanded to know. *How did you arrive into one of my biodomes? Is a Kresh war fleet near our position?*

Klane struggled to hide his knowledge, but he failed miserably.

What are psionics? the Prime asked. *You must explain the concept in detail so I can develop a countermeasure.*

The horror of his new existence gave Klane a last measure of strength. He thrashed about in his new mind. He raved and called upon the old seeker. He sought aid from the singing gods. And there came to him a distant siren sound.

What occurs? I do not understand this. Explain to me—

It was the last piece of coherent thought Klane heard from the Prime Web-Mind. Klane's consciousness ripped free of the biodome. He had a microsecond's flash of vision as massive machines rolled toward his dome. He suspected the Prime attacked him.

The suspicion became reality as the machines beamed the biodome he had resided within.

I want to go home, Klane told himself. *I want to get back into my body.*

His consciousness felt considerably weaker than earlier. There was a weariness of mind, of thought. He couldn't stay here, though. Other bright points appeared in the various ships. They were the minds closest in nature to his. If he remained with the cyborg fleet, which made ready to telejump, he would fall back within another mind.

Gathering his last shreds of resolve, Klane's consciousness began the long trek back to the Fenris System. It was a lone star over thirty light years away. There were closer star systems, but he ignored those, fixating on the planet where his body lay. He had to get back to his flesh before his consciousness dissipated. Yes. He realized that drinking the Chirr psionic force had given him greater mental strength. But that was dwindling rapidly. This was going to be a race, one for his life.

27

Niens stood before a large screen several chambers over from the test subject. He stood with his gaze cast down before the radiance of Zama Dee the 73rd. The Revered One called from High Station 3. Because of the distance, there was a short time delay.

"You have dropped the reality field?" Zama Dee asked, moving her predatory jaws as she spoke.

"I have, Revered One."

"Was there a response from the test subject?"

"Not to date, Revered One."

"Are you ready to raise the field?"

"At a moment's notice, Revered One."

The skin flaps on Zama Dee's crocodilian snout drew back, revealing her blue-pink gums. "You are a mentalist. That means you are the most intelligent of humans. I demand more than these terse answers."

"Forgive me, please, Revered One. I . . . find my situation precarious and it occupies too much of my mental energies."

"Yes, yes, I much prefer to see your deviousness on display as you're attempting now. It settles my mind into believing you aren't hatching some subtle and ultimately foolish design."

I love the Kresh. I love the Revered Ones, the masters of my life.

"I have called for a variety of reasons," Zama Dee said. "The Teleship crew from Earth . . ."

Niens sensed Zama Dee lashing her tail, and it frightened him.

"After seeing them and listening to a data stream from Earth, I have changed my estimation of the test subject," the 73rd said. "He is highly dangerous and volatile. The Resisters I've helped interrogate . . . Klane must never leave that chamber alive."

Niens dared glance up. He'd never heard of any Kresh admitting to the slightest fear regarding humans before. It was unthinkable. Hope flared in his breast because of it. Perhaps he'd chosen wisely to aid—

I love the Kresh. They are my masters.

With a dry mouth and while mentally reciting the love litany, Niens asked, "Should I kill the test subject now?"

The 73rd became rigid, and her reptilian eyes gleamed with malice. "On no account are you to terminate the test subject unless there is a danger of his bodily escape from the premises. If he does escape, you may rest assured that you will perish in a grisly manner for many to witness."

Niens bowed his head. *I love the Kresh. I love the Kresh. I deserve whatever happens to me.*

"I have further orders," Zama Dee said. "You must not allow the test subject to speak. According to High Station 3 Resister belief, he is the Anointed One. As you know, I have been trying to verify that for some time. If he is this legendary one, he will possess a golden tongue along with Herculean strength."

"Revered One, I feel that I must inform you that I am not familiar with the last adjective."

"I, too, found it unusual. Study has revealed that it relates to an old Earth mythos. Hercules was the son of the gods, half man and half god. He delivered his people from several misfortunes by applying his great strength."

"The test subject will possess such physical power?" Niens asked.

"As to that I cannot attest. The Resisters believe so. There are clairvoyants among them who have had many precognitive dreams.

Do all such dreams occur? That is my current area of study. To date, I have found that it depends upon the clairvoyant.

"Mentalist Niens, you have performed as I expected. It gives me greater trust in your predictability and therefore your reliability."

"You honor me, Revered One," he said.

"No, I most certainly do not. In fact, such words from you trouble me. For it shows you still think deviously. I am logical, among the most logical of the Hundred. I hold to facts, data, observable reality."

"I stand corrected, Revered One."

In silence, Zama Dee regarded him. Finally, the Kresh said, "That is all. Continue with your duties."

Shaken, Niens left the communications chamber and returned to the reality field room. Klane still lay as before, an inert mass of flesh, barely breathing and without brain rhythms. From time to time, they had to turn on the reality field. Otherwise, the body, the husk, began to expire.

Niens tapped his chin. The 73rd had let slip amazing data. The Kresh-taught people could not live without someone in authority over them. Who would force the pay girls to their tasks? Why wouldn't the Bo Taw simply take over, since no one could stop them from using their psi-powers with impunity? Yet apparently, people could run their own lives. The 73rd had admitted to seeing the Earth crew. The solar system foundation theory must have a basis in reality after all. It would seem that humanity hadn't always served the Kresh, but had originated two hundred and thirty light years away. That meant his goal of freedom had an actual basis in reality.

"Mentalist," a technician said.

Niens looked up in surprise. The techs usually avoided speaking or looking at him as religiously as their chief did. What could the man want?

The tech trembled and his lips quivered. Slowly, the tech raised his arm, pointing a single finger with a black tip at Niens.

What was the meaning of such indignity? Niens scowled. He would—

A scrap of noise behind him changed the contours of Niens's frown. The only thing at his back was the inert mass of flesh: the test subject.

"H-he's moving, mentalist," the tech stammered. "I-I think his brain waves have begun again."

Niens whirled around. The test subject's left foot looked as if it was in a new position. Then the right-hand fingers twitched.

"Turn on the reality field!" a different tech screamed. "He's back! The test subject's consciousness has returned!"

Three techs were in the room. The one nearest Niens raised a brown-skinned hand, moving it toward a red-colored switch. With a rustle of cloth and a thud, the tech collapsed onto the floor and lay still.

The second tech hurried toward the switch, tripped, and dashed his head against a console. He hammered onto the floor, unconscious, as blood began to pool around the ugly gash.

From the raised level behind Niens, Klane began to groan.

This was the moment to act. Yet Niens didn't know what to do.

Klane sat up. His eyes were lucid. He gritted his teeth and clenched his fists. It appeared as if he battled someone mentally. Of course, Niens realized—psionic Bo Taw had been watching the chamber. They must be attacking Klane with psi-power from the other rooms.

Niens witnessed the same grim determination as before, when Klane had slain Chengal Ras. Bowing his head, trying to remain invisible, Niens backed away. He still watched, though. Intense curiosity compelled him. Their gazes met.

Who are you? The question appeared in his mind.

"I-I'm Mentalist Niens," he stammered.

Why am I lying here?

Help me hold him.

Niens frowned, confused. Then he realized he must have heard a Bo Taw's thoughts, one of those battling the possible Anointed One.

Klane snarled, and his knuckles whitened, indicating a fierce clenching of his fists.

Niens heard a psionic scream. He pictured in his mind a Bo Taw bleeding from the eyes, nose, and ears and slumping backward.

From the raised platform, Klane chuckled. He pointed at Niens. "You'd better answer me, or I'll do the same thing to you. Why am I lying here?"

The man's cold eyes terrified Niens. "I'm your friend," he said.

"You're a liar," Klane said. "And since you won't answer me, prepare to die."

Niens realized he didn't have time to convince the man to spare him. So he spun on his heel and sprinted to the machines. The last technician there tried to slap the red button. The tech's eyes crossed and he groaned, clutching his head before falling and expiring on the floor.

Now it's your turn, Niens.

As the first tendrils of psionic-induced pain touched Niens's brain, another team of Bo Taw invisibly hit Klane. It gave Niens a precious few extra seconds. He reached the switch and stabbed it, hard. The leads above the table and above Klane glowed blue, pink, and then deeply red. A reality field sizzled into place. It shimmered and flickered uncontrollably because there wasn't anyone left to calibrate it properly.

Niens watched in horror, waiting for the end. Alarms rang and a door opened. Technicians raced in, among them the chief. The reality field flickered worse than before, and it might have gone down. The chief tech reached the controls in time, and he acted swiftly, calibrating the field, solidifying it.

Niens watched, and to his amazement, he saw the test subject lie down, beginning to dream while wide-awake. Klane's consciousness had returned, and he—Niens—had captured the Anointed One for Zama Dee.

Had he just foiled humanity's lone chance for freedom? And had he just cursed himself to a lifetime in a cage as boredom drove him to madness?

|||||||||

Niens paced before the shimmering reality field and the prone test subject beneath. On the other side of him, the technicians silently went about their work. The techs treated the machines as if they were gods, and the men the acolytes.

Maybe they operated out of fear. Zama Dee had given explicit instructions concerning Klane. Bo Taw waited behind hidden alcoves, ready to dampen any psi-breakouts. Vomag guards prowled outside the building on the main floor.

The 73rd would soon be in Jassac orbit. She returned from High Station 3, first traveling at maximum thrust from there and then slowing with hard retrofire.

Furrows appeared in Niens's forehead. Twice the door had opened and a Kresh had peered within. Clearly, Klane had the Revered Ones agitated.

Niens licked his lips and sidled closer to the reality field. Klane had shown him mercy once, although the man had tried to kill him this last time. The power Klane had shown and the fear he brought to the Kresh—this was amazing. It seemed conceivable he really was the Anointed One.

That meant there was a chance for freedom. It was time to take risks.

A premonition touched Niens—Bo Taw psionic intrusion. It was like a feather in his mind. *I love the Kresh. I love the Kresh. They give our lives meaning.* Without the Revered Ones, humanity would boil into fevered madness. Men and women—

If we're such illogical beings, why did Earthlings build the first starship instead of the Kresh doing so?

A thrill of pure terror shot through Niens's chest. He shouldn't dabble with such chaotic thoughts, not here in range of the mind readers. Vomags might enter the chamber under the guidance of a Revered One. If the Kresh knew what he really felt, the soldiers would shoot him for being a madman.

Because of his fear of the Bo Taw, Niens shifted his position even closer to the reality field. The feathery feeling departed from his mind. The shimmering thing before him was like a psi-tent, shielding him from intruding probes.

His eyelids began to flicker, and he found that odd. *I'm too close to the reality field. I should back up.* He didn't, though. Instead, he watched a pay girl wearing sequins on her pert breasts coalesce into existence. She swayed in an erotic way and made pouting motions with her lips.

"I love you, Mentalist Niens," she said in a soft voice. "You're so strong and virile and so very smart."

He grinned, and her existence solidified for him. In his subjective view, the chamber lost reality as she became more real.

"I am smart, aren't I?" he asked her.

She nodded in an alluring manner. Then she twirled on her toes for him, letting him see her marvelous buttocks.

Despite her beauty, Niens's fear of the Kresh radiated through the fantasy. He combined the two. "I must use my superior intellect," Niens told her.

"And you must use other things, too," she said, glancing meaningfully at his crotch.

"Yes, yes," Niens said. "I'm not thinking clearly enough." He could use his fantasy—this pay girl—and possibly speak with Klane. He snapped his fingers at her. "I have an idea."

She ran her tongue over painted lips. "So do I, darling Niens."

His eyes shone with lust. This was the loveliest pay girl he'd ever seen. He wanted to disrobe, to make her strip and do things—he shook his head. *Focus, Niens, this might be your last chance to affect your destiny.*

"You're finally ready for me," the pay girl said with a titter.

"Never mind that for now," Niens said. It would appear that all minds were schizophrenic. He was battling himself in a way. "I want you to do something for me." It was a wild idea, but he didn't see why this shouldn't work.

"Of course," she said.

"It's not what you think. You must cross the reality field and talk to Klane."

Something like fear appeared on her features. "I don't think I can do that, darling."

"Yes, you can," he said, wondering if he was battling self-doubt. "You're a figment of my imagination. I power you."

The pay girl began to fade.

"No," Niens said, concentrating on her, believing in her existence.

She solidified, and she glanced at her body in surprise.

"Cross this barrier," Niens said. "I want you to talk to Klane. Tell him he's under a reality field, held in the . . . in the demon city."

"Don't you want to mount me?" she asked with a pout. "We can make wonderful love together."

"Of course I do," he said. "You're the perfect figment, the perfect ideal of what I want to—listen to me. Quit trying to confuse the issue."

"Cross the field?" she asked.

"And talk to Klane."

"You're the one who will do the talking," she said, beginning to sound more serious.

"Don't talk to me. Talk to Klane and give him the message."

"Where will you be, darling?"

Niens laughed nervously. It was bizarre having this schizophrenic conversation with himself. It felt like he was talking to someone else. The reality field was a fascinating invention. "I imagine I'll have to stay right here and continue to power you, to think you into existence. Now, hurry. I don't know how long they'll let me stand here."

She nodded, and she smiled nervously. She turned to go, paused, and glanced over her shoulder, showing off her triangular chin to great effect. "I just want to let you know that you're the bravest man I know. There is no one like you, Mentalist Niens."

"That's true," he said. "And it shows your wisdom that you understand that. Now, go, please."

She nodded, resolutely faced the shimmering field, and slowly sashayed into it.

28

The stars shone brightly as Cyrus and Jana crawled to the edge of the mighty canyon. In the distance, the giant atmospheric convertor churned water vapor into the night sky.

Two days and nights of stiff trekking had brought the avengers across the uplands to the edge of the Valley of the Demons. Three times during the journey, they'd spotted sky vehicles and taken precautions. No one really wanted to try Grinder's suggestion of fooling an alien crew and attempting to kill the Kresh occupants. Skar had been lucky the first time. The soldier didn't want to rely upon luck a second time.

"We are soldiers," Skar had told the others.

"Space marines," Cyrus had whispered under his breath.

After several days of hard traveling, the avengers had finally reached the jumping-off point. Tomorrow morning at dawn, they would begin the descent. Tonight, Cyrus and Jana peered into the depths. The alien city's lights shone far below. It reminded Cyrus of Earth and made him nostalgic.

"Crazy," he said.

Jana turned to him. "What do you find crazy?"

"Actually," he said, "a couple of things."

"For instance?"

"It's crazy that two distinct groups of humans hundreds of years apart left Earth and took off toward the same place, a destination two hundred and thirty light years away. I mean, how did your ancestors' original vessel manage to make it to *this* star system? That seems more than a little coincidental. The odds aren't in our favor that *both* voyages took place by chance."

"Do you mean the Creator caused it?" Jana asked.

"I suppose that's one explanation, but that isn't what I meant. No, I'm thinking along different lines, more nefarious reasons."

"Aliens?" she asked.

"That's right, nonhuman intelligences causing or helping our various ships to head here."

"You can't mean the Kresh," she said. "According to you, they don't possess psionic abilities."

"True," Cyrus said. "But they had a station on the outer asteroids that gave us a false picture of Fenris. It showed us a pristine star system, ready for humanity to exploit. It was the most idyllic, perfect image we could get. Does that make sense?"

"Hmm," she said.

"And your ancestors' leader, the original guy, Attlee, I think the Reacher told me. Why did he see the Fenris System? I bet there are other, closer Earth-like planets. Yet he brought you all the way out here to the Kresh and the Chirr."

"By your earlier tales," she said, "it would seem the cyborgs made it in this general region as well."

"Say, that's right," Cyrus said. "What's going on, do you think? What's the game?"

"I don't follow you," Jana said.

"I'm suspicious of coincidences, especially these," he said.

"Does that change anything about what we should do?"

Cyrus thought about that. "I guess not. It's just that I don't like being led around by my nose. I don't like prophecies, either, which say certain events have to happen. I mean, do we have free will or not?"

"The seeker chose to die so we eight of Berserker Clan could have knowledge."

"Did she choose?" Cyrus asked. "I think she felt compelled to go along with the planned program, with the so-called prophesies."

"That's good, though," Jana said. "The prophesies foretell of our ultimate victory."

Cyrus snorted. "I wouldn't count on winning. Including Skar and me, we're ten . . . outcasts planning to rescue the Fenris System's savior. Ten against thousands are bad odds, my love."

"But better than doing nothing."

"True," Cyrus said.

They peered into the canyon depths. It was a long way down. It was going to be a hard trek to reach the Kresh lights.

"Cyrus?"

"Hmm?" he said.

"Would you have been happy with me if I hadn't received these memories?"

"What do you mean?"

"I was a primitive."

He shrugged. "You were smart. You just hadn't gotten a technological education yet. I used to be in the same boat." He smiled at her. "That's the long answer. The short one is, of course I would have. You're the same Jana."

She'd been watching him closely. "No. I have different memories. We all have them. Well, not exactly. I think you were right the other day when you speculated that each of us received a portion of the seeker's recollections. We each recall different things. My point is that I no longer think like Jana did."

"I'm not sure you're right," he said.

"I am," she said. "You know I'm right."

"Okay. So who are you then?"

"I'm still trying to figure that out," she said in a soft tone.

Cyrus sidled closer. "No. I don't believe that. You're the same Jana, but with more experiences. This isn't like primitive spirit possession. I'm still the Cyrus of the slums, of Bottom Milan. I react with more knowledge most of the time, but it's still me inside here." He tapped his heart. "And it's still you," he said, tapping her heart and ending up by squeezing her right breast.

They embraced, and for a time they kissed.

"Do you love me?" Jana whispered.

He almost told her that he'd already said he did some time ago. When he changed his mind, he would let her know. But that didn't seem like the response she was looking for.

"I love you, Jana, whatever your memories." He kissed her long and lingeringly for emphasis, tasting a hint of salt on her lips.

"Do you still want to marry me?" she asked in a small voice.

"With all my heart," he said.

"When?"

He let go of her and searched her eyes. "Earth customs say that a captain of a ship can marry people. Once we get a spaceship, I'll have the captain marry us. Does that sound good?"

She smiled and hugged him fiercely.

Cyrus breathed deeply afterward. He didn't know what the next few days were going to bring. Probably pain and suffering, maybe death. He knew, though, that he would protect Jana with everything he had. It would be heartrending to lose her now. He was going to make sure he didn't fail her as he'd failed the seeker. That he vowed.

29

Klane frowned and he didn't know why. He recalled something about a hive, and then there had been cyborgs. Yes . . . the cyborgs came in five mighty vessels, heading toward the Fenris System. He tried to concentrate on that because it felt as if he was missing something. A fuzzy dome sizzled above him, and . . . and . . .

His thoughts slowly turned and everything shifted. He was young again. No. What was he thinking? He'd never been old. Clan Tash-Toi gathered at the Red Rock Jumbles. They were reddish boulders piled beside a shale-littered rock formation. Klane examined himself, surprised to see six-year-old limbs.

This happened to me. It's not happening now. Yet it seemed very much to be occurring in real time.

The hetman and several warriors had left a day ago in search of meat. The seeker had cast into the future and foretold about bad omens. At six years of age, Klane toiled for the crafty seeker with his ill-smelling breath. He didn't want to be an apprentice. Klane yearned to be a warrior, carrying a spear into battle and wielding a sharp knife.

It seemed as if he remembered one of the worst days of his life. Yet this felt as if it happened right now. He could feel the cool breeze on his skin. He was always colder than the others were, and had to wear thicker garments to stay warm. Even more embarrassing, he had to breathe rapidly so it didn't feel as if he were suffocating. To him, the air was thin, too thin if he ran or played too hard.

Compared to other children his age, Klane was frail and a sickly pale color. He spied Ram, a seven-year-old and a favorite of the warriors. Ram stood atop a man-sized boulder, with his stout legs splayed wide. Ram sneered at the rest of the children—four other boys—standing at the base of the boulder. But he saved his worst sneer for the fifth child, for Klane, standing among the others and looking up.

Despite his age, Ram's brown face was a slab of sternness. His scarred right hand clutched a knotted club. Klane noticed the clouds drifting high above Ram and the club. There was a taint of ozone in the air, foretelling of coming rain.

"Who is the toughest here?" Ram shouted down. "Who is the hetman of the hill?"

Klane and the other four boys glanced at each other. Each could tell what the other was thinking. They nodded, and together, they lunged up the boulder, scrambling to take Ram down.

Ram knelt and swung his club, hitting the first boy on the side of the head with a decided thud. The boy didn't cry out, although he lost his hold and tumbled down onto the dirt, landing on his back. He lay here, stunned. Another child crawled up on the other side of the boulder. He sneaked up an arm and grabbed Ram's left ankle. With a fierce grin, the boy yanked.

Ram shouted in alarm. He must have been surprised and hadn't been able to swallow the inarticulate sound. The club flew up as Ram hit his head on the boulder. He flailed for a purchase and failed to gain it, falling onto the boy who had tripped him. Together, the two tumbled off, struck a third climbing boy, and all three thudded onto the dirt below.

Klane's young heart soared. This was glorious. The club landed on top of the boulder, rolled, but remained there. He had never been the hetman of the hill. This was the chance of his life.

He scrambled up faster than the last boy and picked up the club, swinging blindly at the other. Luck aided him today. He connected with a meaty thwack and watched the boy of six pinwheel his arms before falling out of sight.

While gripping the club, Klane stood up on the boulder. He laughed wildly. Then he pointed the blunt end of the club at Ram. "I'm the hetman! I rule the boulder."

A warrior happened to be passing by and noticed the interplay. He halted and put both fists on his hips. "Ho ha!" he scoffed. "The pale one has defeated the noble Ram. What ails you, child? Have you been feeding from your mother's teat? Do you lack the strength to defeat the weakling?"

Klane's grin slipped a little. Ram had a terrible temper.

Ram pushed another boy's legs off his chest and scrambled upright. He scowled like a grown-up. Pointing at Klane, Ram shouted, "Get off the boulder! You didn't win it fairly."

Klane was afraid of Ram, but stubbornness boiled in him. A warrior had seen his victory. That was good. "No!" he yelled at Ram. "I'm the hetman of the hill! And I'll knock down anyone who tries to push me off."

Ram growled with rage, kicking dirt. With a savage yell, he shot toward the boulder, and he climbed like a rill.

Klane set himself, judging the moment, waiting for it. As Ram's head came into view, Klane swung the club two-handed. The wood caught Ram on the shoulder. The thud of it numbed Klane's small hands, but the blow only enraged Ram that much more. With a surge, Ram made it up and he shoved Klane in the chest.

Klane sailed backward off the boulder. It was a sickening feeling. He struck the dirt with his back, a stone poking him between the shoulder blades, knocking the wind out of his weak lungs. Ram's dirty feet thudded beside him. Working his mouth, Klane tried to speak. He couldn't. The air had been knocked out of him.

With his blunt, brown features scrunched up with rage, Ram picked up the fallen club. He swung, hitting Klane's side. He swung again, striking the legs. Scrambling around to the other side, he bashed a body blow against Klane's chest.

Klane doubled up, trying to protect himself. He expected the warrior to stop Ram. A glance showed him the warrior nodding with approval. Then knotty wood thudded against Klane's head, and the world spun crazily.

The warrior finally strode forward. With a single blow, he knocked the club out of Ram's grasp. "Off with you, young warrior," the man said. "Don't kill the pale one. It might make the seeker angry."

"No!" Ram shouted. "I'm the hetman of the hill. I'm teaching him a lesson he'll never forget."

The warrior slapped Ram across the face, knocking the boy to the ground. "Don't argue with a warrior, boy. Go. Play elsewhere."

Sniffling back tears, Ram jumped up and ran away, with the other boys following him. The warrior glanced once at Klane, grunted something under his breath, and went his way.

Afterward, after the hurt faded, Klane groaned and spat out dirt. A cut inside his mouth tasted like blood. His entire body ached. To his astonishment, Klane spied the seeker rising from a rock fifteen feet away. Had the old man been there the entire time? Why hadn't the seeker helped him? He was the man's apprentice, right?

The seeker moved near and squatted beside him. He muttered as he tended to Klane's wounds.

"I'm fine," Klane finally said.

"Then why are you lying on the ground like a sicker?"

"Because I'm hurt," Klane said.

"Bah," the seeker said. He produced a stink beetle, putting it under Klane's nose.

Klane shot to his feet, vigorously rubbing his nose and swaying as his vision blurred.

"Come, boy," the seeker said, gruffly. "Let me instruct you in the proper way to play such games."

Klane limped after the old man, drying the tears that trickled from his eyes. No man in Clan Tash-Toi cried—at least they weren't supposed to.

The seeker led Klane to a secluded area among bigger boulders. His ribs ached less by now and his lip had stopped bleeding. The seeker motioned for Klane to squat, which he did.

"Listen to me, boy. You will never become the hetman. The others would kill you if they thought you had a chance of succeeding. Only a true Tash-Toi can be the hetman. Do you understand?"

Klane's little heart beat rapidly. He sat on the ground, feeling alone and outcast. He nodded, though, wanting to please the seeker, the only person who had ever been friendly to him.

"Good," the seeker said. "Remember, you're a lemper, not a rill. The rill is brave and stalks any prey it wants. It fears nothing and uses its power to pull down weaker prey. Yet, because it fears nothing our warriors can easily trap it." The old man held up a gnarled finger as he grinned. Several teeth were already missing. Even so, Klane loved the old man.

"Ah," the seeker said, as he waggled the finger. "Warriors capture the rill, but who captures the crafty lemper?"

"Have you?" Klane asked, softly.

The seeker lowered his head, and whispered, "Once but only once, and I'm the only one in the clan to do it." The seeker reached behind his back into a pouch and pulled out a small, spotted skin. It was lemper leather. The old man unwrapped it and dropped a smooth, oiled stone onto his palm. "The lemper skin holds my most powerful junction-stone. It helps to give the stone cunning."

Klane's right eye had puffed shut. His ribs still hurt and so did his gut. At that moment, he knew he never wanted to be beaten again. He wanted to defeat others. He wanted to win, and to do the beating.

"Yes," Klane whispered. "I want the cunning to hurt Ram, to hurt anyone who attacks me."

"Ah," the seeker said. "The fact that you *want* to be cunning shows you have the ability to be cunning. In time, perhaps, I can teach you the deeper guile."

With his one good eye, Klane glanced up into the old man's face. Pride swelled in Klane's chest. "I'm already cunning. I baited Ram with my words."

The seeker sighed. "Yes, you baited him, but you took a beating in return. That isn't cunning, but stupidity."

"I didn't cry," Klane lied.

"So what?" the old man said. "What does that prove?"

Klane blinked with confusion.

"Listen to me, young one. What you just did was the way of the warrior. But you are not a warrior-to-be. You are a seeker-to-be."

"Which is more powerful?" Klane asked.

"Ask rather, which gets hurt less? Which understands more? Which is more cunning?"

Klane scowled. He wasn't sure he liked those questions.

"Have you ever seen anyone hit me?" the seeker asked.

Klane's eyes widened with horror. "No one would dare hit you."

"Exactly," the seeker said, as he chucked Klane under the chin.

Klane thought about that as the seeker waited, watching him.

"How . . . how can I make it so no one ever hits me again?" Klane asked.

"That is the question," the seeker said. "First, you must never play with the other boys again."

Klane began to sniffle. "Who will I play with then?"

"With me," the seeker said.

Klane stared at the old man, wondering how that would work.

"In truth, you will have little time to play," the seeker said. "You will be too busy learning how to act like a lemper."

Klane nodded, and he told himself he mustn't cry.

"Good," the seeker said. "You can accept hard news. Now, you must begin to make your own junction-stone. Tomorrow, we will search for a suitable rock."

Klane grinned. He knew that junction-stones were powerful—deadly, in fact.

"Afterward," the seeker said, "you need a plan for when Ram comes around to hit you again. You will have to learn how to twist his words, and baffle him and the others with cunning. Would you like to think up a seeker sort of plan for dealing with Ram?"

"Does the plan include hurting him?"

"More than you can imagine," the seeker said.

With his tongue, Klane touched the cut on his lip and recalled how he'd gotten it. "Yes. I want to learn," he said.

"Excellent," the old man said, with an evil grin. "To begin with . . ."

He spoke for a long time concerning cunning: how to use a person's beliefs against them. Klane became weary until his head drooped and his eyelids fluttered.

"Klane, you need to wake up. Can you hear me?"

Klane felt a soft hand on his knee. The hand squeezed and it shook his leg. Drowsily, he lifted his head, and he shouted in alarm, shooting to his feet to stand there trembling.

A naked woman was crouched beside him, with shining things on her breasts. She was exotic, alluring—wasn't she cold without garments?

"Klane," she said.

"How . . . how do you know my name?"

"I'm a figment of Mentalist Niens's imagination. He sent me here to talk to you."

Klane began to tremble. None of this made sense. She took a step toward him. He scrambled back, and he picked up a rock, lifting it, getting ready to strike.

"I'm here to help you," she said.

"Go away," he said. "The seeker was talking to me and now you're here. That doesn't make sense."

She studied him and finally she waved her arm in a wide arc. "All this is false. It's make-believe."

"Seeker!" Klane shouted. "Invaders have sneaked into the camp."

"You stupid little boy, don't you understand what I'm telling you?"

The anger in her eyes and the name-calling made little Klane grin. "The warriors will do things to you, make you scream."

"No," she said. "They won't, because I'm not real."

He scrunched his brow. "That's silly. I see you. I hear you."

"None of this is real. The Kresh have you under a reality field. You're actually a full-grown man thinking this. No doubt you're playing back an old and painful memory."

"Who are the Kresh?" Klane asked.

"The aliens you call demons."

"Why are you here?"

"Mentalist Niens wants to warn you."

"I don't know anyone like that."

"Yes you do. You let him live once."

"What?"

"Don't you remember killing Chengal Ras, one of the Kresh, one of the demons?"

Klane laughed.

"Niens was the mentalist," she said. "He'd been working on the seeker, before you came to save him."

Klane began to blink. He looked up at the sky, looked at the rocks, at his hand, and finally at the pay girl. "I remember the hive, and after that . . ."

"You're a prisoner, Klane. Niens . . . Niens wants to know if you're the Anointed One or not."

Something happened to Klane's eyes. They aged and became

wary. "This is a trick," he said. He'd read Niens's mind earlier and knew this was a pay girl.

The pay girl shook her head. She opened her mouth, but then she began to fade. As she did, Klane's dream also faded and became a sizzling, fuzzy dome above him.

|||||||||

Klane rested under the reality field, regaining his equilibrium and mental strength. He understood the shimmering curtain for what it was now. The pay girl had shown him the truth.

His consciousness had returned to his flesh. This was where he belonged. He was determined never to leave his body again.

Because of the strange field, dreams and old friends tried to call him. Klane studiously ignored the ghosts. He had been to the hive and to the approaching cyborg fleet. He had expanded his mental powers considerably. The best thing would be to gain time to understand all that he'd learned. Right now, he didn't have the time. He had to escape the demons—the Kresh.

I'm trapped under a reality field. My only ally is the dubious Mentalist Niens, a man in love with pay girls.

Klane's understanding of his place in the Fenris System had also grown. A war raged on Fenris II. A Chirr fleet readied itself for launching. *Are the insects and cyborgs allies?* He hadn't sensed that in the Prime Web-Mind, but that didn't mean it wasn't true.

In any case, that didn't matter in the here and now; escaping the Kresh did. Klane didn't think the Kresh would believe him concerning the two approaching threats. Besides, how would it help him or help humanity if the Kresh killed him? *They* will *kill me. Once they realize the extent of my power, they cannot afford to keep me alive.*

Klane tried to sit up, but found that impossible. The reality field played tricks on his nervous system. His mind had likely become the strongest in the Fenris System, but it couldn't operate with full potential under this numbing energy blanket.

You must play within the parameters. You are the lemper, and you must turn your opponent's strength against him. Maybe Niens had shown him the way to do this. His psi-power was useless at the moment. He'd have to rely on simple imagination and craft, just as he'd done most of his life.

Turning his head, Klane stared at the shimmering field. He willed his small, six-year-old self into existence. After a time, a fuzzy image of the boy appeared.

"That isn't good enough," Klane whispered. *Remember . . . remember.* He did, until the boy Klane held a small stone that he religiously polished with gat skin. The boy regarded him.

"Who are you?" the boy asked.

"You know who I am."

The boy frowned. "You're me?"

"That's close enough. Do you know where you are?"

"In a demon . . . *laboratory,*" the boy said.

"Right," Klane said. He wondered if devices picked up his speech. Most certainly, they existed and recorded everything he muttered. He'd seen that in the flash of Niens's surface thoughts. He would have to remember that.

"You know what to do," Klane said.

The boy frowned as he rubbed the stone. "I have to relay a message."

"Then do it," Klane whispered.

The boy heaved a great sigh. He faced the shimmering field and walked into it.

The boy Klane walked out of the reality field and halted. The seeker had never said anything about such marvels as this. Strange men in odd garments worked before flat things with flashing lights.

It was bewildering. At times, the men glanced toward the reality field. Mostly, they watched the . . . the . . . machines.

A different man, a tall, lanky individual in a white coat approached him. He stared down at Klane. Then the man pointed. Klane turned his head, and started at the naked pay girl he'd seen earlier.

"Remember me?" the pay girl asked.

"You're Mentalist Niens's fantasy," young Klane said.

She nodded.

"I want to talk to Niens," Klane said.

"You are, by talking to me," the girl said.

"Wouldn't it be easier if I just talked to him?"

"No," the pay girl said. "The Bo Taw and other specialists record everything in the chamber. But they can't see us, because we don't exist except in our creators' minds. As long as we're near the reality field, the psi-spies can't look into our thoughts."

"I understand," Klane said.

"I know you do. That's why you're here, isn't it?"

Klane thought about it. Finally, he nodded.

"Do you have a plan?" the pay girl asked.

"Explain how the reality field works."

She did, and she indicated the machines and the uniformed technicians.

"Do you understand all that?" she asked later.

Klane shook his head. "But I'm sure my older self will."

The pay girl giggled in an artful manner. "I've told you a lot of things," she said.

"You have," he admitted.

"Now I'd like to know one or two things myself."

"What is that?" Klane asked.

"Where did your consciousness go while it was gone?"

"Oh, that's easy . . ."

"Why do you pause?" the girl asked.

Klane scratched his head, and he glanced at Niens again. The man's face was blank, with his eyes staring. Despite that, Klane sensed the sudden eagerness.

"You know," he said, "I bet it would be a lot easier if big Klane just talked to Niens face-to-face."

"I've already told you why that wouldn't be a good idea or why it's impossible."

"I know," little Klane said. "So why don't you have Niens turn off the reality field. Klane can get rid of the others, and then Niens and he can talk."

She stared at him. "Could Klane defeat all these men with his psionic powers?"

"I think so."

"But you don't know," the pay girl said.

"Not for certain," little Klane said, knowing he was lying and therefore shifting from foot to foot.

"You seem nervous," the pay girl said.

"I have to pee," he said.

The pay girl giggled. "That's silly. You're not real."

"I still have to go. Wait here. I'll be right back."

"No!" she called.

Klane didn't listen. He hurried into the reality field and crossed over to the other side. There, big Klane lay with his eyes open.

Little Klane faded, leaving the real Klane staring up at the buzzing field. Why did Niens want to know where his consciousness had been? Did the mentalist deal truthfully with him? Or was it more likely Niens still worked for the Kresh?

I have to get out of here. I have to get out now.

30

"Something must have given us away," Cyrus said, as he watched a floating APC, an armored personnel carrier, head toward them.

Together with Skar, he crouched behind a lichen-covered boulder. The others hid farther behind. To their left gurgled the demon river: a blue stream as wide as Cyrus could hurl a rock. They'd almost reached the outer perimeter of the puffer fields before the city. For the last two days, the ten avengers had descended into the canyon. It had been torturous and slow work, and the air became thicker by degrees, easier to breathe, and warmer than the air in the uplands.

"Vomags," Skar said, as he peered around the boulder.

Cyrus felt a tendril of psi-power. He knew what it was: searching Bo Taw. As fast as he could, he concentrated, thinking null, spreading it over Skar and him.

"Get behind the rock," Cyrus said in a monotone.

Skar pulled back and looked at him sharply. "Are they scanning for us?"

Cyrus nodded. He was too busy to talk.

"Are we hidden from them?" Skar asked.

Cyrus nodded again.

"What about Yang and the others? Are they hidden, too?"

Cyrus shook his head, and his heart thudded as he thought about

Jana. The null almost slipped away from him then. He fought for calm. If he lost it now . . . there, he had the null over them again.

"They're searching hard," Cyrus whispered. "Can't talk much . . ."

Skar bent his head, perhaps in thought, then he snapped it up. Lifting his torso, he cupped his hands, aiming where the others hid as he kept the boulder between him and the APC.

"Split up!" Skar shouted. "Sneak away. You have to act as decoys."

"Jana," Cyrus said in a tortured voice.

"Keep calm, my friend," Skar told him. "We must outthink and outfight the enemy. Build the null. I have to study what we're facing."

Cyrus lowered his forehead and stroked it with his fingertips, calming himself, calming. The null continued acting as a mirror, reflecting any searching psi-thoughts.

"It's a rover," Skar said in a clipped voice. "It must have one Bo Taw, maybe two aboard. There likely isn't room for more. There will be a squad of Vomags. That's one senior and nine soldiers. They will all bear arms. Ah, they have a stun gun in the cupola. You were right. We must have triggered an alarm. It is as I've thought all along. There are too many of us for a commando raid. Only five of us should have entered the valley."

They had argued about that during the descent. Skar had suggested only five of them go down all the way. Yang and Grinder had disagreed, and they had carried the vote.

Skar drew back and took out his pistol. There was a notch at the end of the barrel, made by a primitive several days ago. He had twelve shots left. Then he'd be down to his hatchet. Grinder still had the heat gun.

Cyrus had a bow. He was an indifferent archer. Fortunately, he also carried his knife. Could he defeat a soldier in a knife fight? Cyrus didn't think he could beat Skar. Why had the Kresh tinkered with human chromosomes anyway and made these genetic supermen?

He heard the rover. It made a low swish-swish sound—the antigrav plates working overtime, no doubt. Then he heard a loud popping sound.

"Relax," Skar said.

Something like a heat wave passed overhead. Cyrus looked over, and he saw one of the Berserkers fall to the ground and lie still.

"Stun," Skar said. "They must want to capture us."

"What gave us away?" Cyrus asked in a labored voice.

"I'd guess passive ground sensors," Skar said.

Cyrus bit his lip. He wished Jana were with them. If the soldiers killed her . . . *I hate this waiting. I hate relying on the null. I wish the space marines were here.* Cyrus twitched. He had to focus. He could feel the enemy minds sliding over him. Were the Bo Taw frustrated? Did they know an enemy psionic was out here?

The stun gun went off again, and the rover sounded closer.

"Lay down," Skar whispered. "And don't move. Keep the null in place."

Cyrus lay on the damp ground. He didn't even have a heat gun. What kind of commando operation was this? It was hard to believe humanity lived or died, remained slave or free, on what the ten of them did down here. It could all be over so easily.

He closed his eyes. The rover was practically on top of them. The swish-swish was louder, and he heard a human shout.

Cyrus held himself perfectly still. *I am null. I am nothing. I am not here. I am a gnat.*

The stun gun fired once more, and he shivered in surprise. Two seconds later, someone from the rover laughed sharply.

Hatred filled Cyrus's chest. If they'd just shot Jana—

"You can rise," Skar said. "But move slowly."

The swish-swish sounds became faint as the rover passed them and headed toward the eight. Cyrus looked up, seeing the tail end of the military machine, a Kresh APC.

"We can't defeat that," Cyrus whispered.

"Not until they land and begin to collect the captured specimens," Skar whispered.

The two of them waited. The stun gun went off eight times. Did that mean the enemy had shot all eight Berserkers? Were the Vomags that efficient?

"Can two men take a squad of soldiers?" Cyrus whispered.

"It is doubtful," Skar said, "but we will try."

"Yeah, let's try."

The rover landed with a thud, and the swish-swishing quit. Metallic sliding sounds occurred, and men bearing equipment stomped onto the ground.

"Are you ready, my friend?" Skar asked.

For an answer, Cyrus drew his knife. He decided to leave the bow and arrows. They would only get in the way. He figured Vomag ears would hear any twangs. He was back to Milan methods, as if he were an enforcer in the Latin Kings.

Using the boulders, Cyrus and Skar began to work toward the rover. "Which team do we take out first?" Cyrus whispered.

Tall reeds swayed between the boulders. The river's gurgle might hide some of their noises.

Skar looked at Cyrus. "I have an idea."

"Let's hear it."

"Who is guarding the rover?"

Cyrus shrugged.

"The soldiers aren't guarding it," Skar said. "They're picking up the stunned captives. The Bo Taw will have remained in or near the vehicle in comfort. We must kill them first. Then we capture the rover and use it to kill or stun the soldiers."

"They might kill our friends in retaliation."

Skar's features became flintlike. "We must move fast and capture the machine before the soldiers reach all the fallen. I see no other way."

Cyrus's pulse began to beat in his throat. *Jana!* "Come on," he hissed. "Let's move."

Skar gripped his arm. "Listen to me."

With a jerk, Cyrus tore his arm free. He had to capture the rover before the soldiers reached his love.

Who are you?

With a curse, Cyrus realized he'd let the null slip. A Bo Taw had found him. He struggled for calm. "They know we're here," he said between clenched teeth.

"Who?" Skar asked. "The Bo Taw?"

The hell with this. Cyrus clutched his knife and broke into a sprint, weaving between the boulders.

There were shouts farther away. Then an instinctive part of his mind gave Cyrus a moment's warning. He threw himself to the ground. A pellet hissed overhead and exploded against a boulder, raining rock chips on his neck. Cyrus scrambled back onto his feet. The air was thicker down here than up on the plains. He didn't tire as quickly. He sprinted so his thighs burned and his feet flew over the ground. He ran into sight of the rover. A soldier stepped out of the back. The opening was like a normal portal on an Earth APC. The Vomag raised his pistol, and then his neck exploded. Skar had shot him.

Cyrus kept sprinting. *One soldier stayed behind. Skar was wrong about that. At least he killed the man.* Cyrus vaulted over the twisting, bleeding Vomag and collided with another rushing out. The shorter man was a mass of compacted muscle like a python. Even so, the two of them tumbled into the narrow confines of the rover.

Cyrus kept hold of his knife, but an iron grip latched onto his wrist. The soldier moved Cyrus's knife hand away as the man reached for his hatchet. Using his free hand, Cyrus jabbed stiffened fingers at the man's eyes. The Vomag had catlike reflexes, for he released the hatchet and grabbed Cyrus's arm before the fingers could dig out the orbs.

With painful strength, the Vomag tightened his grip on Cyrus's wrists. In a physical fight, the soldiers would always defeat him. But Cyrus was from the slums of Milan. A hard upbringing had taught him a grim rule: in a life-or-death match, fight dirty to win any way you can.

Cyrus released the null. In his mind, in that second, he felt the searching Bo Taw, and he felt the psi-master's surprise. There was only one in the vicinity. That was good.

Staring eye to eye with the soldier, acting before the psi-master switched tasks, Cyrus used telekinesis. He twisted matter inside the Vomag's brain. The soldier's grip weakened, and the man groaned in agony.

Cyrus wrenched his knife hand free and slid the blade into the man's gasping mouth. He felt resistance, and put his weight behind it. The knife went in all the way. The soldier stiffened—and then the hidden Bo Taw slammed a psionic bolt against Cyrus.

The former knife man from Milan groaned at the pain. He struggled to reset the null.

No. I won't let you. I see what you've been doing. Sleep—

A physical explosion ended the mind burn. Cyrus blinked, feeling sluggish, struggling to remain awake. Then a tall humanoid with a *baan* around his elongated forehead tumbled onto the rover's floor. He was missing most of his face because a pellet had torn it away in its blast.

As Cyrus shoved up, Skar reached the rover. The Vomag held his pistol and now had only ten shots left. The soldier gave Cyrus a single glance before passing him, heading deeper into the bay.

"Stay down," Skar said.

Why does he say that? I can't even get up. Cyrus squeezed his eyelids together. *The Bo Taw messed with my mind. If I'm going to save Jana, I have to wake up all the way.*

The swish-swish sounds returned. Cyrus could feel the vibration of the antigrav plates under his body and through the palms of his hands. The rear gate began to close. "Jana," he croaked. He fought his way up, shaking his head, pinching himself until he cried out.

The gate clanged shut. How was he supposed to get outside to help her, and how was Jana supposed to get in to safety?

"Hey," Cyrus said. He staggered to the front, finding Skar in the driver's seat, looking through a vision plate.

"Can you drive?" Skar asked.

"Sure. But we—"

"I'll man the cupola," Skar said. "We must hunt down the soldiers before it's too late."

"Don't tell me. Show me. Let's go."

Skar shoved himself out of the seat and hurried to an upper hatch. Cyrus knew it had a bubble canopy protection. Skar had told him a few minutes earlier that it was pellet-resistant.

As Skar rose into firing position, Cyrus settled into the warm driver's chair. The controls looked enough like the needle-ship's panel to make them familiar. He tapped in one spot and grasped a control stick. The rover lifted and swiveled hard to the right. It threw the soldier's torso against the hatch.

"Keep it steady," Skar called down.

"Got it," Cyrus muttered.

The extended stun gun went off, and Skar said, "One."

It didn't take long for Cyrus to get the hang of it. The next few minutes became a one-sided battle, with the Vomags firing at the craft. Their pellets sounded like hail, and they proved completely ineffectual.

"What's the point of their shooting?" Cyrus shouted.

When the first outer camera flickered off, Cyrus understood that they were trying to blind them.

"They're shooting out the vision plates," he shouted.

"Sound tactics," Skar said. "Do you see . . . 12-BB-32?"

"What?"

"Turn on your grid."

"How do you—oh." Cyrus tapped a spot and a grid appeared over the main screen. "What were those coordinates again?"

Skar repeated them.

"Yeah, I—hey, one of our team is there."

"Hurry to him," Skar said. "We're going to change the rules of the game, starting now."

Cyrus sped there, and Skar stunned another two Vomags.

"We have to time this exactly," Skar said. "Do you see the switch to the right of the screen?"

"What's it do?" Cyrus shouted.

"Opens and closes the rear hatch."

"Okay."

"Get ready to open it so I can drag Yang into the rover."

"Roger," Cyrus said. He brought the APC beside the inert body, landed, and opened the hatch.

Skar had already slid down from the cupola. He jumped outside and dragged the big Berserker into the main bay.

Cyrus closed the hatch and started moving for the next Berserker. He searched the screen for a sign of Jana. As he did, the enemy Vomags shot out another camera.

"We're down to two vision plates," Cyrus said.

Skar scrambled back into the cupola, stunning another enemy.

Then Cyrus saw Jana. A soldier stood over her with a pistol aimed at her chest. The enemy Vomag looked up at the rover. It was hard to tell his expression. The sunlight was wrong and the bill of his helmet shadowed his features.

"Let's bargain," Cyrus shouted. "Let's see what he—"

The stun gun sounded, and the Vomag slumped beside Jana.

Cyrus's mouth became dry. Skar had risked his love, the bastard. He throttled the rover wide open so the APC strained, and he flew over two large boulders.

"Steady," Skar shouted.

The rover wobbled, and it threatened to flip. Cyrus clenched his teeth. And he played the craft, riding out the shaking and shifting, and he brought it down so near his woman that dirt exploded, some of it raining onto Jana's face.

"Skar!" Cyrus shouted.

"I see him," the soldier said. He shot and missed, the Vomag ducking out of sight too quickly. "It must be the senior," Skar said. "You'll have to get her this time while I keep him busy."

The rear hatch had already opened. Cyrus launched out of his seat and sprinted through the bay. He darted into bright sunlight.

Ten meters away and hidden from the stun gun, the senior Vomag appeared, brushing past two tall plants. The man aimed his gun at Jana.

Cyrus launched himself airborne, thudding onto her body in protective covering. He clenched his teeth, waiting for the end, but nothing happened. He looked up. The senior toppled onto the ground, with a burn on the back of his head and a curl of smoke rising. Cyrus didn't understand. He hadn't heard the stun gun go off. A second later, Grinder stepped past the tall plants where the Vomag had been. The former primitive held the heat gun. He had robbed the fallen Vomag and then shot the man in the head.

Cyrus didn't have time to worry about that. He lifted Jana, clutching her in his arms, and staggered into the bay. He set her down and dove for the driver's seat.

The stun gun went off again.

"This is bad," Skar said.

"What?" Cyrus asked, seeing Grinder hurrying within and beginning to close the hatch.

"Our friend killed a Vomag. Now the soldiers are butchering some of their captives."

"How's that any different than before?" Cyrus asked.

"The soldiers held back from murder. Now Grinder has made this a killing match."

"I've paid back the demon slaves in the only way they understand," Grinder muttered.

Cyrus turned, grim-faced, and the next several minutes proved deadly. They stunned the rest of the soldiers, but the enemy killed three more Berserkers.

It left Cyrus and Skar with Jana, Yang, Grinder, and Darter: six people to achieve the impossible.

After looting the fallen soldiers, killing them, and retrieving and reviving their friends, they had a council of war inside the rover.

"We have modern weapons," Yang said. "And we have a war vehicle. That is greater luck than we could have expected."

"We've also lost four good people," Cyrus said.

"It is amazing we have anyone left at all," Yang said. "We are in the Valley of the Demons. Now we must attack while we can."

"Attack what?" Cyrus asked.

"Attack whoever holds the Anointed One in thrall," Yang said.

"We must scout out the situation first to find out who that is exactly," Cyrus said.

"What does that mean in terms of action?" Yang asked.

"It means Jana and I will infiltrate the city," Cyrus said. "We'll discover where they're keeping Klane and then send for you."

"We lack communicators," Yang pointed out.

"I'll have to use telepathy," Cyrus said.

Skar glanced at him.

"I know," Cyrus said. "We'll have to risk some of the Bo Taw hearing the message. I'll give you a code word."

"I don't approve," Skar said.

"So what do you suggest?" Cyrus asked. "Do we barrel in with the rover and just shoot up the town?"

"Those would be poor tactics," Skar said.

"Exactly," Cyrus said. "This is a snatch and grab. We have to get one man and get out. That's it."

"Klane will likely be well guarded," Skar said.

"Meaning two people will have a better chance of sneaking in than six driving up in a rover," Cyrus said.

Skar and Yang exchanged glances.

"It is a wise idea," Yang said. "I agree with Cyrus's plan."

Skar pointed out that, as a Vomag, he could blend in better. He should go into the city.

"You're right about blending in," Cyrus said. "You're also our best soldier. When that rover comes in, you have to be in it."

The others agreed with Yang and Cyrus. They also agreed that the rover should stay well out of the city, to stay out of both visual and Bo Taw range. It meant that Cyrus and Jana had several kilometers to go on foot.

"Let's get started then," Cyrus said. He shook hands all around, and he wondered if he'd ever see any of these men again. Then he and Jana headed for the city of the Kresh.

31

Niens stood frozen with indecision near the reality field. The pay girl had disappeared, leaving him with his hopes and fears.

What should he do? He wanted to make a stab for freedom, but now that he stood on the threshold of it, fear incapacitated him. The other choice was to run to a comm and demand an audience with Zama Dee, with the Revered One. He had priceless information. Klane was on the verge of telling him where his consciousness had fled. Surely, the 73rd would delight in such arcane knowledge. She would reward him commensurately.

One who belonged to the Hundred would surely keep her word, wouldn't she?

Would she keep it to one of us cattle, though?

It was hard to tell. He had no doubt she could destroy him without compunction. The Kresh . . . it was difficult to read them, to fully understand the higher race. If he could speak to someone knowledgeable about them—

Niens gobbled in fear as a gigantic Kresh solidified before him. The nine-foot creature with its metallic streamers and the agonizer in its talons—

"Chengal Ras," Niens whispered. "W-what are you doing here? The s-savage killed you. I witnessed it."

Chengal Ras snarled, waving his arms and clicking his talons in agitation.

Niens turned away, his muscles tensing as he made ready to bolt. Instead of running, he frowned. Techs adjusted the machines, recalibrating, perhaps. Techs . . . technicians . . . the reality field . . .

The mentalist exhaled in relief. Yes, yes, what kind of idiot was he? He faced Chengal Ras, realizing the Kresh was a figment of his imagination. Yet maybe it could tell him things from his subconscious that he couldn't face in any other way. That was an interesting concept. Even so, Niens considered stepping several paces away from the field and getting rid of the ghost. Chengal Ras had always been difficult and would likely prove so now. Yet if he stepped away from the field in this stressed state, it would put his mind in range of the Bo Taw. That was a bad idea.

Therefore, Niens tilted his head as he regarded the imposing 109th. "Can I trust a Kresh when one gives her solemn word?"

Chengal Ras quit waving his arms, clicking his talons, and lashing his tail. The alien lowered his dinosaur-like jaws until he breathed in Niens's face. The musty odor nauseated the mentalist. For a fantasy, this felt far too real. Yet he held his ground.

"You played me false, mentalist," Chengal Ras said. "During combat, you sought mercy from the human instead of coming to a Revered One's aid. How long do you suppose you can keep that hidden from Zama Dee? She is cleverer than I, or at least she was when I lived. Otherwise she would be dead, and I would be alive."

"You're saying I can't trust her?" Niens asked.

"A human does not *trust* a Kresh," Chengal Ras said, while gashing his teeth side to side. "He obeys. He serves. You have served her and fulfilled your usefulness. That is enough for one like you."

"She promised me rewards, though."

"Yes. A good master knows how to motivate his cattle. The promise was the thing, your completion of a task. For a human, nothing else matters beyond that."

"You're saying I can't trust her?" Niens repeated.

"Consider your position," the ghost said. "You have knowledge she desires. As long as she wants something from you, she will likely treat you well—given it's the easiest way to acquire what she wants."

"Is that logical?" Niens asked. "If she rewards me, she can point to it and show others that she keeps her word."

"It is difficult for me to understand such foolishness from such a crafty and deceitful creature as you," Chengal Ras said. "Others of your kind already believe she keeps her promises, just as you believe. After this is over, you will disappear. No one will ever see you again or ask about you."

Sweat trickled under Niens's collar. He tugged at it in order to ease his breathing.

"If you consider my logic in detail," Chengal Ras said, "you will find it impeccable."

"What do you suggest I do?"

The ghost snorted. "There is nothing you can do, as you have no options."

"Untrue. I can help Klane. He let me live once. He was merciful to me."

"Such actions will make no difference," Chengal Ras said.

"No, no, you're wrong," Niens said. "He would keep his word. He had no reason to show me mercy the first time, yet he did. Besides, he's human like me. He would feel gratitude if I helped him escape. For such an act, I might even become a hero to the human race. Yes, yes, I think he's the Anointed One. I think humans can live on their own without Revered Ones, without you aliens mocking our humanity."

"It is a vain hope. The Kresh are invincible. Have you counted the number of spacecraft in the so-called Anointed One's camp? None. The Kresh have many and can build more."

"But Earth—"

"Is ripe fruit for the Kresh to pluck," Chengal Ras said. "Humanity is a slave race. Admit it to yourself and live life the best you are able. Anything else is sheer futility. Do you want me to administer the agonizer? It will be a pleasure compared to what will happen to you if you help the test subject and fail."

"I—"

Before Niens could finish his words, rough hands jerked him away from the reality field. At first, he didn't understand what went on. By degrees, he became aware of two Vomags dragging him away from the field. Chengal Ras became ghostly and then disappeared. The Vomags cast him onto the floor before . . .

Niens looked up at a tall, sneering Bo Taw. The man wore a red robe and had the elongated cranium of his kind. He wore a silver *baan* around his forehead and kept his hands hidden in voluminous sleeves held before his body.

"You truly are a vain creature, Mentalist Niens," the Bo Taw said. "I have watched you for several days now, wading through your chaotic thoughts. How could you have believed the tripe about an Anointed One? It is a silly hope."

Niens licked his lips.

The Bo Taw smiled and laughed. The techs at the machines studiously avoided looking at the duo. The Vomags had retreated several steps, keeping their beady gazes on Niens.

"How can a man with your intellect believe that a Revered One was going to leave you in charge of the test subject?" the Bo Taw asked. "She knew you begged for mercy from him and let Chengal Ras die a hideous death. She knows you are devious and utterly bent."

The Bo Taw shook his head as if he couldn't believe such things possible.

"We don't have to be slaves," Niens said, raising his voice so the techs would hear.

"They won't help you," the Bo Taw said. "They know their place. They know the Revered Ones give us peace and meaning. Man on his own is a miserable creature."

"Those aren't your real thoughts," Niens said. "From your youngest years, mentalists forced you to love the aliens."

"You poor, pathetic creature," the Bo Taw said. "Don't you understand that the Revered Ones realize humanity is a broken reed? Can't you comprehend the altruism of their actions? They have mended humanity and integrated us into their advanced society."

"They're using us like cattle."

The Bo Taw shook his bald head. "If that were true, why did they fashion us? We have psionic gifts that humanity wouldn't have developed in thousands of years of change."

"Why are you telling me this?" Niens asked.

With one of his long fingers, the Bo Taw stroked the side of his mouth. "You still have a modicum of intelligence. No. You are clever, mentalist. You have use, and maybe the 73rd will show you mercy."

"Do the Kresh know the meaning of the word?" Niens asked, bitterly.

The Bo Taw frowned. "Have a care, Niens."

"Why? All is lost."

"But I just told you that it isn't." The Bo Taw motioned to the Vomags. "Bring him along."

"Where are you taking me?" Niens asked.

The Vomags plucked him off the floor and hustled him after the swiftly marching Bo Taw. They exited the reality chamber, went down a long corridor, and entered a comm room. A tech swiveled around and hurriedly faced her screen.

"Put me through to the 73rd's Attack Talon," the Bo Taw said.

There were beeps, a flash of light, and soon, Zama Dee appeared on a large screen. Behind her, another Kresh moved into view and stalked out. They were on the bridge of the Attack Talon.

The Bo Taw motioned the Vomags, showing them where to place Niens. Then the lanky humanoid bowed low before the screen.

"Revered One," the Bo Taw said in a subdued tone. "The mentalist indeed followed your 'A' prediction. I have apprehended him and now hold him for your judgment."

"Bring him into full view," Zama Dee said.

The Vomags shoved Niens beside the Bo Taw.

"Revered One," Niens said in a rush. "I have discovered a method of communicating with the test subject while he is under the reality field."

"Is he practicing his love litany?" Zama Dee asked the Bo Taw.

"No, Revered One. His mind is fully open."

Fully open, Niens thought. *That means my love litany was partly successful.*

"It made no difference," the Bo Taw told him. "Over time, I picked up everything."

"Your statement is factual?" Zama Dee asked Niens. "You have communicated with the test subject while he is under the reality field?"

"Yes, Revered One," Niens said. "I asked him where his consciousness went while it left his body."

"I'm amazed you could communicate," Zama Dee said. "My experts have said it is impossible. Well, supposing this thing is true, what did the test subject say?"

"He became nervous," Niens said. "He's very distrustful by nature."

"Does he trust you?" Zama Dee asked.

Niens almost lied. He glanced at the Bo Taw. The man didn't look down at him, but he wore a superior smile. Niens wished he could cut the man's throat.

"Tsk, tsk," the Bo Taw said. "You're a violent little slug, aren't you?"

"I've gained the test subject's partial trust," Niens told the Revered One.

"He speaks the truth," the Bo Taw added.

From her place aboard the Attack Talon, Zama Dee glanced to the side. Niens could imagine her tail lashing. After a time, she regarded the Bo Taw. "Yes. We will continue to use him. Put the mentalist in temporary confinement." She spoke to Niens now. "You will continue your experiments while in my presence. This is a priority issue and I will land directly . . . in one hour."

"We await your glory, Revered One," the Bo Taw said.

The screen flickered out.

"Cut my throat, would you?" the Bo Taw asked Niens.

"Gladly!" Niens spat, before shaking his head. He needed allies, not enemies. Oh, this was a disaster.

"Take him to detention," the Bo Taw told the soldiers. "Then watch him. The Revered One is coming and we must be ready to perform for her service."

32

Shrouded in stolen gray cloaks, Cyrus and Jana attempted to imitate the other humans: head bent forward, shoulders slumped, and moving with a half shuffle. Cyrus had used such tactics before in Milan, imitating the natives. That time he'd entered a costly pavilion to deliver Dust to a rich merchant.

Today he approached a Kresh city by a fine wide avenue, surfaced with a rough blue substance that rasped underfoot. They had overpowered some workers earlier and stolen their baggy garments and black produce bags to hide their weapons.

Cyrus practiced his null. It was hard work keeping it up; he felt winded and his legs were shaky. Jana looked around, gawking at the sights.

The avenue led to the main street. On either side rose spires, red and purple. They looked glassy and reflected the sunlight with hurtful brilliance. In places, crystals scintillated within the spires, giving it a fantasy feel, as if the structures cost priceless sums.

Their feet scraped across the rough substance. It was like nothing Cyrus had seen before. Perhaps it had originated on the Kresh home world many light years away. Cyrus put a hand on Jana's arm, keeping her from heading down a side lane.

"We'll keep on the main avenue for now," he said.

She nodded, and continued to stare right and left.

"Don't do that," Cyrus whispered.

"What?"

"Look around like that."

"I've never seen a city before," Jana said.

"You twist around like a tourist," he whispered. "You have to blend in or someone is going to report us."

The avenue led close beside a two-hundred-foot shaft of silver. It was much more slender than an Earth apartment complex. Surrounding this was an expanse of clean orange sand upon which rested half a dozen peculiar objects of rusted metal. Were they art things? Perhaps they were Kresh fetishes or trophies.

A Kresh stood on a circular steel platform in front of the spire. The alien regarded one of the rusted objects. The creature held a box, slowly twisting a dial.

Cyrus took one of Jana's hands and squeezed hard enough so she looked at him. "Concentrate on the road for now," he whispered. "You'll have a chance to look around later."

She was a hunter, a warrior. She understood and stopped gawking unnecessarily.

The spires increased in height the deeper they moved into the city. In places, large glass boxes seven or eight stories high and just as broad stood in place of the towers. Humans entered and exited those. Were they cube apartments? Cyrus didn't see any windows.

The process of movement among the various people seemed to depend on type. The regular, genetically unmodified humans like Cyrus and Jana shuffled with a defeated spirit. The Bo Taw strode importantly but slowly, like flamingos Cyrus had once seen in a zoo. The Vomags had a military bearing. No one had skin as white as he did, although some were lighter skinned, the Bo Taw the most so.

Beside some of the glassy boxes were plazas composed of stone tiles. There humans ate at round marble tables. A few of the tables boasted awnings. He spied only a few Kresh. They always stalked like predators, ready to strike with incredible speed. The humans stopped in apparent reverence whenever an alien neared.

Once, Cyrus and Jana halted. The raptor-like alien didn't notice them, with its streamers glittering in the sunlight. The three-toed claws scraped across the rough surface. The two Vomags following at a discreet distance gave Cyrus a second glance, but nothing more.

"What are we looking for exactly?" Jana whispered.

That was a good question. Cyrus didn't know. Where would they keep Klane? How close was the Anointed One? As he moved through the alien city, a dull feeling of despair began to grip him.

Don't listen to it, he told himself. *You've been in worse spots and won. Remember, not that long ago you were in High Station 3. You didn't have any friends, either. Now you have Jana, Skar, and the others.*

"Cyrus," Jana said, tugging at his sleeve. "Look!" she pointed into the sky.

Craning his head, Cyrus saw a distant bright speck. His woman had terrific senses. He recalled that she had been the one to watch for demon sky vehicles. The speck grew, and it looked as if it was headed straight down toward them.

Had cyborgs broken through the outer asteroid belt? Was this a nuclear missile taking out a Kresh stronghold? No one else noticed or ran screaming in panic.

Even so, he expected missiles to loft or beams to fire, intercepting the thing. But that didn't happen. Soon, the speck became a large round object and it slowed, with shimmers or heat waves before it. A minute later the object floated, still headed straight for the city.

Cyrus looked around. The streets were deserted. Where had everyone gone and why? They'd disappeared without screams or panicked movement. How the populace had accomplished the disappearance without their noticing it didn't matter. He needed to keep calm and keep his wits.

"We have to hide," he said.

Jana looked around. "The people—"

"Have done a bunk," he said.

She stared at him.

"They're hiding for some reason. Maybe we should hide, too," he said.

Jana dragged him to a niche between what seemed to be two sheds. As he craned his head, watching the thing, Cyrus began to ponder the odds. This was as long a shot as there was. It was crazy, but he was the Tracker. He was supposed to find and free the Anointed One. They had wondered how to get into space. Maybe this was the ticket, the descending vehicle.

Cyrus took a deep breath as he composed himself.

"What's wrong?" Jana asked. "You seem tense."

"Just a minute," he whispered.

Maybe she heard the urgency in his voice. She said no more, letting him concentrate.

With his fingers splayed apart and touching his head, he strove for calm. He wanted to do this quickly but thoroughly. This was their chance, and maybe this was their gift.

Skar, bring the rover. Come into the middle of the city. When you see a lander, something that can go up and down from space, capture it. You have to come now.

Cyrus exhaled and rebuilt the null. He forced himself into a calm state and stared at nothing. The ground shook under his feet and a strange odor roiled over him. He didn't look up to check; he strove for the ultimate null. When the Bo Taw mentally began searching—he felt a whispering mind and then nothing.

Finally, Cyrus looked up and found that Jana was at the edge of the alcove peering around a corner. He tiptoed to her.

"What are you looking at?" he asked.

"Demons," she said. "Demons came out of the spaceship. You can see the last one entering that spire over there."

Cyrus peered around the corner. He saw the ship. It was a circular craft almost completely filling a plaza, resting on stone tiles. Two glass buildings surrounded the spacecraft. The ship appeared to have several decks inside. He couldn't believe anyone would have tried to squeeze such a vessel down between the buildings. In some places, only ten feet separated the craft's hull from a glass wall. The craft had a ramp coming down out of its belly, touching the plaza. The Kresh must have exited the ship from the ramp. Behind the last Kresh followed a squad of Vomags. The group entered the nearest spire, the tallest he'd seen, with a greater girth than the other towers. The spire was half a block beyond the glass buildings surrounding the plaza and three blocks from Cyrus and Jana.

"Why are they going into the spire?" Jana asked.

Cyrus's eyes narrowed. When the seeker had been alive, she'd said they had to move fast. Time was critical. If the aliens had the Anointed One, would they realize whom they held? Maybe. Would they want to study the human in detail?

Cyrus Gant nodded. "I think we know where they're holding Klane."

"In the spire?" Jana asked.

"Yeah. It's the tallest, seems the most important."

Cyrus squinted. He counted several Vomag soldiers up there on terraces. Why hadn't he noticed them earlier? Maybe because he hadn't been looking up. The terraces looked artificial, as if they'd been glued to the spire. The Vomags there held long-barreled rifles that might have scopes. Were they sharpshooters?

"Did you get through to the others?" Jana asked.

"I don't know. I'm not that good at telepathy. I sent a message. We have to hope it went through and that no one else caught it."

Jana searched his face. "Do you really think we're the ones the prophecies foretold?"

"That's hard to know," Cyrus said. "We're here, though, and we have to do something."

"What?"

"Come on, follow me," Cyrus said, heading onto the street. No one else was outside. Maybe this was the perfect moment to make their move.

Jana hurried beside him, whispering, "What's your plan? Do we follow the Kresh into the building?"

Cyrus blinked twice as he strode purposefully down the street, mulling that over. Could he and Jana defeat unknown numbers of Vomags, Bo Taw, and Kresh? Did the aliens have precise protocol or metal detectors in the building? The more he thought about it, the less this seemed like a good idea, just barging into the tower. But if that wouldn't work, what would?

While chewing his lower lip, Cyrus thought furiously. He remembered the first time he'd seen an alien aboard Teleship *Discovery*. He'd used psi-power against it, but the Kresh had worn a device, blocking him. The aliens were unbeatable, raptor-like dinosaurs with ultralogical minds.

Two people couldn't rescue the Anointed One here in a high-security area, at least not while using regular commando tactics. For a commando operation to work, they needed overwhelming surprise and fierce firepower at the concentrated point. What he hoped to do here would be like a Latin King figuring he could travel all the way up to Level 1 Milan and kidnap the city governor. For a Latin King to do that, he'd have to do something utterly original. That meant Cyrus had to do something original here.

Cyrus noticed prowling Vomags near the targeted building's entrance. They couldn't go through the front door, not brazen as could be. His step slowed.

"What's wrong?" Jana whispered.

Inspiration came, but Cyrus rejected the idea even as he thought it—too crazy and insanely wild. Yet what other chance did they have?

He was stuck on an alien moon, two hundred and thirty light years from Earth. Everyone he'd known from Earth was dead or captured. The aliens had psionic wizards and supersoldiers. He had a gun and a knife and the most beautiful woman anywhere. If the Kresh captured them, the result would be torture for Jana and him for the rest of their short lives.

A Latin King would do something crazy. That was better than dying, right? He nodded, and he turned to Jana. "We're heading for the lander," he whispered out of the side of his mouth.

"But the Anointed One is in the building," she whispered back.

"Yeah, and we're not going to get in now, are we? Do you see those soldiers? No! Don't stare. Do you see them near the entrance?"

"Yes," she said.

"We're going to hijack the lander," Cyrus said. "Then we're going to lift off and get our friends."

"We can't leave the Anointed One behind."

"We're not going to," Cyrus said. "Once I have Yang and Skar aboard, we're going in."

"Going in how?" she asked.

"You'll see."

Jana stared at him.

Cyrus ignored her, because he saw out of the corner of his eye the soldiers studying him. He had a crazy impulse to wave, but he held it at bay. Letting his shoulders slump a little more, he headed for the plaza with the lander. The open ramp had given him the idea. No one stood on guard there. Why should they? No one would dare enter a master's lander.

He tried to settle his nerves, but his stomach roiled with butterflies. This was just crazy stupid, but then, he was from Level 40 Milan. Everyone in the city knew that Latin Kings were the wild men of the slums. You didn't want to mess with them, because you never knew what insane stunt they would pull to take revenge.

"It's go time, baby," Cyrus whispered under his breath.

"We hunt," Jana whispered.

Cyrus squinted. He could hardly feel a thing, emotionally speaking. He felt numb. When in doubt, brazen it out. He was a Latin King, the lord of the streets and alleyways. Now the aliens were going to find out the hard way that they shouldn't have messed with an Earth ship.

Cyrus's booted foot stepped onto the ramp. Keeping his stride steady, he went up, with Jana beside him. Inside the craft, he spied a mechanic by his coveralls. The man carried a toolbox, or what looked like a toolbox.

"Wait a minute," Cyrus called.

The man stopped and turned around, regarding him.

"Where's the control room?" Cyrus asked.

"Did the Revered One send you?" the mechanic asked.

"That's right. He wants you to show me the control room."

"He?" the mechanic asked.

"Oh yeah," Cyrus said, wondering how he'd screwed up like that. "I mean the Revered One."

The mechanic shook his head. "Our Revered One is female."

"Of course," Cyrus said. "Now take me to the control room."

The mechanic made a strange face, opened his mouth as if to protest, and then shrugged. Maybe he was thinking things through. "This way," the man said.

"Is the crew still on duty?" Cyrus asked.

"The Revered One ordered them to stand by," the mechanic said. "You should know that if she sent you."

"Hurry," Cyrus said.

"I've never seen you before," the mechanic said, finally looking suspicious.

Cyrus drew his gun and jammed the barrel against the mechanic's ribs. "Do I have to kill you?"

The mechanic looked at him blankly.

"Show me the control room," Cyrus said, shoving the barrel hard into the man's flesh.

The mechanic stumbled and dropped his toolbox, making it clang on the floor and things rattle inside it. Raising an arm, he pointed down a corridor. Cyrus shoved him in that direction. Then the three of them hurried, the mechanic tight-lipped, Cyrus with his free hand on the man's collar, and Jana bringing up the rear, her gun out, too.

A door swished open for them. Cyrus pushed the mechanic through and to the floor and strode in after him. Four uniformed men and women turned around at their stations.

"Who are you?" the oldest woman asked. She wore a cap and had stars on her shoulder boards.

"I'm taking over this ship," Cyrus said.

"I don't think so," the woman said.

Cyrus was out of time and had decided to revert to Latin King methods. He shot the woman point-blank, her chest exploding as she toppled out of her chair.

"Does anyone else wish to die?" Cyrus asked, brutally. "If so, tell me now to save time."

The remaining men and woman stared at the dead woman and then at Cyrus Gant.

"How can we serve you?" a trembling man asked.

"You will take the ship up," Cyrus said.

"And go where?" the man asked.

"That way," Cyrus said, pointing with his gun in the direction of the puffer fields.

"The Revered Ones will destroy us," the man said.

"Look at her!" Cyrus shouted, rushing the man, aiming the gun in his face. "I am your Revered One. Obey me or die. The choice is yours. I'm done asking."

"We will obey," the man said. The others nodded.

"Then take this thing up and follow my directions," Cyrus shouted. "How many other people are aboard?"

"Us, him . . ." the man looked questioningly at the mechanic still lying on the floor.

"The others went to the kiosk for iridium," the mechanic said. "They won't be back until—it's only me."

"Just us," the temporary captain told Cyrus. "This is just a shuttle."

"Yeah," Cyrus said, "fine." For a shuttle, this thing was huge. But maybe that's how Kresh looked at such things. "I want you to take us into the air, but not too high. We have some passengers to pick up." He grinned. They would pick up the Berserkers. After the others were aboard, they would attack the tower.

The captain or pilot gave him a funny look before applying himself to his panel. "We will do what he says and tell the Revered Ones later he forced us. Our master will understand."

"Shut up," Cyrus said. "You talk only if I give you leave. Now let's go."

33

Mentalist Niens staggered away from the reality field, having interviewed the test subject for an extended length of time through his pay girl ghost. The techs stood at attention at their stations, while the Bo Taw with his smug superiority watched from the back of the chamber.

Two lesser-ranked Revered Ones stood with Zama Dee. They served her in an apprenticeship, and were smaller Kresh. Lining the chamber walls stood several squads of Vomags with two seniors present. Each of the seniors wore red shoulder boards.

Niens found that intimidating. What did Zama Dee expect? This wasn't a war zone, but a laboratory. Did she fear the test subject? That seemed absurd.

I love the Kresh. I love the Kresh.

The Bo Taw's smug smile grew.

"Mentalist Niens," Zama Dee said. "Approach me and make your report."

Niens rubbed his forehead. He felt off, and strange, while odd thoughts tumbled inside his brain. He was supposed to remember something. Klane had said . . . something.

"Revered One," the Bo Taw said, sharply. "The mentalist has been compromised."

Zama Dee pressed a clicker. The soldiers along the walls drew their sidearms, aiming them at Niens.

"Explain," the Kresh said.

"I sense foreign brain patterns in him," the Bo Taw said. "I believe the test subject has suborned the mentalist in some manner."

"Impossible," a different Kresh said. "The reality field nullifies psionic activity."

"No," Zama Dee said.

Torture, Niens thought.

"The Resisters claimed magical powers to their Anointed One," Zama Dee said. "The Resisters were most insistent, increasingly so under painful stimulation. They are awaiting a new day and expect our test subject to deliver them from what they term . . ." The Kresh lashed her tail, glancing about the room at the humans.

Niens rubbed his forehead. He needed to acquire a pistol. Once he had one . . .

"Assassination, Revered One," the Bo Taw said. "The test subject has rewired the mentalist's thought patterns. Perhaps he has even imprinted his own on the mentalist."

"Has the test subject's consciousness moved into Niens?" Zama Dee asked.

The Bo Taw shook his bald head. "I do not think so, Revered One."

The 73rd studied Niens. Finally, she motioned to the Vomags, and the soldiers holstered their weapons. "How is it that a mentalist of your stature allowed a test subject to dominate your intellect?"

Niens cocked his head. Is that what happened? He felt fine. No, he wasn't fine. He was in peril. "Revered One, I implore you to reconsider. The test subject has amazingly vital news for you. He is our friend."

"Indeed," Zama Dee said.

"He wishes to trade the news for his freedom," Niens added.

"That is ludicrous," the 73rd said.

"His consciousness went to several interesting locales at odds with Kresh interests."

"Does the test subject believe himself a slave?" Zama Dee asked.

"In truth, he considers you demons," Niens said.

The three Revered Ones lashed their tails in agitation.

"If he believes that," Zama Dee said, "why would he warn us?"

"Because he has found greater dangers than you Kresh," Niens said.

"Remember your place, mentalist," Zama Dee warned.

"You Revered Ones," Niens hastened to add.

"I suspect the test subject has corrupted our mentalist," Zama Dee told the other two Kresh. "That shows the test subject has hidden talents. It would be a waste to destroy such a specimen. Yet . . . logic now dictates the wisdom of such a policy."

"But he is a mere human," one of the other Kresh said. "He is a wild. Surely, such a being cannot hold any danger to Kresh society."

"A reasonable thesis," Zama Dee said. "I also find myself intrigued by him. I begin to wonder, however, if the reality field is the best place for the test subject. I think we should rewire his brain and put him in a submersion tank."

"That would risk his health, his longevity, and his brain," the other Kresh said.

Zama Dee hissed, "I have no desire to grant him long life. I want to know what process has given him these extra psionic abilities. It is most strange."

"Revered One," the Bo Taw said.

Zama Dee lashed her tail, and she took her time turning toward the tall humanoid. "Niens appears placid. Are the test subject's thought patterns still evident in him?"

"Please forgive the interruption, Revered One," the Bo Taw said. "I just detected a foreign psionic presence. It has vanished, but it was near. I think it homed in on my thoughts."

"This is certain?" Zama Dee asked.

"I know what I felt, Revered One," the Bo Taw said. "The mind came from outside the building."

Zama Dee lashed her tail. "Recommendations?" she asked the other two Kresh.

Before anyone could answer, the three Kresh turned toward the north wall. Loud swish-swish antigrav plate sounds grew tremendously in volume. Then the wall exploded inward and everything in the chamber heaved violently.

34

The shock of collision threw Cyrus against his restraining straps. From outside he heard explosive metallic scraping, crashes, bangs, and thuds, and breathing became impossible. He slammed back against the cushioned couch, his head ringing. It was difficult to hold the null under these conditions.

With a gasp like a swimmer who has held his breath several seconds too long and finally broken the surface, he sucked air into his lungs. Grinding metallic sliding sounds told him the shuttle shoved still deeper into the building's upper floor.

It had been his idea to use the ship as a battering ram. He had located a psi-master, and decided that was the place to strike.

No klaxons wailed on their ship. No emergency noises of any kind rang. Instead, the old hetman Yang shouted the battle cry of the Berserkers. At the same time, the bottom ramp made crushing noises as it opened. A billowing wave of choking mortar dust rolled into the shuttle.

Cyrus burst into explosive coughing. He should have thought of that. He yanked the release, and the restraining straps fell away. Feet thudded. Yang appeared in the dust cloud, and Skar and Grinder. Cyrus joined them. Each of them wore body armor. Cyrus had his knife tucked at his side, and he gripped a Vomag pistol in both hands. The others had similar weapons.

"Kill the Bo Taw, Vomags, and Kresh," Skar said in a loud voice. Cyrus's head pounded and he breathed too fast. Jana and Darter remained with the bridge crew, making sure they stayed at their posts. Choking and spitting dust out of his mouth, Cyrus entered a disaster. Dust drifted everywhere. Men groaned from the floor. Others screamed. Heavy beams, equipment, pieces of flooring pinned humans and Kresh. Some of them looked dead. Others stirred. Twice, Cyrus shot men. Once he used both pistols and slaughtered a helpless Kresh, blasting the alien so flesh and blood spurted like a volcano.

That was for Captain Nagasaki.

Yang, Skar, and Grinder likewise killed the enemy.

"Don't shoot! Don't shoot!" a man in a dirty white lab coat shouted, staggering toward them.

Cyrus aimed a gun in the man's face. Blood ran from a gash over his right eye. "What are you?" Cyrus shouted.

"I'm Mentalist Niens," the man whined. "Are you Klane's friends?"

"Where is he?" Cyrus demanded.

Niens screamed, clutching his head. "Stop! Stop it!"

Cyrus scanned through the dust. He spied a psi-master with his long head bent and pinned by a broken beam. Cyrus raised a gun—and a mental bolt struck his mind. He heard interior laughter. He vomited, and he emptied a magazine in the psi-master's general direction.

The mental attack ceased. With blurry vision, Cyrus witnessed the mutilated, lanky body twisting on the floor, still pinned by the beam.

Cyrus dropped the spent pistol and grabbed the front of the mentalist's coat. "Where's Klane?" Cyrus shouted. "Tell me before the same thing happens to you."

Niens stared at him in a daze.

Cyrus shook the lean man, and shook him again, making his teeth rattle. "Talk to me. Where's Klane?"

"Right here," a man said.

ALIEN SHORES

Cyrus spun around. He saw a man about his height with short hair and open features. His eyes seemed to swirl with power, with hidden knowledge.

"You're the Anointed One?" Cyrus asked.

"Yes," Klane said.

"I'm Cyrus Gant from Earth."

Klane raised an eyebrow.

"I'm also the Tracker," Cyrus said. "I'm here to rescue you."

"To take me where?" Klane asked.

"Into space," Cyrus said.

"You have a ship?"

"You see our shuttle. It's taken a little damage, but the armor held well enough so it can still fly. I plan to use it again and storm onto an Attack Talon. Then I'll own a spaceship, yes."

A smile spread across Klane's face. "Yes. That will work. Let us leave."

"Follow me," Cyrus said.

"What about me?" Niens asked. "You can't leave me here. The Kresh will torture me."

Cyrus turned and studied the mentalist.

"He comes too," Klane said.

Cyrus shrugged. Then he shouted, "I've found him! Let's get back to the shuttle and leave this place. Come on, let's hurry!"

||||||||||

Antigrav plates hummed. The shuttle slid out of the building, leaving the dead behind. Without fanfare and without challenge they raced upward.

Cyrus stood in the control chamber, watching. The Kresh city dwindled. Soon, so did the canyon and then the wide uplands. Finally, they saw the moon's curvature as the stars began to appear.

"We're really leaving this place," he told Skar.

The soldier said nothing.

The pilot turned to Cyrus with an imploring look. During the attack, the pilots had each been bound.

"Take us straight to Zama Dee's Attack Talon," Cyrus said. Niens had given him the Kresh's name and told them the alien had died during Klane's rescue. "You know the procedure," Cyrus told the pilot, "so follow it to the letter."

"This is blasphemy," the pilot complained. "You slew Revered Ones, branding us all with certain death."

"Do you prefer to die this instant?" Cyrus asked.

Tight-lipped, the pilot maneuvered toward the Attack Talon, opening channels and following procedures, as Cyrus had ordered.

Klane, the Anointed One, sat in a chair. He had been silent since boarding the shuttle. He glanced at Cyrus, saying, "The Attack Talon lacks Bo Taw. This could work."

The ship assault proved anticlimactic. Seventeen personnel were aboard Zama Dee's Attack Talon. With Klane's psionic help, Yang, Skar, and Cyrus moved from compartment to compartment. They disarmed the few Vomags and put the techs in what passed for the brig. There were no Kresh aboard, thus none were slain.

"We won't be able to hide our vessel for long," Niens told them an hour later.

"Why?" Cyrus asked.

The mentalist threw his hands into the air. "In case you failed to notice, the Kresh have more than one Attack Talon. They have hundreds. They will track us down no matter where we go."

"I have the null," Cyrus said.

"What is that?" Klane asked.

Cyrus explained it, how it had hidden them from psionic tracking.

"I can expand on that," Klane said, shortly. "It will make us invisible. Yes. I'm beginning to perceive the way."

"How about you explain it to us," Cyrus said.

Klane studied him, finally saying, "Wait a few days. Let us see if we can disappear. Then I will explain what I'm thinking. I don't want to risk capture and losing valuable information to the Kresh. I know they'll never pry it from me."

Cyrus put it to a vote, and they decided to trust the Anointed One. On low power and with Klane providing the null, they piloted the Attack Talon closer to Pulsar.

It was a massive gas giant, twice the size of the solar system's Jupiter. Pulsar emitted intense amounts of radiation and heat, which would help cloak them.

After discussing it for several hours, Klane and Cyrus agreed that near-Pulsar orbit would be the easiest place to hide.

Days passed as Klane informed them of frantic psionic activity, searching for them. Later, radar sweeps bounced against the ship, but they were not found. Klane locked himself in a wardroom, and didn't emerge until several hours later.

All he would tell them was, "I took care of it."

"I don't see how that's possible," Yang said. With his transfer knowledge, he diligently began studying astrophysics and other space-related sciences.

"I don't understand it, either," Cyrus said. "But I believe he has the ability to do it." He recalled how psi-masters had fashioned laser-resistant shields with their minds against *Discovery*. Why couldn't Klane have figured out a way to thwart radar pulses?

Niens began to interview the captured crewmembers. "I'm a mentalist," he told Cyrus later. "Give me enough time, and I will turn them from Kresh love to Humanity Ultimates."

"You're going to brainwash them?"

"At first, perhaps," Niens said. "In time, they will understand it was for the best."

"Very well, proceed."

Five days after leaving Jassac, the Attack Talon entered into close orbit around Pulsar. With careful piloting, they brought the vessel down to the highest atmospheric clouds, the antigrav plates working overtime.

Only then did Klane bring Cyrus, Jana, Yang, and Skar into his wardroom. It was lit with a single lamp on a center table, showing pen marks of odd symbols on the plastic top. Klane had listened to Cyrus's story some time ago and gone over it with him in detail.

"We are hidden for the moment," Klane said. "I have ranged with my telepathy, searching between here and Jassac. Your null was a brilliant idea, by the way," he told Cyrus.

"I can't take credit for it," Cyrus said. "I learned it from a lady on High Station 3."

"That's interesting," Klane said. "In any case, my point is that as long as our antigrav plates last—and with constant tinkering, they should—and enough food and water remain, we can stay here, hidden from the Kresh."

"How does that help us free humanity?" Cyrus asked.

Klane grinned, and it made him seem like the young man he really was. "There is a war coming to the Fenris System."

"Do you mean the cyborgs?" Cyrus asked.

"Yes," Klane said.

"You had a clairvoyant dream about them?" Cyrus asked.

"No," Klane said, "nothing like that. I went to their fleet and spoke with their leader, the Prime Web-Mind."

Cyrus paled. He knew his solar system history. That's what the cyborg leader had been called: the Prime. "You went to their fleet?" Cyrus asked. How was that possible?

"I think it's time I told you what happened to me," Klane said. For over an hour, he spoke about the singing gods in the caves, his attack in the demon city, the Kresh response, his consciousness fleeing his body and his dreadful visit to the Chirr hive, and later, the cyborg fleet.

"So you see," Klane said, at the end of his tale, "the Chirr are going to launch their war fleet soon enough. They have hundreds of thousands of vessels. They have planned the attack for generations. It will be a bloodbath in space."

"And the cyborgs?" Cyrus asked.

"They have five ships tougher than Doom Stars," Klane said. "Are you familiar with those?"

"I've heard of them," Cyrus said.

"Doom Stars were dangerous?"

"Extremely," Cyrus said.

"Well," Klane said, "those two coming attacks are the cornerstone of my plan. That means we have to wait until the Chirr strike and the Kresh bring their Attack Talons and other craft to Fenris II. Or we wait until the cyborgs arrive and begin their gruesome procedure. That, too, will occupy the Kresh."

"Okay," Cyrus said. "And then what?"

"Then we attempt to slip near High Station 3 and rescue your Earth crew and the Teleship," Klane said. "That will radically alter the equation."

"Equation?" asked Cyrus.

"Of man's standing in the Fenris System," Klane said.

"Okay . . ." Cyrus said. "I have a question. What if the cyborgs begin winning their war? That would be a disaster for the humans. The cyborgs will strip their flesh and give them metal bodies and programmed minds. That would be worse than being a Kresh's slave."

"It will be a bloodbath," Klane said again, his features hardening. "Many will lose their lives. Remember, I have been to the hive and I have been to the cyborg fleet. I have a good idea of what is in store for humanity. Millions of humans will die. We're not fighting to save them. We will be fighting to save humanity from extinction. We will be fighting to give our kind a future in the universe."

"You think it's going to be that bad?" Cyrus asked.

"I see two possibilities. No, three," Klane said. "We can throw our lot in with the Kresh. That may be the most reasonable, but it would be fraught with the peril of them coming out on top."

"You're talking about them and the solar system humans, too?" Cyrus asked.

"Of course," Klane said.

"All right," Cyrus said. "That's one possibility. You said there are three."

"The second is that either the Chirr or the cyborgs prove victorious," Klane said. "Neither side will allow humanity to live. They will exterminate us root and branch."

Cyrus flicked out a second finger, waiting for the last one.

"The last possibility is that humanity wins," Klane said. "Then we survive to populate the stars as our own masters."

Cyrus nodded. "Which do you believe is the most likely outcome?"

"Given the odds," Klane said, "either the Chirr or the cyborgs win. That means the end of the human race."

Cyrus sat back. In time, he took Jana's hand. The stakes were still astronomical, weren't they? They had a bigger ship now, and more people, but the odds had turned grimmer. Yeah, the Anointed One was right. They had to get *Discovery*'s crew and get out of the Fenris System. But what about the millions of humans here?

No! There had to be a better way than fleeing back to Earth. He'd met Skar, Yang, and Jana. There were millions more like them in the Fenris System. They had the Anointed One, likely the most powerful psionic around. They had mind transfers and exactly one military vessel. Was there a way to start a mass rebellion as Spartacus had once done in Italy? That was worth some careful thought and possible planning.

Cyrus stood up, and he went to a port, staring down at Pulsar with its banded colors. For the moment, he was safe. Soon, though, he would have to enter the fray again. It was going to get hairy all right. Cyborgs, Chirr, and Kresh—this was proving to be a deadly, dangerous universe.

Jana came and stood beside him. He put his arm around her. Tomorrow, or the day after tomorrow, he would marry her. He had found his woman, but he had yet to find a peaceful place to live.

I wish we really had discovered New Eden here. Yeah—that would have been a thousand times better than these grim alien shores.

ACKNOWLEDGMENTS

Thank you, David Pomerico, for wanting to see the Doom Star universe continue in a new series. Thanks, Brian Larson, for giving me advice during the writing of the story, and thank you, David VanDyke, for the first round of editing. Thank you, Jennifer Smith-Gaynor, for you excellent editing advice. I'd also like to thank my copy editor Michael Townley for her hard work. A hearty thanks to the entire 47North team. You are an easy and enjoyable group of people to work with. Thank you, Evan Gregory, for your advice on the business end. And I want to give a special thank you to my wife Cyndi Heppner and to Madison and Mackenzie: two of the nicest girls in the world.

ABOUT THE AUTHOR

2013 © CYNDI HEPPNER

Vaughn Heppner is the author of many science fiction and fantasy novels, including the Invasion America series and the Doom Star series. He is inspired by venerable sci-fi writers such as Jack Vance and Roger Zelazny, as well as by *The Nights of the Long Knives* by Hans Hellmut Kirst. The original *Spartacus* movie and its themes of slave rebellion color much of his work. Among his contemporaries, Heppner counts B. V. Larson's military science fiction novels as the most akin to the Fenris series. Canadian born, Heppner now lives in Central California. Visit his website at www.vaughnheppner.com.